A Sound of Rushing Water

Agnes Fisher

A Sound of Rushing Water

A Sound of Rushing Water

Agnes Fisher

WIPF & STOCK · Eugene, Oregon

Wipf and Stock Publishers
199 W 8th Ave, Suite 3
Eugene, OR 97401

A Sound of Rushing Water
By Fisher, Agnes
Copyright©2014 by Fisher, Agnes
ISBN 13: 978-1-5326-1725-6
Publication date 1/18/2017
Previously published by Inkwell Productions, 2014

CATHERINE

Dedication: for Sarah

Agnes Fisher

Chapter 1

Westie

Inside the little cottage on Ocean Drive, Catherine West-Cedar awoke and tried to rub the sleep from her eyes. *Forty years*, she thought as she rubbed her hands over her face in an attempt to iron out the wrinkles and lift the sagging jawline. She rose to the knowledge she had just entered the next generation. Fear and anticipation curled around and through her stomach. She sighed, then threw the covers off her body with a grand sweep of her long arm and sat up in bed. This was finally the day. She smiled her private, secret grin as she walked to her closet, got out a robe, covered her long, naked body, and reached deep into the back corner, behind the clothes and under the quilt, into the deepest recess, her private hiding place.

On the morning of her sixtieth birthday, Catherine took the ball out of its hiding place and whispered "Westie" to herself. The old thing had acquired a bit of mildew, grown quite hard, and come to smell very musty in the forty years it had lain in one or another of her closets, always in the darkest corner.

Catherine had moved around a bit in the forty years since the ball had been placed in her hands. Her school-teaching years in the Midwest and on the East Coast had kept her focused and busy. Teaching had been her lifeline; it had sustained through the long wait. She hadn't had time to reflect too much about her personal life, but the ball and the promise it held was always in the back of her closet as well as her mind. The promise directed her life.

On this southern New Jersey island, Brigantine, crowded by the world of fame, fortune, and despair that is Atlantic City, Catherine had found a haven by the sea for her early retirement a few years ago. The Ocean Drive house was her heaven on earth. She expected to get some peace here, and time to do the things teaching had never allowed. She expected to take some painting classes and perhaps a little sculpture. After she had accepted the more than adequate severance package, the move had seemed just right.

She carefully placed the ancient pigskin on her robe-covered lap, gently put a finger on it, and traced the outlines of the seams and cord that still held it together. As she reflected, a small tear ran down her cheek and onto the dirty surface, creating a crooked line down the side of the ball. Memories bounced back into her brain and made fresh wounds she thought had scarred over years ago. Love had been rich in its youth, its innocence, its passion, and its pain.

Laughter was always a part of that pain. The short guttural giggle that accompanied the tear eventually erupted into laughter. A few more tears ran down her still-fleshy pink cheeks. Oh, what fun it had been. Football with the guys, she was as good as any of them; lover of the man in charge, the big handsome quarterback who paid attention only to her; the pain of loss that followed; and then the promise.

Catherine gathered up her birthday-celebration treasure and walked out through the French doors onto the deck. She squinted into the rising sun and perused the long yellow beach just beyond the dunes. She wished she could throw this football all the way out to the ocean, and then run after it like fury on those long legs which now hurt a bit with every step. She would run till the wind blew her hair into her face and the air refused to go down into her lungs. She would run with the ball until she fell laughing onto the sand, and wait for her best beau to come and haul her up and away. She would run faster than Herman, faster than Bill—the men on the team, the friends of her Zachary. The memory was so strong she could feel it in her being, and then she laughed at herself as the ball left her hand and went flying a few yards beyond the deck. It fell with a thick thud onto the moist morning sand. Catherine went after it, snickering at the comedy of her years, trying to get that ball out to sea. The memory of days when it would have gone just where she wanted bothered her just a little. Then a voice behind her forced her back to the present.

"Hey, Mom. What are you doing out there with that dirty old ball? Where did you get that thing? I thought you hated sports."

"Oh, oh," Catherine muttered under her breath. "I told her to come at ten. What is she doing here so early?" Then she called to the young woman standing on the deck. "Hey, Tina. What are you doing here so early? I told you ten, remember?" She hid the ball under her robe and walked up the steps to where her daughter waited. Tina scrunched her nose and squinted her eyes so that her whole face appeared to be pulled up from her bottom lip, exposing front teeth that were just a little crooked in an otherwise perfect oval face. This was her exasperated-with-her-mother look; Catherine knew it well and hated it. What right did this twenty-five-year-old child of hers have to be exasperated with her much wiser mother? "Never mind the ball. Ask me no questions I'll tell you no lies, remember? Now tell me why you're here before I've even had my first cup of coffee," she said and gave Tina her teacher look.

Tina quailed a little at her mother's sharp tongue and forbidding eyes. She was fully aware of her mother's moods and recriminations. She had been taught years ago that you neither cross Catherine West-Cedar or go against her wishes; nor do you ask too many questions. "I wanted to surprise you on your birthday with breakfast in bed, but I see you can't be surprised. What time did you get up, anyway?" Tina put her arm around her mother.

"Early. You should know better than to try to surprise me." She took Tina's hand, methodically removed her arm from around her shoulder, and turned to face her daughter. "Now that you're here, let's see what breakfast I'll get. Shall I go sit in bed before you show me? Just to make it worth your while?" She was still bending forward, trying to hold the football under her robe with her other hand. Tina looked at her quizzically, raising an eyebrow, but said nothing. Catherine suddenly felt foolish standing with her hand on her robe with the big bubble under it, exposing her bony knees. "Wait until I put this ball away. And don't follow me!"

When she got back, dressed in pajamas, she grinned into her daughter's face. "Okay, Tina, I'm ready for my surprise breakfast. I'll get back in bed." She turned to go back into the bedroom when Tina stepped in front of her.

"Why do you have to be so...so—oh, you know. So...sarcastic. Always. Why do you have to be like this? Put your robe back on, Mom, and go sit on the deck. We'll have breakfast together while you tell me about the ball you just threw onto the beach and retrieved. Why is it even in your house?"

"Oh no you don't. That's none of your business. Don't even ask."

The two women sat across from each other at the little café table on the deck. It was a cozy summer scene. The sun was coming up over the ocean, brushing its brilliance onto the tops of little whitecaps as they floated to shore, creating a sparkle like the dazzle of a gem-studded dress dancing under pulsating lights. Catherine sipped her coffee carefully, almost as if the hot brew would further damage her scarred top lip. It had never healed properly after the surgeon stitched it up in her youth. She'd refused advice from friends and family to have the surgery redone; she figured one flaw was all right—it would help keep her humble. Her wound had been inflicted in the glory of her youth, in the best game she had ever played. These days, it reminded her of the promises and failures that had shaped her years. People still stared from time to time, but Catherine had not minded once she'd philosophized about how flaws and hardships worked. She felt powerful because of her little badge of triumph.

She grinned as she inspected her daughter. There had never been much power evident in her child. Why had she been born with such perfect looks? "Mother, why are you staring and grinning at me?" Tina now asked.

"Just wondering why your features are so perfect. I think it might have been better if you'd had a bit of a flaw to contend with. Makes you strong, you know. Oh well, never mind."

"You're so weird sometimes, Mom. And I can't understand why you keep a filthy old football around when you're so meticulous about your house," Tina replied, trying to ignore the remark about her appearance.

"Don't try to figure it out, because it has nothing to do with you." Catherine was using her teacher tone again, and realized that she used it too often. Tina squinted into the rising sun, which now embraced a long strip of ochre sand.

"To change the subject then, what are you going to do for this milestone birthday, besides having breakfast with me and doing lunch with that old man down the street?"

"He's not as old as you think. I was thinking that I might get that old man into bed with me this afternoon. That would be some birthday present, don't you think?"

"Mom! You embarrass me."

Catherine laughed again. She found a kind of wicked glee in making her daughter uncomfortable, but she didn't know why. She knew it was somewhat cruel: she tried to stop, but it kept happening. The girl seemed to open herself up to it. She was just like her father, really—a little too kind, a little naïve, and a lot too accommodating. If only Tina had been raised by Zach, it might have made all the difference. But now Catherine just looked at her and thought her old thoughts.

Perhaps Tina should be a little more like me, Catherine sometimes thought. Perhaps then she'd understand herself better. Too bad, too, that she had never gotten the chance to know the father she resembled so much. Catherine had guarded the truth about Tina's birth from the very first. It was better that way, Catherine still believed.

Tina was smaller than Catherine by inches, fine-boned, and dark-haired with intense, deep brown eyes. Her hair was cut very short and highlighted at the tips; she gelled it into place and just let it dry. Catherine, on the other hand was tall, angular, thin, and long of limb. She had worn her deep red hair long all her life, and had only recently taken to keeping it short. It was so much easier for swimming. Her green eyes were like glass marbles—almost like a cat's—with long yellow specks in the middle which reflected deep, large, and expressive images. Both women had oval faces, but the resemblance stopped there. Tina's lips were bud-like; whereas, Catherine's were full and long. Tina's eyes were large, but set not terribly far apart; Catherine's were very wide set and almond-shaped. All Tina had had to compare herself with for most of her life was Catherine, but they were so different. Catherine was a difficult role model for any child, but for Tina, she was impossible. The child simply could not measure up to her mother, in neither her own eyes nor her mother's. Tina suffered self-doubts, more as an adult even than when she was a child.

Catherine said, "Well, Tina, I'll tell you something. Since I moved to Brigantine, I've felt like a different person somehow. Maybe it's the sea air; maybe it's the lack of daily pressure. But this is the best thing I've done since I was twenty. And having you move down a few months later—well, I'm sorry for your earlier loneliness, but I'm glad to have you nearby."

"I think I've got some options here, Mom. Bergen County is way too expensive for me to support myself, and I need to be close to some familiar part of my life. This seems to be the best option for now. I'm still in touch with Saskia, though." She bit her lip and changed the subject. "By the way, what did you do when you were twenty that was so good?"

"Oh my, some really amazing stuff. Maybe I'll tell you sometime, but not now. I'm having a birthday and I've got company coming. I'm going in for a swim first, though." She took her plate and cup, put them in the dishwasher, and walked off to the bedroom to change. Tina followed, carrying her dishes, and put them in the sink.

"Don't put your dishes in the sink!" her mother called from the bedroom. Tina sighed and opened the dishwasher. "Who's coming later, Mom?"

"The old guy, as you call him, and then Zach Bekker, a man I knew a long time ago."

"When you were twenty? Does he have anything to do with that football? I thought you hated sports!" Tina called into the bedroom.

"Ha! You're not going to give it up, are you? Maybe he does and maybe he doesn't. And next time I tell you ten, come at ten!" Catherine emerged from the bedroom in her modest black tank swimsuit with a very large red towel draped around her neck. "And, for your information, I don't hate sports. I hate what this culture has done to sports. I hate the materialism and idolatry of it, among other things. I especially hate what it does to nice young men. You should know all that by now.

"I'm going swimming. See you in a bit." She exited through the French doors and ran over the dunes and down to the beach.

Tina watched her mother go. The long legs still carried the older woman with grace, despite the aches. She ran like a mature doe to the shimmering waves, which always seemed to anticipate her. Catherine and the ocean were one. She slid and glided like a dolphin, playing

7

in the waves as if nothing were more natural. Tina did not care for swimming in the ocean and seldom accompanied her mother. She shook her head as she watched the older woman plunge into the waves. Tina never could figure her mother out. Even when she was very little, Tina had wondered about her mother—and her father. Everybody else had fathers, but not Tina. She felt cheated her whole life

After Tina left, Catherine began cleaning and arranging the little house for her guest. As she wiped down the spotless counter lest a crumb remained, she thought about her day. First was lunch with William, the "old man" Tina had referred to. Zach was due to arrive later; she didn't know exactly when, but that was typical of Zachary. She hadn't seen or heard from him since the football had been a part of their life, and then, last week, he'd called. Had he remembered her birthday, or was it just a coincidence that he was coming today? She didn't know and had no way of telling.

She wondered how he looked now. She hoped he hadn't gotten fat or bald. Well, bald would be all right, but she would not be able to endure a big belly hanging over his belt like a sack of pudding. He had been such a handsome man, such a fine specimen, such a hunk, as the kids said. Some men in their sixties, like Sean Connery or Paul Newman still were, she knew; perhaps Zachary Bekker would be like one of them. She hoped he had improved with age, as these men had. Maybe he'd turned out like a Sean Connery or Paul Newman, both of whom looked better old than young. At any rate, it would be a lark to see him again. She'd certainly surprise him with that old relic in her closet. He would probably not think to ask if she still had it. She felt like she was still twenty, and hoped he did too. But the years had made her slower, she acknowledged.

The stiffness in her knees had not always been like this. Running after the ball this morning had made her knees hurt, which made her disposition ornery. It was not easy for Catherine to admit she was, more or less, "old."

After wiping off the café table, she returned to her kitchen and sat down at the butcher-block table to indulge in a second cup of coffee while thinking her Zachary thoughts instead of hurrying off to do the housework. Tina had left in a bit of a huff, and Catherine reddened a little at the thought. She had these hot flashes often—since her early fifties—and when least expected. They could be triggered by any number of things, even thoughts. Annoyed, she thought, *Poor Tina. If only she could latch onto a good man.* It hadn't been possible for her, but Catherine was sure Tina would thrive in a nice, solid marriage.

Turning the cup up over her nose as she drank the final drops, Catherine then placed the second mug of the morning in the dishwasher and ran the load. She wiped the front of the appliance with a damp cloth and, as she worked, noticed a smudge on the counter and went to work on that. Her curtains hung a little unevenly, but not for long—her still-agile long fingers pulled them into perfect matching widths. She wanted her house tidy for Zachary's arrival.

Back when she and Zach had been together, he had often teased her about her "cleanliness phobia," as he'd called it. They had even had a pretty gruesome fight about it.

"You're absolutely anal about this cleaning stuff, West. Put that vacuum away and relax! Damn it, you're a pain in the ass!" He'd then plopped on the floor in front of the vacuum and turned on the TV. She couldn't get around him; the apartment was too small. She tried to budge him with the end of the vacuum, but he didn't move. She ran over his foot; the machine growled, and Zachary yelled. He grabbed the hose and twisted it until it broke.

Catherine screamed, "Zachary, you idiot! We can't even afford to get this fixed. How could you?"

"Tough shit, West! Sit down!" he'd commanded.

"No!" she replied, and hit him over the head with the end of the hose. She hadn't meant to, but she had drawn blood. He put his hand to his head, touched the wound, and put his finger in his mouth. When he tasted blood he gave her an odd look and slowly got to his feet. She retreated. "Zach. I didn't mean it. I'm sorry, but…"

He was too fast for her, and got her arm behind her back before she could stop him. He pushed so hard she thought it would break. When she screamed in pain, he let go, but it hurt more to straighten it out than to keep it behind her. In a little while, she was able to move it. She looked at her lover through tears. How could he have retaliated like this?

Then she was in his arms, and he was kissing and caressing her, telling her he was sorry, that he had retaliated in response to his own wound. "Please, please, forgive me, West," he'd whined into her ear. Then they were on the floor, all was forgiven, and mad, passionate lovemaking followed. She told herself he had never meant to hurt her; she knew she'd deserved it. The housekeeping stopped for the time being. But the incident did not change her habit, and smaller spats about it had followed. Cleaning was her personal need to control.

To her, it was just a way to be in charge. And what better way to manage your environment than by keeping it in the order that suited yourself? She polished her fine wood furniture to a patina reminiscent of reflecting pools in ancient Roman gardens; the arms on her dining chairs were worn from the daily exercise of rubbing them clean despite there being no dirt on them. So she had been a little anal about it. But she would show Zachary that, if nothing else, she was consistent, even after forty years.

Forty years! She could hardly believe it. It was really only one day, wasn't it? How could one feel like a silly teen at sixty? How could these feelings, this weird desire, still be there? When one is twenty, life stretches beyond the horizon of dreams and hopes, promising a forever of romance, energy, and time. At sixty, the promises, like the dreams, have melded together into one day, and the hope for tomorrow is to find joy, peace, and a promise that it's not over yet. So she felt the desire of her twenties in her sixty-year-old body and was amazed.

Tina had not even been a thought then. Catherine had been younger than Tina was now, but she thought she'd been so much more mature, so much more daring. During that first fairy summer, she'd even had the guts and strength to play football on the team with the guys. She ran like the wind, her long legs outpacing the best Back on the team. And these were not just guys, they were pros.

When she got tackled for the last time, her lip had been split and half her nose hung loose like a flag from her face. The guys didn't notice until the game was over. They then took Catherine to the emergency room and her face was repaired—somewhat. Her many stitches gave her an emblem of strength. Then, at the end of that same year, Zach was drafted into the big time.

What a great star he'd been then. And she was his special girl. Mature and able to handle anything, or at least she had thought so. When he left, they said their goodbyes without tears. Zach would return for her; he'd promised. She believed him and went on to begin her career. Then she waited and waited.

But now she allowed self-doubt to have its way. She made a mental note to ask Zach if he had thought she was mature and wise back then, if he'd had some special thoughts about her, if he'd considered her exceptional in some way. What had he thought of her, really? He never called or wrote. She often feared that she'd lived completely deluded about his feelings for her. She had always quickly forced those thoughts away without looking at them, as one did a spider web for fear of encountering the spider. But now she had so many questions that it boggled her brain.

She shook herself from her reverie. She had work to do and herself to prepare for lunch with the old man.

Poor William. If he only knew he'd been referred to as an "old man" that morning. He too had retired early, and now, at sixty-five, he still felt so vital he'd taken a part-time job at the local CVS. He loved his new job, enjoyed the people he met, and regularly brought Catherine whatever items she wanted. He also volunteered at the marine saving station. She enjoyed his friendship, and they had lunch or dinner together once or twice a week. His wife, Bernice, had been in her grave for more than five years. William didn't pretend he wasn't lonely; he was, and he admitted it. He spoke of Bernice often and told Catherine that he missed her terribly. Cancer, the devastation of the modern age, had taken her far too young. William liked to mention it, but did not offer details.

He was one of the first people near Ocean Drive who'd come to introduce himself and welcome Catherine when she'd moved to Brigantine. He lived on one of the streets leading to the dunes and, from his deck, he had a view of Catherine's place. That's how he'd known she was a new neighbor. He'd taught her so much about the island— from its history, including the Speidel house, the families associated with it, the various fires which had devastated the island, and the murder case of almost a hundred years ago—to its present, including the Edwin B. Forsythe National Wildlife Refuge and the Annual Flower and Art Show. He had given her much companionship and expanded her social network in the short time she'd been a resident. She wanted to be ready to go today when he came by for their "special celebration luncheon," as he called it. They were to have it at the Pirate's Den, a cozy, intimate, and homey seafood and breakfast place on the north end of the island.

As she busied herself vacuuming, dusting, making beds, and arranging flowers and fruit bowls, she thought of Zachary. She felt like a schoolgirl getting ready for her first date with someone she'd had a crush on for a long time. When the phone rang, she jumped. "Oh nuts," she muttered. "What if that's him? I'm not even dressed." Then she realized it didn't matter. "Hello?" she almost whispered.

"Hello, is this Catherine West-Cedar?" said the voice, with an emphasis on "West."

"Yes it is, Zachary." She recognized his voice immediately.

"Hey, Westie, how are you?" came booming through the phone.

"Well, Zach, I'm fine. How are you?" she asked in reply, "and where are you?"

"I'm in Boston; I'll be in Atlantic City at five-thirty. Think you can get me?"

"Sure, I was expecting to." She paused. "Will you be alone?" she found the courage to ask.

"Of course I'll be alone! I thought I told you that when I wrote you last week."

"I don't think you mentioned it, but not to worry. I've got everything ready for your visit. I'm really looking forward to seeing you, Zach." She was glad he couldn't see her red face.

"Yeah, me too. We can do old times, huh? See you in a few, then." And he was gone.

She was a lot more flustered than she wanted to be. This guy really unnerved her. It was one part of her life she was never able, in the past, to keep under control. She was unhappily surprised to discover she had not outgrown it.

She dressed for lunch in jeans and a yellow-and-green striped Polo top; nothing fancy, just lunch with William. *He really is a dear*, she thought. When he rang the bell, she let him in.

"Happy birthday, Catherine," he said, and gave her a warm, friendly hug and a bouquet of her favorite wildflowers. He was nearly the same height as Catherine, but quite a bit heavier. This was a problem for her, but she never mentioned it. After all, she seemed to attract the type.

"Well, thank you, Will. They're beautiful. Let me get them right into some water." She grabbed a rusty old metal coffee can from under the sink, ran some water, tore the paper from around the flowers and stuck them in the can without seeing to the arrangement or stems. She placed it on the counter, turned, and said, "That's that. Ready?" He looked at her quizzically. "Yes, okay, I guess so. Let's go, then," he replied and followed her out the door, taking one last puzzled glance over his shoulder at his gift left orphaned on the counter.

William had moved to Brigantine years ago to be near the wildlife preserve, the bay, and the birds. He was an ecology and ornithology enthusiast to the core. But lately he was more interested in being near Catherine than birds and other wildlife. Although she didn't share his natural enthusiasm for animals, she'd often gone bird watching with him and expressed delight at his knowledge of the various species as they appeared during the different seasons. But she was distracted this morning.

"Look, Catherine, there's a Northern Pintail! Marvelous, isn't he? Quite interesting, don't you think?" William enthused as he pointed to the ducks in the bay. Catherine muttered something unintelligible in reply and didn't even look out the window. William looked at her; her disinterested response brought a frown to his otherwise placid, round face. "Catherine, are you all right?" he asked.

"Pardon?" She turned to him. "Oh, yes, just fine. I'm sorry, Will, I haven't paid attention to a word you've said. I'm a little preoccupied. Tina came over much too early and interrupted my morning plans." She sighed. "No, that's not even it. I'm being unfair to Tina to say it but, well, I didn't expect her until ten—and, well, I am an old lady today. Another whole decade to contend with. That's a distraction, don't you think?" she lied.

"Yes, I guess that's it. But we'll celebrate anyway. Bernie never made it to sixty, you know." Catherine cringed at another reminder of his wife. "I'm glad you did, and I want to make you happy today. Let's order the most extravagant thing on the menu and get a bottle of Champagne on the way."

"Oh dear, Champagne. This early? I don't know if that's such a good idea," she laughed. William replied, "Since when was having a nice drink any time of day or night a problem for you? You surprise me, Catherine. Maybe sixty is too big a number for you to digest. Don't start getting prim and proper on me now!" He said this in jest, but looked over at her without a smile. She hummed an old tune to herself and didn't return his gaze.

They ordered a large shrimp cocktail to share as a starter, swordfish steak for the main course, and a wonderful Caesar salad with paper-thin slices of Romano and Pecorino cheeses on top. Conversation was sparse during lunch, and Catherine refused to drink more than one glass of Champagne. When it was time for dessert, they shared a piece of homemade blueberry pie with extra whipped cream.

During their second cup of coffee, William put his elbows on the table and leaned closer to Catherine. He smiled. She smiled back. With a bit of hesitation in his voice she'd never heard before, he said, "Catherine, I've been thinking." He paused and put his hand on hers. "We see a lot of each other," he continued. "We're both so alone, and I thought it was time, perhaps, that we might consider..." She pulled her hand from under his so fast that a glass went tumbling off the table.

"Whoa! Back up, William. Don't say another word; I can't handle whatever's on your mind. Please don't say it. Let's just do the friend thing and forget this conversation ever almost began. So sorry, Will, but no, I do not even want to hear where you're going next."

Visibly shaken, William bent down to pick up the fallen glass. He put it back on the table and wiped it with his napkin. "Okay, right. I'm sure you're right. Let's just pay the bill." He searched his wallet to find his credit card, which seemed to be hidden somewhere; it took him a long time to locate it. Catherine felt awful, but relieved that it had not gone further. How would they ever be comfortable again?

"Shit, William. I don't know how to feel now," she finally whispered.

"Don't feel any different. It was my mistake; I'll do the feeling. Let's be the friends we've been. I do enjoy your company, so let's not let this incident stand between us."

"Right," she replied, and they left the restaurant trying to be friends.

Chapter 2

Zach

Catherine peered through the crowd as she waited at the gate, standing on tiptoes and scanning the heads. She was so nervous she could hardly stand still. She rocked from one foot to the other, wrung her hands, and twisted her ring around her finger a number of times. She had taken extra care with her appearance, even putting on some makeup. Her green dress perfectly complimented her deep auburn hair which still had only a few strands of gray, even at sixty.

She wondered if she'd recognize him and if he'd recognize her. She'd tried to hide the slight heaviness under her eyes with a very expensive concealer she bought after the William fiasco, and had taken extra care fixing her hair. She almost wished it were still long; she knew what Zachary Lee Bekker would be looking for.

The people from his flight began to come into the terminal. Catherine again stood on her toes to see above the heads. Suddenly a voice boomed from behind her, "Westie!" and two strong arms encircled her waist from behind. She was momentarily lifted off her feet and, when she was back on the ground, she turned to look once more into those smoky gray eyes. She couldn't believe what she saw.

Zach was thinner than she remembered; he was now tall and lanky instead of tall and muscular. His great shock of black hair was still there, but as white as titanium. His beautiful long, straight nose pointed to another shock of white hair above his once-visible full top lip. The hair extended to his chin in very small, tufty beard. He looked like Colonel Sanders or Santa Claus, but so much thinner. The smoky eyes stared at her through wireless glasses. His shirt hung open to reveal a thick gold chain around his neck, and a small tattoo of an elaborate football trophy with a naked woman holding a football at the top. How totally contemporary and exciting he looked; no jock appearance for him any more.

"Hey, what are you staring at, West? Say hello, for John's sake."

"Hello," she replied, laughing. "My, it's good to see you."

"Likewise. How in the world did you get that gorgeous red hair to stay that way? And you're wearing my favorite color. You're still a wonder." She blushed at his memory of her.

She could hardly believe she was holding his arm; she'd waited such a long time. If it hadn't been for the wonderful distractions of teaching and her daughter Tina, as well as the strength and determination to simply wait, Catherine might not have made it. *What if I had married?* she now thought in a panic. She'd come close, but knew Zachary would always be in the back of her mind. She couldn't let some other guy be in her house or her life as long as she had her dream and her career. And now here he was—and she was free.

When they drove up to her house, he let out a whistle. "Nice place, West. How did you afford this? Teachers doing well these days, huh? Been married and got all his money?"

"Yeah, right. Money like sports figures, maybe. And no marriage. You got a bundle somewhere, Zach?"

As they got out of the car he put his arm around her shoulder. "Sorry to disappoint you, Westie," he said into her ear. She could feel his nose in her hair, sniffing its fragrance. "But I got nothin'. Nothin' but what you see right here beside you." She laughed in response. He had teased then, and apparently still liked to tease now.

Catherine opened the front door, took a long step inside, and turned to see if Zachary fit into her décor. He walked into her slightly prissy, slightly-too-feminine living room, dropped his duffle bag on the floor and himself into her best blue-velvet chair, and then motioned her to sit on his lap. He looked oversized and terribly masculine. Nothing had changed, except age and years of experiences not shared. But Catherine took the opportunity.

The phone rang just as she was adjusting her mind and body into her long, longed-for lover. She jumped up and ran to pick it up, but Zachary ran faster and answered it before she got there. She stood next to him with her hand out and a frown on her face. He grinned and whispered into the phone, "I'm not sure she's available right now. I'm planning to keep her busy." Catherine snatched the phone from his hand, and he dropped back into the chair, laughing.

"Hello?" she said, hoping it was a telemarketer.

"Hey, what's going on over there? I call to wish you a happy birthday and I get a guy on the phone? You are celebrating! Who is he? Do I know him?" Gwen, Catherine's older sister who lived in Michigan, never forgot her birthday, and always remained nosy about the details of her life. Now she felt cornered. What to say?

"Oh, hi, Gwen. So glad you called, but your timing is a bit awkward." Honesty was best with Gwen. She'd be able to tell if Catherine were lying; they had been raised almost like twins. They were barely a year apart in age and had always shared a bedroom, clothes, school, friends—everything. When Gwen got engaged, they'd hoped for a double wedding until Zach had decided his career needed to come first. She didn't quite know what to tell Gwen now. "He's just an old friend who flew in today."

"Right. Has he got a name? Do I hear any familiarity in that voice? Who is it?" the voice demanded, and Catherine blushed. She knew her sister would not approve. Zach grinned at her embarrassment, flicked her on her behind, and tried to pull her down. She swatted him away with her hand.

"Gwen, just say 'happy birthday' and ask no questions, okay?"

"Don't tell me!" was the incredulous response. "You wouldn't, would you? Catherine, please tell me there is no Zachary Bekker in your house after all these years!" Silence. Then, "You're blushing, aren't you?"

"Say 'happy birthday,' Gwen. That's all you need to do. That's what you called for. Leave me to my own private business."

"Catherine, Zach is there. Who would have believed it! How many years have you pined for him? Forty? You crazy woman, you! He abandoned you, remember? You gave Robert up for him, remember? Get real, sis. Throw the bum out. Forty years is too long, and who knows what creepy stuff he's been doing all that time!"

"None of your business, Gwen." She peeked at the chair to see if Zach was listening, but he appeared to be sleeping. "Leave it alone, Gwen. You know I've been waiting. You know I never married because I didn't want to. After Zach, I didn't have the heart for anybody else— you know that. He's back, and what's it to you? What I do now is none of your business or anyone else's, either. Say 'happy birthday' so I can thank you and get on with my life again."

"Happy birthday, Catherine. Don't do anything stupid in that little beach house of yours! Let me know how it goes, though."

"Fat chance! Goodbye, Gwen. Thanks for remembering my birthday."

"Bye." The phone went dead. She turned to Zach, who was already sound asleep, naked and snoring. His clothes lay strewn on the floor His socks smelled, and there were holes where the toes should have been.

Catherine sighed; he hadn't changed in all those years.

Yet she felt her old desire return as she looked at his long, thin body lying limp in her living room. Forty years had done little to change Zach. There was some loose skin where tight abs and pecs had been, and his arms were not as firm and muscular, but for the most part he was recognizable.

What will this visit bring? she wondered. She hoped for closure, for a future which had so far eluded her. Could life start at sixty? She damn well intended to give it a shot.

Chapter 3

Change

The humid, ninety-four-degree weather put them both in miserable moods. It had been difficult to sleep, even with the air conditioner on. Catherine got up early and made coffee. She took it out on the deck, hoping to catch an ocean breeze. But the air was still, and the ocean hung like rags on the end of the beach. It made a few feeble attempts at rising to its usual morning glory, but the little waves soon lost their strength and collapsed back into fatigued sheets of humid flatness. Catherine understood them. She also felt limp, wet, and flat. She sipped her coffee and thought about the past month.

Zach had been so cool, so sophisticated, so engaging, and such fun. Even though he kept most of the details of his life to himself, she continued to caress her image of him. She still could not figure him out completely, but she had again been fully seduced—even at sixty—and taken in by his exciting charm.

Then after, four weeks or so, and completely to her surprise, some of the thrill had begun to wear off. After four weeks of fun, they lessened their activities. And Zach was drinking too much. Catherine mentioned it and got nowhere. "Don't even think about running my personal life,

Westie," he said. But she was uneasy. He slept too much and began to become irritable. This was a side of him she'd experienced only once in the year they had lived together, but the moods seemed to be more frequent now. If she refused to do something he enjoyed, he became far more angry than warranted.

He now sauntered onto the deck wearing only his briefs, clutching a cold beer and interrupting her thoughts. "Don't mention it, Catherine. I already know what you're going to say. I'm too hot for coffee and too ornery for conversation. The beer might help the latter."

"Fine" she replied. They sat in silence, enduring the humid heat of a Jersey July and each other.

After each had finished their drink, after about a half-hour of sweating silently side by side, Catherine went inside. She felt upsets by his mood and responded in kind. She took her coffee cup to the dishwasher as she did every morning and looked at her kitchen counter. Beer was spilled all over it; glass rings had dried to crystalline circles. Catherine couldn't help yelling out to Zach, "Hey, can't you just pick up a cloth and clean up after yourself? Can't you just wipe up this crap so I don't have to do it for you? Wipe it up the minute you spill it? What's the big deal?"

"Hey, West. Cool it, will ya? It's no big deal. Why make it one? I'll clean it when I'm ready," he yelled back.

She reached up, took a small bowl from the cupboard and a box of Wheaties from the pantry. Then she poured some milk on them, and sliced half of a brown, mottled banana over it. She took the bowl out to Zach.

"Thought you'd like some of the stuff made for champions. Might go well with your beer." She plopped it on the table in front of him and went back in for a cool shower; she thought she'd have a better appetite afterwards. Zach frowned at the bowl, stuck his spoon in, and spilled about half. "What a lousy day," he mumbled to no one.

Catherine thought things out while enjoying the cascade of cool water which washed her body and bathed her thoughts. The past month had been decadent. Catherine was so thrilled to see him after such a long time that she agreed to anything. They did Atlantic City and all its wonders almost every night, losing a ton of money one evening and winning a few dollars back the next. They saw shows and found places to dance, drink, and laugh. They went to bed at the odd hours of youth and made love like a couple of pubescent kids. Zachary had even had the gall to ask Catherine to a nude dance show, and the night that followed made even Catherine blush. As she thought about it now, she wondered what had possessed her.

It had been a hot night, almost as hot as this morning. They'd driven all the way up to Camden, where some of the best nudie bars were. When Zach had suggested it, Catherine had declined the invitation. But, as usual, he'd been able to convince her.

"C'mon, West, don't be a prude. It's exciting to see these beautiful bodies perform. Nothing wrong with that. It's just acting, just a show," he insisted.

"It seems a bit more than that to me, Zach. It seems like exploitation," was her response.

"Don't be nuts. It's an act. It makes people happy, and the girls do it for the money. They don't have to do it, you know. Come for my sake. I'll make it worth your while. Promise," he'd sworn, and so she'd agreed.

She went, feeling very apprehensive. All the way to Camden, her heart throbbed and her stomach churned. She remembered how she'd hoped for a car problem or even a minor accident to keep them from the inevitable evening of embarrassment and pain for the young women they were to see.

They pulled into the parking lot, and Zachary had been the gentleman and walked to the passenger side to open her door. He took her by the arm and, with his usual grin, led her to the door. She was sure the Mafia was waiting for them on the other side. The place looked like an old abandoned warehouse but, to her surprise, the interior was quite elegant. Small cocktail tables with matching chairs were placed throughout the room, and elegant candle holders, each holding two long tapers, decorated each table. Men and women were seated here and there, enjoying drinks and conversation. Soft, romantic music filtered through the room, lending an ambiance of class. Sinatra crooned, giving the place a sweetness contradictory to what was to come.

Catherine told herself it wasn't going to be so bad after all. They sat down and ordered dry gin martinis with lots of olives—her favorite. Zach leaned close and warmed her ear with his breath, and then put an arm around her, pulling her close. He whispered that she was the gamiest broad he'd ever met, and thanked her for the opportunity to show her this part of his life he had enjoyed for many years.

Then the lights dimmed, and a girl much younger than Tina danced into the light. She wore an elegant, shimmering-green gown which covered her from her ankles to her chin, and very spiky heels. As she danced to the now-loud music with a heavy beat, she dropped her skirt and threw it aside. Her legs were bare except for green netted stockings which went all the way to her thighs, but her top still covered the rest of her.

More of her clothing came off at intervals before she undid her top and threw it to the audience. Catherine gasped as she watched the girl slowly remove her bra, the stockings, and her green lace panties. Then she was naked except for the shoes. She flung her arms up and out, spread her legs, and gave everyone the opportunity to see all there was of her. She turned her back to the audience and lit a match, which she then used to light a candle. The lights went even dimmer. One could hardly see the girl now. She held the lit candle up to her very exposed bottom as she bent forward and spread her legs wide to expose even more. Catherine felt her face turning red and wished the heat would be turned down.

The lights came back up slowly, and the girl stretched forward and grabbed a pole which had descended from the ceiling. She shimmied up it like an athletic chimpanzee and turned over, holding on with her legs, and did all kinds of ridiculous contortions. Catherine wanted to be embarrassed for her; she wanted to stop this child from exposing herself like this.

Then she looked at Zach and back at the girl. The pulse of the music and the lights, the rhythm of the girl's movements, played on Catherine until she became intoxicated with the event. She knew her continuously refilled martini glass contributed to the sensation, but she began to experience excitement. She tried to fight it; she'd never felt anything quite like it before.

When the number was over, she excused herself and went to the women's room where she ducked into a stall and did what she could to get rid of the feelings she knew were somehow impure, not quite honest, and perhaps even dirty. *Maybe I am a prude*, she thought. She came out of the stall and splashed cold water on her face, but she knew she wouldn't mind seeing a little more. Maybe she and Zach were made in the same mold. Maybe she was more like him than she was willing to admit. How could this be? Because of a naked girl? Because of Zach's leering look? What? Her self-doubt followed her back into the room.

Now there were three poles and three very lovely young women, all naked except for the spiked heels, all extending limbs, turning somersaults to expose their breasts even more, and bending forward so their buttocks were in full view. None of them smiled. Their faces took on expressions of lasciviousness, but not one of them smiled. That was one thing Catherine thought odd, besides her own very unexpected response. The only smiles in the room were those on the faces of ogling men and some women who might have identified with the girls. *Is that what I'm doing?* Catherine wondered as she looked around.

When they got home, they made use of the experience. She quickly found out what Zach had meant by making the experience worth her while. He believed she was as lascivious as he was. *How could this old guy still have so much ability?* she wondered. Could be drugs, of course, but she never asked.

"What a comedy for two old farts like us, huh, West?" Zach observed, laughing, the following morning. But for the first time in her life, Catherine felt shame because of what she'd done with Zach. All she could think of that morning was what William or Tina would think of her if they knew.

On another very hot evening, they'd driven up the coast to Asbury Park to take in a concert. New Jersey's number one rock icon, born and raised in the Asbury area, was to perform at the old, broken down concert hall. Zachary loved the guy, had met him years ago at a celebrity function, and insisted on taking Catherine. He assumed that because he loved this kind of performance, she would also.

When the musician mentioned Zachary from the stage, all the women turned to the aging football star, who visibly swelled like a cock dropped into a hen house. Catherine came away too sweaty for words, but impressed by the energy of the performance. She understood the appeal the glitz, the hype, and the raw power of the performance had for Zach. It was Zach himself, his own vitality and hot, overpowering energy in the game. She knew what effect the insane worship of the crowd had had on the performer, and Zach had also gotten lost in it. He had taken her to remember himself at his peak, but he told himself—and her—he was only a faithful fan of The Boss.

The gambling at the blackjack tables, poker, craps, and the one-dollar and five-dollar machines had cost them both a lot of money, but when Zach put a thousand dollar piece into a big one-armed bandit, Catherine had a fit.

"How could you? Zach, where did you get that?" He'd shushed her with his hand over her mouth and pulled the lever. When the thing rang out a win, she collapsed onto the floor and sat with her legs straight out and her face in her hands. Zachary jumped up, whooped like a cowboy on the range, and landed on the floor beside her. "Want another spin, Westie?" he asked, and they laughed and fell into each other's arms.

In exchange for Catherine's willing excursions into Zach's indulgent world, she had taken him to art galleries, little artsy stage shows—which were not some of Zach's favorite haunts—and to what he called a "ridiculous" wildlife preserve to look at ducks. "Ducks!" he complained, but Catherine insisted on pointing out the various species she had learned to identify. William had taught her, she explained, and Zach smiled sardonically. He made a rather quick assessment of William after their first meeting at the center.

"William is a first-class wimp, Catherine. Don't tell me you go to this little fishy duck thing just to please him? I can't believe you're friends with a guy like that," he remarked, adding, "You don't sleep with this guy, do you? Although if you did, I'd guess you'd just sleep, if you know what I mean," and winked.

"He's a sweet man—moral, very lonely, and a nice friend. Don't criticize what you don't know." That had ended the conversation. But Zach had not warmed up to William, even though Catherine had him to dinner once after that.

She'd also introduced Zachary to Tina, and they were at odds almost immediately. Catherine had hoped for more, but Tina became completely withdrawn and silent in Zach's presence. Zachary had introduced himself as the "football hero of the age," and tried to flirt with Tina. "How about the two of us lose your mother for a while and kind of get to know each other better?" he'd suggested with a grin that would have turned Catherine to mush. Tina turned bright red and backed away from him.

"I was only kidding!" he later told Catherine. "Can't she take a joke? I'd think she'd be flattered." "She's never met anyone like you before. Give her a break," Catherine said, upset and embarrassed. When she tried to defend Tina, Zachary turned his back and walked away. She wasn't sure which of the two embarrassed her more.

Zachary showed no fondness for Tina after that. "She's a looker for sure, West, but not like you. You're beautiful and athletic. I loved watching you with that ball—you ran faster and better than Herman and Bill. They were jealous, remember? It was good to have you on my team. That summer between school and pro ball—well, I'll never forget it. I think I've carried that image of you with me all these years. And now I love to watch you walk or run down the beach and jump into the water. You're a great swimmer, still a strong and lovely athlete. But your daughter—well, she's more like a Victorian doll. Breakable, you know? She could do with a little experience. I'll bet she doesn't even know what end of a ball to hold!" He laughed, relishing his own joke.

Catherine did not laugh. Her daughter was not fair game, even for Zach. Maybe sweet, vulnerable Tina was somewhat lucky not to be like her mother. Catherine preferred her daughter, at least in some ways, to be like her father, who was proper, submissive, not overly passionate, thoughtful, and a little withdrawn, almost as if apologizing for his own existence, but not quite. He could be assertive if pushed, and Tina was very much like that. Better for her; it made for a much easier life, Catherine was convinced, even though it had kept them as polarized as a mother and daughter could be.

So Catherine and Zachary had spent a month together after a forty-year separation. They had wined and dined, loved and laughed. She had forgotten how wonderful and cleansing a rally good laugh was. They'd laughed until tears rolled down their cheeks and Catherine's side hurt when Zach's knees buckled on the dance floor and they had almost, in slow motion, gone down and landed on top of each other. They laughed when Zach fell off the bed and twisted his ankle during one of their more daring episodes.

For a month, it seemed there had been no separation at all. But now, today, in this hot July, the relationship was beginning to cool. Zachary began to withdraw again. Wednesday morning, Catherine made the inevitable mistake of asking about future plans. She intimated that marriage would be a just conclusion to all her years of waiting, to this month of intimacy and fun. Zach instantly recoiled, and she couldn't get him back to his former mood. This morning, Friday, was the worst.

When Catherine returned with a towel wrapped around her head, Zachary looked up from his musings about the misery of the impending day and winked at her. "Guess what I've been thinking, West?" Before she could answer he continued, "I've been thinking we should go somewhere where it'll be perfect weather all day and longer. Where do you think that would be?"

"I can't begin to imagine," she answered as she unwound the towel from her head and ran her fingers through her hair. The thick, short hair fell right into place. She considered her aging beau as she asked, "Well? What are you thinking?"

"I'm thinking," he said as he stood up and put his hands on her shoulders, "we should run away to Hawaii so we can get away from your entanglements here and build a new, private little love-nest just for ourselves for the next month or so. What do you say? Won't that be fun?"

"All my what?" she inquired in disbelief.

"Your entanglements. You know, that William guy down the street. You really need to unload him, Westie. He's such a wimp. Not your style at all, you know. And Tina needs to have the opportunity to distance herself from you, don't you think? Give her a month or so to grow up without you."

"And give you a month of my exclusive time and attention for your enjoyment?"

"Well, yeah. For old times' sake. We used to have such a good time. We had a great time this month, right? We could both stand a bit more of that. It'll rejuvenate us even more."

"Zachary, I don't need any more rejuvenation. I need stability, commitment, and some peace." She couldn't restrain herself anymore, even though she felt her candor might be the death knell of his ardor. "I needed that when you left me the first time. I've not had it since, because I only saw it being possible with you. I never got it. I waited for you to fulfill your promise to me; I've waited for forty years. I denied myself marriage to Robert—for you!"

"Don't be ridiculous, West," he retorted. "Who the hell is Robert anyway?" His emphasis on the name was not lost on her. "That fat little guy I saw you with—when was it? Twenty or so years ago? Robert! Not 'Bob' or 'Rob,' but Robert ? Like William, perhaps? You didn't do that denying for me; you could never live with anyone that dull. You know that."

"I did it for you," she insisted, not missing a beat. "I thought it better to be alone than with someone other than you. I came to this island to get my 'entanglements' as you call them, into perspective. William recently entered my life because he is a nice, caring man. And I might as well tell you now that I've written to Robert Scotland. He's the man I met some years after you left, and also a very nice man. William reminds me of him in many ways. Anyway, I've finally told him who Tina really is—that she's not your daughter, as he thought, but his."

"What? He thought Tina was mine? Did you tell him that? How many other people think that? Does Tina? Holy cow, no wonder she backed off in horror." He banged his beer down on the table. "Let's talk this out."

Zach slammed the French door back and almost took it off its trolley. "Hey! Easy!" she cautioned as they moved from the deck to the kitchen, where Catherine sat down with a sigh. It would have to come out now. "I never told him anything; I just let him believe what he wanted to after I refused to marry him. Probably the biggest mistake I ever made in my life."

"Not a mistake, Catherine. Not marrying him, that wimpy-like-William father, was not a mistake. Letting him think this kid could be mine—that was the mistake. Writing to him now, after twenty-five years—that is a mistake. You did tell him we hadn't been together in any sense of the word since we were twenty, didn't you? Why would or could he possibly think Tina could be mine?" Zach shook his head in disbelief. He knew Catherine had tried many times through letters and calls, as well as a very embarrassing visit, to get him to come back to her, but his career and freedom were much too sacred to him, even if it cost him the "love of his life." He had made up for that in so many ways.

"He thought I'd gone back to you. He believed, because he knew I was still in love with you, that when I went away that time during my summer break, I'd gone to find you. He believed I'd been successful and we had had an affair. I never told him you didn't want to see me then. I was too hurt and ashamed." Tears welled up in her eyes at the memory. She couldn't forget the pain this guy sitting across from her had caused. He had told her he loved her, and then rejected her. When she finally got the nerve to search him out fifteen years later to remind him of his promise, she found him with someone else. He'd easily dismissed the whole thing, but sent her on her way just the same. She had never understood, never forgotten his last words to her. "Catherine," he had said, "let's not complicate our lives with commitments now. It's best not to see each other, but when I'm ready, I'll be there. Wait for me. I'm just not ready to be entangled with you now."

Now she remembered. The same word. What a lousy word to use for relationships—entanglements!

Maybe Zachary, the great pro-ball star, is really screwed up, she thought. "What would you advise now? About Tina, I mean?" she asked, hoping he would offer support.

"Beats me, kiddo; no problem of mine, as you know. What are you going to do if Scotty boy shows up? Wants to know about and meet his kid?" His grin and tone twisted her heart. He had no idea how difficult it all had been, nor did he care.

"Zach, do you have any idea how hard my life without you has been? I've been waiting for you. You told me to wait, you'd be here someday. I've waited forty damn years! Now you're here and you still don't understand what commitment, what love, means. Why did you come?"

"Because you're the greatest dame I've ever been with. You're gutsy, you're beautiful, and the sex—well, why even mention that. You know how great that was. And man alive, lady, you've still got it! I wanted that back—maybe for a long time—is what I thought."

"But you don't think it now," she reminded him. "Well, it took me a long time, but I can see I've been a fool to wait. I think really need you; I always did. but I guess now, when my entanglements may also include Robert, you'll let me work out the mess alone. Would that be about right?"

"Westie," he whined, "you know this has nothing to do with me. This is all your own doing. Why involve me?" Then, abruptly, he changed his tone. "I take it we won't be going to Hawaii?" He got up, finished his beer in one gulp, and moved off to the bedroom. A few minutes later, after Catherine had cleaned up her little kitchen, she heard his voice from her bedroom. "Hey, West," he called. "C'mon in here. Let's forget all this heavy stuff. I've got the solution right here."

She slowly made her way to the room. Everything had seemed so perfect. She had decided to finally put her life in order, to get all the lies straightened out, so she and Zach could finally have that life he'd promised. She figured they could have maybe twenty good years together, considering the present lifespan of most of her friends. But as she turned the corner into her room, her sanctuary, she saw him stretched out, naked, on her bed. She took one look at the skinny lothario and walked away, closing the door behind her. "I need a little time to adjust to my new mood," she said, more to herself than to him. She was at a loss to know what do with him. *Keep him or throw him out? Go to Hawaii and maybe rekindle, or get rid of him?*

When the phone rang, Catherine hesitated to answer it. She heard Zachary getting dressed in the bedroom. She hoped he wasn't angry, but knew he would be. When she picked up the receiver, she was taken aback.

Chapter 4

Sisters

"Hi, Catherine. It's Gwen. I'm in Atlantic City. I was going to surprise you, but thought I should call first. Got time to see me?" Catherine's jaw dropped in surprise. "You there, Kate?"

"You have an uncanny knack for calling at just the wrong time. You're in Atlantic City? Now? Why?" was all she could think to say. Gwen must not know that Zach was still with her; that would mean nothing but war.

"Because I want to see you. I want to see Tina. Want to do dinner tonight? Shall I come there?"

"No! Don't—I mean, you don't need to do that. Where are you? I'll meet you and we can do the town. Okay?" Catherine tried to sound normal, but she was afraid the strain in her voice might give her away.

"I really don't want to do the town, Kate. I just want to see you, talk a bit, catch up, see Tina, do some nice family time. You know."

"How on earth did you manage to get away? I mean, won't Warren worry? You've never done this alone before." Catherine did not know quite how to handle her sister. Gwen had always been the wise one, the one to give advice and live the perfect life while she was doing it.

Warren was a good, stable man. They met and got married as normal people do, according to Gwen, and had a family. And a nice Christian family at that. Gwen had called Catherine often, but resorted to too much preaching as far as Catherine was concerned. Zach was anathema in Gwen's eyes; when they met there was fire. Now why would she have come to Atlantic City?

"Listen, sis, I don't know what you're up to, but I'll meet you and we'll talk. That's apparently what you want to do, yes?"

"Kate, don't be suspicious. Warren went on a fishing trip with his brother for the first time in their lives, and I thought I'd drop in to see you and Tina. She's expecting me."

"What? She never said!"

"I asked her not to. Let's just do coffee and talk about it when you get here." They decided to meet on the boardwalk outside the Wild West Casino. After closing the door on angry Zach, she yelled through it to let him know he could take an hour or so to cool off. "I'm running into AC to meet a friend for coffee. See you later. We'll talk, okay?" She heard something like a mumble in return and left.

The coffee shop was too warm for them to endure, so they took their cool frappes down to the beach and sat right on the sand, near the water. Catherine squinted into the glare of the waves, took a sip, and sighed. Gwen pushed her hand through her short-cropped boy-cut. "Even my scalp is wet with sweat," she complained.

The sisters sat sipping their cool coffees without a word for quite some time. Anyone walking on the boardwalk might have thought the women were twins, but no one would have guessed they were in their sixties. Their beautiful long legs stretched out toward the sea, the only difference being that one set was tan, the other nearly white. Their short hair was identical in hue, but so unique a deep, dark red it was difficult to define. They faced the sea, hoping for a breath of air.

They accepted the heat as best they could, but New Jersey

Julys can be brutal, and this was one of the worst. Things indoors mildewed; outdoors, they wilted and burned. Grass turned brown weeks before it normally did. Sweat poured off bodies able to sweat, and others succumbed to weakness and listlessness. Silence was the most tolerable communication in this kind of humid, oppressive atmosphere. But Gwendolyn broke the silence with the dreaded yet anticipated question. "Zach still here, huh, Kate?" she asked, looking out to sea, not even turning to see her sister' reaction. She could feel it. "So, what about Zach and you? Finally going to marry this guy and have a lovely retirement together?"

"I guess. Tina told you he was here? We haven't decided anything yet. Is that why you came without warning—to check up on me?"

"No, honestly, to both. I figured that he was still with you when you insisted on meeting me here. I know you, Kate. You have something to hide when you can't find words, and what in the world would give you reason to hide anything these days except Zach?"

"Well, okay, yes, he's here. We had a great month. But no, there is no marriage in our plans."

"Why? It's only been forty years. Still can't make a commitment, huh?"

"Sarcastic! Who are you referring to, Gwen?"

"Both of you, I think."

"I don't know. And it's really none of your business."

"Right." Gwen took a deep swallow of her drink and closed her eyes in thought. "Right, but…you know what I think? I think he's coming to you now in a last-ditch effort to save himself. Is Zach wealthy? From his years as a pro, as the great star? The man with the legs great enough to sell pantyhose? Any money left from all that?"

"What? What's that got to do with anything?" Catherine showed her embarrassment by reddening, which was visible even in the heat of the day. Her sister looked at her.

"Huh! Thought so. He's using you, you know. The old fart, who always was a fart, by the way, although now an appropriately old fart, is using you, Kate. He spent his goods on women, and who knows what he might have gotten in return. And now he's using you. Yes?"

"Gwen, just leave it alone. I've waited forty years for this guy to show up. I've spent my whole life wondering every day if this would be the day he'd call. I've refused marriage because I couldn't bear to be tied to anybody else, just in case. His sporadic cards (not even letters, but so what) kept the flame alive. As it turns out, I've been fine and my career has been good. I really didn't need him or anyone. But now that he's here, let me at least enjoy it, okay?"

"Whatever you say, sis. If you can call that enjoyment." Catherine was satisfied this would end the conversation, but Gwen broke the quiet again. "He's a gigolo, Catherine, and you're his meal ticket as well as his pet. Get it? Is this what you've been waiting for? And what about Tina? Surely this guy is not her father. Going to tell me who yet? You're living a monstrous lie for this guy, do you know that?"

She hated Gwen's assessment. She would never admit to her sister that doubts which had already formed now grew overpowering. Had she lived a lie all these years? Yes. Even her daughter had not been told the truth. Was Zach a man or just the empty shell Gwen painted? He certainly looked good, and Catherine knew she had always been a sucker for good looks. He complimented her all the time. Who wouldn't love that? He did know how to laugh and enjoy life. That had been good. But...

"Listen, Gwen, I can't talk about this right now. You've always been opposed to Zach, so you can't be trusted to give an unbiased opinion. I've got him and I plan to keep him as long as I can." Gwen shrugged. "And don't tell me you didn't fly all the way out here from your pathetic little Michigan town to check up on me and Zach." She'd always hated her Midwest upbringing since Zach had made fun of her provincial attitudes and speech. He never let her forget her roots. "Westie, get over it, will you? The rest of the country has class; go get some," he'd said after their first few dates. After that, it had become ongoing mockery which he claimed was just a joke. She'd let it seep into her being and make her disdain it as much as he did. Gwen, she knew, did not deserve her last comment. But, Gwen being Gwen, she grinned and patted Catherine's arm.

"Right on, Kate. Let me get back to my pathetic little life—which is what you really meant—with Warren, and let you go back to the excitement of figuring out who means what to whom."

"Don't be sarcastic, and don't be so judgmental. I'd invite you to my house, but I can't let you ruin what I've got. I never told Tina about her father, you're right. And I'm not telling you the entire story, either. But for now, his name was Robert Scotland, and he never knew about Tina until I wrote to him a week ago. Don't look so surprised! Go see Tina; she'll be very excited to see her favorite aunt. And please don't discuss me and Zach with her."

"Yes, well, I can't exactly promise that. She'll certainly want to talk about her mother, and right now that includes Zach. You're living in sin, you know." Gwen gave Catherine her best lifted-eyebrow look, said goodbye, and ran up the beach to the casino where she'd left her rented car.

When Catherine returned home, she gave Tina a call to let her know Aunt Gwen was about to arrive at her apartment, but Tina had been expecting her. Catherine felt the old jealousy take hold. Gwen had always been so good with Tina; Tina had gone to her or called whenever she really needed to talk. Catherine had tried to be there for her daughter, but somehow always misunderstood her and said the wrong thing. The inevitable call to Aunt Gwen would follow, and long conversations from behind Tina's closed door after that. Catherine had often tried to eavesdrop, but Tina's quiet voice allowed no success.

She made another phone call, noted some things on a pad on the counter, and frowned at her own determination. Then she wiped a tear from the corner of her eye and walked into her bedroom. Catherine took one long look at Zachary, who was awake and in an entirely different mood. As always when he napped, rested, or slept, he lay uncovered and unclothed. When he saw her, he grinned his anticipation. She hated his naked body on her clean bedcover. She looked him up and down, considered his obvious anticipation, and leaned against the door, looking him in the eye, letting him think she was game. Without a smile or frown she stared at him, and then suddenly turned away.

"Hey, tease. You never did that before. You're no good at it, you know that?" he yelled.

A few minutes later, she called from the kitchen, "Better get your clothes on, Zach. I think your plane leaves today."

"What?" He flew out of the bedroom. "What did you say?"

She took his face into her hands and held him for a moment, then very quietly enunciated, "I said, your plane leaves today—at seven this evening, to be exact. Better get dressed; you're deflated, you know. Cover yourself." He threw her hands away from his face and stalked into the bedroom.

They were not on speaking terms for the rest of the afternoon. Zachary behaved as though he felt as totally deflated as an old football that had seen too much play. He worked mechanically at getting his stuff together and ate the small meal of tuna and a tomato slice with rye toast Catherine fixed for him, but did not look across the table at her. He guzzled beer all afternoon. She drove him to the Atlantic City airport at five o'clock.

They said little on the way. While they waited for the plane, she mentioned the football. "Why did you give that to me when you did?"

"Oh, I guess so you wouldn't forget me," he said without emotion.

"That's it? I thought it meant more. You had said something about engagement at the time."

"Did I? Well, maybe I did. I don't remember the details anymore," he answered blandly.

"Uh-huh."

When it was time for him to board, she took a step toward him so she could stand close. "One thing, Zach, before you go. You are and always have been my first and only love. I waited for you to grow up and come for me, but you haven't grown at all. I'm sorry it turned out this way. I want you to know that if you ever find that you really do need me, or might even love me as a man, give me a call. And we'll see." Her weakness still controlled her.

"Right," he said, and turned to the gate.

Chapter 5

A Voice from the Past

The phone rang in Tina's apartment at three minutes past nine on Monday morning. She almost tripped over a chair on her way to get it, since she was already late getting started for work. "Hello," she breathed into the phone.

"Hello. Is this Tina West-Cedar?" a man's voice asked.

"Yes. Who's this?" She swallowed her last bit of coffee and picked up her toast to eat on the way.

"I'm Robert Scotland. Are you the daughter of Catherine West-Cedar?"

"Yes, I am. I'm also in a terrible hurry. Are you a telemarketer? What do you want?" She shoved a yogurt into her bag with the chicken and lettuce sandwich she'd made the night before, and then walked to the sink and dumped her dishes in. Her first customer would get there before her and that always irritated them. Tina wanted to get there on time.

The voice hesitated, sighed, and then said, "I think I'm your father."

Tina hardly heard him in her hurry to be off. "Yeah, right. My father's dead. I don't have time for this," and she hung up, disgusted with the insensitive attempt on some man's part to get her attention. "My father, right," she muttered on her way out the door. "He's been dead for years. What a creep to take advantage of me like that."

As she drove down Brigantine Boulevard toward the bridge, she wondered how this guy could have known her mother, too. As she approached the bridge, she scrambled in her purse with her free hand and took out her cell phone. There was one way to clear this up. As she dialed Catherine's number, she veered to the right to let faster traffic pass her, and then pulled off the highway to be able to pay full attention to her call.

When Catherine said hello, Tina hurriedly said, "Hello, Mom. I'm on my way to work, but I need to ask you something. Some guy by the name of Robert, I think, called this morning to tell me he's my father. Do you know any guy by that name who'd pull a sick joke like this?" There was dead silence on the other end. "Mom? You there?" Tina yelled. She did not have time to lose the connection and dial again. "Mom?"

"Yes, Tina, I'm here. And I do know such a man," came the unexpected answer.

"What? Mother, what is this about?"

"Honey, I can't talk about this over the phone," Catherine replied.

"Well, when, then? Mom, I'm late for work as it is. I can't come by now." Tina's confusion brought irritation into her voice. "Just tell me it's a joke and I'll be on my way."

"Okay, dear, I guess it is sort of funny in way, but it can wait until tonight. Stop by right after work so I can explain this to you." Catherine sounded too serious for Tina to dismiss her, but she was late.

"Goodbye, Mom. See you later," Tina concluded, and hung up. All the way up Route 30 to her shop in Absecon, she mulled over the two calls. Why hadn't her mother simply blown it off as a bad joke? What was she going to talk about after work?

Tina was upset all morning, and her two best customers both complained about their hair. Tina took some extra time to spritz and restyle each. Her tips were not as generous as usual, either. She decided to take her food and go for a walk at lunchtime.

When she walked out of the shop, she noticed a short, rather stout man standing across the parking lot. He was staring at her. She looked away and headed for her car, having decided a walk might not be the thing after all. By the time she got around the back of the building, the man was right behind her, calling her name. Tina jumped. *Who is this guy?* she thought. After the morning phone call, she didn't know what to think. Her fear was palpable. She dove for her car, shot into the driver's seat, and locked all the doors.

She was about to start her car in case she needed to get away, but just as she turned the key, she heard a rap on the window. The man was standing outside her car, and he motioned for her to roll down the window. She wasn't sure what to do. He rapped again and called to her. "Don't be afraid. I just want to talk a minute. I'm Robert." It was the creep on the phone this morning. Now she really didn't know what to do.

She picked up her cell phone and dialed 911, but before the call went through her boss came out of the shop on her way to the diner down the street. Freda took one look, walked over, and approached the man as Tina looked on.

"Is there something we can do for you, sir?" Freda asked, hands on her hips, arms akimbo, attitude written all over her face. Tina felt relieved and rolled her window down.

"I'm Robert Scotland. I was once a close friend of Tina's mother, and I would like to talk to Tina for a few minutes. I'm sorry to have made this look suspicious, but I mean no harm. Trust me." The short, overweight man certainly looked harmless enough, but who knew these days?

Freda looked at Tina. "Wanna talk to this guy, Teen? Says he knows your mama." Tina got out of her car and slowly approached Freda and Robert.

"Freda," she began, "this man called me on the phone this morning. That's why I was late."

"Want me to stay out here with you while he explains his business?"

"Please."

"I find it very uncomfortable standing here in this parking lot. Could we sit somewhere so we can talk privately? I don't mind if this other lady wants to come, but you might mind, Tina, when you hear what I have to say." Robert's voice was reassuring. He spoke softly and calmly, but Tina was nervous and asked Freda what she should do. Freda looked at the man, then at Tina, and then at the man again. His brown eyes looked more like a needy puppy than a predator. Freda also saw the uncanny resemblance. *Surely this man is somehow related to Tina*, she thought.

"Why don't you both come inside? Tina, you can use the back room; there's some coffee in there. Leave the door ajar. No one will hear you if you don't talk too loud, but we'll all hear you if you need anything. How's that sound?"

Tina looked at the man. He raised an eyebrow as if to question her approval. She shrugged. "I guess that will be all right," she ventured. "Okay. Let's do that then."

Robert agreed and they went into the beauty shop. "Just to authenticate things," he said while they walked, "your mother is tall and beautiful, but has a scarred lip. I really do know her." Tina said nothing; she screwed up her face at the description, but did not stop.

The two walked through the little beauty shop as colleagues and customers stopped their chatter to watch the man with the dark thick hair with graying temples follow the young woman with the same hair, facial features, and walk. Freda put her finger to her lip to indicate there were to be no questions or comments.

When they got to the back, Tina gestured to a chair for Robert, pulled the door almost closed, and asked if he wanted coffee before she sat opposite him. "I'm staring at you, Tina, because..." He hesitated. "Well, haven't you noticed it?"

"Noticed what?" she asked.

"That you look just like me. Your hair, your eyes, your mouth and nose, all like mine—only younger. You even have my body shape, except for the weight. Catherine is tall, angular, and athletic. Can't you see the resemblance?"

Tina shuffled her feet and tried to get comfortable by crossing her legs. The table was too low, and she banged her knee. She bent down to pull her denim mini over that knee, and then managed to look up at this man who was trying to tell her he was her father. Her father was dead, and had died a long time ago; her mother had told her so. Why was this guy here?

"The resemblance you seem to see is coincidental. Why, exactly, are you here?" she asked. "My father has been dead for years; I think he died before I was born."

"Did your mother tell you that? She let me believe Zach was your father all this time. Imagine that!"

"Zach! You mean that creep who was with her last month? He hates me. She never told me he was my father, and he certainly never suggested such a thing. Why would she let you believe that? Who are you, anyway?"

Confusion filled her brain. Surely there was something about her past here. This guy would never know about Zach and her mother otherwise.

"I don't know why Catherine does anything, but she had this thing for him, and she wouldn't—"

"Um, listen. Robert, is that your name?" Tina interrupted. "I think you're confused. I know I sure am. Let's talk to my mother. She can explain all these misunderstandings." She did not want any more information about herself or about her mother from this stranger. Who knew who he really was? Although she did have to admit his familiar face…it was disturbing.

"I don't think I want to see Catherine. I'm a happily married man, Tina, and I don't need to open old wounds or create new ones for my family. I'm sorry I've come. I needed to see you, but I can see I've done more harm than good. I thought Catherine had told you about me long before this. I'm not here to claim you, if that's what you think; I just needed to see you myself. My own—I mean, other daughter—is younger than you, of course, and is so ill, and…well, I just wanted to see you. You really look very much like her. Catherine only informed me about you're whereabouts in a letter a short time ago. I'm so sorry she's done this to us."

"I can't believe what you're saying. My mother did this to us? Are you saying my mother lied to me all these years?" she questioned, incredulous.

"It appears that way. I'm sorry; I'll go now. I'm glad to have met you and found out the truth at last. I'm just sorry it's too late for us," he said. Then he added, almost as an afterthought, as if he had lost something precious, "You certainly are a Scotland if ever I've seen one.

"I'd better be going," he sighed as he shoved his chair back from the table and made a swift move to leave. She did nothing to stop him or even say goodbye. She sat, stunned, in the little room.

Freda came in to see how she was. "Honey, what happened? You're white as sheet. What did that man say?"

"Huh? Oh. He said he was my father, but my father is dead. I don't know…" Tina's words were almost inaudible.

"Listen, kid, take the rest of the day off. Jean will cover your customers for you. Go talk to your mother. She'll straighten this all out for you." Freda placed a hand on Tina's shoulder. "Go on. Go."

Tina regained some control and stood up. "Thanks, Freda. I guess that's what I'll do."

Chapter 6

Robert

When Robert Scotland had first come into Catherine's life, she had been more vulnerable than usual. Zachary was still a star, and she was tired of hearing, seeing, and reading about him and his exploits. He was a number one womanizer; that much she knew for sure. When she read about his latest affair with a very young ingénue in Hollywood, she thought she would lose her mind with jealousy and loneliness. She'd taken a couple of personal days to get away and think.

That was when she'd gone to Brigantine for the first time, on the recommendation of one of her colleagues who spent his summers there. She stayed in one of the small hotels which had since been demolished to make room for a mansion built by some wealthy family in Philadelphia.

It was there she had met Robert.

Robert Scotland was in Brigantine for much the same reason as Catherine; he needed some time alone to rethink his life since his dead-end job had just about done him in. He knew he had to do something other than keep books for a small engineering firm which promised him no future. His love life was also at a dead end since his girlfriend had dumped him for a much younger man just the month before.

These two unlikely friends met at a sparse "continental breakfast" of one bagel and one pat of butter in the run-down little hotel near the ocean which happened to be just right for both Catherine and Robert. They both fell in love with the island immediately upon discovering it, but neither had the least intention of falling in love with each other—or anyone else, for that matter.

Catherine came to breakfast early, at six-thirty, since she enjoyed walking on the beach right after coffee. She found the almost-deserted beach a joy. She would fill her pockets with small treasures the ocean had coughed up during the night, and delight in watching the seabirds pecking into the sand or flying overhead only to dive down nearly into the water for their own breakfasts. The sea air, the waves, the rhythm of the ocean all helped in washing the cobwebs from her brain. Jealousy seemed farther away in this atmosphere. Even a robust storm, with wind whipping her hair into her face and rain pelting her with shotgun precision, made her spirit soar. These were the kinds of days she loved best; high waves shooting their foam onto the beach, soaking her booted feet, gave her delight no sunny beach day in July ever could. This was the stormy Catherine whom Robert met on that fateful morning.

Their initial conversation was tentative. "Hello, I'm Robert. May I share this table with you?"

"Why not?" Catherine asked, smiling. "Please sit down."

"Rather a sparse breakfast, don't you think?" Robert commented.

"Indeed, yes. Very sparse," was her terse reply.

Catherine lifted a mug to her lips, took a short sip of the hot, black coffee, and continued eating her bagel. Robert opened his with his fork and began spreading butter on one side. Then he opened a second butter square and spread all of it on the other half. Catherine watched, bemused by the amount of fat this slightly overweight man was willing to subject his heart to.

"Do you think I'm overusing the butter?" he asked with a smile in his voice. "I noticed a look of bewilderment on your face when I went for the second pat. I love butter so, yes, I overindulge."

"None of my business, I'm sure," Catherine responded, and to make things lighter and more comfortable she asked him where he was from.

"Pennsylvania." he muttered through dough and fat.

"Oh. I'm from Michigan originally. I've been teaching for a few years, and took a couple of days off to regroup, as they say. I've been a little freaked for a while. Sorry if this is more information than you need. Feel free not to offer any more of your own." Catherine began to feel foolish about saying so much; she had not intended to, but she had.

Robert took some coffee and swallowed hard to get the large bite of bagel down quickly. "I'm glad to talk with you. I've been a bit bummed myself. It's nice to be able to relax with someone you don't know and let a few things hang out without fear of judgment, don't you agree?"

Catherine laughed. "I do."

"What are you doing for the rest of the day?" he queried. "I'd planned to take a ride out to the Cape May Zoo later. Do you think you'd like to join me?"

"Sounds rather nice. Yes, I think I might like to join you, but I'd feel very awkward if I didn't know your last name." Catherine said this, she realized, in what she knew to be a flirtatious tone, and kicked herself under the table.

"Oh, right. I'm Robert Scotland. And you?"

She smiled. "You won't believe this, but I'm Catherine West-Cedar. You're a country and I'm a street, of all things." They both had a good chuckle as they gathered up their cups and plates to take to the sideboard.

"Ten o'clock, down here, sound okay?" Robert asked when he'd deposited his dishes and turned to face Catherine. He was surprised at how tall she was. She was almost regal with her thick reddish hair and svelte athletic figure. He almost laughed at his own height, because they literally stood eye to eye. Catherine said ten was fine and left to change, take her walk, and read for an hour or so prior to her date.

When she got to her room she looked at herself in the mirror and said in disgust, "What the hell did I do that for?" She changed quickly and decided to call this Robert person to cancel. Then she thought better of it when she remembered what Zach was up to, and ran down to the beach. She allowed herself some time to think about Robert. He was not very tall; that was a con. He was very nice looking, though, with dark eyes and almost perfect facial features—small straight nose, lips full and a little prissy, wide-set eyes, strong jaw, and great dark hair which was almost Kennedyish. All pros. The perfection in his face did suggest some femininity; another con. He was very kind looking and obviously interested in her—another pro. So Catherine figured what the heck, go for it.

As he drove to the zoo, he sort of prattled on about himself and his life. He had gone to the University of Pennsylvania, which he claimed was way out in the boonies, where he'd gotten a degree in business. From there he went to the small company which he now rather disliked. He had almost been engaged when he was suddenly jilted for a very young man.

Catherine responded with a little information about herself, not more than Michigan, sister Gwen, and teaching English for a year and a half. He offered his commentary on college football, which was the least of his interests; she told him she rather liked it. They had had a very pleasant day and made plans for more time together.

That was the beginning of the affair. They saw each other off and on for over a year after that, until Robert started making noises about marriage and Catherine felt the old panic return. What if she were married when Zach came back? So she told Robert about Zach, and he suggested she go find him to be sure about her feelings.

Robert had offered to go with her, just for company. He was curious about this guy, and was a little anxious to see just what Catherine was so crazy about. They found where Zach was, but Catherine never connected with him. She learned he was still the playboy and she was unable to deal with that. She would wait. She didn't tell Robert what Zach was up to. Robert had agreed to wait for her in the motel they shared until she'd seen and talked to Zach. They had one short lunch together when Robert saw from a distance the great hero sitting with others at a table, but he saw no hero characteristics in him and said so. Catherine did not care what he thought of Zach, even though Zach had not even looked at her. And then she found out she was pregnant.

Catherine returned to her work; Robert went back to his home and began looking for better work in the hope of getting Catherine to be his wife. But she wrote Robert a letter in which she lied about being with Zachary, told him she was pregnant, and wrote him off. She never saw him again. He never knew he had fathered a daughter, he assumed the football star was the father, and Tina had never met him.

Chapter 7

Tina

When she stopped her little red Volkswagen in front of Catherine's house, Tina realized she could not remember having driven there. All she could think about was that man who claimed to be her father. She had never had a father, and didn't know what to do now. She sat for a while thinking about the past. She remembered, when she was six or seven years old, asking her mother about her father. Catherine had made it clear there simply was no such person for Tina.

"Tina," she'd said when Tina inquired about her own daddy, since all the other kids had one. "You have—or had—a dad just like everybody else, of course. But he is not a part of our lives. He is gone. You'll never see him, so forget it. I'll give you everything you need, don't worry. You don't really need a father as long as you have me—isn't that right, sweetie?"

"I guess so, Mommy," Tina had replied.

"Okay then. Let's never talk about this again." Catherine had permanently closed the subject, and Tina had been afraid to bring it up again. She had made the automatic assumption that whoever he was, her daddy was dead and gone. Why talk about it?

She bit her lip at the memory, knowing they had to talk about it now. Catherine could not turn her off this time. She looked in the rearview mirror, thinking maybe he had followed her. She was acting paranoid and felt annoyed with herself. She adjusted her clothes and pulled at her hair, and got out of the car.

Catherine met her on the front steps. "Tina!" she called before the car door had slammed shut. "I'm sorry, honey. I just got a call from Robert; he had no right. I'm so sorry." All this erupted from Catherine as she flew down the stairs to hug her daughter. Tina stood stiff in her mother's embrace. "You lied to me my whole life, didn't you?" she whispered in her mother's ear.

Catherine released Tina and looked into her eyes, reading the hurt there. *Was there hatred there as well?* she wondered. She wasn't sure, but she knew she had a lot of talking to do to make this right with her child. "Come in the house, Tina. I have some explaining to do." Tina walked woodenly behind her mother as if she were a doll.

Tina went into the living room and dropped into the large dark blue chair. She flung one leg over the arm, put her head back, closed her eyes, and said, "Okay, Mom, explain. This should be good after all these years." Her voice lacked emotion. Catherine had never seen or heard her like this. Tina's posture and tone frightened her. What could she say that would restore things between them? She decided on complete candor.

"Tina, I know now that I have been wrong. I need your forgiveness, but after you hear the truth, you may not be able to forgive me. I pray that you will." Tina shot her mother a look of disdain.

"You never pray, Mother."

"Please don't be so angry. Here's the truth and the reason. I fell in love with Zachary, you know, when I was still in my teens. I was head-over-heels in love with him; maybe you can understand that. He was a big football star in high school, and then in college. He formed his own team in the summer one year, and I was a star on it. I was the only girl, but I was better than many of the guys—faster, you know. I was always fast."

"Get on with it, Mother," Tina demanded, with emphasis on the word "mother."

"Yes. Zachary said he loved me, and we lived together for a year because he promised marriage. He gave me that old football sort of as a commitment present, or maybe as an engagement thing— like a ring, only more significant, I thought at the time. Well, to make a long story short, Zach was drafted into one of the pro leagues after college, and he said he'd have time for our relationship after he'd made it in his new career. He became very famous and very wealthy. He built a reputation as a womanizer, and I was constantly in pain over it. When I called him after the second year, he said no big deal about not having been in contact, but he never came to see me and he never called, until finally—"

"Really, Mother. What does this have to do with my father?" Tina interrupted.

"I'm getting there. I began dating other men. One day I met Robert Scotland, who was sweet, attentive, loving, kind, and honest. He was, in short, everything Zach was not. He had a wonderful face with near-perfect features, but he was short and tended to be pudgy. When I told him I was pregnant, he wanted us to marry. I refused. He went back to Pennsylvania; I went back to Michigan. But he kept writing. I made up a lie that I'd caught up with Zach and slept with him that summer, and that's how I got pregnant. Robert wanted to raise you as his own, but I absolutely refused. 'What if Zach came back for me?' I'd said. He let it go, and I never saw him again."

She paused to look at her daughter, gauging the effect this had. Nothing. "I found him through the phone book, and wrote him some weeks ago to clear the air before Zach came. I think Robert's probably married."

"He is. He has children. My siblings, I guess," Tina added. Then she yelled, "Why would you refuse to marry my father?"

"Tina, you sound so awful; I don't know you like this. Please find it in your heart to forgive me. I meant no harm. How could I marry one man when I was still in love with another? What would I do if Zach came for me and I was married to someone else? I couldn't bear the thought."

"What about Robert? What about me? What about the relationship you took away from us? We could have loved each other all this time. You only loved yourself and that disgusting man who played you for a fool all these years. Mother, how could you? And to have lied to me! You let me believe my father was dead!" Tina burst into tears.

"Honey, don't you see? I was trying to protect you from my own past. I thought it was best for the two of us just to go on together." Catherine pleaded—something she had never done with her daughter before.

"Right. And if Zach had come back at some point? What about me then?"

"He would have loved you like a daughter," Catherine answered weakly.

"Oh, Mother. He isn't even capable of loving you." With this last stab, Tina got up and walked to the door. "You're still waiting for him to come around. Admit it."

"Tina, don't go like this. Let's make this right somehow. We have too many years invested in each other for you to be so angry now. I do love you. Please." Catherine's words fell on deaf ears. Tina was halfway to her car by the time Catherine finished them. She did not turn around to look at her mother; her heart was too sore and her tears too plentiful.

She got into her car and took off. Driving was difficult; she could hardly keep her mind on the road, much less the tears from her eyes. She felt like a rag, a dirty, wet rag, all wrung out, which nobody wanted. Her mother couldn't be trusted, and the father she thought she didn't have just checked in to see what she looked like, then took off. "Nice going, Daddy!" she sneered at the windshield.

When Tina got home, she found it impossible to settle down, to concentrate, or even to eat. She tried taking an aspirin and going to bed in the hope of falling asleep, of forgetting. But aspirin was not enough for this agitation. She tossed and turned, and then got up and turned on the TV. The late-afternoon fare only worsened her mood. Judges were dealing with family problems—divorces, suits against former lovers, child support, and all the things Tina was struggling with. Severely obese girls and boys sat angrily accusing each other of infidelities and all sorts of other sordid behavior on the other shows. She needed fresh air.

Tina walked from her small apartment to Deebold Boat Yard, which was just around the corner. The boats were bobbing up and down in the cool bay waters. Tina sat on the bench for a short time, but even the serenity of this place did not give her peace. At three o'clock she left, not knowing what to do with herself any more. She ran back to her house, up the stairs into her apartment, and wept with agitation, anxiety, and fear. Heavy depression and an awful shaking threatened to take over her body.

Tina did not know where to go with her confusion. She tried reaching one of her old friends up north, but the line was busy. All her former friends were far away—some in Indiana, where she'd gone to middle school while her mother taught high school. Those kids wouldn't even remember her. Some of her friends were in Ridgewood, where she'd gone to high school, but after her mother moved and most of her friends got married, she'd moved to the island to be near her mother. She needed identity—the one thing only her mother could give her.

Now what? No new friends, no trust in her mother, no father except a little fat guy who came, looked, and ran. She did not know where to turn. Her friends were left behind, her mother was anathema at the moment, and her coworkers were not close friends. She considered her Aunt Gwen, who would listen, but she was also too far away. If only she could have stayed for another week or so. They'd had such a good time together a week ago. She always felt that she could say to her aunt everything she could not say to her mother. She decided she needed to hear a loving and familiar voice.

"Hi, Auntie Gwen," she said tentatively when her aunt picked up the receiver.

"Tina! Hi, honey. How are you?"

Before Tina could answer, she began to sob. "I just feel so awful," she finally managed.

"Take a deep breath, Tina. Then tell me what's troubling you."

Tina inhaled, and then slowly let the air out. "Auntie Gwen, I met my father."

"What? When? How?"

"He came to my salon—you know, where I work—at lunchtime."

"How did he know who or where you were?"

"My mother wrote him a letter," she sobbed. "He didn't even know until then that he had a daughter. My mother had never bothered to tell him!"

"I'm so sorry, Tina. I wish I could come and help you. Where is Robert now?"

"He has a family. He went back to them. He didn't want to see Mom; he just wanted to verify what she'd written. Apparently I look like his side of the 'family.' Did you know, Aunt Gwen? Did you know all this time?"

"I begged Catherine to tell you, Tina. You know how stubborn she is. I would have told you myself if I'd known all the facts or thought it would help you. I only knew that she was pregnant, and Zach had nothing to do with it. I just got Robert's name from her last week."

Tina laughed into the phone. "It isn't funny, is it? We got his name almost at the same time."

"Listen, Tina, before you decide to hate me—the telling was not up to me. It was Catherine's responsibility, and as long as Robert Scotland was not aware, I couldn't see how my interference would have helped. Besides, Catherine, being who she is, did manipulate a vow of silence out of me. I'm more than sorry for you, honey. This was not the way to find out. I can hear how upset you are."

"I don't think anybody knows how upset I am. I hate my mother for what she's done. I can't even bear to talk to her. It's always, 'But Zach…' What a creep!"

"I know. Catherine is obsessed, but don't be too harsh on her. She is your mother, and I know she loves you very much. Why don't you put all your thoughts on paper—write a letter to her. You never have to send it. I think that might help to start. Then find somebody to talk to."

"Yeah, okay. I'll see. Bye."

Finally, after an hour of thinking, hating, and crying, she called the only person on the island whom she thought might understand, the only person who knew both her and her mother, and might be willing to lend an ear. The one kind face she might be able to trust.

Chapter 8

William's Advice

William's phone rang and rang. He rushed from his back yard, where he was tending to his little flower garden, to answer it, but the party had hung up without leaving a message. He shrugged it off, and then wondered if it had been a person he wanted to talk to or just another telemarketer. They called at the most inconvenient times. In fact, they called all the time. But William had a feeling he might need to know who this caller was. He didn't know why, but he picked up the phone and dialed *69. He got an unfamiliar number from the service, but he dialed and waited. Finally a trembling voice said, "Hello."

"I'm sorry to bother you, miss, but I think you just called me and I couldn't get to the phone on time. Who is this?"

Sweet, considerate William. He bothered to find out who it was, Tina thought. "It's me, Tina Cedar." Tina had dropped the "West" right after high school. "I'm in sort of a quandary, and I don't know who to talk to."

"Well, Tina, I'll be glad to help, but what about your mother? Shouldn't you go to her?"

"She's the trouble," Tina answered.

"Oh? Well." He hesitated. "Will this little chat get me into trouble with Catherine? I mean, should I know about whatever is bothering you?"

"I need you to know."

"This sounds serious. But I do have time and I do love company." He paused to think, and then said, "Tell you what, Tina. Why don't you pop by and we'll have a nice cup of tea. Will that do?"

"Thanks, William. Tea is good. I'll be right over."

William was not at all sure about his place in Tina's life, especially where trouble with Catherine was concerned. He only knew Tina from a few meetings at dinner with Catherine, and the few times he'd seen her at church. He anticipated her arrival with a bit of apprehension; he moved around his kitchen, bumping into the table then rubbing his thigh, and almost dropping the teapot on the counter. *Catherine has been acting oddly lately, what with this strange man she's been entertaining and all. I wonder what this has to do with me?* he wondered as he arranged the things for tea.

The road to William's house took Tina from the bay to the center of town, around the lighthouse and down Brigantine Boulevard. She drove by the various restaurants where she'd had dinner with William and her mother, and then past the shopping center. She hung a quick left into the parking lot of the little mall, almost hit a pickup she never saw, parked outside the Shop and Bag, and ran into the store to pick up some sweets for William. She didn't even remember to lock her car. She thought it would be nice to bring something to have with tea.

She surprised herself with her ability to do even this much thinking about something so ordinary. She even thought to give Freda a call so she would be apprised of the situation. As she fumbled for her cell phone while at the checkout, she heard the woman behind her complain, "Can't these people talk where there's privacy? Like outside?" She said the last word a little too loud. Tina ignored her as she paid for the donuts, and then dialed on her way out of the store.

Freda told her to take the next day off if she felt she needed it.

When she passed her mother's house, she felt a wave of nausea and hoped she'd passed by unnoticed. She parked as far down Sunset Court as possible, on the opposite side of the street, and walked to William's. She didn't want to risk the chance her mother would see her car. Right now, she didn't want her mother to know anything she was doing. She needed space and distance.

Tina rang William's doorbell and moved into the shadow on his front step. When he opened the door, he didn't even see her until she stepped forward.

"Were you hiding, Tina? What on earth for?" he asked.

"Oh, William. It's my mother. I just don't want her to know I'm here." Tina hurried inside.

"Well, come in. I've made some tea, Tina. How would you like it, hot or iced?" He directed her into the small sitting room which looked out over the beach and ocean. It was painted light green, with white trim around the windows and narrow French doors. The blinds were also green, as were the rug and other accessories. White and light yellow accents were provided by curtains, pillows, and a luscious wool throw. This room was designed to calm.

She sat down with a sigh and peered out the window. The ocean was calm and glistening with sparks of light. People were walking on the beach with small children in tow. Some were lying on blankets, letting the sun do its work on their already bronzed bodies. Still others, children mostly, boogie-boarded their way out into the water in the hope of finding a wave or current to take them back in. The scene before her was familial and tranquil, and she wondered how all these people could be so happy when she felt such pain and confusion. Life is full of mysteries, and Tina felt caught in the maelstrom of one.

"Tina?" William interrupted her thoughts. "Will that be iced or hot?"

"Oh, I'm sorry. Hot, please. And I brought some donuts to have with our tea. I thought you might like that."

"You didn't have to do that, but thanks. It's very thoughtful of you." He chuckled, "Now that I think about it, I guess you already told me you preferred hot tea on the phone. My brain is getting a little mushy, I'm afraid." William poured two cups of tea, and went to the cupboard for some cake plates and napkins. He set everything down on the table, which was fast becoming overcrowded. William had furnished this little room to be a kind of nook, creating a cozy intimate atmosphere; he'd placed a small café table and two chairs near one window, but it could accommodate only one diner. The rest of the room contained a bookcase, telephone table, and a telescope on a large tripod, as well as one easy chair. This was William's special place for watching the beach and the wildlife, and for reading. Tina felt very special to be sitting here with him. He apparently thought she needed some tender loving care to have provided this welcoming spot to talk.

Tina opened the bakery boxes and offered William his choice; she was too upset to eat. She cradled the teacup in both hands, her elbows resting at the edge of the little table. She sat so close to the edge of her chair that William was afraid she'd fall off.

"So, Tina, tell me what's troubling you about your mother." William had a teacup in one hand and a French cruller in the other. He took a bite from the cruller, a sip of tea, and waited.

Tina tightened her grasp on the cup and began. "My father showed up at work this morning."

"You mean Zachary is back already?" William was incredulous. The guy had only just left.

"No, William. Zachary is not my father," she reported slowly and methodically. "A man named Robert Scotland is, apparently." She paused to measure the effect of this revelation on William. His forehead wrinkled in confusion. "He got a letter from my mother telling him that he was my father, and he came looking for me. He just wanted to see who I was, but he didn't want to see mom. He thought I knew; he thought surely my mother would have told me. I think she should have. Now he's gone, I know my mother is a liar, and I can't figure out who I really am or how my mother could have done this to me. I hate her right now!" Tina cried.

"Let me get this straight. Your mother has always claimed to be in love with this Zachary person who spent the past month with her. She told me that much, to my chagrin. But now we find out she had had an affair with this Scotland man? Is that what you're telling me? And you're this other man's daughter? And neither he nor you knew anything about it?"

"That's how it seems."

"Did you talk to Catherine about this? What did she say?"

"Yes. She said she did it to protect me. She wanted me to stay and talk, but I couldn't." Tears welled up in her eyes.

"Well, this is a bit of a mess, isn't it?" William put his teacup down, chewed thoughtfully on his cruller, finished it, and wiped his mouth and hands with his napkin. He sat back and considered Tina as though she were one of the rare birds he so loved to study. "You feel betrayed," he began. "I can understand that. Did Catherine tell you whether or not your father had wanted to marry her?"

"He did," was the curt reply. Tears spilled from Tina's eyes.

"And she told him she was waiting for Zachary, I take it," William said knowingly.

"Yes, of course. That weird man has dominated her whole life, and he wasn't even around! She denied me a family, siblings, and all that goes with it for this guy who never even showed up. Can you believe it? And then she lied on top of it. How will I ever be able to be decent to her again?"

"Hmm. That will take time, of course." Then he continued, "Tina, are you asking me for advice, or are you just venting? I'll listen, of course, but I'll also tell you what I think if you want to hear it. I've been thinking a lot about Catherine myself for the past few weeks."

"I don't know. I guess I need to hear what you have to say. But don't tell me to talk to her again, because I'm not going to do that. She manipulated my entire life in a way she had absolutely no right to. I don't want to see her." She banged her fist on the table and sent one of William's china teacups sailing across the room. It landed with a bang on the little circular green rug, but did not shatter. She looked over to see the result. "Oops! Oh, William, I'm so sorry," she cried.

"You're obviously overwrought right now, Tina. My guess is that you're in a state of shock of a sort. You've just found out who your true father is; you met him and he left. Not a good thing, I'd say. On top of that, your mother has admitted she has lied to you your whole life—also not a good thing. You have a lot to digest, and you may be right; it is probably best that you don't see her for a while. However, would you give me permission to go and talk to her about our visit? It may help in the future."

"What future? I don't want a future," Tina said petulantly.

"Yes, you do. You're just not ready to face anything right now." William reached over and patted Tina's hand, but not in a patronizing way, and she felt it.

"Go see her, then. She'll probably tell you some lies anyway. What can anyone believe that comes from her mouth anymore?" Tina spat.

"Tina, I know it's impossible for you to do this right now, or even to think about it, but someday you're going to have to forgive her for all of this. You'll need to for your own peace of mind. She is your mother, and she was not trying to hurt you. Even in her deception, she thought she was doing the best for you."

"She was only doing the best for herself—in case Zach came."

"Yes. Well, try to keep in mind what I said. You'll need strength, but I'm sure you'll get it in time. First, you need to give yourself time, and probably some distance." With that he got up and cleared the table. He leaned on the counter in the kitchen, took one more pastry from the box and chewed it methodically as he worried about the woman, still a child in many ways, sitting in his sanctuary, at his table. He went back into the room. "What are you going to do with the rest of today?"

"I don't know. Maybe I'll just go sit on the beach for a while and think."

"It might be a good idea to get together with a friend or two and take a little vacation— get away from your mother entirely for a while. Why don't you call a friend from up north and see if you can't arrange something?"

"I don't know. What about my job?" Her voice was still sullen and weak.

"Did your boss seem sympathetic today?" he asked.

"Yes. Freda is wonderful, really."

"Well, then, I'm sure she'll understand and find someone to cover for you. Have you ever been to Italy?" William asked with a smile.

"Italy?" Tina said incredulously. She had never been abroad, never even considered it. The sound of the word shocked her. "Why Italy? How do I do that?"

"Italy for the colors, the warmth, the food, the clear cobalt-and-green Mediterranean, for antiquity and art and distance. For Venice, Florence, Orvieto, Assisi, Perugia, Rome, Capri. You should see it all. It will get into your soul and cleanse you in a way that will leave you entirely refreshed. Italy is a paradise, and just the kind of environment you need." He waited to see her response, and was pleased to see her smile just a little. He continued, "Get cut-rate airfares on one of the Internet sites and just do it. If you need a loan, I'd love to help." He looked at her now-interested expression and drove his point home. "You need the time and a complete change of scenery. Try it. What do you say?"

"Do you think I could?" she asked tentatively.

"If you want to, you can," William assured her.

"Well, maybe I'll call Saskia Van Ryn. She's always up for anything," she replied, musing. She pondered for a minute, and then saw the possibility take shape. "Thanks, William. I'll get right on it. God knows I need to get away from here, and this weight that threatens to bury me." She got up, hugged William, and ran out the door.

Tina was careful to take an alternate route home. She did not want her mother to see her. When she got home, she called Saskia at her small Bergen County studio right away. She was immediately receptive.

Saskia had had a yen to get back to Italy since she had studied art there a few summers ago. She could also speak enough Italian to get them by in a pinch. "What fun this will be!" she added as the two finalized their plans.

Saskia promised to take care of the details and get back to Tina as soon as she had. Tina had not told her friend why she wanted to get away, but Saskia was such a free spirit it never occurred to her that anyone needed a reason to pick up and go off to Italy for a while.

Tina hung up the phone and went into the bathroom to wash her tear-stained face. Her reflection brought back the pain. While washing, the phone rang. *That must be Saskia*, she thought, which lightened her mood again. "Hello," she sang into the phone.

"Well, I'm glad to hear you're feeling a little better than you were a few hours ago," Catherine intoned.

"Oh, it's you." Tina's voice had changed immediately. Her disdain disarmed Catherine.

"Yes, it's me. Why not? Are you ready to talk about our misunderstanding? I still have a few things to say about it." Catherine used her usual masterful tone and expected it to manipulate Tina into submission.

"You call lies and deception 'a little misunderstanding,'

Mother? I don't. I'm going away for a while. I don't care to see you right now or to talk about this any more. I need distance and time. William will explain."

"William? Why William? What does he have to do with this?" Catherine was angry now. How could Tina have been so stupid as to involve William in their personal life? What had happened was certainly none of his business.

"He's a friend, Mother. I need to go now." With that, Catherine heard a click as the phone went dead. She felt as if ice water had poured into her heart at the distance she felt from her daughter. She never expected Tina to be able to react like this. What strength had suddenly possessed her child?

When she tried to reach Tina later that evening, she got no answer and no opportunity to leave a message; the answering machine had been turned off. Catherine was furious.

She went to her painting class on Tuesday and threw every color combination she could mix onto the large canvas. She knew this might create nothing but mud, but that was the way she felt. Splash—on went the red; splash—on went the ochre; splash—on went three different blues mixed together, followed by raw umber, lemon yellow, and magenta. When her teacher, Edvard Boucher, a retired professor from New York came to check on her, he got splashed on the cheek with a rude mix of alizarin crimson and raw umber. He was so taken with Catherine's exuberant abstract that he hardly noticed what she'd flung onto his cheek. "This may well become your masterpiece, Cathy," he enthused.

She flung all her fury on him. "Never call me 'Cathy'! Never, never, never!" When she saw his face with the brown-crimson stain on his right cheek, she suddenly stopped and laughed. "Oh, I'm sorry about the paint." She began to wipe at his face with her dirty rag with the result that he looked more comical the more she rubbed. Edvard caught her hand, placed it at her side, and said, "Don't do that! I apologize for calling you 'Cathy.' I just want you to know you are developing into a real artist at last." Then he picked up a paint rag, dipped it in Skin So Soft, wiped his cheek clean, and moved on to the next student.

Catherine was left with a cheek redder than her teacher's. Her fury had somewhat abated, and she stood back to look at her painting. She thought she would call it "Tina," but first it needed tears. She took her most powerful white titanium, dipped her brush in linseed oil and right into the tube of paint, and then threw little blobs of white all over the canvas. As they ran and formed natural-looking tears, she smiled at the process. She stood back and observed her work. "Tina!" she said, and wrote her signature in bold letters across the bottom. But Tina was not available to her for a long time.

Chapter 9

Admission

In the week that followed, Catherine tried to get William to come and talk to her. She got all kinds of lame excuses, from "there are egrets out today" to "I have to paint the bedroom." He finally agreed to meet with her on Saturday for breakfast at his house.

On Saturday morning, William greeted Catherine with a smile and a hug, as if he had not been putting her off for an entire week. She stiffened at his touch and spoke coldly. "You think you can put me off for a whole week with silly-ass excuses, and then get a warm 'hello' as if nothing is wrong? You think you can let my daughter confide in you, tell me nothing about it, and then go back to our friendship as if everything were normal? No, no, no, William. It isn't that simple—not with Catherine West-Cedar, let me assure you. Now, what's for breakfast? Then we'll talk!" She moved through his kitchen and out onto his little deck with the authority of a drill sergeant, placing herself at the table facing the beach. There she turned an imperious look on William and pointed to a chair.

He smirked and did not sit. He ignored her nonsense, which he knew it to be, and went inside to get a tray with coffee, bagels, cream cheese, and smoked salmon, which he knew Catherine loved. He set the tray down and poured her a cup of coffee. "Here, drink this first. It'll calm you down." He sat across from her and looked her in the eye. "Drink," he repeated, "you need it." She was incredulous. How had these soft people suddenly become strong? What had happened to her best weapon?

She picked up her mug and swallowed some coffee. It was some of the best she'd ever had. William did make great coffee. She couldn't stay angry, but she wasn't going to give an inch either. "Okay, William. Let's eat and get this conversation under way."

"Yes, well, have some lox; I got the best I could find. It's your favorite. Eat!" She had never known William could be so commanding.

She enjoyed the bagel and lox; it was a real treat. She knew she was being manipulated, but lox could not be resisted. "I'll eat and you talk, okay? Where is Tina?"

"In Italy," he said between bites.

"Italy? Tina? What the hell is Tina doing in Italy? Is she alone?" She almost spit her bagel out with her words.

"Don't get excited, Catherine. Tina can take care of herself. She's not alone. Saskia Van Ryn is with her."

"What? That artsy trollop? She's after every man who crosses her path. A lot of good she's going to do Tina—in Italy, yet. You know what those Italian guys are like? And what they look like?"

"Stop it right now, Catherine," William demanded. "Tina is in Italy with her friend to get away from you for a while. You can hardly blame her after what you laid on her last week." She opened her mouth to speak, but he put up his hand to keep her quiet. "Just think for a minute. You told your daughter that her father was dead. She believed you'd loved him, and he'd died. Then she met Zachary, who was not a warm glow in her life, although you seem to think he is in yours. Then her real father shows up at her work, tells her he has a family—in essence, that she has siblings—then takes off. And you give her Zachary as your reason for lying. Are you getting the picture? Your daughter is hurt, confused, angry, and very upset. I advised her to go to Italy. I even gave her the money. Be as mad as you like about it."

"I hear a distinct tone of judgment in your little speech," Catherine surmised.

"Catherine, I think the world of you, but I find your behavior rather abominable, especially where your daughter is concerned. She should have known the truth from the start, when she was still very small, in my opinion."

"Oh, really? In your opinion, eh? And what do you know about my life? Zachary and I were engaged, you know. That means something. I promised I'd wait for him. And that meant something to me, too. He gave me his lucky football as a symbol instead of a ring, because it meant so much more. I still have it in my closet. I don't know what business of yours any of this is!" she suddenly shouted. William munched a bagel quietly and calmly looked at Catherine. "Anyway, by the time Tina's father came along, Zach was already a major football star. I knew that football meant more to him than anything else, but I also thought he'd have to quit by the time he was in his thirties. So I saved a place for him in my life. You blame me for that?"

"You're right. It really isn't any of my business," he admitted. "Tina made some of it my business, but you don't need to tell me any more than you have."

"Right. And you'll draw your own conclusions, half of which will be wrong! Well, let me tell you, William, I had my reasons. And you're in it up to your neck, so you're going to hear them whether you like it or not."

"Go ahead, Catherine, I'll listen. I'll try not to judge."

"All right, then. As I was saying—by the time Tina's father came along, Zach was already a major football star. I knew that meant more to him than anything else, but, as I said, I also thought he'd have to quit soon, so I saved a place for him in my life. Do you blame me for that?"

"No."

"Then why that look? You said you weren't going to judge!"

"I'm only judging for Tina. She should have been told some of this early on in her life. You have only yourself to blame for the present mess." Catherine looked as though she would explode. "Don't be angry with me, Catherine; Tina came to me broken. I told her to go to you, but she refused." William needed to make her understand that he did not invite himself into the private life of either of the two women, nor did he enjoy the part he'd been forced to play. But he'd felt Tina's need and knew he had to respond to it. He would do what he could for her sake, and maybe help Catherine see herself in the process. One cannot change without understanding one's own foolishness.

Catherine was quick to respond. "All right! I'm not angry with you, really. I'm sorry, of course, that Tina refused to talk with me, and I'm really upset that she left for Italy without telling me. But I'm going to assume that wasn't your doing. I am upset that you helped her accomplish it without telling me. William, let me tell you what I'm really mad about, what I really hate."

"You don't have to tell me anything, Catherine, if you don't want to. Don't entangle me in your life any more than you feel comfortable." William was exercising caution; he felt he already knew more than he needed to.

"And please don't use the word   entangle.' I'll tell you what I really hate, and that's what pro ball has done to my life. I hate what it did to Zach; I hate what it did to Tina. I hate the way it takes young men and exploits them for money, for capital gain. These young guys see nothing but fame and dollar signs. They willingly forsake everything else in their lives for fame and fortune. And then there's the sports scholarship. What an oxymoron that is. Think about it—sports scholarship! Get it?

Now what in the world has sports to do with being a scholar? And when they get into their thirties, sometimes sooner, they wreck their knees or some other essential body part. I despise pro ball for what it does to lives, for the hypocrisy of it."

William interrupted Catherine's tirade with, "Hypocrisy, hmmm? Did Zachary have a sports scholarship, by any chance?"

"Of course he did."

"But he wasn't much of a scholar, I take it."

"Well he's not a raving intellectual, if that's what you mean, but he's no lightweight, either. He could have been a fine lawyer or something if that glowing carrot hadn't been hung in front of his nose by the team that drafted him." Catherine was still smoldering.

Interesting metaphor for this guy, William thought, and then continued, "Did he give you that engagement football you spoke of earlier when he left college to go pro?"

"Yes. It had been given to him by his favorite coach as a reward for an outstanding play. It meant the world to him, so I believed he'd come around when he was done with the big time."

"But he never did. And you turned love away all these years for that empty promise in the back of your closet. Catherine, I believe you're blaming sports for a whole lot more than it deserves. Pro ball has a lot of issues to be sure, but wrecking your love life and messing up Tina's life are is not among them. That responsibility is your own."

"What? How dare you, William!" Catherine was livid, but William put his hand up again.

"Let's leave it. Hear me out and then I'll quit. For Tina's sake and your own, try to understand that Zachary, as you perceive him, does not exist. And he never has, I'm sure. It seems obvious that he never meant to come back to you. He never meant to love you exclusively. In fact, guys like Zachary probably don't have the faintest idea of what that kind of commitment means. You're in love with an ideal on which you have placed his face; you've made a god out of a man. You love your fantasy.

"Get over it for now. Let's just quietly mull these things over and consider the best for Tina, each in our own way."

"I don't know about mulling; I've mulled it over most of my adult life. You just don't understand Zachary. I don't think anybody does."

"Shall I tell you why?"

Catherine squinted into the sun. "You already did. Is there more? I'm sure it'll probably be something like Gwen's thinking. All right, go ahead. But I'm not promising civility afterwards."

"Okay." William took a long breath and a swallow of coffee. He wasn't at all sure he wanted to get into this morass, but his feet were already wet, so he decided to wade all the way in.

"For Tina's sake and for your own, try to understand that Zachary—or what you've made him in your mind—doesn't exist. As I've said, he never has. He never meant to come back to you; he never meant to love you exclusively. He always meant to seduce every woman he could. I'm sure he doesn't have any idea about the kind of love that makes a marriage successful. It's about sacrifice and giving, about compromise, about the other person. He didn't think of you all these years; do you believe he is now? Let it go, Catherine, before some irreparable damage is done—worse than has already been made. You may still be able to reclaim some of what you've lost over the years. Just let go of this guy and what you think he is, and get on with real life."

"Real. Like you, perhaps?"

"Don't be obtuse. Tina needs you, but came to me. Take what I said or leave it. It's your life, Catherine; I didn't and don't mean to interfere. I was involved against my will, and so decided to run with it." William brushed some crumbs from his lap, placed his napkin on the table, and stood up. "Enjoy the rest of your breakfast. I've got some wildlife to look after." He grabbed his coffee cup, got into his car, and started it up. When he hit the remote, the kitchen door flew open just as the garage door was beginning to rise.

Catherine ran out and knocked on the window. "I'm sorry for that last comment, William." Catherine knew this was a friend she could not afford to lose, even in the present circumstances. "Thank you for breakfast, especially the lox. And for helping Tina. Really. I'll lock up for you," she added, and went back inside.

William watched her back stiffen as she threw her shoulders back and walked into his house. He shook his head and drove away, not knowing if he'd made any impact at all.

Chapter 10

A Short Message

Just when Catherine was hoping Tina would return from her trip, she got a postcard. "Mom, we've extended our stay. See you next month. T." That was all; a cold missile from a warm climate. Catherine went to throw the terse message away, but thought better of it. She tucked it in a kitchen drawer under some bank receipts, and decided to go for a swim to cool off. Her art lesson would not start for another hour. She needed a little time before she could engage in artsy small talk, but she was upset enough to again produce what Dr. Boucher would call "masterpiece." The first was drying in the attic, and no one outside the class was destined to see it, if Catherine had her way. She made her way to her bedroom to change and, in a déjà vu moment, thought she saw Zach on the bed. She smiled as she changed into her swimsuit.

The water was icy this afternoon. The current must have shifted, because it had been wonderful just twenty-four hours before. Catherine shivered but did not get out until she'd dived through at least three large waves and let the fourth skim her to shore, landing her on her belly in the wet sand. The undertow would have taken her back out, but she was quick to get to her feet and onto sturdier ground.

The cold water had done her good. She toweled herself down and rubbed her hair. With an audible sigh, she walked up the beach to her house, and showered the salt and sand out of her hair and off her body.

When she was ready to leave the house, she went to the drawer where the postcard lay, and took it out to re-examine it. On the front was a picture of Capri rising out of the shimmering Mediterranean. *Tina must be having the time of her life*, Catherine thought, and put it away.

Chapter 11

Italy

When Tina and Saskia got into the large boat with the other twenty-or-so tourists, Tina thought the Blue Grotto would be a large cave the boat would just sail into. They were very surprised to find tiny rowboats with jovial men carrying long poles in each awaiting them. Only one rowboat could enter at a time, and four to five people at most fit into each. When their eyes were directed to the little hole in the bottom of the island through which they were to go, Tina gave Saskia a nervous look. Saskia was getting used to Tina's nerves, and so paid little attention to her friend's anxiety. "This is going to be fun!" Saskia exclaimed. "I can hardly wait. I wonder if we can take our cameras in there." Another passenger leaned over and assured her that was the thing to do. Saskia thanked him and hung her Nikon on her back. Tina did the same with her little camera.

One person at a time was helped into a little boat, handed down by the local tour guide and helped by the rower of the smaller vessel. Tina was surprised at the strong hand of the Italian who guided her. His gleaming white smile and burning dark eyes unnerved her for a moment. *Wow,* she thought, *these Italian guys are something else.* Saskia, of course, couldn't let it alone, and gave him a wink and her most engaging smile. "*Grazie*," she said. "*Prego*," he responded. He held her hand a little longer than necessary and seated her close to himself. Tina felt a twinge of jealousy. She wished she could be more like Saskia—totally unselfconscious and a bit of a flirt. But Tina was reserved, tight and unapproachable, especially since her encounter with her father, a man she did not know. She felt positive she would now never really know herself either.

The little boat bobbed on the clear water as the handsome young Italian pushed it towards the hole in the cliff. The closer they got, the more convinced Tina was that they would never fit through. Suddenly the man caught hold of a chain on the side of the rock, yelled for everyone to duck, and with one great pull slid the boat inside. Gasps of amazement and delight echoed through the cave. The cave was pitch black on one side, and brilliant blue on the other. The sunlight shed an azure and cobalt glow through the water, as if the sun shone up from the depths. Tina was delighted. The beauty grabbed her and lifted her imagination to new levels. No one could imagine this; it had to be experienced.

The guide broke the silence with the announcement that he would sing for them for a dollar. Saskia immediately pulled a single out of her pocket and pressed it into his hand. He began to sing a lovely Italian tune Tina could not understand, but which was directed straight at Saskia. One could only guess what it was about. Saskia was delighted at the beautiful tenor voice as it reverberated in the massive cave. Tina wouldn't have missed this for anything; Saskia was equally taken, but not with the scene alone. Cameras took shots from all the little boats. "Capture what you can in case your memory fails you" seemed to dominate the atmosphere.

When they arrived back at the island, Saskia admitted that she'd had as much fun flirting as observing the natural phenomenon. Tina laughed at her friend's consistency, but she did not laugh when Saskia told her she would be seeing Vanni, the oarsman, that evening. "Saskia, how could you? You don't even know anything about him," Tina complained.

"I know," answered Saskia with a smirk. "That's why I told him I wouldn't see him alone. I told him you'd be with us. Just think, Tina. Won't it be fun?"

"If you call me chaperoning you and some Italian hunk whose language I can't even understand fun!" Tina exclaimed.

"Don't you get it? He won't come alone if you're going to be there. You, my dear friend, are going on a blind date with another Italian hunk!" Saskia put her arm around Tina's shoulder and laughed.

Tina did not respond in kind. She wanted nothing to do with anyone who spoke a different language and she had never met, let alone let him take her somewhere unfamiliar in a foreign country. When Tina voiced her protests and misgivings, Saskia laughed. "Don't be such a prude, Tina. I speak Italian, and we won't go anywhere unfamiliar, I promise. It'll just be a little fling to laugh about when we get old."

"I can hardly wait," Tina answered sarcastically.

As it turned out, the two young men were perfect gentlemen, and Tina indeed had a good time. She even gave her address to Alessandro, her very polite blind date. He wasn't a typical hunk; he was tall and lanky with sort of beige hair, dressed in a black tee over black jeans. His eyes took her by surprise, though—deep blue with flecks of light yellow, amazing eyes that looked at her with kindness and fascination. He was cool, interesting, and very infatuated with Tina. He walked her up and down the narrow streets of Capri, explaining everything. He bought her the most wonderful limoncello, and got her a bottle to take home. Lemon trees were ubiquitous; lemons the shape of footballs, and almost that size, hung everywhere. Alessandro picked her one and told her to sniff. No lemon had ever smelled so fragrant to Tina. She found him charming and warm.

Saskia was not impressed with Vanni once she got to talk with him; she found him shallow and a bit too full of himself. While Alessandro swept Tina away with his commentary on their surroundings, Vanni regaled Saskia about his many talents, exploits, and dreams. He was obviously used to having women fall all over him. Sometimes exceptional good looks were more a bane than a boon. When Vanni hinted at breakfast together, Saskia smiled and whispered in his ear that he was very nice, but she thought not. He smiled, shrugged, and left. Alessandro kissed Tina's hand and followed his friend.

Following the trip to Capri, Saskia suggested a return to Florence, the medieval city from which they had driven south. Of Rome, Venice, and Florence, the three famous cities they visited, both girls loved Florence best. Not only was it the most beautiful place, filled with art and antiquity everywhere one turned, but the gelato was absolutely exquisite. Tina thought the trip worth it for that alone; she could not get enough of it, and was sure she'd gained ten pounds because of it.

When they returned to Florence, the first thing Saskia wanted to do was take some pictures of the statues, which were everywhere. Tina was amazed at the angles Saskia was shooting from. "Why the backs?" she wanted to know.

Saskia giggled. "I'm doing a butt series. I'm even going to do some writing to go with it. Let's go to one of the leather stores and buy a souvenir. Hey, let's get one of those hats with our initials written on the underside of the visor in gold. What do you say, Tina?"

Tina's money had run out the first week, but Saskia covered her for the rest. A loan among friends is sometimes more than simply a loan, Saskia told Tina, when they decided to stay longer than planned. Tina asked what that meant and Saskia would only say, "Don't ask. We'll deal with it later."

When they left the store, each wearing a leather cap—Tina's black, Saskia's red—they laughed and laughed. Some boys playing guitars in the piazza stopped to stare and smile at the two American girls having what appeared to be the time of their lives. "Look." Saskia pointed. "Every piazza in the center of the old town is filled with sculptures." And she shot the backside of every single one.

The buildings they visited also contained sculptures, paintings, and frescos. Every building was a museum, every street history. Saskia, in her artistic exuberance, snapped picture after picture of the backs of sculptures. She caught the magnificence of Neptune in the Piazza della Signoria, all the backsides of the sculptures in front of the Palazzo Vecchio, and the musculature of the men in *The Rape of the Sabine Women*. She concentrated on Michelangelo's *David*—the original in the Accademia Gallery as well as the replica, also in the Piazza della Signoria, where the world had first seen him.

Tina took in the art and architecture with eyes wide open in constant wonder, and her little digital camera became almost attached to her right cheek. When she stood in front of the Battistero San Giovanni and heard the guide explain the *Gates of Paradise*, she nearly fainted. A tourist from Iowa caught her just in time. He held her up, walked her to the outside of the crowd, and handed her over to Saskia, who was close behind. Saskia thanked the man, who told them this was not uncommon among tourists in Florence.

"I'm Sol Apel," he said, introducing himself. "I teach art at a university in Iowa. Your friend may be suffering from Stendhal syndrome." Saskia had heard of this; it is a psychosomatic reaction to the abundance of art in Florence or other places. Professor Apel further explained that when Stendhal experienced it in the nineteenth century, the sight of the artworks transported him into a state of ecstasy. Another artist, Anselm Feuerbach experienced similar symptoms in 1856, when he was overwhelmed by tears in the Uffizi Gallery and the Palazzo Pitti.

Tina hoped that she would be able to endure; she felt totally wiped out. Only an exquisite double-dip caramel-mocha gelato cone from the *gelateria* managed to bring her back to herself a bit. It set the girls back about six dollars each, but they knew no price could be set on superb fixes for the palate and psyche.

They returned to their hostel later that afternoon. Tina took a much needed nap while Saskia busied herself with her journal. When Tina awoke, Saskia exclaimed, "Hey, Teen, listen to this." Saskia recited a poem she had written in her most dramatic voice:

> The beauty
> of bones
> muscles, veins
> and butts
> Carved from
> marble by
> men like
> Michelangelo
> Would inspire no
> awe, show no
> beauty if Adam
> had not first
> been carved from
> mud and stood
> butt-naked
> perfection before
> his Creator.
> "And this one."
> The Statues of Florence
> Oh, statuary
> Florentine mastery
> of naked masculinity.
> Chiseled artistry
> solid butts
> stationary. More fun if alive!

"How do you like them Teen?" she laughed. Tina had to admit it was fun. "Yeah, and I've got more. I'm going to do some illustrations and call it my *Book of Butts*. What do you think?"

Laughter brought Tina back to earth, but nothing could ever erase the memory of this place and the ecstasy it had produced.

One of the secret things she hid even from Saskia was her last few minutes with Alessandro. They had exchanged addresses and e-mails, just in case either felt they wanted to stay in touch. They'd agreed to wait a month to see if the desire to communicate was still there. Tina was sure it would be.

Chapter 12

No Reconciliation

Through the rest of August, Catherine kept busy with her art and volunteer work in an effort to avoid William. She knew she needed to keep his friendship, but she also knew she needed time to assess her feelings. She tried to tell herself she was angry for his interference in her private life, and angry too because of his audacity to be judgmental. But she had to admit to herself—although never to William—was that she was embarrassed. She knew deep down she had done her daughter a great injustice, but she also knew she had not been able to risk losing Zachary, even if only as a hope for some future time.

As soon as Tina returned from Italy, she called her mother to tell her she was home. It was a Saturday evening, very late. Catherine asked if she had had a good time; Tina simply answered "Yes," and ended the conversation with that. Catherine refused to accept her daughter's cold shoulder any longer. She got into her car the minute Tina hung up and tore across the island to Tina's house, and then stomped up the two steps to her front door and banged on it. Tina opened it very slightly to see who it was. The banging made her nervous, but when she saw her mother, her nervousness turned to anger. "How dare you come here at this time of night and bang on my door like that. You scared the wits out of me, Mother!"

"Well, you scared the wits out of me when you ran off to Italy for a month—"

Tina interrupted, "Three and a half weeks."

"Whatever. Too long, at any rate, without communicating anything at all—"

"I sent a card." Tina interjected.

"One lousy card with no information during almost a month's absence. And then this little phone call just informing me you're back. You hung up on me!"

"I said goodbye."

"Tina, when are you going to let me talk to you? We need to get back what we had. We can't live like this. We are our only relatives."

Tina was almost too quick to reply, "Apparently not. I seem to have more somewhere."

"That's not fair, Tina."

"You're the one who's not fair, Mother." She still held the door open just a crack. "I always trusted you. And then I find out, in a weird incident, that the guy following me to work is my father, and that I have siblings. I never even knew it. I'm twenty-five, Mother, and I grew up without knowing!" Tina cried the last part, tears flowing down her cheeks. The dam had finally broken; she sobbed and sobbed as she had not done since she was a small child. Then, the awful pain had been a child's. This pain was the child's as well as this woman's, and it reached to the depths of her being. She'd lost faith in her mother, the only parent she had ever known, and she'd lost touch with herself. Italy had been a good salve for her wound, but it had not healed the deeper infection.

Catherine pushed the door open and came in. She wanted to reach for her daughter and pull her onto her lap to protect her from harm as she had done so often in the past. But this time, she was the harm and Tina was a grown woman. She finally found the courage to say, "Tina. honey, you need help with this, and I'm obviously not the one to give it to you. It was good that William could be there initially, but now you need more. I think you should see a professional to help you sort things out."

"Like a shrink?" Tina raised her head to ask.

"Maybe. I think so. I've done a lot of thinking while you were away, and I believe the damage requires more than I can do to repair you. Perhaps you could go see Reverend Wisekirk first. You like him, right? He might be able to recommend someone. Tina? Are you listening?"

Tina sat up and nodded. Her face was swollen with tears and unhappiness, but at least the racking sobs had stopped. "You seem into the church scene, Tina, so that's probably the best place to begin. And a minister is, of course, bound to keep whatever you tell him in confidence, so we don't have to worry about that."

"You mean you don't have to worry, Mother." Tina could not let go of her accusatory tone. "Okay, maybe I'll go," she acquiesced.

The women tentatively said goodnight, and each returned to her own version of the problem. Catherine was upset that her daughter had taken the news and meet Robert so hard. *Why can't she be strong like me?* she thought.

Tina went to bed shaken and nervous beyond her control. It was all too much for her to take. She felt she'd been torn apart from the inside out. She wanted so badly to trust her mother again, but deep inside knew she couldn't. That was the greatest of her pain. She tried to get to sleep, but waves of uncontrollable panic rolled over her. Italy had been so wonderful that she'd virtually forgotten her pain, and now her mother had had to show up. She was a trigger.

Catherine was struggling in her own way. The fact that Tina had lost faith in her was what Catherine did not get. Why in the world would Tina not be able to trust her anymore? For Pete's sake, hadn't she taken care of her all her life? What was the big deal now, except that Robert had shown up? She certainly had not wanted him to find Tina as he had; she had expected him to call her. They could have had a nice chat and cleared everything up, and she would have shown him pictures of Tina, both growing up and now. He could have heard all about the years he'd missed, and perhaps even have met her—with proper preparation. But look what he'd done, what a mess he'd made of it! She had not thought he would do such a thing. If she had, she wouldn't have written. She was trying to protect Zach in case the lie about him being Tina's father came out now that he was back in touch. She would expect Zach to be angry about something like that, but not Tina, who had had a very good childhood with her mother.

Catherine was glad Tina had at least been amenable to her suggestion to get some outside counseling, even if it was only the local pastor. Perhaps he would guide her to a professional.

At any rate, Catherine had done her best, and now she had to work on William. She knew he was not someone to throw aside although she was not able to articulate why. She decided to call him on Monday.

Chapter 13

Getting William Back

William always volunteered at the animal rescue station for a few hours each Monday, so Catherine knew it would do no good to call in the morning. She decided it might be best to find him there, to show him how happy she was to be with him again.

As she drove up the boulevard, past all the extravagantly huge beach estates and condominiums, and around the bay where excessive condo building was in full swing, she thought of how best to approach her friend. Why he should be miffed at her was not the issue anymore, although she didn't get that, either. All these people who were only peripherally involved in her life with Zach should not be so sensitive or judgmental, but there it was.

Now what could she do to cajole William into a nice lunch and a friendly chat? She thought she would show some real interest in what was going on at the rescue station first, ask William some questions, and then invite him to lunch at that nice Italian place, Venticello, which had recently opened. Neither of them had been there as far as she knew, so that could be the ticket to get him out with her. He had not seen her since the talk about Tina, and she realized how much she depended on him for some of her entertainment and much of her companionship.

When she pulled into the parking lot, he was standing by the outside pool, talking and gesturing to a group of about ten people. There were children of all ages and sizes, and a few adults. William loved to tell children about the animals that had been helped, and especially enjoyed showing them a real rescue case when there was one.

Today the pool was temporary home to a lost baby seal. William was busy telling his audience about the needs and probable release time for the animal, about how they'd have to wait until she was old enough and strong enough. Then he saw Catherine and ended the talk.

The people thanked him and began to go back to their cars. A few of the children reached over the fence, but were quickly told not to by both William and one of the other volunteers. They explained that if the animal got too familiar with humans, it would be very difficult to release her back into the wild where she would have to adapt and be adopted back into the group.

When he was finished, William turned to Catherine. "Well, what brings you here?" he asked with a smile.

"It's good to see you smile, William. I thought perhaps I wouldn't see that any more, considering the way you've been avoiding me. I came specifically to see if you would go to lunch with me. Please don't say no."

William took her arm and guided her to his car. "Let's take mine," he said. "It's good to see you. I was hoping we might get together soon, anyway."

"Well, what kept you? I thought I'd offended you for life!"

"No, I'd just seen a side of you that really took me by surprise. I needed some time to think and sort out my feelings about you."

"And now?"

"And now I've decided that you're the same person you were

when we became friends. Nothing has changed, except my knowledge of your past and my feelings about you as a result."

"Your feelings have changed, then? Are we still friends?"

"Somewhat changed, yes. Let's eat. Where to?"

"I thought that new Italian place in the center of town, Venticello's. What do you say?" Her favorite food had always been Italian, and she knew that William preferred Italian over anything except really well-prepared seafood.

"Sounds good to me. Hop in." He held the car door for Catherine and she got in. He went over to his side, got in, and started the motor.

"William, are we going to be okay again, do you think?" Catherine ventured.

"I think it'll take some time. We'll see. Let's just have lunch and work on understanding each other."

William drove the few blocks in silence. Catherine felt comfortable and in control; things had worked out fine for now. One step at a time, she told herself.

They ate fat, succulent shrimp over capellini in a light cream-tomato sauce and the wonderful house salad in congenial comfort. They chatted amiably about nothing but the weather, the tides, the baby seal, and the food. During a dessert of cannoli and cappuccino, William talked a bit about his volunteer work with church and wildlife, and Catherine talked about her painting. Neither spoke of Tina or Zach or Italy or Robert.

The lunch went well, and when William dropped Catherine off at her car, they parted on good terms. Each expressed a desire to see the other soon, and William said he would call within the week. Catherine smiled her approval and drove off a satisfied woman, for the time being.

When she got home there was a note stuck in her door. It was a scrawl of almost illegible script. She squinted to read it and gasped when she saw who it was from. "I've done some thinking. I really need you now, like you said. Please call." There was a local phone number. Catherine did not know whether to laugh or cry.

Chapter 14

Reverend Wisekirk

Tina took her mother's advice and went to see Reverend Wisekirk. He was a man of about fifty, tall and thick around the waist, with an angular face bearing a bit of facial hair like younger men wore in many of the fashion magazines. He had served on the island for about ten years, and he seemed sympathetic. She had been to his church a few times, usually in response to William's urging. Tina knew she needed a base and more structure in her life than her mother could provide. She'd always believed there was a God and, when she was still a teen, had sought out an active church life. Here on Brigantine, she'd done a little church shopping on her own, and then found comfort at Wisekirk's Presbyterian church, at William's suggestion.

She went to him. His name suggested he might be the right man for the job.

She told him her story. He showed no surprise, asked few questions, and nodded from time to time during the explanations. Tina omitted nothing. Her feelings about her mother were obviously her main problem, and the reverend agreed that real concern was warranted. He knew Catherine only slightly. She had come to church on a pretty regular basis for a short while, sometimes with Tina and sometimes with William. Then, sometime during the summer, her attendance waned. He had not seen her for a month, maybe more.

Tina told him about her sleepless nights, her waves of panic, and anxiety-ridden days. She had lost weight since he'd seen her last. He began, "Tina, you're obviously overwrought by this new knowledge about your parentage. I think your inability to trust your mother is also a major factor in causing the symptoms you've described. I can help by listening. I'm glad you went to William, too, but you need more than either of us can give you. Have you had similar symptoms before?" She said she couldn't remember. She didn't want to remember her panicky childhood nights when she would wake up and stand by her mother's bed, hoping Catherine would wake up. She didn't think Reverend Wisekirk needed to know about that.

He explained that she was obviously suffering from some kind of depression and was in need of professional help, so he recommended a doctor. Tina thanked him for his help and left with the doctor's number in her hand.

She was so tired of telling her story that she waited a week before she called. When she finally did, it was because she felt so awful. She could not believe that information about one's self could cause so much physical pain, but something was wrong. It was more than a problem with her mother—it had triggered into severity whatever else had been going on for much of her life, and she needed to know what it was.

The psychiatrist assessed her, spent two hours talking and listening, taking her medical history, and conferring with her family doctor in Bergen County before he made a diagnosis. He gave Tina a prescription for an antidepressant medication, as well as appointments for therapy scheduled over a number of weeks.

Tina seldom missed work due to her illness. All the girls at the salon were supportive and friendly, but Freda was a gem. She offered

Tina time off, but also understood that working would be better than staying home, doing too much thinking. When Tina got home in the evening, she was so tired that she was usually in bed by eight. She would fall right to sleep, but she'd wake up in an hour or two, and that would be it for a couple of hours. It often felt as though she'd spent the whole night tossing and turning. She seldom felt like eating, but forced herself with soup, tuna salad, nibbles of cheese, and anything else that would go down easily.

The pills didn't take effect for a few weeks, but she slowly felt her strength returning. Then she suddenly had troubling thoughts of suicide and nightmares so her doctor prescribed an older medication. How glad she was for anything that could help her get better and be able to think about and deal with her problems. The strange fear in the pit of her stomach slowly subsided; the waves of panic which had washed over her in her worst nights were over. What a tremendous relief it was.

Chapter 15

Rake and Lothario

One day in early September, the doctor told Tina she might soon be ready to talk to her mother. It was on Shoebie, the day traditionally celebrated by native islanders in honor of tourists returning to their own homes. Tourism was a necessity, the islanders knew, but how nice it was to have their streets and homes to themselves again. They'd named the celebration after the tourists' shoebox lunches. Tina enjoyed watching, but did not join in. She knew the doctor was right, but even the thought of seeing Catherine was not comfortable for her.

As she was getting ready for bed after a nice day of watching the activities, doing a little shopping, and talking with Saskia on the phone, her doorbell rang. She thought it was probably her mother, who had the uncanny habit of coming over just at the wrong time. She ran down the stairs, her unfastened robe flying out behind her, unbolted the door, and opened it with a jerk.

"What do you want at this hour?" she yelled.

"Hey, Tina. Sounds like you were expecting me." It was Zachary, grinning into her astonished face. "Now don't look so grim. I just came to have a little chat with you since your mother and I are getting back together. Mind if I come in?" He pushed through the door and bounded up the stairs. Tina didn't know what to do, so she followed him upstairs and into her small apartment. He had already made himself comfortable on the sofa. His long legs reached almost to the door, and Tina had to step over them to get to the other side of the room. She stood as far away from him as she could, with her arms drawn tightly across her middle in an attempt to hide the nightgown beneath her robe.

There wasn't much room in her small apartment; she had only two rooms and a small cooking area in one corner of the main living space. It was furnished with a sofa and beanbag chair, as well as a small TV and a garden table made of wrought iron and bronze which held a vase and some books. Other than that and two prints from Italy, the space was fairly spare. The bed was behind a curtain and through a small entryway. Tina hugged the wall between the prints. She wasn't sure what frightened her more—the time he'd showed up, the fact that he'd almost forced his way in, or the ugly leer on his face as he looked her up and down.

"Relax, girl. Sit down." He patted the seat next to him. She didn't move.

"What do you want? Why are you here?" she asked, almost whispering.

"Don't be such a mouse, Tina. I only want to talk about our future relationship. I'm going to be your stepfather, you know. Thought I'd just come over and get to know you a little better. I'm sorry people thought I was your real father. That really wouldn't do, would it?" He continued to leer at her. Tina moved tighter against the wall. *This is too bizarre,* she thought.

"I'm just about ready for bed. I wish you would go now."

At this, he stood up and moved over to her. "Why can't you just be friendly? Give your future old man a little kiss. What about it?" She tried to move away, but he caught her against the wall.

"What are you doing? Leave me alone!" she yelled.

He clamped his large hand over her mouth, and then replaced that with his mouth. She squirmed to get away. When he stopped, he covered her mouth with his hand again. "Don't yell; I'm not going to hurt you. I just want a little taste, and I think you need the experience. I'm just going to help you grow up a little."

Tina began to struggle and kick, but Zach was too strong for her. He picked her up and had her on the couch before she knew what had happened. With one hand on her mouth and the other holding her wrists behind her, he used his legs to move her into position for what he intended. When he moved his hand from her mouth, he had his mouth on hers so quickly she could only whisper a scream. She felt his hands wrapping tape around her wrists and thought she would faint. Then he began whispering in her ear.

"Relax, Tina. You're too pretty. I just want to see a little more of your sweetness, maybe taste a little. Don't be afraid. Daddy Zach is going to take very good care of you. Now just lie back and relax so we can both enjoy this. Everything in life is better if you relax. Here, let me help you get more comfortable." With one hand, he tore off her robe and then her nightgown. "Oh yes, this is worth my trip," he said as he took her in with his eyes. His hand now began to undo his own clothes; the other hand remained over her mouth. She tried to bite him, but he was too quick for her. He slapped her so hard that her head rammed into the back of the sofa. She arched her back against the pain. "Ah, yes, little one. Perfect position. Look at how pretty they are. Think I'll just take a little nibble from each one."

Tina's face stung from the slap, and she could taste blood. She twisted against his assault, trying with all her might to ward it off, but she fought in vain. He seemed to enjoy her resistance. When he had her pinned tightly under him, he whispered, "By the way, your mother is going to marry me. If you ever breathe a word of this to anybody, I'll be a widower before you can say my name. Now let's see how exciting we can make this." She froze with horror. When his calloused, crusty finger slid inside her, she gagged. She thought she would die from the stench of this old man's filthy body and slow steady attack. Her head burst with the onset of a migraine and then she lost consciousness.

She wasn't sure how long it had lasted, but when she came to she was in bed, her clothes thrown over her. Her hands were free, although her arms and wrists ached, as did her whole body. She felt as though she'd been torn in two. The burning in her groin and the pain in her head nearly made her faint again.

When she began to remember what had happened, she shuddered and wept. Then she willed herself off the bed and into the shower. She turned it on full blast, hot. She scalded her flesh in the attempt to get his smell, his filth, off her. She scrubbed until she was too tired to stand. If she could have turned herself inside out, she would gladly have done that just to get all of him out of her body. Then she slid to a hunched position in the shower and let the water assault her. It was a cleansing heat, mixed with hot tears and shaking she thought would break her.

When she'd had enough, she wrapped a towel around herself and lay on her bed as waves of fear and nausea rolled over her. She ran to vomit. When she was finished, she called Saskia.

Chapter 16

Plans

As Catherine dialed the number on the note, she felt a bit uneasy.

"Yeah, hi, who is this?" Zach asked.

"Hi, Zach. How are you?" she answered.

"Hey, Westie, never been better. How's all by you? Ready for your old lover boy to come home?"

"That depends on his plans."

"Well, let's take it a day at time and maybe make it a permanent arrangement in a month or so. What about that?"

"Are you serious? Are you capable of this commitment?"

"Yup. I've tasted most of the sweetness of the single life, and I do believe I need to settle down."

"I'm not sure what that means, but come on over and let's begin settling down. When can you get here?"

"How about tomorrow morning?"

"I'll be waiting."

When he finally came to the door, she rushed into his arms. "I hope this is the last of the goodbyes," she whispered.

"I think it is," he responded, and clamped his mouth on hers. She felt a hint of fear, of some kind of warning deep in her gut. She didn't know why. She pushed it aside and took Zachary into her home and into her life one more time.

Catherine was still deceitful enough not to tell William that Zach was back again. When he called for her to have lunch, she told Zach she needed to do some shopping. When William asked her to dinner, she told Zach she had church meetings to attend. He wouldn't understand her continued friendship with Will.

Zach didn't seem to mind her evenings out. He just settled into her big blue chair, flipped on a sports channel, gathered beer and chips or pretzels, and settled in for the evening.

The routine seemed to serve them both, but when Zachary, after a few days of this, asked about wedding arrangements, she put him off. "Of course, Zach, but not right away. Let's get used to being together for a while first," she replied. This was not like Catherine, and Zach was puzzled. He changed the topic to feel her out.

"Where's your daughter, anyhow? I haven't seen her. Did she finally move somewhere to be on her own?"

"No, Zachary, she is where she was the last time you were here. Only she's under the care of a professional who says she shouldn't see me for a few weeks."

"What, she's seeing a shrink? Why?"

"I didn't say she was seeing a shrink. I said—"

"I know what you said, Westie, and I know what you meant," he interrupted in a cynical tone. "Why can't she see her own mother is what I want to know."

"Seeing Robert so unexpectedly caused a shock. She needs time to heal, that's all." She'd half-explained the reason, and let it stand at that. But Zach had other ideas.

"She hates you now, doesn't she? Admit it Catherine. Your little girl isn't tough like you."

"You know, Zachary, you have a real cruel streak. I never saw it in you before. I wonder why," she said aloud, thinking she'd mused to herself.

He laughed and grabbed for her. "Westie, we were so good together. Nothing else stood in the way. I had no reason to let you see that side, understand?"

"Yes, I'm afraid so," she answered, and moved from his reach.

"Oh, come on. Don't be upset. I'm sorry. Really, I am. I won't be cruel anymore, I promise. You know, I really do like Tina. I think I know her a little better now than when I came the last time. I'm going to be a real good father to her, wait and see." He took a sip of beer and grabbed the remote. "When Tina comes around, I promise I'll be really good to her, okay?" He switched on a sports show, and the conversation was over.

Catherine went to the kitchen to get herself something to drink. She took some ice water from her fridge, poured it into a glass, squeezed fresh lemon into it, and added some sugar. As she stood stirring the lemonade, she stared at the man in her living room. He had hardly moved from that chair since he returned a few weeks ago. He had not even mentioned going to Atlantic City, nor had he tried to ambush her in his usual sex games when she least expected it. Nothing. She had some serious misgivings, but did not know quite what to do with them. She told herself that they were both in their sixties now and that would account for his different behavior even though, earlier in the summer, he had been much more his old self.

She began to question him a little at a time.

He responded to all her questions with what seemed viable answers. He was tired. He wanted to rest after a really active life. He knew he had done her wrong. He loved to sit and watch her do her daily things.

One evening, she decided the next day it would be time to confront

Zach with her misgivings. She went over what she would say and how she would say it all night. William's words resurfaced with her every resolve to give Zach a chance. Tina's pale smile interrupted her thoughts continually. Even Gwen haunted her night of tossing and turning. But she held on and knew she would take Zachary at his word. She just hoped it was the right word.

When morning came, Catherine did not get a chance to deal with Zach.

Chapter 17

Tina's Issues

Mom, it's early morning, and I couldn't sleep.

I can't say all the things I need to say, so I'm writing this all down as both Aunt Gwen and my doctor suggested I do. Dr. Albert says I'm suffering from clinical depression. He also said it is something I probably have had to some degree all my life, but the recent incident with my father and triggered the worst episode.

I have to tell you, Mom, that when I was little and when I was in my teens, I had what I guess are called anxiety attacks.

Remember when I was a little kid, I would sometimes wake up in the middle of the night and come to your room? I was terrified to be alone, so I came to be near you. I'd stand by your bed praying you'd wake up. I was afraid to wake you. Sometimes you did wake up, and once or twice I remember you let me stay in your bed with you. But Mom, sometimes you didn't wake up, and I had to go back to my own room. I fell asleep, but always with a stomach full of fear. I don't know how else to describe the feeling. I learned to pray then. I believed Jesus would make me be able to sleep. It always worked. Thank you for at least taking me to Sunday school every week.

I had the same episodes when I was in high school. I was afraid a lot of the time, but was not afraid of anything specific. I didn't tell anybody because I thought there was something wrong with me that nobody else could possibly have. Sometimes I thought I was going to die, and sometimes I wanted to get rid of the awful feelings by dying. Remember how quiet I was at times? You would try to get me to talk, but I just wasn't there. I was depressed and didn't even know there was a word for the way I felt.

My doctor says it might well be hereditary, so this must be from my father's side of the family. You see what I'm trying to say? If I had known him, maybe I would have understood myself and been able to get help long ago.

I'm sorry to lay this on you in this way, Mom, but I'm really hurt and hurting, and don't know how else to tell you. I really can't bear to see you now. I don't know what to do about you and me except that I'll have to find the strength to forgive you at some time. I don't know when that will be. I'm on medication right now, and I think it's beginning to help a little bit. I'm going to go live with Saskia for a while. Don't call me; I need to be far away from you for a while.

Tina

Catherine got up very early. For some reason she felt apprehensive and decided to get some coffee and sit for a while in living room to quell the feeling. She sat in a chair near the front door, just to be in a different place where Zach would not look for her. Her mood this morning was intolerant for anything and anyone. She looked around the room she barely ever used and saw something under the door.

The note, stuffed in a used envelope, was lying on the floor just under the front door. Catherine read and reread the letter, unbelieving. Her daughter had been depressed her whole life and she, Catherine, had not been aware? How could this be? She was a teacher, damn it, and sensitive to kids! Now Tina and some shrink were trying to lay this on her? "Who's the guy who's messing with my daughter's head?" she exclaimed. The note couldn't have been there long; it was dated that morning, and it was still so early.

When she had read it for the third time, she slowly folded it and tried to remember the nights of Tina's childhood anguish. She did recall the child asking to sleep with her and remembered having allowed it a few times, but then she put her foot down and told her she needed to be a big girl and sleep alone. Catherine had been sure this was the right approach, and even talked to her pediatrician about it. The doctor had agreed, and had even said it was wiser for Tina to sleep alone since it would strengthen the little girl's independence. Was this psychiatrist now trying to put false memories into Tina? Had she really felt all these anxieties when she was young? Catherine decided it was time to get some answers.

"Hey West, what are you doing? Did you get the mail?" Zachary came out onto the deck with a beer in his hand and the paper under his arm, wearing only boxer shorts. His long, thin legs looked like they were covered in onionskin, with long inky scribbles running up and down. The crooked white scars on his knees attested to his years of pro ball. His enormous bare feet slapped against the wood of the deck as his long, crooked toes caught his balance with each step. He shivered in the September air. "What were you reading, West?"

"Huh?" Catherine said, startled. "Oh, nothing in particular. I've got to go out for a while, Zach. Get yourself some cereal, okay?"

"Hell no, that's not okay!" he responded with some irritation. "You promised me a nice breakfast this morning, remember?"

"Something came up, Zach. I need to go. Sorry." She turned to go into the house, and when she brushed by him, he caught her arm.

"Is this something more important than me, West?" he dared to ask.

"My daughter needs me. And yes, she is more important than you right now."

"Wow. Who would have expected this from my long lost lover? Well then, go. By all means, go!" He thrust himself past her and into the house where he took a six-pack from the fridge, stomped into the bedroom, slammed the door, and retreated back into bed.

Catherine ignored him, filled the dishwasher, and ran out to drive over to Tina's apartment. She couldn't be gone yet; it had only been about an hour, Catherine guessed, since the letter had been written. But Tina did not answer the door when Catherine rang the bell. Tina and her doctor had finagled a way for her to get a day off from work every so often so she could work on healing, Catherine knew. She banged on the door with her fist, then took her shoe off and banged even harder. There was no answer. She tried the door, but it was locked. Next she checked the windows; all were closed, and the drapes as well as the blinds were drawn.

Catherine decided to go to Tina's landlady's house next door to ask to be let in. She was becoming fearful now. When the woman opened her door, Catherine didn't wait for her to speak. She yelled, "Where is my daughter? I can't get her to open the door!" Mrs. Hanrahan was taken aback.

"Tina? She moved out very early this morning," she answered.

Catherine let out a loud sigh. "What? I'm too late?" Catherine turned to walk to her car, leaving Mrs. Hanrahan bewildered at both mother and daughter.

Catherine got into her car and tried to decide what to do. William would have to come to the rescue one more time. He probably knew all about this. William would never agree to keep such a thing quiet, but at the same time she was sure. She still tried to keep Zach's presence from William too. *What a mess*, she thought. *How did I ever...?* Then she started her car and headed for home.

She knew Zach would be out of his mind with irritability by this time, but she couldn't let William know he was at her house. Well, she guessed he knew, but he wasn't going to hear it from her. Zach was out cold in the living room when she got home. The placed reeked of him and of beer. Her meticulous housekeeping was rapidly deteriorating once more. Her wonderful oak floors were still in good shape, but she had the fleeting thought that sometime soon they might sustain beer stains or worse. She would have to do some serious work on Zach if this was going to last. Otherwise, she'd have to get some throw rugs and place them strategically.

Why was she thinking this? She kicked herself into action and called William.

"Tina moved out of her place. I might need your help later."

"Wait a minute, Catherine. What did you say? Is Tina gone?"

"You bet she is, and I'll bet you know more about all this. I certainly hope you do."

"I really don't, but my guess is she went to Saskia's. I'll call and get back to you as soon as I know anything. Please calm yourself."

"Yeah, she said she's going there, but I hoped not so soon. It's easy for you to tell me to keep calm; I'm the one who went to her apartment. Empty! You call Saskia and call me back!"

Zach was so out of it that he didn't hear the phone when William called back. "Yup, she's there. Saskia said Tina just got there a minute or so ago. She must have driven like the wind, according to Saskia; she got there in only an hour, and she seems pretty upset. But Saskia said not to worry; she'll call if they need anything or if there's a serious problem. I think she'll be fine. Maybe we should plan to have a little lunch tomorrow. What do you say, Catherine? We can talk, and you'll feel better about things."

"What a mess, William. I'm really sorry it turned out this way, and especially that you had to get so involved."

"Yes, well, I'm sure there's a reason for it. There's a reason for everything, you know."

"Don't get religious on me, William!" Catherine could not stand to hear what she considered patronizing talk from William.

"Not at all; I wasn't even considering it. Let's do lunch, we can talk. Italian okay?"

"Fine."

Chapter 18

William's Concern

When they got to the restaurant, they ordered coffee and asked the waiter to take their order a bit later. Catherine let go a long, painful sigh. "Well, William, it looks like I've done some number on my daughter, huh? I don't think I've ever felt worse than I do right now."

"Your priorities have been a bit confused, Catherine. I think Tina will be all right, given time and the help she's getting," William consoled, hoping Catherine was the wiser for wear.

"It seems you've had a major hand in her help these past few weeks. First you send her off to Italy; now I discover she's gone north without calling again."

"Well, I had nothing to do with this last episode, but you're right about the other, of course. I'm sorry that she needs to be away for a while; it must be very painful. I gave her my cell number, and I'll let you know what's happening. In time, she'll want to talk to you and be with you as she was, I'm sure. You've given Zach forty years; you can be patient with your daughter for a while."

"Ouch! She has your cell number? Must be on pretty friendly terms for that, I'd say." Catherine tried hard to sound nonchalant, but inside she was tearing herself apart that William had turned out to be for her daughter what she had always dreamed Zach would be.

William himself had not expected to be Tina's confidant. He and Bernice had not been blessed with children, although they'd desperately wanted them. After many tests and diggings into Bernice's body, they'd called it quits and accepted their childlessness as God's will. They'd been blessed with a very happy union, and learned to be satisfied with that.

William thought about himself in contrast to the educated, sophisticated woman sitting across from him. He'd always wanted to go to college, but his parents, having immigrated to the United States in the late fifties, needed him to go to work at sixteen to help support the family. This was William's one great grief in life. He had educated himself, but still felt inadequate all his life. He'd been taught carpentry as a trade, and even been in business with his father. They were not tradesmen so much as craftsmen. William had designed and built some glorious kitchens and dining rooms in Ho-Ho-Kus, Ridgewood, and even Saddle River and other towns in Bergen County. He was proud of his work, but Catherine's education awed him. And now he found her needing him.

William leaned forward, elbows on the table. Catherine knew something serious was coming and braced herself. "Catherine," he began. "May I be very frank with you? Give you my assessment, so to speak? Are we friends enough for me to be honest?"

"Try me," was the only answer she had. She picked up her coffee cup and held it to her face as a kind of shield.

"I gave Tina my number in case she needed someone in an emergency. Her doctor told her she'd need to have a relative or close friend on the island to whom she could go if she needed to. You weren't an option, especially since Zachary is back in the picture." William paused to evaluate Catherine's reaction. She colored slightly but said nothing. He took a sip of his coffee, put the cup back down, and waved the approaching waiter away.

"Well, go on," Catherine finally said.

"I saw your friend on your deck a few days ago. I couldn't help it."

"Yes. So?"

"Catherine, why? Why do you keep deluding yourself? Zachary Bekker is not who you think he is. What you have in your head is a dream. You have lived in a romantic dream all your adult years. You built an icon out of this guy and worshiped the image. You've sacrificed your daughter's and your own happiness to this idolatry. The man who is in your house right now is not even close to what you've dreamed him to be. He seems to me to be a whipped old ball player who's come back to suck the last of the goodness out of you. I suspect he's fully aware of your weakness for him and will play on that for as long as he needs you. Besides that ridiculous old football in your closet that you mentioned so often, has he ever given you anything? Has he ever given any of himself?" Catherine had tears in her eyes as William continued to hammer the truth home. She wanted to throw her cup at him, but she gripped it tightly and sat through it all.

"Catherine, come back to reality. Ask Tina to forgive you. One day soon she'll be ready. Be there for her without that piece of male baggage hanging onto you. He's in the way. You may still be able to salvage a few years of honest happiness for yourself. Let go of the phantom. Take a good, close look at what you have in your closet, and throw him out." William stopped to put his hand on Catherine's. He knew that wrenching away an idol which had been a part of her very being for so many years would be very painful, akin to surgery but of the heart. Catherine was doing admirably well, considering her ready tongue which could lash out so swiftly, so effectively, and so cruelly. It now lay paralyzed.

He saw her struggle. His words had been delivered quietly, but he'd thought about them for a long time. He'd even gotten so involved in her life as to have met her sister, Gwendolyn. Tina had insisted on Gwen calling William to figure out what to do about Catherine, or at least to let William get a better handle on the situation. He had serious reservations about this, but for Tina, he had allowed it. Now that the words were out, he could do nothing but wait for the effect.

"I'm so sorry," he said as he patted her hand. The waiter was hovering over them again, not sure what to do. William beckoned him over and ordered a simple marinara-based pasta and a salad for both of them.

Catherine wiped her eyes, pulled herself up to her full sitting height, and thanked William for his candor as well as the order. She put on a smile and said, "Well, let's eat, and then we'll see what comes of all this. I suppose I ought to thank you for being there for Tina, but frankly, I feel somewhat betrayed by both of you."

"I'm sorry, Catherine. I surely did not want to get involved in anything like this. I had no idea you had this particular skeleton in your closet—excuse the obvious—and I certainly had no understanding of your relationship with your daughter. I only helped because she called and I couldn't turn her away. She and I have been going to the same church for a short while, and we have that important connection. She trusts me. That's the way it is. I still cherish your friendship; I'm not sure about anything else."

Chapter 19

Revelations

Zachary was not pleasant when Catherine returned home after running off to see about Tina and then having lunch with William.

That same early afternoon, Zach awoke from his morning booze snooze to find Catherine gone. He got out of the blue chair and walked around the house. She was nowhere to be found. He yelled for her. Nothing. Then he went out onto the deck. She was not on the beach or in the ocean. Then he went to her bedroom and looked around. *Wonder what she's got hidden in here?* he thought. He opened the drawers of her dresser and rummaged through her personal things, and then threw them aside to search underneath. "Nothing of interest there," he murmured.

Next, he went to her closet and looked through her clothes. "Westie does have class," he admitted. Then he wormed his way deeper into the closet, behind her clothes, and found the old football. "Well, well, look what we have here. Who would have thought? My Westie is really a piece of work. Who would have thought the dame would hold onto this old thing all these years. Ugly as sin and smelly as hell by now," he said to himself. Then he looked under the bed and found a pair of his dirty socks. "Oops," he whispered. He continued on his search and picked up a box from behind the beautiful blue and gold oriental screen. It was a heavy box. He put it on the bed, sat down beside it, and opened it.

Inside were what appeared to be photo albums. He took one out, which was dated 1965. When he opened it, he realized it was a scrapbook filled with things about him. As he paged through the first book he saw his life catalogued here. The others were all dated, and contained pages similar to those in the first.

The first thing he read was a short biography of his early years written by a sports writer about famous quarterbacks in the 1960s. It read:

> Football was in his blood. He had wanted to play pro ball ever since he threw his first forty-yard pass as a sophomore in high school. The coach yelled. "Hey Bekker. Do that again!" This time he made the ball fly fifty yards, and the coach made him the new quarterback.

He reminisced. From high school, Zach had gone to college on a full sports scholarship. His fame did not grow immediately; he had had disappointments on the way. He was too slight of build to impress any university coach, so his scholarship took him to a college school in the South. As a sophomore, he led the team to the Cotton Bowl, but then he suffered a back injury and sat out most of the games during his junior year. Instead of losing confidence, as most would have done, Zach sneered and quit the team in the last half of his junior year. He managed a transfer to a northern state university, where he'd met Catherine, he recalled, and where the coach used him as his star quarterback despite his injury. His performance had suffered with his back problems and by the time he was ready, the Pros were not. Through sixteen rounds, no NFL team drafted Bekker.

But The Northern Black Bears made him their number seventeen choice for the 1962 season. Playing for a small team in northern

Wisconsin was not desirable for any serious draftee; the town was too small and the climate too cold, but Zach didn't care. He wanted to play football. She had clipped all the information about his early career; he guessed there had been a lot more.

He'd said goodbye to Catherine at this point and moved out of her life—at least out of the immediate physical part of it. He did remember giving her the football. It was the football, the one his coach had given him, the one he'd let fly, the one that got him his first real break. Was engagement mentioned? He thought not.

As he scanned the clippings and turned the pages of these thick scrapbooks, he saw all his past accomplishments and failures highlighted, circled, and underlined. Years of hard playing, back trouble, knee operations, relationships with stars and starlets, coaches and teammates, were pasted in perfect columns, each under its own specific heading, like soldiers standing ready to march on parade. There were headings for winning years, for hospital stays, for failures, for celebrations which showed pictures of Zach with champagne pouring down his face. There was a page dedicated to the Rose Bowl, and one to his trophies. There were columns from sports writers, complimentary and not. There was a double-page feature showing Zach with his parents and his sister, apparently taken after some great win, all of them grinning from ear to ear. The last three or four pages of each scrapbook made even Zachary Bekker blush. He flipped through the back of each book, and then quickly picked up the next and the next. He was appalled by what he saw. There were pages filled with scraps torn from tabloids, exaggerating his sexual exploits and failures. There were excerpts from *The National Enquirer*, *The Star*, and the more obscure and notorious *West Central Mars Report*. The pictures showed many of the women he had ever known, and some he had not. His relationships with all of them were told graphically or tragically. Catherine had not lined these up, but had made arbitrary collages with torn scraps of women's heads, sensational headlines, and almost pornographic details overlapping one another at random. The pages looked like jaggedly torn injuries which had left multiple scars. Each page suggested that his life away from the game had been one great, empty orgy. When he finally looked up, Catherine stood in the doorway. She was amused at his blushing. "You embarrassed about something?" she asked. "Does your life embarrass you?"

"I'm appalled, Catherine. How could you have done this? Why? Most of this stuff is not true, and what is, is grossly embellished. Even the sports writers did that. Surely you didn't believe all this?"

"It was all I had of you. You had promised to come back, so I filled empty hours with that bit of you I could get. Now you're back. I've been waiting as I wrote, but things are not quite right, are they?"

"I'll tell you what's not right; these books. These books are not right. I feel weird about these. Why do they make me feel weird, Catherine?"

"Well, let me think. Because you are weird, Zachary Bekker. You're pissed over these stupid books. You use and discard. These pages expose that side of you."

"No, no, no! That's not entirely it. What's weird is your obsession. You weren't waiting for me; you were obsessed by something inside yourself, not me."

"What I've carried around with me all these years was a promise from a guy who said he loved me and always would. He said he would come back but he never did until now, now that he's old, spent, and who knows what else. I couldn't wait to see you again. I fell right back into the old routine, but now—"

"Now I'm here, and look what I find; a shrine to somebody I don't even know. The sports stuff is one thing, but the other? Lies, Catherine. Almost all of it. Nothing but media lies"

"Really? **Almost** all of them?"

She closed the bedroom door, ran to her car, raced out of the drive, and went shopping the rest of the day. She couldn't face his nonsense. The day had brought enough.

She wandered through the streets of Atlantic City; then she drove to Ventnor and bought herself some sinfully lovely boxes of homemade dark chocolates. After this she drove east, parked at the Hilton, and went to the boardwalk where she first bought some jewelry. "Maybe Tina will like this," she said to herself. Her need for Tina grew stronger as she walked and bought. She filled bags with sweaters, skirts, books, and jewelry. She sensed her own foolishness, but these gifts brought her closer to her daughter. When it was dark and cold, she finally returned home and went to sleep in her guest room. She had no room for Zachary this night.

Chapter 20

New Promises

Catherine's morning began with a start when she found herself in the guest room. She'd almost forgotten why; then she remembered. No Zach the night before. When she saw him getting a cold one and a banana, she didn't talk to him. He shrugged. She smiled at him whenever she ran into him the rest of the day. She got his meals, went for a swim, worked in her sketchbook, and virtually ignored him. He, in turn, went about his business of drinking beer, watching games, and eating bits and pieces of what she prepared.

Zach didn't know how to deal with this aloof, smiling Catherine, so he retreated into sports mode. Women were a brand of people he knew how to enjoy, but he did not pretend or even try to understand them, and Catherine had always been a greater enigma than most. Maybe that was the lasting attraction; he had to admit that he'd never really forgotten her, either.

But she was a puzzle to him. She seemed to enjoy him, and then suddenly turn on him about some trifle he could not fathom. But she was always fun and apparently always waiting. The last time she kicked him out for no reason, he'd been flabbergasted. But at least, thankfully, she'd left the door ajar.

But last night and those scrapbooks really threw him for a loop. He wasn't sure how to get it all right in his head.

On Sunday afternoon of that first week of September, Zachary Lee Bekker did what he most loathed to do; he opened a conversation with a woman about their relationship after a rather profound misunderstanding. Usually he left, let things cool off and, if she was worth it, come back with a grin and a gift. But now he sought Catherine out asked her to sit down. He intended to get things right again.

Catherine also knew that the conversation of the previous evening needed finishing. She knew she had to confront him.

"Okay, Zach," she began, "you want to talk? We'll talk. All the weirdness and prying into my private thoughts about you aside—out with it. What's wrong, and why are you here?"

He had not expected this. "Nothing's wrong, West. I'm here so we can finally get married and end our lives together in rapturous joy and fulfillment," he said, laughing.

"Right. Now tell me the truth, because I know you're not all right. Your humor is wrong. Your attitude has changed. Your over-willingness to be cooperative makes me suspicious. Am I your last resort, maybe?"

"Okay, you've got me," he answered with total honesty. "I'm broke. My sister kicked me out claiming I'm an alcoholic. She said no more room and board without Alcoholics Anonymous. Now, Westie, you know I can hold my beer. You know I can go without if I feel like it. So I left Boston, walked around for a few days, and decided to make you an honest woman. I'll even be good to Tina. Sorry about last night, by the way. I was just a bit overwhelmed by the books, you know."

"I think your sister may be right about you. I've been as much in denial as you have. But no more."

"Even if I do have a 'problem,' as she put it, what's the difference? You're getting what you've been waiting for all these years. Your dream can now be realized. This drinking never bothered you before. If it does now, I'll cut down and do better. Then we'll take up where we left off," he said without apology.

"Will you join AA?"

"I'm sure I can, West. We can have this time with just the two of us, finally, you know. I've been thinking. This little house you bought is now worth a lot more. We could probably sell it for close to a mil, then find someplace cheaper and live like a king and queen. What do you say? What could be better? Retirement with the old flame, huh? You need me—you've said that often enough. Now I need you too. You don't have anybody else to take care of."

Catherine was incredulous. "I still have Tina!" she exploded.

"What, Tina? She's an adult. What does she have to do with anything now?" *Westie needs to learn to cut her daughter free*, he thought.

"She's in a crisis. It's mainly my fault—and yours, in a way. We need to be there for her now."

"We? I don't think so, Westie. There's no 'we' where Tina is concerned. She's your baby, in every sense of the word. But I'm willing to, you know, be nice. I'll be very nice, but I'm not responsible. Know what I mean?" Zach got up from the table with a beer in his hand and walked out to the deck.

Catherine had expected this attitude about her daughter. She followed him out.

"I've had a very productive life, Zach. My teaching, my students, meant everything to me. I was really good at what I did. I love the classroom; I even love the smell of it. But when early retirement was offered—an incredible package plus a bonus—I couldn't resist. I love this ocean life. But I had not anticipated you coming here totally broke and with a negative attitude about my daughter—who, by the way, means more than my life to me."

"Want me to leave, Westie?" he asked as his arm circled her waist.

"I said I'd be very nice to Tina, and I meant it. I find her quite delicious, but not a daughter figure for me."

She turned to look at his face but made no reply.

They leaned on the railing and looked out over the quiet beach to the lapping waves beyond. A small dog ran madly back and forth, trying to frighten the waves into some sort of submission by barking and biting at nothing. The owner stood a short way off, making a video of the action. When a larger wave suddenly appeared, the little dog scampered in retreat, but got caught in a deluge of salt and sand. The man with the camera bent double laughing and welcomed his tiny wet pet into his free arm. Catherine snickered at the sight. Zach commented on the wuss who would buy such a lame excuse for a dog. "If I had a dog," he remarked, "it would be a real dog, like a Rottweiler, or bullmastiff. At least you'd be able to see a dog like that."

"You know what, Zachary Lee Bekker? I think you need to go to rehab for treatment," Catherine said with little emotion in her voice. She'd simply stated a fact.

"You think?" he asked.

"Yes, I think. Let's get dinner and talk about how to go about this." Zachary nodded and they went in to get dressed. Catherine suggested they try a Thai restaurant in Atlantic City, but Zach said 'no' almost too fast. "Why not? I thought you liked exotic food."

"I do, but not Thai. Too much done with peanuts for my taste."

"You don't like peanuts?"

"Look, Westie, I never told anybody because it's such a wimpy thing. I think I'm allergic to peanuts."

"You think you're allergic?"

"Well, I know I am, but I have some stuff with me to take, just in case. Don't tell anybody. It's my own business, nobody else's, okay?"

"I guess. So where to?"

"Let's do that great buffet at the Borgata."

"Okay."

While enjoying their first course of shrimp and crab cakes, Catherine again broached the subject of rehab. "So, Zach, what do you think? Rehab for a while?"

"How long do they make a guy stay in a place like that?"

"I guess you'll have to go get assessed. Then they'll tell you what you need. What do you think?"

"Will you marry me once I'm clean?"

"We can talk about it."

"No, now! Yes, I go; no, I don't."

"Yes, Zach, I will. Will you be good to Tina?"

"You bet I will. I'll be very nice indeed, and I bet she'll be very nice to me too."

"Well, we'll see about that. But okay, you get out of a rehab program and we get married. That's a deal."

Chapter 21

Bad News

When they got back, there was a message on Catherine's machine. "Hi, Ms. Cedar, it's Saskia. Call me right away, no matter what time it is. It's urgent." Catherine turned to Zach. "What could this be about? There must be something wrong with Tina."

"I don't know. Call and find out."

"Yes, I will," Catherine said as she picked up the phone. She dialed Saskia's number hoping she would finally get a chance to talk to Tina. Maybe she would now be able to convince her to listen to her mother's side of the mess she felt she was in.

"Hello, Saskia, this is Catherine. Is Tina there? Is she all right?" she asked before Saskia could even say hello.

"Oh, Ms. Cedar. Oh, no. No, no, no. Tina is not all right. I hope you're not alone."

"What? What? Tell me. What's wrong with Tina?"

"How do I tell you? Tina, well, Tina is...she was so unhappy and...we think she committed suicide. I found her about an hour ago."

Catherine turned white; her hand went numb and she dropped the phone. She turned to Zach and said, "I have to call William." Then she picked up the phone again. "Saskia, what did you say? Tina is what?"

"They tried to revive her, but they couldn't. She took a lot of pills. Please come as soon as you can."

"Yes. Please take good care of her until I get there, Saskia. Thanks."

Saskia had no answer for that, and hung up.

Catherine began to cry. "I have to talk to William, I have to tell him what happened to Tina," she sobbed.

"My God! Woman, you haven't even told me what's going on," Zach said frantically.

"What? Oh, Zach. Tina is gone."

"Gone? Where? What do you mean, 'gone'?"

Catherine dialed William's number. "Hi, Will. I have a real problem. Can I see you right away?"

"What about me? Can't I help? I'm sure she'll be all right…well, maybe I shouldn't come," Zach interrupted.

"This is one for me and William, Zach. Tina is rather close to him. Forgive me. I've got to go."

She grabbed her keys and ran out the door. Zach shrugged, walked to the fridge, and took out a beer.

When Catherine and William arrived at Valley Hospital two hours later, she was met by a weeping Saskia, Gwen, and a young man who hung back awkwardly in a corner. Saskia ran to Catherine and embraced her forcefully. "Oh, Ms. Cedar, I'm so sorry, I'm so sorry. I wasn't home. I didn't know she was that bad off. Oh, forgive me, please." She sobbed her distress into Catherine's neck.

Both William and the stranger stood aside, looking at one another and waiting for the women. Finally Saskia pulled away and introduced Alessandro. "He came from Italy last week to see Tina," she explained. "Now she's dead, and Alessandro is as heartbroken as I am."

"Yes, well that may be, but where is Tina? I want to see her." Catherine stormed through the corridor to the desk. "I'm Tina Cedar's mother. Where is my daughter?" she demanded. Gwen followed close behind and put a hand on Catherine's shoulder, which was quickly removed by Catherine's deft shrug. "Don't touch me, Gwen. Why are you here?"

A doctor approached from behind and addressed Catherine. She turned to face him as he offered his condolences. "I'm so sorry, Ms. Cedar. We did everything we could to save her, but she took too many pills. Her heart gave way almost immediately."

"Where is she?" Catherine demanded.

He led the way to a little room and opened the curtain for her to go in. There lay Tina with her pallid, peaceful face. Not until she saw the pale face and touched the cold hand and forehead of her daughter did Catherine realize what everyone had been saying. She kissed Tina's lips and slowly raised her head to stare at William, who had followed her in. "I think Tina has died," she said.

William caught her before she fainted.

He and a nurse helped her to a seat. When she was revived, she turned her grief-stricken face to Gwen. "Why were you here before me? Why?" she whispered.

"Kate, I'm so sorry. I'm so sorry. Tina called me a couple of days ago and asked me to visit. She wanted to talk about you. She wanted to know what her mother was like at her age. She just wanted to talk, so I came. I'm so sorry I wasn't here when it counted."

"All of you people—her friends, her helpers—left her alone?"

"Catherine, don't blame them. They—"

She furiously cut William off. "Don't blame them? Then who do I blame? Me? This is my fault? Tina was betrayed by her mother, is that it?" she sobbed. "Yes, that's it, I know."

"I'm sorry, Mrs. Cedar, but we need to know what to do with the body. Do you have a funeral director in mind?"

"The body? My beautiful baby's body? No pathologist, no funeral director is going to touch her! No cutting up, no makeup—she's beautiful in her own right. No tubes, no messing around. Just a beautiful burial. That's it."

"I'm sorry to have to tell you this, Ms. Cedar, but an autopsy will have to be performed due to the circumstances."

"Exactly what circumstances would that be, doctor?" Catherine's sarcastic tone was not lost on anyone.

"It seems as though Tina committed suicide," he replied.

"Impossible!" Catherine yelled, but was restrained by William and Gwen. Her voice echoed through the hospital corridor before she could be calmed.

"What the hell do you mean? Tina would never..." and then she collapsed, sobbing uncontrollably. "It's all my fault. All my fault."

The autopsy officially confirmed an overdose, but Catherine could not accept it.

When the body was released, the final arrangements had to be made.

"Saskia , help me here. I can't think." Catherine stood up, left the room, and went outside, where she took a great breath of air into her lungs.

Saskia tried to think. "I guess the place in Wyckoff, up on Godwin Avenue, is as good as any. Vander Plaat, I think it's called. Try them."

While making the arrangements, going through the motions of a funeral, and thanking supportive people, Catherine was in a daze. Most of the decisions had to be made by Gwen and the others. All of them worried about Catherine and tried to console her, but that was not possible yet. She was beside herself.

The cemetery was about a fifteen-minute ride from the funeral home. Catherine had bought a plot for herself there years ago, when she was still working in Bergen County. She would never have imagined the present use. Gwen and William stood beside her as the final words were said.

She still could not figure out why her daughter would have found life so unbearable as to do this. *Why? Why?* she kept asking herself. Surely her depression was not so serious as to cause this. She had been on antidepressants, hadn't she? And in therapy? Why had she run to Saskia in such a hurry? None of it made sense. Her grief was so profound that all she could do was blame herself over and over again.

When the last person had left the gravesite on that hot, humid morning, Reverend Wisekirk, who had been kind enough to come from Brigantine, took Catherine's hand and walked her to his car. They drove in silence to Saskia's little apartment where William, Gwen, Alessandro, and Saskia met them. Saskia had ordered a light lunch from the deli and made coffee. No one was very hungry, but the salads were cold and the coffee a welcome lift after the mourning of the last few days. Friday night seemed years away, but it had only been a few days.

Catherine could not believe she would never see her daughter again. She blamed herself. Saskia, in some way, blamed herself. Alessandro felt so out of place that he kept repeating in broken English how much he had wanted to get to know Tina better. He blamed himself, too. Tina should never have been left alone, but Saskia had a date, and Alessandro had spent a day in the city visiting friends. Gwen had gone into town, and Tina had refused to come along, making some excuse about a TV show she needed to see. Tina had been alone.

On the following evening, when Alessandro and Reverend Wisekirk were gone and Saskia was alone with Catherine, Gwen, and William, Saskia asked William to go out and get some tea. "I'm all out, and I think we could all use some. Why not go with him, Gwen? He doesn't know Ridgewood like you do," she suggested.

That was when Catherine heard the worst of it.

"I have to tell you, Ms. West-Cedar, the real reason Tina was so severely disturbed. She said I wasn't to tell anyone, especially not you.

But, well, I think you need to know."

"Okay, out with it, then. I think I can take just out anything after this," she responded.

"Well, you know that guy Zach that you have around sometimes? Tina said you were going to marry him. She said he would kill you if she told—"

Catherine interrupted. "What? Told me what? Zach, kill me?"

"Please don't interrupt. This is hard enough for me." She looked at Catherine as though she were going to die. "You see, he came to her house one night and he told her he wanted to talk to her...about you and your impending marriage and all that...so she kind of let him in. And then—well, he forced himself on her. He...well, he raped her." She almost whispered the last few words, but Catherine heard it as though all the bells of Notre Dame had clanged them into her ears.

After almost five minutes of silence, Catherine finally asked, "Did Tina tell you this? Did Tina say that he had—had—had done that to her?"

"Yes. Two days before she died. I should never have left her alone when I knew. She said she had no right to even go out with Alessandro; she was too dirty. She said she could never get the stench of that creep off her. I should have guessed what she meant to do. I'm so sorry."

"Shh. Be quiet, Saskia. None of this is your fault. It is mine and his." She almost hissed the last word. Saskia saw the most awful expression on Catherine's face, a mixture of grief and something ugly that Saskia couldn't place. "Well, it all makes sense now. 'I'm going to be very nice to her.' Yes, it makes a lot of sense now," Catherine murmured before she turned to the frightened girl on the sofa. "He said he would kill me if she told?" Saskia nodded. "We'll see about that. We'll see who kills whom," she said, almost to herself. "We'll just see about that," she announced to the frightened girl sitting next to her. "Listen, Saskia, not a word of this to William or Gwen. We're leaving as soon as he gets back."

When William and Gwen returned with the tea, they were surprised to see Catherine at the door, holding her little overnight bag, ready to leave.

"What's this?" Gwen asked. "No tea? Why the rush all of a sudden?"

"I don't have time to explain. William, can we go now?" she asked, then addressed her sister. "I'm sorry, Gwen, I have to rush back to Zach. I have to see him. I'll call you later, and then we really do need to visit for a long time, okay?"

"Zach? Are you crazy? At a time like this?"

"Don't worry about me and Zach. I know what I have to do."

She ran down the stairs and into William's car. They drove in complete silence for the first hour. William knew Catherine needed space, and he still didn't know how he fit into her life since Zach remained a part of it.

Finally he dared to break the silence. "Do you think it's permanent with Zach? I mean, now that you really do need him?"

"Who said I need him now? Now is exactly when I do not need him."

This almost brought a smile to William's face. "Well, this is new. Then what?" he asked.

"William, can I tell you something in complete confidence?"

"Yes, of course, Catherine. You can tell me anything. What is it?"

"I really don't know how to say this," she began. "I'm so terribly confused and guilty that I just want to start over from the day Tina was born. I want to be the mother she should have had. I've been the biggest fool there ever was. I've been stubborn and blind and an idiot! I've caused pain and death to the one person I always loved the most."

William consoled, "Now, Catherine, don't be so hard on yourself. You..."

"William! Zach molested Tina. He raped her!" she screamed.

William looked at her, aghast. He stepped on the brake and steered the car to the shoulder. The parkway was not busy on a late Monday evening; only one or two cars went by, some with passengers who craned their necks to see what appeared to be two lovers locked in an intimate embrace.

Catherine sobbed and sobbed. When she was finally finished, William released her.

"You've got to go to the police about this, Catherine. This is serious."

"Oh, it's serious, all right. But no police. No one will ever convict him; there's no proof, no evidence. It would be Saskia's second-hand information with no one to corroborate it, and Zach would lie and charm his way out of it. Don't forget, Tina was in therapy and severely depressed; he'll claim she made it all up just to impress a friend, or something like that. No, no police," she said with finality. "No police. I think I'll just deal with this in my own way.

"Catherine, I don't know what to say. I'm so sorry for you and for all this mess. But please, please don't blame yourself for Zach's evil. He hid it from you."

"Yes, well, I think I know what I have to do," she repeated.

"You'll have to get rid of him immediately, of course." William stated. "If you need any help, Catherine, now that you know what he's capable of, please call me. Please."

"If I need you, I will call. I promise," she said through fresh tears.

William started the car and they rode the rest of the way to Brigantine in a more comfortable silence. Catherine had her hand on William's shoulder all the way, and she thanked him for being a true friend when he dropped her off. Waiting for her on the front step was Zach, a beer in his hand and a grin on his face.

Chapter 22

With Impunity

"I'm so glad to see you. How is Tina? She's all right, isn't she? It was a false alarm, I take it," Zach said in a rush as Catherine swept past him and into the house.

"She's probably better now than she ever was in her life," Catherine responded. She walked into her bedroom, which was a total disaster. The sheets were smelly, the floor was covered with newspapers and beer cans, the window was wide open with no screen, and the dresser was piled with dirty underwear and socks. She screamed, "Zach! Get in here!"

"Now, Westie, don't get yourself into a tizzy. You should have called and said that you were on your way. I would have had the whole place cleaned up."

She rounded on him. "You wouldn't know where to begin!"

"Hey, I said I was sorry. I'll take care of it, okay? What's wrong with you anyway? Gone for four days, no call, no kiss when you get home—just a cold shoulder and nagging."

Catherine took a deep breath and tried to fix her face into an appropriate expression. "Yes, Zach, you're right," she responded as she turned to face him. "You clean up this mess; I'll sleep in the guest room until it's done. And tomorrow evening, to celebrate me being back and you entering rehab, I'll fix your favorite dinner."

"Well, now you're talking. Let's have a beer together since it may be one of my last." He wandered to the fridge, took out two Guinness— Catherine's favorite—and popped the tops.

Catherine sat at her kitchen table and took the beer. "No kiss first?" he asked.

"Let's save all that until the big dinner tomorrow. Then we can really finish this homecoming properly. After all, it is really a big homecoming for you, you know. I've only been gone a few days; you were gone for forty years! Now we can finish the whole thing up right."

Zach lifted his can. "I'll drink to that," he said. Catherine smiled and took a deep drink of the dark stout.

The following morning, Catherine dressed and went shopping for dinner. She bought a small turkey, potatoes, salad, bread crumbs, apples, spices, onions, garlic, and bread at the Shop and Bag. She also bought a small jar of peanut butter to add to the stuffing. She felt pretty safe about this since she had once had apple pie baked by a friend who always added peanut butter to the pie. Very strange she had thought at the time, but now that little addition would come in very handy.

When she got home, Zach was on the beach, enjoying the final warmth of summer. She poured herself a cup of cold coffee, nuked it, and stood on the deck holding the steaming cup to her lips while staring at the old man sitting on her best red beach towel.

Later that day, she began to prepare his favorite dinner. While he took a shower, applied aftershave and a touch of cologne, she prepared the dressing, adding some of the peanut butter. Then she stuffed the turkey with it, poured some oil into the deep fryer on the deck, and immersed the bird before she applied the match to the propane nozzle. "That should do it," she whispered to the passing clouds. Standing on the deck, she almost found the ability to enjoy the fine sunset. If one stood on the beach and turned toward the bay, he was met by an array of colors more varied than Van Gogh's palette splashed across the sky.

When Zach came out of the shower, it was obvious he expected a very special evening. Catherine smiled at him. She wanted him to believe just that, and she certainly intended to give him the time of his life.

"I'm really glad Tina is okay," Zach said as they sat down to the feast. "I thought you were overreacting when you said she was dead. Wow, what an overreaction that was, huh, Westie?"

She smiled. "You bet, Zach. Eat."

She watched him take big bites of the turkey and dressing. "Good, huh, Zach?" she asked.

He did not answer; instead, he clutched at his throat. "My medicine," he croaked. "Get my—peanuts? In turkey? Get…"

Catherine sat back and watched. "What did you say? Tina is okay? Is that what you said? After what you did, you think she could be okay? She's dead, Zach, just like you." He looked at her in horror as he slipped off the chair and onto the floor. These things apparently did not take long, Catherine observed.

Chapter 23

No Guilt

After the paramedics left and the ambulance had taken his body away, the police questioned Catherine.

"You say you didn't know? How could you not know?"

"Well, when I called his sister, she said he felt it was wimpy so he never told anybody. He just kept his medication nearby," she explained.

"And you never saw the injector?"

"No. I never even knew he had one until she told me. Apparently he kept it in a case. I trusted him, so I never went through his things."

"Didn't he ever check ingredients on things he bought when you were with him?"

"Of course he did. But he never said what he was looking for, and told me to mind my own business when I asked. I don't eat peanut butter, so the issue never came up."

"Just out of curiosity, do you always put peanut butter in stuffing?"

"No, but I found a new recipe for an apple stuffing that also included peanut butter. I wanted to make the very best meal for Zach, you understand. It was a celebration of sorts." Catherine wiped tears from her eyes as she explained this to the officers. Then she blew her nose, more to get the stench out than anything else.

The men stood up, offered their condolences, and left. After the autopsy had been performed and anaphylaxis due to a peanut allergy confirmed, Catherine was off the hook. Although the officers were suspicions, her story was plausible, and the information offered by Zach's sister helped confirm that he had not ever acknowledged his allergy.

Zachary was flown to Boston, where he was attended to by his sister. Catherine said she was too distressed to go to another funeral so soon.

After the police had gone, the phone rang. "Catherine. I saw the police and the ambulance. What happened? Are you all right?" William sounded concerned.

"Not to worry, Will. I'm fine. It seems Zach is—was—allergic to peanuts, and I used a new stuffing recipe that included peanut butter. Can you believe that?"

"Did they get to him in time?"

"No. I'm afraid he's dead. Gone for good this time, William."

"Catherine, oh, Catherine. What did you do?"

"I couldn't help it, William. I didn't do anything, really, except cook his favorite meal. He loved turkey with all the trimmings, so I made it. He began with gusto, and then he fell over and off his chair. I called 911, but it was too late.

"When I called his sister, she asked if he'd eaten peanuts in anything. I explained about the dinner and told her I'd used peanut butter in the dressing. Then she told me he was allergic to peanuts, but had always been too proud to tell anybody. She said she knew this would happen someday. That's it," Catherine explained.

"And you were not aware of his allergy, Catherine? Why would you cook for him? Why would you do that after all you've suffered? After all you knew? After Tina? Why?" William fired a barrage of questions at her.

"William, what are you suggesting?"

"Nothing, Catherine, nothing. Are you all right? Do you want me to come over?"

"No. Not right now. But thanks." She said goodbye and hung up.

Catherine sank into her big blue chair and immediately smelled his odor in it. It made her nauseous. She felt an awful chill come over her whole body; it felt as though every fiber in her body trembled. She was too exhausted to get up.

After about a half-hour, she managed to wrest herself out of the chair.

She slowly made her way up the stairs, put her hand around a cord, drew down some stairs, and went into the attic. She unwrapped the large container of peanut butter, stared at it, and wept. She slowly and carefully took down the painting she'd called *Tina*, carried it into the living room, and set it on a chair up against the wall. She looked at it for a long time and then fell to her knees, lifted her hands high, looked up to heaven and sobbed, "Oh my God. What have I done? What have I done? Forgive me. Forgive me. Oh, please, please, please. Can you forgive me?" Then she collapsed in a heap on the floor. Her energy, her vitality sapped, she lay for a long time before crawling into her bedroom.

Chapter 24

Out to Sea

William stood on his back deck wrapped in a jacket for the first time of the season, delighting in the sunset. When he noticed a slight movement up the beach, he turned to the ocean side to see what it was. Walking toward the edge of the water was a tall, athletic-looking figure, slightly hunched over now. Long strides hinting at a kind of silent determination apprised William of who it was. He stared into the coming darkness, tried to adjust his eyes, and could just make out the lifting of one long, dark arm, an oblong ball in the raised hand, and then a powerful swing that propelled the thing far out into the waves which curled white frothy tongues around it and swallowed it with satisfaction. The sea became calm; not a bubble or burp erupted.

William watched the small projectile disappear, bob back up for just a second, and then disappear into the darkness, perhaps to reappear on some distant continent. "It's finally over." Then he murmured his epitaph to the silent sea. "The idol was found wanting; the idol has been torn down."

He pulled his jacket tightly around him and shivered as he walked into the house. The cozy little room he'd shared with both Catherine and

Tina had taken on an atmosphere of its own. Memories bounced off the walls now, and his peace had been seriously shaken. As he looked out over the dark and silent beach, he reached a new resolve.

In the wisdom acquired from years of quiet observation and deep contemplation, William found the strength not to reach for the phone, but instead for the teakettle.

Chapter 25

Moving

The ocean swells turned into strong breakers farther out than they had been all summer. The late October air on Brigantine reminded William of his wife's favorite time of year, her favorite weather. The cool breeze blew through his thin hair, sending its combed-over strands flying in different directions as the sun made the silver in them glisten. He stood on the beach in the early morning sun, facing its eastern rising as though he expected something special, and his face shone with the prospect. But William had no clue what his expectation was. He turned toward Catherine's house and saw her long arm reach up and wave to him from atop her dune. He quickly turned away, wishing she had not seen him. He didn't know what to do with her. He thought he had successfully swept his life clean of her, but now, a month later, he knew he missed her company He'd often reached for the phone but stopped. William no longer quite trusted Catherine, so he resisted.

The little room he'd built as his personal space was now part of the whole house. The main wall had been removed, allowing the early-morning sun to suffuse the entire main living area. William had bought a new white leather sofa and love seat with matching ottoman. These faced the little gas fireplace. Behind the sofa, facing the beach and the sea, he'd placed a green wrought-iron table and four chairs. The glass on the table was beveled and etched with a lovely dolphin scene. Under the table was an exquisite, round, hand-tied carpet in hues of pink and pastel green accented with white and gold.

The walls were newly painted also. The wallpaper was gone, and blue and ochre replaced it in the kitchen and dining area. One wall in the living room was a deep pumpkin—his most daring move in redecorating. The other walls were a restful, very pale, green. William had placed some large plants in the bay window. The only places he had not touched were the bedroom and guest room; otherwise the beach house had taken on a whole new character. William had successfully erased all physical memories of both his wife Bernice and his friend Catherine.

William's goal was to rid himself of the guilt he felt about Tina's death and the Catherine's subsequent behavior. He knew it was a little insane, but he still felt a sense of responsibility. Tina had come to him for help when she'd discovered her true parentage, and now she was dead. He must have failed her. Catherine had been his friend, and she might have done something so horrendous he could not even allow himself to think about it. Zach was dead, too.

Catherine was left with no one and nothing. What a devastating series of events. He felt he'd failed her too. Yet how could one solitary man have carried these women through their problems? Had he been expected to? He put up the "for sale" sign with a sigh of resignation. His house had been redone and tastefully staged.

Catherine had tried to call him and had left a message asking about his intentions, but he had not been able to return her call. He felt like the wimp Zachary had so often said he was.

Now he sat at his new dining table with a hot cup of tea in his hands. He thought about Catherine, about leaving, and about his new house in Pennsylvania, close to some old friends. At his age, he needed community more than he needed the ocean. He thought about what a waste it all was—Catherine's lifelong wait for her football hero, Zach; Tina's fatherless childhood and her early death; Robert's ignorance of a lovely daughter.

The consequences of one person's decisions reach deep into the lives of so many others. The devastation resulting from Catherine's life-choice to wait forty years for her lover had culminated in misery, death, and separation. William knew some of it and surmised the rest. The sooner he could sell his house and move home, the better he would feel, he believed. He'd considered a move north to Bergen County where he and his father had worked at remodeling homes. He'd thought of moving to North Carolina to be completely renewed. But he had settled on Pennsylvania, the place of his birth. He hoped to forget; he knew he never would.

Chapter 26

Guilt

"I hate you. I hate you! No! Don't touch me!"

"Oh, oh, oh. What have I done? Tina, what have I done?"

Catherine stirred on her disheveled bed, opened her eyes and sat upright, and then screamed and stared, without seeing, at her sister. She sank to one elbow before she lay back down on her sweat-drenched sheets. She hardly knew where she was. "What are you doing? Who are you?" Then recognition entered her wary brain. "Gwen, what are you doing here?" she whispered.

Gwen was sitting at the edge of the bed. The tidy little room had taken on a sour smell from an awful mess of dirty clothes on the floor, dust on the dresser, and a wet towel hanging over the single antique wooden chair. Gwen had been trying to clean it all before Catherine woke up, but had been instantly distracted by her sister's loud and anguished cries.

"Are you awake now, Kate? You called me on Tuesday, remember? You were depressed and terribly unhappy, so I came as soon as I could. I'm sorry it took so long for me to get here. I was so worried about you."

"Ooh, my head hurts. I'm so confused." Catherine rubbed her

eyes and pushed the hair back from her forehead with a trembling hand. Then she again sat straight up and eyed her sister with suspicion. She came entirely to herself, then said, "I'm so sorry, Gwen. I didn't mean to call you. I'm so sorry. I can get through this by myself. It's just these damned nightmares. I called you after one of those, I guess. I'm hardly myself then, and it takes a bit of time for me to pull it all back together. I didn't mean for you to come all the way out here. Forgive me. Go home. I'll pay your way back."

"No, Kate! I don't think it's as simple as that. I think you need a lot more help than you realize. I'm not going to let you send me away—not this time. After Tina, and then your Zachary dying—well, it's all too much. You need time, and probably some grief counseling."

Catherine sighed deeply. It seemed that all the battles of all her years were stuck deep inside her belly, threatening to travel to her brain and explode. She sighed again as she had so often the past few weeks. She had had bouts of vomiting, and thought they might help get rid of a bit of the burden from time to time. She did get relief for a very short time, but it was just a tease. It all soon came back—a great burden, like a great black sack filled with fear, anger, and guilt lodged deep inside her. She still ached from the inside out, just as she had before the purging. But she was not going to tell Gwen any of this; it was none of her busybody business. The perfect sister was not going to get wind of this new, weak Catherine.

Her daughter had been the most precious part of her life. She knew her obsession with Zachary Bekker had contributed to her daughter's death, and had certainly put a wedge between them. Zachary, the famous jock, the man who had promised her so much but had taken every bit of her dignity from her, and then her daughter as well. His death had been some recompense, but now she felt only emptiness and guilt.

Why? No one knew what she had done. No one knew how clever she had been. No one even guessed how she had watched Zachary die while eating his favorite meal—turkey, but with a peanut-butter stuffing. He, so proud, so fearful of losing even a smidgen of his macho reputation, told no one was of his allergy. He saw it as a weakness. Well, she had learned of it just in time. If Zachary could ruin her life by making her wait forty years for him and by raping her gentle, vulnerable daughter, then she had every right—no, she had a duty—to do something about it. So why did she now suffer these awful nightmares? These awful feelings of loss and guilt? Well, whatever. No one was going to be privy to any of it. No knowledge, no judgment.

"Listen, Gwen, I'm all right now. Thanks for coming. Can you get a ticket home, do you think? Did you get a round-trip ticket? As I said, I'll pay. No problem."

"I'm not going home without you," Gwen said firmly. "No ifs, ands, or buts about it. You're coming with me or I stay here." She said this quietly but seriously, and Catherine could not believe her ears.

"You've got to be kidding me! You can't stay here. What about Warren? And why would I go to that little burg of yours? Why would I leave this island for the Midwest, where there's no sea? Why would I leave an exciting place like this for a dull, provincial one like yours? Galey, of all places. Tell me that!"

Gwen was ready for this; Kate had always disdained her place of birth, especially after Zachary had made a joke of it. It was high time she got over that. "Listen, Kate, that's nothing but Zachary's nonsense talking, and it's about time you recognized that. But consider this. You don't have to come back to the 'little burg,' as you put it. Find a spot on the lake. You'll still be near the water and you'll be able to leave these bad memories behind, at least somewhat. Brigantine was never your real home anyway."

"How can you say that? What would you know about it, anyway?" Catherine felt her old annoyance about her sister's interference. Not only had Gwen married the "right" man at the "right" time, but she had always been the person to whom Tina had turned in her moments of crisis. Catherine could not forgive this because she could not understand it. Gwen had been the perfect daughter; Catherine had been the wild one. But she'd called Gwen here herself, and was angry at her own weakness. What did Gwen have that she didn't? Sisters who looked so much alike would have some personality traits in common, one would think. But Catherine felt as far removed from her younger sister as she did from William.

"I can always call William and get things on a good footing with him again. I can still make some kind of a life for myself here. Leave me alone. And if I call you again, just chalk it up to momentary dementia. I'll snap out of it, just as I have today. Go already."

"Sorry, sis, not this time. I'm insisting, and you had better take a good, hard look at yourself. William does not want to see you. His house is for sale; I'm sure you know that. You're suffering terrible nightmares. You've lost a considerable amount of weight, and you're not able to make a life here or anywhere else by yourself at the moment. You need help."

"Yeah, well, maybe," she quietly acquiesced, then added, "but I don't need it from you."

"Of course not. But you do need to get away, and you need someone to talk to."

"Like a shrink? Look where that got Tina."

"Kate, please. The shrink had nothing to do with Tina. Something else was bothering her, and I bet you know what it was. I'm just sorry I couldn't get her to tell me before she died."

"Oh? You think you had the almighty power maybe to save her? Really, Gwen, this is too much. Besides, it wasn't suicide anyway." She was proud to be able to lay this on her sister. "And, yes, I do know what was bothering her. I know everything about my daughter and her death. You could not have saved her. It was just an accident. Even though she was terribly upset, it was not suicide. I'm sure of it."

The sun was just rising over the water, and a ray of light shot into the room, illuminating the bantering sisters. The radiance it shed on the two heads gave the illusion of halos, but it disappeared as quickly as it had come. Angels did not lose their halos so quickly. Gwen and Catherine ignored the light and continued the debate.

"What?" Gwen was pained and totally floored by Kate's words. She didn't know what to say, except "What?" She was unsure if she was responding to Kate's accusation or information.

"That's right. I know exactly what was bothering her. I know exactly what killed her. And the two are not related. I knew she would never take her own life, and she didn't!"

"Are you going to enlighten me on any of this? The result of the autopsy was that she'd taken two kinds of meds." Gwen wasn't sure what was to come; Catherine could be so smug and evasive.

"Tina was depressed. She was taking one drug, but it didn't seem to be working for her, so the doctor changed her medication. Well, she felt so bad that she didn't wait long enough for one drug to leave her system before starting to take the other. She was also drinking wine as well as taking an over the counter cold medication. The combination was lethal. It's rare, but it can and does happen. It was not a suicide, it was an accident," Catherine explained, a little triumphantly.

"Are you sure you're not grasping at straws?"

"Isn't this just like you, Gwen? I come up with a good solution to a really difficult problem, and you refuse to accept it." Catherine's hackles were up. Her nerves could take no opposition just now, especially not from Gwen. She fought back tears—whether of anger, desperation, or a keen sense of loss, she could not be sure.

"Kate, please. I've just never heard of such a thing. Please don't go on the offensive. I'm concerned about you, and hope you have some evidence for this."

"I spoke to her doctors," Catherine retorted, looking her sister in the eye. "They both reluctantly agreed that this could happen. Get it?" She tossed these last words at Gwen, hoping her sister would catch them.

"So we can all stop feeling guilty about not helping her. But she was left alone, and that was a serious mistake any way you look at it." This final dig made Gwen wince. Kate was right, but she could not live with the guilt of Tina's death on her shoulders. She had only left the house for a short time; the others also had only left for a few minutes to walk up town on an errand. Tina's death was not their fault; it was an accident. She would believe this and help her sister as best she could.

"Kate, we all left her alone. We all believed, as you did, that she would never resort to taking her own life. Now we can get some peace at least in the knowledge it may very well have been an accident, as you described. I thank you for giving me this information."

"Yeah, well, she's still gone."

"Please don't stay here alone any longer, Kate. I need you in Michigan. I need to be able to reach you, and I think you need that too. Just live on the lake. I'll be a couple of hours away. We don't need to be close enough to get into each other's hair, you know."

Catherine stared at her sister. She thought about her nightmares. She remembered her terrible pain when thinking about Tina, and William too, now lost to her. She felt waves of guilt and fear wash over her too often. She knew she shouldn't be alone all the time. But Michigan? Shit! How could she go back there after all she'd said about it? Yet she knew the lake could offer her the solace water always gave her. She shook her head as she considered the possibility and stared straight through Gwen. Maybe…maybe it was the answer now. Money was not an issue. Prices on Brigantine had skyrocketed; the early 2000s had brought housing prices to a peak. Zach had been right about that when he'd suggested she sell for about a million and move away together. Well, doing it without having to share it all with a penniless alcoholic seemed like a viable possibility now. But Michigan?

"Okay, Gwen, you win. When do we leave?"

"Just like that, you decide? Great! Well, let's go as soon as you sell. Call a realtor." Gwen smiled with delight. The heavy atmosphere seemed completely dissipated. What a relief. They both felt it.

Catherine laughed. "I hate Michigan. I'll call my friend Grace right away."

Chapter 27

On the Dune

Catherine walked through Van Wickes furniture store, looking at sofas, chairs, dining sets, and bedrooms. She hoped no one would bother her; she had no intention of letting some overbearing sales person influence her. Catherine preferred no one following her around or making suggestions. She knew exactly what she wanted, and she knew exactly how much she needed to pay for it. As her hand slid over the back of an elegant silk brocade couch, a very short, black-haired youth approached with a chart and a smile wider than his height. Catherine stared down at him. He was undaunted by her severe look and quickly said, "Great fabric and color you've chosen. One of our very finest. You have exquisite taste, if I may say so. French Provincial is so elegant, don't you think?"

"I'd like to browse for a while, if you don't mind," she replied sternly.

"Certainly. Here's my card. Call me when you're ready to purchase or if you have any questions." With this he smiled and walked off.

Catherine was impressed by the salesman's tact and willingness to leave her alone. She wandered through the store, making mental notes of what she liked and how each piece could be used in her new cottage. She enjoyed the freedom of being able to buy whatever she liked. What a difference from her younger years, when every penny had to be counted twice. Now she simply chose and paid, and not even with a credit card.

She realized that she was having fun. The furniture wasn't the issue; the looking, the choosing, the lack of restraint—these were the things which gave her some joy. Total freedom. When she was ready, she summoned the salesman. "Just call me Big Jim," he introduced himself, "everyone here does." He chuckled at his own joke.

Catherine smiled and began pointing out the things she'd decided to buy. There was a small red sofa for her family room, which was really a wonderfully designed closed-in porch. A large round cocktail table with leather in the center for her formal living room, twin wicker beds for her guest room, and four nightstands. She also chose a small drop-leaf table for her family room so she could have breakfast overlooking the lake. She would probably use the same space for any eating she did alone. And the four chairs she chose would accommodate a few guests in that same space.

Her bedroom would need a king-sized bed. She chose a simple Shaker style in warm birch tones, and a small dresser to match. She decided she'd finish the decor with a few odd pieces from an antique store she'd passed on her way. She asked Big Jim to add up her purchases. She thought he looked ten feet taller after he calculated her costs. "Wow," he said. "You certainly made my day." She smiled and took out her wallet.

Catherine found the town of Good Heavens acceptable, with its little shops, restaurants, galleries, and proximity to Chicago. Her new house on Camelot Drive, atop a dune overlooking a Lake Michigan beach, gave her some pleasure. She had never, in this lifetime, wanted to move back to Michigan, but under the circumstances and given her need for a complete change, the lakefront did offer a suitable option. The excessive paleness of the locals was a bit of a downer for her, although she figured she could avoid closeness to these people if she wished. She wasn't right next door to her sister either, but she had come to understand she did need some kind of community to reach out to if she were to become whole again. She wasn't sure how she would handle this.

William had moved from Brigantine and left no forwarding address. Robert Scotland, her daughter's father, was married and off-limits. She'd just barely found the nerve to let him know of Tina's death, and what a fiasco that had been—grief compounded by guilt and remorse, blame heaped on her for all the years of lies and deception. Robert had been appalled. He was red with anger and grief when she'd told him, hurled horrible accusations at her, and then stormed out of her presence. Her guilt tasted acrid in her mouth, and she understood his anger. But she could not forgive him for laying so much blame on her, so she'd left. She told no one except her sister where she was off to.

Now she was living in a contemporary house above the beach, which she could never have afforded if Brigantine beach-front-property prices had not gone crazy. She was sure her lovely little house was already a thing of the past, and that bulldozers were busy clearing the land for some massive structure which would be lived in for a few months a year, if that. But she didn't need that guilt trip either, so she brushed the thought away and continued decorating.

Every piece she purchased opposed what she'd had on Brigantine. No more blue velvet, no more white, no more light, airy things. Her present life demanded solid wood, contemporary lines, and some decorative Asian touches. These she found in unique chests of drawers painted with flowers and leaves. There would be no window treatments. Her yard was dense with pines, and her front windows stretched from floor to ceiling, overlooking the beach and the lake. If she forgot for a moment where she was, she'd have thought she was looking out over the ocean. The dune was higher than her ocean dune, but she was limber enough to scale it without using the stairs after her cold morning swims. It was almost as if she were torturing herself in her adamant pursuit of morning swims in the frigid lake waters, but she felt cleansed each time.

She browsed daily through every furniture store she could find. She loved leather, but could not buy it; Zach had been a leather man. She could not bear the elegance of most French Provincial—it was just too fussy. And, of course, Tina had loved it. Catherine was on a quest to find herself and rid herself of daily reminders of her recent past. It was all too horrible, too heartbreaking. So she moved on to the sleek contours of contemporary. She initially found them cold, but figured with the proper accents and art work, cozy might be accomplished. She loved Eames chairs, and had already purchased two. In this case, leather would not be an issue. They sat in her glassed-in family room overlooking the lake.

She was glad she'd bought the king-sized Shaker bed, just in case. One could become sick and need lots of room to toss around, or her nightmares might take her on a fling to the opposite side. She knew she wanted plenty of room. Sometimes she got so hot and sweaty she had to throw the covers off, even though the room temperature was only fifty degrees. Then she'd get cold and move herself to the other end of the bed and burrow under the covers. Yes, a big bed was a definite need for her present self.

Gwen had volunteered to assist with the buying and decorating, but Catherine had quickly squelched that idea. "No, Gwen, this is a personal quest, and you don't fit in now." Gwen knew better than to feel hurt. She would bide her time, give Catherine her space, and be ready for the inevitable call.

Chapter 28

Setting Up

After the last delivery had been made and the last truck had left the driveway, the doorbell rang. "Who could that possibly be?" Catherine muttered. She went to the door, opened it a little, and peered around the corner to see a somewhat past-middle-aged couple standing, grinning, on her front step.

"Hi!" the round-faced man said. He was too jovial, and Catherine's guard immediately went up. "We're Sam and Betty MacMurtle. We live next door, and we want to welcome you to the neighborhood. We saw all your deliveries and thought we'd pop by to introduce ourselves now that you're all moved in."

Catherine felt obligated to open the door a little farther. Without an invitation, Sam and Betty barged into her space. "We've been watching the activity from our house. We're certainly glad to have someone living here. It's been almost a year since the Carsons left. It's been too quiet for us. Right, Sam?" Betty said and grabbed Catherine's hand, giving it a great shake. Sam took her hand next. "Good to have you here. I don't believe I've caught your name."

Catherine thought she'd better be friendly since these were

her closest neighbors. "I'm Catherine Cedar. I just moved here from New Jersey."

"Wow, that's a long way. What brings you to Good Heavens?"

"Guilt," she said, without thinking.

"Oh." Betty looked around. "But you didn't buy any gilt," she observed. *Very funny*, Catherine thought, but then realized Betty was serious. *What an incredibly stupid woman*, Catherine silently observed.

"Yes, well, I couldn't find what I liked, so I had to settle for ordinary wood." Catherine played along, knowing that, in her haste, she'd said the most inappropriate thing she could think of. "Maybe I'll find a nice gilt mirror for my bedroom one of these days."

"Ooh, you know what? There's a very nice antique place on 105th Street. They have all kinds of stuff like that. I'll take you there sometime if you want." Betty was far too enthusiastic, and Catherine had to find a way to nicely put these two off.

"That would be great, Betty, but I'm not quite ready yet. I still have so much to do. Maybe I'll drop by sometime when I'm ready for a little antique shopping."

"Well, we're so glad to meet you. We've been without neighbors for almost a year, and I bet we'll be great friends. Here's our card. if you need anything, just call." With that, Sam handed her a card with their pictures on it as well as their names, address, e-mail, and phone number. Catherine thanked them and deposited the card in her pocket.

As they moved down her driveway and across the lawn and sand to their rather massive home, Catherine sighed with relief and regret. She'd come to this lake home out of guilt, and had not realized how much until it suddenly erupted from her mouth to these strangers.

She'd always used water to calming agent the turbulence in her life. Even as a young girl, she would take her woes and fears to the river just down the hill from her house and sit for hours, letting the sound of the rippling flow heal her brain. Now she knew she would sit often, perhaps too often, on the beach, hopefully in the wind, and let the rushing sounds clear the cobwebs from her brain. She felt as Macbeth must have felt after the murder of Duncan, when he told his wife his mind was full of scorpions. Catherine was beginning to learn that there is no such thing as an action with impunity. Everything one did had consequences. Everything.

Since the devastating events of the past months, which seemed more like years, she could not be sure if her pain was a result of her grief over her daughter or guilt over her lover. She could not organize or categorize her feelings. Sometimes Zach would enter her dreams bigger than life and ten times scarier; sometimes Tina would be standing by her bed, tugging at the sheets until she woke up to find herself alone in the dark.

Chapter 29

Nightmares Again

Catherine tossed and turned. She was extraordinarily tired, and yet sleep would not come to her. She opened the sliders to her deck. The sound of growling waves, angry-sounding at night, from the lake offered no comfort. Catherine went out and sat in a lounge chair. She let the wind blow through her hair and nightgown. She was sure she looked like some romantic Victorian waif out of a novel, soon to be rescued from impending doom by the long-haired Fabio. A close look would reveal her lack of youth and innocence, but she knew there would be no close look from the black beach at three in the morning.

As she pined away her time listening to the black, lonely waters, soaking up the moon's incandescent half-light, she felt the calm she'd longed for all night. She opened her eyes and looked out to the end of the beach. As she did so, she noticed a dark shape forming near the water's edge. It seemed to crouch, then grow larger as it straightened to its full height. She wasn't sure if it was man or beast or a combination of both. She felt an odd anticipation not akin to fear so much as yearning, yet she knew she must never allow the yearning to take her. She stood as the specter approached and, the closer it came, the more Catherine recognized the gait, the posture of her lover, Zachary Bekker. *How can this be?* she thought. *I watched him die.*

"Zach!" she called. He began ascending the stairs. The closer he came, the more Catherine anticipated his touch. The more she anticipated, the more a growing dread formed in her stomach. She felt the warning fear and tried to get up, tried to turn from his grasp. She tried to run, but her legs would not move. When he hovered over her and picked her up off the lounge, she tried to scream, but it stuck, impotent, in her throat. His smell was of death, she was sure. Dead fish in a barrel were perfume compared to this. She gagged and called his name. Then he flung her over the rail.

She landed with a terrific thud on her bed; she could feel it shake. A cold sweat had soaked her pajamas, and her pillow was saturated. She lay still for what seemed like hours; the fear that had overtaken her had paralyzed her. She was afraid that if she moved, he might come back, or that she would die. As light slowly began to drift into her room, she realized it was morning. She moved her head. She looked around her room and saw there was no one there. No one had been there, either, she knew.

Another horrible nightmare had taken her to hallucinatory heights and dropped her, sweating, into her bed. Why couldn't they just leave her alone? She wept as she staggered into the bathroom. She leaned over the sink, vomited, and looked up to see her tear stained face. Lines of fear were etched around her eyes and mouth; she opened her mouth and jutted her jaw to flatten them. She tensed the muscles at the bottom of her chin and cheeks, and then let them relax. Facial exercises were a routine with Catherine ever since the lines of guilt, grief, and pain had begun to appear. She'd aged since Brigantine. She'd looked younger than her age for a long time, but not any more. She knew the nightmares caused some it. She also knew that this one's intensity would trouble her the entire day. It would follow her like an ugly black dog, close on her heels, and try to trip her up. She feared entering the day, but moved into the kitchen in an attempt to ward off these feelings.

Catherine made herself a strong cup of coal-black coffee. The new stuff from Columbia and Kenya and who knows where else amazed and delighted her. She'd bought many varieties, and chose one of the strongest this morning. She omitted her usual cream in the hope of warding off the dog. She sipped slowly and frowned at the bitter taste. Yet, as the heat descended into her stomach, she believed it was doing some good, that the black coffee brought some warmth and perhaps even light to her dark awakening. She thought to carry her mug to the outside and sit on her deck, but the memory came back. What if the deck were wet? What if there were footprints? Big, Zach-like prints? What if?

Then her doorbell rang. She jumped a mile with fright, but this also shook her back into the morning. The sun was shining. The breeze off the lake cooled the kitchen too much. She shut the glider and went to the front door. Her mug still in hand, she peered through the glass to see who it was. Only Betty. *Thank God for that*, she thought. Against her will, but with the knowledge she might need her someday, Catherine opened the door to her neighbor.

"Good morning, Catherine," Betty almost sang.

"Yes, well, come on in," Catherine responded. "What can I do for you this morning?"

"What can I do for you?" Betty answered. "I saw you out on the beach last night, it must have been about three o'clock, so I thought maybe you needed some company or something. I couldn't sleep last night either, you see, so I was on my deck. And there you were running along the beach, nightgown blowing in the wind behind you. I must say, you were a lovely sight in the moonlight," Betty giggled.

Catherine was stunned. "I wasn't on the beach last night. It must have been someone else you saw."

"Oh, it was you, all right. Tall, elegant, running like an athlete, just like you do when you take your dips in the morning. Even in this freezing water. You are something else, Catherine. Oh, yes, it was you. But at that hour?" Betty would not let it go.

Catherine insisted she had not been out. Finally Betty shrugged and said, "Well, I'm sorry. It did look like you, but I guess at three in the morning anyone could be mistaken. Aren't you going to offer me some of that coffee?" she asked, pointing to Catherine's tightly clenched mug.

"No, I'm not," was the too-quick reply.

Betty backed up a step and looked hurt.

Catherine tried to recover the situation, "I'm so sorry, Betty. I really don't feel well this morning. Please forgive me. I'll call you later and we can have coffee another time soon, okay? So sorry. Really."

Betty retreated with a smile and closed the door softly behind her. Catherine put both hands in her hair and screamed, "How could I have been so rude!" And then she remembered what Betty had said. Shivers crawled up and down her spine. Had she really been on the beach? Had her dream driven her there? What was going on? She gulped down the rest of the coffee, which had cooled down by now, and bent to check the hem of her nightgown. It was damp. She took a closer look; there was sand. "What the hell?" she murmured, and fresh tears began to form. "Am I losing my mind?" she heard herself say as she ran into her bedroom to check the bed. Sand! "What am I going to do?"

She sank down into her Eames chair. The odor of leather nearly did her in; it was Zach's smell. Why had she indulged in leather? She got up. Maybe getting dressed and doing daily things, ordinary things, would set her mind at ease. She opened the closet and walked in. She rummaged through her clothes, tore a pair of jeans from a hanger and pulled them on under her nightgown, which she then hauled over her head and threw on the floor. Then she grabbed a far-too-old bra and strapped it on. Next she grabbed a blouse, not even looking to see which one it was. The one piece of simply designed, purple Prada clothing she owned or would ever own now graced her long body, adorning a pair of old jeans. "Tough," she said to no one. Barefoot and almost elegant, she went back into the kitchen and put the dirty mug in the dishwasher. At least some things never change, she thought. No matter what, you have to wear clothes. The dirty dishes need to be washed. And laundry required washing as well. So she moved to the laundry room and started a too-small load in the hopes of bringing normal sounds and activities into her overly agitated present.

Then a sound from the past entered through her phone. When she first heard the ring, Catherine was afraid to pick up the receiver. The caller ID read " Phillis Ver Hage." She had no idea who that was, but she picked up and said hello.

"Hi, Kate," twanged the high, friendly voice. "How are you? I'm Phillis Sonderfan—from school, remember? My married name is Ver Hage. How in the world are you?"

Catherine shook her head to try to jar an old memory from a dusty shelf in her brain. The voice sounded familiar. "Squeaky" was the nickname she recalled from junior high days. That had not been kind, but somehow stuck to Phillis. "Oh, yes. I remember now," Catherine answered with a bit of hesitation in her voice.

"I know," the little voice said. "You're probably thinking, 'Oh, it's Squeaky,' right? Well, don't be embarrassed. I named my dog that just to get over some of the early pain, and to remember that I'm a rather wonderful person made in the image of God, regardless of what my peers thought of my voice. Anyway, Gwen told me you were in Good Heavens and might need some company once in a while. I've been living here for fifteen years and really love it." She paused long enough for a breath, and Catherine found the time just enough to get a word in.

"Yes, Phillis. That would be really nice, but right now is not a good time. Can you call back in a few days maybe?" With that she hung up.

"Leave it to Gwen," she muttered, "hooking me up with one of them. I never really loved Squeaky anyway. But…" She remembered what a fast friend Phillis had been. She always quietly took all Catherine's digs and stood by her when Catherine had had boy trouble in high school. "I guess some things never change." she breathed to herself as she remembered those turbulent years. It was always men who caused her problems. Always. And Phillis had listened and made her laugh.

But she had been annoying, too, always wanted Catherine to go to church with her. The few times she did, Phillis positively beamed, as though she were personally responsible for saving Catherine's soul. Nothing had come of that, of course, but it had given Catherine the incentive to send Tina to Sunday school. She never questioned her own motives in doing it, but somehow knew it was one of the best things she could do for her child. "Poor little Tina," she whispered as she wiped a thick, wet tear from her cheek. "My poor, sensitive daughter."

Catherine spent the rest of the day polishing furniture, scrubbing the floors on her hands and knees, wiping counters, dusting, and washing windows both inside and out.

She vacuumed until her back hurt. Then she fixed herself a cold supper of beans and tuna and ate some of it on the deck, loving the brisk, cold air off the lake, and took some time to think about her high school friend and Tina. The wind ruffled her hair and nearly froze her ears, but it always felt like the cobwebs were blown from her brain for a while when the cold air cleansed her like this. She went inside, threw the remains of her meager supper away, and put her dishes in the dishwasher. Before she retired, she took her now-usual small shot of brandy and stood on her deck until she could feel its warmth, and then fell into bed exhausted. Once in bed, she took the time to do a bit of the daily crossword puzzle in what she called "the lame little town paper" she'd subscribed to, but soon turned off the light and fell asleep.

"Mommy." Tina tugged at the blankets. Catherine fought to stay asleep. When she opened her eyes, the child had turned into the adult Tina. Catherine asked her what the matter was, and Tina slowly changed into the white-faced, blank-staring cadaver Catherine had last seen. She screamed herself awake. Nothing was there; only the darkness and the sound of the swishing lake, which now sounded welcoming, beckoning.

Chapter 30

William

William woke up with a start. He was stunned. He could not believe what he'd just experienced. For years, while living on Brigantine, he'd had recurring dreams of his wife. They'd been sweet dreams, echoing the years of commitment he and Bernice had shared. Their life together had been quiet and filled with tender satisfaction, but not passion. William had sort of accepted this, thinking perhaps it was the best kind of marriage to have. He had never experienced anything different; neither had Bernice. So they lived together in mutual respect, friendship, and occasional intimacy. But the latter seemed to embarrass Bernice, so William restrained himself often. No fighting, no harsh words, no fire in the bedroom; just a relaxed, simple daily life of work and home. Sometimes they went out for dinner, occasionally with friends. When he'd retired, Bernice had suggested they invest in a little house at the shore, and they'd discovered Brigantine. The few years they'd shared there were uneventful until Bernice got sick and had to undergo treatments that depleted her body of everything substantial until she finally died. That had changed everything.

William met Catherine about a year after Bernice had died, and he discovered a whole other kind of woman. This one was strong-willed, passionately in love with someone else, willing to share her time with William, and converse with him. It was always fun and intellectually entertaining. But now, he'd come to believe she might be dangerous. After the death of her daughter, William had seen another side of Catherine. Her determination to get back from Ridgewood, where Tina had died, to Brigantine after the funeral; her lapse into tears and recriminations on the parkway on the way back; her resolve not to involve the law after she'd learned of Zach's abuse of Tina and the subsequent death of her long-awaited lover made William so fearful and suspicious that he'd decided to end the friendship. After his move back to Pennsylvania, he'd had some doubts about his decision concerning Catherine, but now he felt undone.

He sat up in bed, shielded his eyes from the glare of the rising sun, and frowned at his dream. What could it mean? Catherine had displaced Bernice in William's dreams for the first time. Would there be more? He could not wrap his mind around it. He felt fear; he felt joy; he could not discern the difference. He scanned the details.

William and Catherine sat on the beach. Atlantic City was to the right, and the stretch of clean, unspoiled beach lay before and to the left of them. It was autumn, but the days were still warm, and they sat together, arm in arm, on the moist sand. It must have been noon; the sun was high in the sky. He could feel the coolness of the wet sand through his khakis and knew Bernice would never have sat on the sand; she would never have allowed him to get his clothes wet and sandy, either. But here he was, with this exciting woman and a wet seat. He was exhilarated.

They laughed at some of the other people on the beach who were running or playing with their dogs or children; they talked about everything from dolphins to ducks—two of William's favorite subjects. They also talked about Tina and all Catherine's hopes for her daughter's future. She asked William what he thought of Tina, and then she brought up Zach.

The cold of the wet beach slid up his back and reached all the way to his face. He got up and walked towards the boardwalk. She followed him, and he could sense it. When she reached him, she told him not to worry about Zach, took William's face in her hands, and smiled. His warmth returned as he anticipated her next move—and then he woke up. He felt his cheek with his left hand. It was warm. A blush? From a dream? Why?

William's life had not been fun since his return from Brigantine. He missed his daily walk on the beach, his volunteer work at the wildlife preserve, the yearly migration of the birds, and he missed his friends. He attributed his dreams, especially the last one about Catherine, to his loneliness. This particular morning, it was palpable.

As he made coffee, he tried to figure it out. He remembered the trip from Ridgewood the night Tina died. That in itself had been a great shock. He could not believe Tina had killed herself; this was not the young woman he'd come to know. And then Catherine told him about Zach's assault on Tina, which was beyond comprehension. As William reflected on Catherine's next words, which he had done so often in the past few months, he shook his head and tried to erase his suspicion. But it kept coming back, more forceful each time. What if? And now this dream. He'd actually felt desire—at his age, yet. He shook his head again. There was too much to contemplate this morning.

During his reverie, William filled the coffee cup too full, and now the hot, dark brew was spilling all over his counter. He was not even aware of it until he felt the heat on his bare feet. At first he thought it was just another reaction to his dream but then he looked down, seeing what he had done. Meticulous William, thrown off by Catherine again. *Nuts!* he thought. *How can this be? I don't even like her anymore. I'm too old for this stuff.*

He decided this would be a good day to go to the library and immerse himself in some bird books. Birds and their behaviors always helped calm William. He had often found himself to be somebody new in Catherine's presence, but now he needed to be free of that. He drank his coffee and decided to have brunch a bit later, maybe in town with some of the guys from his past.

He showered and dressed in yellow khakis and pink t-shirt. His hair was still thick on the sides, and he did a quick comb-over. He somehow felt younger with a little hair on the top of his head. When he drew on his jacket he looked in the pocket for his keys. Not there. Nuts again! *What is going on with me*, he thought. *I never misplace anything. Why now, all of a sudden?* He retraced his steps from the previous evening, and found his keys in the bathroom—another weird thing. William never took his keys past the kitchen.

On his way to the library, he thought about the dream and his own absentmindedness. It was all so uncharacteristic that he decided his feelings of guilt and grief must be causing the changes. His age did not occur to him; only Catherine could cause such atypical behavior. So instead of searching for bird books, he began browsing the dream and psychology stacks.

Chapter 31

The Psychiatrist

"The reason I came to see you, Dr. Landman, is not because I think I'm crazy. You see, I need to know something about the effects of guilt. And about dreams." Catherine looked straight into the doctor's eyes, just to let him know she was tough and didn't need a shrink at all. "I've been having these strange dreams, and I wonder what's causing them. Also, I need to know what I can do to make them stop."

"What kind of dreams, Ms. Cedar?"

"Nightmares. Horrible nightmares about dead people."

"Any particular dead people?"

"Some people I knew."

"People close to you?"

"My daughter."

"Oh." He paused. "I'm so sorry. Recently?"

Catherine nodded.

"And you mentioned guilt. What about that?"

Dr. Geoff Landman sat in his oversized red leather chair with his legs crossed. He had a pen and notebook in his hands; the latter was much bigger than Catherine had expected. His black hair was perfectly styled—not a strand out of place. It made Catherine nervous. She wanted to put her fingers in it and mess it up. Instead she said, "Oh, that. Well, I really don't have a lot to say about that except that, like any parent, I think I could have done a better job of raising my daughter. I feel a bit guilty about that."

"Uh-huh. And that's it?" He stared at her for a few moments. Then he looked down and did not look up from his notes for quite a while as he pushed his pen.

He might just be doodling in there, Catherine thought as she watched him. He kept scribbling even when she'd stopped talking. She decided to wait to see if he kept on writing even when she was silent. He did. After what seemed like an hour, she finally broke in. "What are you writing, exactly?"

"I'm sketching a picture of you, Ms. Cedar. I very often see more in people's faces and postures than I glean from their words, so I like to keep a sketch of each patient from their first visit in their file."

"What do you mean, 'a sketch'?" She assumed he'd been writing; now she wasn't sure what he was doing.

"Drawings, Ms. Cedar. A drawing of you. My interpretation, in a drawing of you when you came in and began speaking. Would you like to see it?"

He'd been using a pen. He'd not even attempted an erasure. nor had he looked up at her more than maybe three times. She expected to see some grotesque caricature of herself, one which would resemble no one at all, especially not Catherine Cedar.

"And by the way, I'm not a patient. I'm a customer."

"Oh, really? Well, you must be in the wrong place. I'm a psychiatrist, and I deal with patients. Customers go to stores and buy over-the-counter medications, or go to pop-culture quacks for advice." With that he held up the sketch.

Catherine gasped. It looked like her, but at least twenty years older. The shoulders were stooped. Her hands lay in her lap, tightly interwoven, as if dominated by fear. There were deeper lines between her brows than she remembered having seen in the mirror that morning, and the circles under her eyes were far too dark. But the thing that really frightened her were the eyes. They were anguished, filled with pain, fear, or both. She couldn't be sure where, but she knew she had seen those eyes before. He'd gotten her thick hair exactly right, laying partially over her forehead.

She stared and stared, then averted her eyes as tears welled. When one dropped onto her lap, she stood up. "You've been very unfair. I'm not that bad looking, and I resent that picture. I'd like to have it, please," she said firmly as she stretched out her hand.

"No, Ms. Cedar. It is a part of your patient record."

"I don't think it's legal to keep a picture of someone without their consent," she retorted illogically, and when she put her hand out again, again he refused.

"Is this a good resemblance of you? It's really only my thoughts on paper. It has nothing to do with who you really are, does it?"

She sat back down in the chair and looked down at her hands. She clasped them together, and suddenly realized they were interwoven much too tightly. She felt a pain shoot into her shoulder and neck as she shifted her weight. She knew tension when she felt it, and was as angry with herself as with this young fiend of a doctor. Maybe 'fiend' was too harsh; maybe 'manipulator' would serve better. At any rate, Catherine felt her tension grow as she realized he might be right on target. All the more reason to steer clear of him.

"I came for a few easy answers, and you embarrass and discredit me with this so-called portrait. What are you, anyway?" She spoke evenly and quietly, working hard to maintain control, and felt she had achieved it.

"As I told you, I'm a doctor. If you have mental or psychological problems, I am equipped to help you. I can give you a pill for your sleeping issues; I can give you a pill to ease your fears and tension; I can give you a pill for depression, or whatever the case may be. If you're suffering from some kind of serious guilt, I can only advise you about that if you are honest with me. There's no pill to wipe out guilt, I'm afraid."

"I don't want any of your pills and I don't want your advice. I want two answers—what are nightmares about, and what are the ultimate effects of guilt—or rather, feelings of guilt?"

"All right, Ms. Cedar. Nightmares may stem from unresolved life issues. The dreams may symbolize some aspect of these issues. That's all I can say without knowing more. As for feelings of guilt—if one carries them around too long without resolution, serious depression can result. So serious, in fact, as to lead to suicide. They can also be manifested through physical illness. What else can I tell you?"

He looked down at his sketch and waited. They sat in silence for a moment, and then he addressed Catherine. "Ms. Cedar, you came here for a reason. You're in some kind of pain; that is obvious. I might be able to help you. But you must be willing to receive help, and you must be honest. You must be absolutely candid with me."

"I told you, I have guilt about not having been a perfect parent. I also have nightmares. That's as candid as I can be."

"What is it about your daughter that you feel you haven't done well?"

"She isn't as happy as she should be, that's all."

"What makes you say that? I thought she'd died."

"I don't want to talk about it any more. I've got to go. Thanks for listening. I'd still like that picture; I'll be back for it. Bye." Catherine got up and left, slamming the door a little too hard in her hasty retreat.

The man in the elevator heard Catherine mutter, "Shit. I knew this was a mistake from the beginning. Let me out of here," under her breath.

When she got home, Catherine called her sister. "Gwen? I went to see somebody. It didn't work out."

"Hi, Kate. What do you mean, 'somebody'?"

"I went to a psychiatrist, but it didn't work out. He wants to know too much."

"What do you mean?"

"He wants to know about Tina. I told him I felt guilty about not having been a perfect mother, but he wanted more. I just couldn't, so I left."

"Oh, Kate," Gwen sighed, "maybe you just need a little more time. Did you mention your grief about Zach? Did he say anything about that?"

"I never got to that. I don't want to, either."

"Maybe you could give it another shot in a week or so. I'm sure there's help for you."

"Yeah, well, not from him. Talk to you later." She hung up.

Gwen shook her head. Kate became more of an enigma every year. What was this Zach thing all about? She seemed to be experiencing more grief over his death than Tina's. Gwen couldn't figure it out. She hoped that someday she and Catherine could have an open, honest conversation about the events of the past year. Heaven only knew how much Kate was suffering.

Catherine was sorry she had called Gwen. She felt she couldn't trust herself any more. She decided she needed something frivolous, perhaps even some shallow conversation. She picked up the phone one more time.

"Hello," Sam almost sang into the receiver.

"Hi, Sam. It's your neighbor, Catherine Cedar."

"Well, hi! So glad you called."

"Really? Well, I'd like to go out for a light supper this evening and thought perhaps you could suggest a place."

"What a coincidence! Betty was just saying how nice it would be if we could go to the Western Café on Route 31 and have a nice big hamburger. Theirs are the best. We'd love for you to join us. What time shall we pick you up?"

"Oh, well." Catherine hesitated. She wasn't sure if she was doing the right thing now either. The Western, indeed. With Sam and Betty? Hamburgers? Catherine didn't do hamburgers, but tonight it might be the release she needed from her stressful afternoon. "Okay, Sam. I guess around six. Is that okay with you?"

"We like to go a bit earlier to avoid the rush. Would five-thirty be okay instead?"

That was a little early for Catherine, but she gave her approval and hung up.

When Sam and Betty drove up in their Jeep, Catherine was ready. She wore a pair of old but clean jeans and her favorite green tee. The MacMurtles also wore casual clothing, and grinned from ear to ear when Catherine entered their car. "Soo glad you called," cooed Betty.

"Thank you for inviting me along. I've had a rather tiring day, and this is wonderful."

Catherine really did feel grateful that these people had been so readily available. This too-garrulous couple was just what she needed tonight.

The Western turned out to be as hokey as the name suggested. It was constructed from logs and had beams showing everywhere. There were saddles and other tack hung from the rafters and attached to the walls. The faux Texas scene made Catherine giggle. There was a small salad bar in the center of one of the large rooms. People left it with plates piled high, JELL-O on top of beans and bread, with loads of butter heaped on top of that. Catherine opted for a bit of lettuce, a few olives, and a slice of onion—a small salad, even for Catherine. But the hamburger she received turned out to be half the size of Texas. "How do you eat such a big hunk of meat?" she queried of her neighbors.

"Oh!" Betty exclaimed, "wait until you taste it! You won't be able to put it down."

Sam nodded an enthusiastic assent as he took his first great bite. "Wonderful food here," he said as he chewed. Betty delicately cut her burger into four pieces, doused her fries with ketchup, and ate with lusty zeal. She savored every bite, Catherine could tell. Their enjoyment of food lifted Catherine's spirits. The conversation too, was filled with food and wonderful places to eat. In fact, the entire evening revolved around food. The MacMurtles regaled Catherine with stories of all the restaurants they frequented in Good Heavens, and the light conversation turned Catherine into a mellow chuckler. She'd somehow known Sam and Betty would be a good balance for her heavy thoughts and burdens. She nibbled at her burger while listening to their chatter, and realized she'd eaten half the thing when it was time to leave. Food and conversation, along with a nice bottle of wine or beer, can help one forget even the greatest guilt for a short time.

When Catherine got home, her memories attacked her and she vomited that wonderful burger into the toilet.

Chapter 32

William's Resolve

A few of William's friends were seated in a booth in the far back of the little diner when he entered. He smiled when he saw them, and one of his old friends waved a greeting. As he slid into the booth next to Joe Cushman, both Tom Packer and Jack Visser said hello and then continued their conversation about their last golf game. William was not terribly keen on golf, but his buddies lived it day and night.

Joe motioned the waitress over, and they ordered coffee and breakfast. William ordered his usual oatmeal with raisins and just a touch of cream. Joe wanted his eggs over easy with hash browns. Tom and Jack both ordered the big western omelet with loads of potatoes and bacon on the side. These guys were the most avid golfers, and William figured they needed the calories and grease to build the stamina to sustain a strenuous all-day game. As they ate, Joe kept an eye on William, who ate little of his oatmeal and sipped his coffee, his face down over the cup.

"Hey, Bill," he said. "You feeling okay, old man?" Joe had been William's best friend all during childhood and high school. He had been best man at his and Bernice's wedding. In fact, if it hadn't been for

Joe Cushman, William would not be sitting here this morning. But as soon as William had moved back to Events, Pennsylvania, Joe had made a point to visit and invite him to the once-a-week breakfasts with his friends. The men were people William had known most of his life—they'd double dated, or gone bowling or to games together. William felt awkward with these guys he knew but didn't know at all. The years change so much, internally and externally.

His answer sounded false, even to him. "I'm fine, Joe. Just a little tired. Didn't sleep too well last night, but I'm fine now." William didn't want to go into any more detail about the difficult nights he now too often had.

"Yeah, I know about those sleepless nights," Tom interjected. "Sheila snores like crazy and no matter what I do, I can't get her to stop." He laughed. Jack laughed too, but Joe just looked at William. He raised his cup to his mouth, sipped at his coffee, and put the cup back down.

"You still miss her, don't you, Bill?" he asked.

"What? Miss who?" William replied, somewhat surprised.

"Bernice, of course. Who else?" Joe answered. "Maybe you're a bit lonely."

"Well, yeah, I am a little lonely."

"Man it must be hard to lose a wife—when you're so young, I mean," Jack added. "I'd be lost without Nancy. So sorry about your loss, Bill."

"It's been a number of years now. I'm really not grieving anymore. Not for Bernice. But thanks for the sentiment, guys."

Joe caught the nuance of William's response. "Are you lonely because of someone else, Bill? It's none of my business, of course. But I thought—"

"I do miss some friends I had in Brigantine, but we've all moved on. I'm just trying to find my place here again. You guys never left, so all your connections are in place. I've moved quite a bit—first with my father, and then with Bernice—so I just have to find my groove. I guess it'll take some time. And, by the way, thanks for letting me in on your weekly breakfasts. I really appreciate it."

"I get that, Bill. Events is not exactly filled with events, if you knew what I mean. Not a lot to do here." Jack laughed at his own joke and patted William on the back. "You're going to do fine, though. Just wait and see."

"I used to volunteer at the wildlife rescue, and I did a lot of bird watching, especially sea birds. I miss that stuff. You know."

"You can always do some volunteer work with kids, Bill," Tom suggested. "Reading at the library, or even doing some teaching about birds."

"Or I could introduce you to my sister-in-law's friend. She's about your age, and a widow. You could just have some friendly times together, if you want. I could do that," Jack offered.

"No thanks. No more women. Really, Jack, that's a nice offer, but I'll be fine. Thanks, all of you." William wiped his mouth with his napkin, folded it neatly on the table, and asked for his check. "I'd better be going," he said.

The other men had barely begun eating and looked at one another. Jack raised an eyebrow. "I didn't offend you by suggesting—"

"No, no, not at all. I need to get a haircut and I have loads of errands to run. Thanks. I'll see you next week, then. Thanks again." With that William slid back out of the booth, smiled at the astonished faces, and walked up to the register. He paid his bill and went out into the street.

"What do you suppose set that off?" Tom asked. The others shrugged.

"The guy always was a bit of a loner." Jack commented.

William hurried to the barber shop, and used the time while he was getting his hair cut to think. His silence did not seem to bother his barber, who whistled amiably as he snipped away. It didn't take long. William had not needed a haircut at all, but thought he'd better get one in case the guys were watching him. He wanted no more questions and no more suggestions.

He reflected on what had disturbed his sleep; another surprise visit from Catherine. He dreamed that she'd called and asked him to come to her. The dream had been so real that he checked his phone's caller ID list when he got up. Her number was not there. He thought he'd gotten her somewhat out of his system in the last month; he'd worked hard at dismissing all thoughts of her. Then, last night, there was the familiar voice on the phone, just as real as it had always been. "Hi, William. I thought I'd call and see how you were. I think I'm going to be all right now, so I'd like to see you. Please come out for a visit, okay?" Then she'd hung up.

When William woke, he still had her voice in his ear. He was sure the call had been real, but knew he had not gotten out of bed. It disturbed the rest of his day, saturated it with the sound of Catherine. So William sought relief, after his haircut, in buying as many bird books as he could find at the local bookstore. Anyone with any sense of humor would have chuckled at the sight of this short man with a buzzcut hauling a large, heavy bag of books that he nearly had to drag home.

But there was nothing funny in William's life at the moment. He stacked his books on the kitchen table when he got home, and then made out a shopping list and drove to the nearest grocery. He could have gotten better prices at the discount market, but never shopped there. Ever since it had opened, the small mom-and-pop stores in town had, one by one, closed. William knew this to be the case nearly nationwide, and he resented it, choosing his battle. He would never even drive into that parking lot.

That evening he fixed himself a peanut butter and mustard

sandwich, poured himself a glass of Merlot, and then pored over his books for the duration. He immersed himself in the one passion that might clear his mind of the recent past, and a most disturbing past it had been. Zach's sudden death in Catherine's house was an enigma to William, and he fled in the assumption she might have instigated it. He had not been able to clear his mind of that suspicion and, if it were true, he certainly was not going to pursue that friendship any longer. But he felt his loss every day. Bernice had been replaced by this somewhat crazy woman, and William felt guilt about that as well. Poor Bernice; if she only knew. She'd turn over in her grave for sure— maybe even twice.

Chapter 33

Bernice

"I'm here, William. Remember when I used to call you Will? I know about Catherine. I know what you need to do. You need to go to her. You need to find out about yourself with her. Go, Will. Go." The sound of Bernice's voice receded from the dream slowly, quietly, as William began to ascend into dawn.

He came awake as quietly as Bernice had left. He opened his eyes to the bright morning light in his small bedroom Pennsylvania. He could hardly believe where he was; he'd lost track of himself. He twisted around in his bed to see where Bernice was—he'd even forgotten for a moment that she'd died. He had heard her voice. He had even sat at her grave to ask what he should do. Had she come from her rest to answer him? Impossible. Had she been buried in Brigantine? No. In Events, then? Yes. He was fully awake now. It had been in Events. He'd had her body shipped to Pennsylvania. He remembered it all now, and he remembered going to the cemetery. But for her to answer him like this? He didn't know what to make of it. He wasn't ready to see Catherine, that was for sure. He had too many doubts about her. And yet his dreams were constantly about her.

He sat over his morning tea, meditating on the dreams and events of the past few years. His loneliness after Bernice's death had been almost physical, and his interest in Catherine had been immediate. He'd found a lost world in her. Her language was often raw; her behavior impulsive, spontaneous; her laughter, infectious. Her commitment to another had been his great sorrow and her undoing. If Bernice knew any of this about the woman she'd told William to see, he was sure she would not have advised that.

As he analyzed the dream, he began to see it for what it was. Bernice had not come to him; she had not given that advice. He had given it to himself. Dreams come from your subconscious, don't they? He scowled in thought. But why, after what he knew and suspected, would he have this subconscious desire to see her? This was something William wanted to figure out. He wondered if he should talk to someone about it. Maybe he would give Reverend Wisekirk a call; at least he had been there. He knew Tina from church in Brigantine. He'd known Bernice very well, and he had even met Catherine and Zachary. William mulled this thought as he finished his tea and prepared himself for the day. He was to read children's stories to toddlers at the library this morning, and he was looking forward to the diversion. Children had a way of keeping one completely involved with them instead of one's self.

Chapter 34

Gwen's Suggestions

"Maybe you should think about volunteering somewhere, Kate," Gwen suggested. "Use your years of experience to help some less-fortunate kids and keep your mind busy."

"I could. I don't know if I'm ready for more kids right now."

"Are you still having nightmares, Kate?"

"Yes, from time to time."

"Now don't get mad at me, but have you thought about going back to that doctor?"

"I don't want to."

"Is there anything I can do? Would you feel more comfortable if I went to see him with you?"

"Oh, hell, Gwen, this is getting too complicated. Why can't these damned dreams leave me alone? Even Tina is in them, still a little girl. Why?"

"I don't know. I'll go with you if you want."

"Maybe you've done enough. You even sicced Squeaky Sonderfan on me. For Pete's sake, Gwen, what did you do that for?"

"You need friends, Kate. I knew she lived near you. You were always good buddies; I thought you might be able to talk about old times, if nothing else."

"Crap, Gwen. She did call; I may have been a little curt with her. I can't remember. My mind is mush. I even had a dream about William, if you can imagine that. I dreamed that I wanted him to come see me. I don't, but the dream was as real as if I'd been standing next to him. Oh, these awful dreams!" she sighed into the phone. Gwen could hear the frustration in her sister's voice and tried once more.

"Kate? The doctor?"

"Okay!" Catherine nearly yelled. "I'll call him. I'll see if he's okay with you coming along. I'll call you back. But don't hold your breath."

"I won't think of it. Later, sis." Gwen hung up and smiled at her success. Manipulating one's sister can be very difficult, but Gwen had learned a few tricks from her older sibling.

Catherine wasn't smiling. She'd not told Gwen the worst of her nightmares. Two days ago, she'd gone to bed around ten o'clock, but could not find sleep. She tossed and turned until she saw midnight on the clock. Then she heard a noise in the room. She could barely make anything out, but there was enough light from the moon to show weak shadows. Her closet door slowly opened; a brown, hairy hand pushed it open, and a man like a werewolf came out. She knew it was Zachary Bekker. He did not look like him exactly, but he was carrying the old football he'd given her years ago with his promise to return. She'd kept it for forty years and then had flung it out to sea when he'd died. Now here it was again—and in his hand. The mildew from years of hiding in her dark closets, deep in the farthest corners, was very visible.

As he approached the bed, he began to grin, and she recognized that. His white, perfect teeth gleamed in the moonlight. This grin used to drive her mad with desire for him; now it threatened to drive her mad with fear. The closer he came, the more he grinned, until finally he reached the bed and leaned over her to give her the ball. Only it wasn't the ball anymore; it was Tina, hanging limp in his outstretched hands. Catherine recoiled in horror and rolled away from the sight in such a fury of fear that she landed on the floor, fully awake and trembling in every fiber. When she sat up, he was gone.

She knew now, without a shadow of a doubt, it was time to get to the doctor again. Someone had to help her with these terrible dreams or she would not make it. The temptation to run from it nearly overwhelmed her. The dark two o'clock roar of the lake had begun to invite her. She feared herself.

She sat on the floor next to her bed well into the early light, crying. It took her hours to acclimate to reality. She knew she needed a whole lot more sleep than she was getting, but who could sleep again after a nightmare like that? When she did finally get up, she went to the bathroom and washed her face, which looked more like a rag than the washcloth she used to cleanse it. Then she slowly made her way to the kitchen. She felt dizzy with the effort. *Perhaps I hit my head when I fell,* she thought. She felt her head, putting her fingers through her hair, but found no bump or other evidence of injury. Moving on, she made a pot of very strong coffee. No food, though; she knew that if she tried to eat, she would vomit, so she ignored her growling stomach.

The phone rang. She let it go until the machine kicked in and walked out onto the deck to avoid hearing the message. She held her mug of hot, strong, black coffee in her hands, placed both elbows on the rail, and leaned over to view the lake. It was so glisteningly clear and clean with the sun dotting each tiny ripple that it brought tears to her eyes. "How can such peace and beauty exist alongside such fear and horror in my soul?" she wondered aloud.

She stood there for more than an hour, unmoving, staring out at the blue horizon as if she could see beyond the edge of the earth. When she finally turned, she slipped and fell to her knees. Her mug shattered, having hit the edge of the iron-and-glass table. Catherine looked at it with such shock that it could have been thousand-dollar antique crystal. Then she looked into the sky, and tears rolled down her cheeks as she called to whatever benign deity might be out there. "Oh God, surely this is not all my fault. Surely you can't lay the blame for all of it on my back. I can't carry it all. Did I kill my daughter? Wasn't it just and right that Zach should die? Who else would have made it right? I did what I had to. For her, for Tina! Surely you can see that. Help me!"

She'd not told Gwen any of this. When Gwen mentioned her weight loss and dark-circled eyes, Catherine admitted her lack of sleep, but not the details.

Catherine knew the doctor might be able to help, and Gwen's offer to come along made a lot of sense. Her competition with her sister had had to come to an end some time ago. They were old women now; everything they'd competed for was gone. It was time.

Chapter 35

Landman Again

"Do you have a different chair I could sit in?" Catherine asked as she stood next to the large leather recliner in Dr. Landman's office. She and Gwen had just been asked to come in, and each was offered a large recliner by the doctor. Catherine had immediately reacted with nausea the overwhelming odor of the chair. "Could I perhaps have a cloth chair, Doctor?" she asked again, rather apologetically. Gwen looked at her in puzzlement. She'd already settled into the lush, overstuffed chair set out for her.

"Sure, if you like. I'll get one from the waiting room. Be just a minute," Dr. Landman responded and left to retrieve a cloth-covered waiting room chair. "There you go. Less comfortable, but less noxious, perhaps." He moved the leather to the far corner of the room and Catherine moved her new seat a short distance from Gwen.

"Are you settled now? I'm glad you called and asked your sister to accompany you, Ms. Cedar. The more comfortable you are, the more we can accomplish. So where did we leave off last time? Dreams and guilt, right? Anything you want to say about those today?"

"First of all, I think I'd be more comfortable if you would call me Catherine. My students always, of course, called me Ms. West-Cedar, and the formality reminds me of them. You wouldn't want me to respond to you as if you were one of my students, would you, Doctor?" She smiled at her own remark. Gwen gave her a raised-eyebrow look, but the doctor simply smiled.

"All right then. Catherine. What would you like to say about the guilt you mentioned earlier?"

Catherine hesitated; this was going to be very hard, she knew. She and Gwen had gone over her inability to discuss Tina with the doctor, and Gwen had made it clear that without the utmost candor, he would not be able to help her. Catherine really knew that, but still, it was so hard.

"Okay, well." She paused to grab a tissue from a table, and coughed a few times to clear her throat and her mind. "Guilt. Yes, I feel guilt over what I did to my daughter," she began. After another long pause, Catherine continued. "You see, Tina is dead. She died last summer. Quite unexpectedly. The death certificate reads that the cause of death was self inflicted." Another pause. "Suicide."

Dr. Landman looked up from his notes. "I see," he responded quietly.

"No, you don't see; I'm not finished. I did a lot of research, spoke with doctors and figured out that Tina did not, in fact, commit suicide. She died as a result of a drug reaction. That's how she died. I'm sure of it."

"Well, that's very interesting. I'm so sorry for your loss, Catherine." He wrote something on his pad, scratched his head, and leveled a sympathetic look at her. "What I don't understand completely is why you feel so guilty about your daughter. Loss, I understand, but why guilt?"

Catherine twisted the tissue into fuzz in her lap. She did not look at either the doctor or Gwen; she looked down at the destroyed tissue and saw a wet drop fall onto it. She tried to control the tears. She reached for another tissue and began, without looking up, "Terrible things had been done to Tina. I can't talk about them right now." After another long pause in an effort to keep control over her raw emotions, she added, "And all of them are my fault." She looked up at the doctor to see his reaction. She did not dare look at Gwen, who knew nothing of Tina's real reason for having run away from her mother.

Gwen had assumed it had been because Catherine had never told Tina the true circumstances of her birth, and when her real father had appeared, the truth had been too much. Tina would naturally seek asylum for a while. Her trip to Italy made sense, but her later escape to her friend was a little much. Her desperate call to Aunt Gwen began to make a little more sense, but what terrible things was Catherine hiding that were making her so sick?

"Would you be able to talk a little more about your feelings, if not specific circumstances?" the doctor asked.

"I dream. I see her in my dreams. She is accusing me, I believe. I'm suffering. Everyone around me seems so perfect. Everyone is happy and living life as if nothing was ever wrong. Then I find myself disturbed about my own rotten life, and the guilt and fear overwhelm me. That's really all I can say about it. Except for the awful dreams."

Doctor Landman wrote all this down, continuing to scribble for what seemed like a long time. Finally Catherine looked up and over to Gwen. "I'm sorry, Gwen, but I can't tell even you everything. I'm glad you're here. It helps for now."

Dr. Landman stopped writing and addressed his patient one more time. "Catherine, we can leave the details until you're ready to talk about them. But I find your comments about suffering and other people's lack of it very interesting." He paused for a moment, and then continued, "I'm going to give you an assignment. Will you try that? It's simple and might help with your feelings of isolation due to your pain."

"I guess I'll try just about anything, except pills. Pills are out of the question."

"All right—for now." He turned to Gwen. "You're welcome to accompany Catherine on her next visit if she wishes, Mrs. Konynbelt. I'm glad you were able to come today." Then he addressed Catherine again. "You have heard the old expression 'misery loves company,' I'm sure. Okay, this is the assignment. Go to lunch or coffee or dinner, whatever you prefer, with family members, friends, and acquaintances. Sit and talk with each them. But you need to listen, listen very closely to what these people have to say about their own burdens. It won't be easy to get them to talk about personal things initially, but if you steer the conversation in that direction and promise, if only by gesture and expression, to be a sympathetic listener, you'll find most people willing to share some personal pain or grief. Try it, and you will discover company. You'll see that others also carry burdens and how they cope."

"Yes, I will, but I assure you no one on earth has the baggage I have."

"We'll see. Call me when you're ready for your next appointment." And with that he ushered the sisters out of his office.

When they got to the car Gwen suggested lunch. Catherine nodded.

Gwen suggested a little bistro on Madison Square called Two Friends. "They serve wonderful cappuccinos and sandwiches," she added. They walked the few blocks in amicable silence. The center of the small city on the Grand River was almost dead. A few business people carried laptops and briefcases to buildings or restaurants, but most of the streets bore little pedestrian traffic.

They entered Two Friends, which was very small, with five tables along one wall and a grand counter opposite. They were greeted by a young woman with massive dreadlocks who must have been about Tina's age. She smiled, showing straight, sparkling-white teeth and equally bright brown eyes. "Looks a little like a young Judy Garland," Gwen observed, "who, by the way, was born here. In this city, I mean."

"I think I read that somewhere. She does look a little like her, I guess. Let's order and sit. I need really strong coffee and a bowl of soup."

Gwen ordered for both of them and sat opposite her sister. "So, Gwen," Catherine began, "what do you think of the assignment Dr. Landman gave me?"

"Sounds interesting. I think it will offer you a lot of insight into the human condition."

"Really? Well then, here we are at lunch. Let's start with you. I can't imagine what you might have to offer with your perfect husband and life, but I'll listen to whatever you might think is your burden. Couldn't be Warren Konynbelt, the fine Christian man who was the love of your life since you were a kid. So what might it be?" She was almost sarcastic as she spoke, but Gwen didn't care about that.

"You really care? Are you really serious about listening to me? You never have."

"There's a first time for everything."

"Perfect Warren is the most dishonest man I know," Gwen began, and then took a huge bite of her liverwurst, mustard, tomato, and onion sandwich.

Catherine wrinkled her brow and opened her mouth in utter disbelief, but restrained herself from commenting. She sipped her coffee as she waited for the explanation.

"I was so jealous of you when you had Tina," Gwen said. "I wanted nothing more than to have children of my own, you know. As happens to so many women, I went through the battery of tests—not one of which was any fun. Well, the doctors said there was no reason why I didn't become pregnant. I never told you this. Warren was so sympathetic; he even cried and prayed with me about it. Then it was his turn to be tested, but he made all kinds of excuses why he couldn't do that. He assured me there was nothing wrong with him. When you had Tina and refused to tell anyone who the father was, I was furious—mainly because you were single and didn't even want a baby, and I was married and had every right to one."

"What? You're saying I had no right to Tina? Maybe I should have given her to you, is that what you're saying?" Catherine exclaimed.

"No. I'm not finished, Kate. That was then, anyway. We were young and I felt betrayed. Not by you; by God. How could He have given you a child out of wedlock and not given me one? That was my dilemma. And I began to doubt all I'd ever believed. You never wanted God, and He gave you a child. Not fair, I thought."

Catherine wasn't too thrilled about hearing this from the sister whom she had always envied. Things are not as they seem, she knew, but now she had ample proof. It was all she could do to keep her tongue still.

After another bite of her sandwich and a long pause, Gwen continued. "Well, after a while, my doctor insisted on testing Warren. He refused to deal with me any more until Warren came in." She took a swallow of her coffee, gulped a piece of sandwich, and almost gagged at having swallowed too much too fast. "Warren refused, saying he didn't want to masturbate, not even for testing, because he knew it was a sin. I had to leave it alone, and I did. I thought about adoption, of course. You know how I love children. Again, Warren opposed me at first. But I continued to hope and pray. And then, of course, we finally adopted Doug. Years later, when Doug was already a young adult—"

Gwen found it hard to continue, and Catherine could not imagine why. She put her hand on her sister's arm—one of the first gestures of caring she'd shown Gwen since they were children.

"Thanks, Kate. It wasn't so long ago that we got a phone call from a man. I never told you because it was just too much. He asked for Warren. When Warren hung up he told me it was a mistake, he wanted some other Konynbelt. Naturally, I believed him."

Catherine sighed. She was becoming really bored by this. But with a great deal of effort she continued to focus on Gwen. She knew how to keep her side of a bargain.

"About a month or so later, after I'd completely forgotten the call, a man came to our door. He was very tall, a bit thin, in his forties or so, with grayish blue eyes. His sandy hair fell across the left side of his face."

Now Catherine found she could not restrain herself. "Gwen," she almost shouted, "you've just described Warren!"

"Please, Kate. This is difficult. Yes, he does look a lot like Warren. He asked if Warren was home. He wasn't. I asked who he was. He said he was Conrad Wilson. He said Warren wouldn't know him, and then he left. That evening I told Warren about him.

"He was here? He actually showed up here?" Warren must have forgotten himself, because that response told me more than I wanted to know.

"I said, 'Okay, Warren. What have you go to say? You'd better tell me all of it.' He did. After all those years of married life together, I never knew my husband as anything but a loving, honest man in spite of his reluctance to bring children into my life. So when he told me all he had done, I thought I would die. He'd gotten a girl pregnant while in high school. Don't look so embarrassed, Kate. Yes, it was while we were going together; he said that's why he could never tell me. Anyway, she was only fifteen, and her parents made her give the baby up for adoption. When Warren turned eighteen, he had a vasectomy. He never told me. He just said, 'I never wanted children after that.'"

"How utterly stupid. He had no right—" Catherine interrupted, but Gwen put her hand up to silence her.

"Of course, he had no right to marry me without telling me, but he did. That's why I say he is the most dishonest man I know. He almost made me lose my faith, and he certainly destroyed my faith in him. We've lived a quiet, amiable life. He apologized and asked for forgiveness, and he cried and pleaded with me. I thought I forgave him. It's a thing of the past, but I still feel distrust. Can't help it."

"I don't understand, Gwen. Why did you never let on there was a problem? You always knew about Zach and Tina and the rest of my life. Why didn't I know anything about you?" Catherine was appalled.

"I found out too recently. You weren't really available emotionally. I don't know. Let's face it, Kate, you never did listen to anything I had to say anyway."

"What? I would have listened to this!"

"You think so? Without having had your own great pain and someone to tell you it was time to listen?"

"I don't know. Maybe. I'm really a lousy bitch, aren't I?"

"Wow. You've always been so hard on everybody else that now you're overdoing it with yourself. Lighten up on the judgments. See humans as the frail beings we are."

"Yeah, well, frail is not the word I would use for one of those beings, who thankfully does not exist anymore. I found out too late."

"You opened your eyes too late is more like it. But yes, the pain of finding out something rotten about a man you totally trusted—well, it's overwhelming. I know," Gwen answered.

"As it happens, I know too."

"So, Kate, It might do us both a whole lot of good to be more honest with each other. We both need support; let's give it to one another. What do you say?"

Catherine bit her lip; she had to think for a minute. "I always felt you were interfering too much in my life, especially with Tina. I'll have to give it some time."

The women paid the bill and left Two Friends being better friends themselves. Each drove home thinking about the turn of events. Catherine knew she needed time to rehash what Gwen had told her;

she'd had no idea Warren was such a duplicitous character. Apparently Gwen had not known, either. *How could you live with a guy for over thirty years and not know him better?* she thought. But then she thought of her relationship with Zachary, which was hardly the same, but still she had made herself believe things about him she'd always known were wishful thinking. He was a womanizer, a liar, and a user, and she'd always known it. Waiting for him her whole life, only to be used after forty years—and by an ex-football hero, yet. Well, she knew she'd been wrong. And then Tina, and then Zach's death. She would have to give Gwen a little more credit based on her own experience. There was one thing for sure—she was very glad she'd listened. All this time she'd thought Gwen had the perfect life.

On her way home, she stopped at the local D&W Fresh Market to pick up a salad for dinner in case she got hungry later. She knew she had to eat more, but her emotions were still so raw that it was hard to get involved with food.

Chapter 36

William Going

William ate his lonely supper with more gusto than he knew was proper. He did love food. He couldn't help but think of Catherine while he ate. They had had some wonderful meals together on that little Jersey Shore island and beyond. He was also still wondering about his dreams. In the dream, Catherine had called him, and Bernice had approved. He was disturbed, but food was not to be ignored. If anything, it gave him power, the ability to see to it all. Before he opened his books, he'd fixed manicotti with meat sauce, a green salad, a side of Kalamata olives with chopped onions and garlic, and a nice Chianti. He savored every bite. For dessert, he treated himself to two custardy chocolate Napoleons from Pallatucci's bakery, which he downed with a couple of hot cappuccinos. This food and his bird and wildlife books helped him through the evening. Then he went to bed.

He smiled in his sleep as he dreamed of Italy. He found himself on the Grand Canal in Venice. He walked alone over the bridge in the cool of the evening and stopped to look over the railing. He stood and let his mind wander over the wonders of the city as his eye took it all in. Soon a gondola passed under the bridge. He enjoyed watching the gondolier push his pole into the murky water as if it were a soft, quiet dance he was performing for the two lovers in the boat. He looked at the lovers and smiled at their obvious delight in one another. But then something strange caught his attention. The lovers were Catherine and Zachary. He couldn't believe his eyes. "Hey, Catherine!" he tried to call, but no sound came from his mouth. Then he saw her turn around, look straight up and into his eyes for a moment, and with one swift, deft movement she hurled Zachary overboard. Zach tried to get back in, but the gondolier pushed Zach under with his pole. Catherine turned to William again and smiled.

He woke up in horror, yelling Catherine's name into the darkness. Then he realized where he was, and that he'd dreamed it all.

William got up and put on his red tartan wool robe and black slippers, knowing there would be no more sleep for him that night. He went into the kitchen, filled the shiny chrome kettle with water for tea, and awaited the cozy sound of the whistle. He hoped it would help bring him back to himself. When the water boiled, he made himself a pot of black tea, allowing it to steep for ten minutes before pouring himself a mug. He added the requisite three heaping teaspoons of sugar and filled the mug to its brim with cream. Then he moved to the sitting room and sat in his recliner, sipping the tea and trying to get a handle on the recent assault on his peace by these awful, realistic dreams.

He still didn't want to believe what he suspected. Catherine could not have had a hand in it; yet his subconscious was obviously not convinced. The call for him to come to her was even more disconcerting than the crazy night he dreamed of Bernie's encouragement to go see Catherine. It was all too bizarre. He put his two chubby hands around the big mug of tea. The warmth offered a touch of comfort, but the greatest contentment came from drinking the sweet brew. Even so, his mind was still in turmoil. What was he supposed to think? What was he supposed to do?

Chapter 37

Sam's Story

Catherine wanted to call William. She had the desire, but knew she could not. After her talk with Gwen, she wanted to clear the air with William. She wanted to see him, but she didn't know why. He lay heavy in her thoughts, and had begun to do so on her way home from Two Friends.

She sat at the table on the deck and listened to the little waves curling up to the beach; they reminded her of a tight perm on an old lady. If only she could hear the roar of the ocean. Oh, what a cleansing she thought she'd feel then. But the lake was here, and it would have to do. At least it was a great expanse of water, one she could not see to the other side of. There was a beach and the great dunes to offer her some peace; natural beauty could do that. If you looked at nature, she thought, you could imagine a greater reality than yourself and your own problems. So she sat atop her dune and pondered the water. But the smell was not there. There's nothing like the Jersey Shore, she knew.

After a while, she felt hungry. She was grateful, and hurried inside to get the purchases of the afternoon and a fork along with a bottle of Guinness before the feeling subsided. She placed everything on her patio table and quietly offered thanks to whomever might be out there for it all. Then she looked up in surprise.

What had she just done? Prayed? No way! She knew this was a response to nature, which she loved—that was all. She ate in a comfortable silence she had not experienced in months. It was suddenly and shrilly interrupted by a loud "Yoohoo! Well, hello!" from her neighbor's deck.

"Oh no. It's that Betty person," she murmured, her forkful of potato salad suspended in mid-air.

"Would you like to come over and enjoy some ice cream with us? Sam just made it and it is scrumptious! Cherry vanilla—with real Michigan cherries!" The voice squealed through the barrier of trees, shattering her peace. Even the little waves seemed to jerk back into the lake at the interruption.

Catherine took quick stock of the situation, knowing she very much needed to be patient with these people who meant nothing but kindness. She hesitated for just a moment and responded rather more loudly than she liked, "I'll finish my supper a minute. Then I'll stop by, all right?"

"Great," came the reply, and Catherine knew her evening would not be what she had planned. But homemade vanilla ice cream did sound good. She'd rather have a tall, cold Guinness, but this would have to do. She reminded herself to be polite.

Her quiet evening pondering the lake was now out. She finished her salads and took her dishes inside. After she'd rinsed them and put them in the dishwasher, she made her way over the dune path to the MacMurtles, who were on their back deck. Catherine climbed the steps to the deck and managed a gracious smile.

"Hi, Catherine," they said in unison. "We're so glad you could stop by. Sam makes the most wonderful ice cream. Wait until you taste it," Betty said as she pulled up a wicker chair for Catherine.

Sam opened the big bucket of ice cream and scooped out a large portion, slid it into a soup bowl, and handed it to Catherine. "Here you go. Enjoy!" he said with a grin. Betty handed Catherine a spoon. She could feel their anticipation of her response to the first bite. She smiled and licked her lips.

"This is truly the best ice cream I've ever tasted," she said. She took another large bite, savoring the cool sweetness. "Mmm. Fantastic job, Sam. Thank you."

"Oh, good. We're so glad you like it," Betty affirmed. "There's also a place by the bridge that has the most exquisite butternut ice cream you've ever had. Right, Sam? "

"Right," he answered, swallowed a big spoonful, and then continued, "There's also a shop in Furryville. Wow. To die for. We've found the most spectacular places to eat. We'll take you on a tour sometime, Catherine."

"Yes," Betty cut in, her mouth still full. She put her hand to her mouth to catch the overflow, and with a giggle she forged ahead. "We'll show you all the great places to eat. But how do you like living here so far?"

Catherine could see that these two lived for eating. That was certainly not her favorite form of entertainment, especially now, but she wanted to be gracious. She answered them as best she could.

"Well, it isn't the ocean. But living on a dune this size is new and rather remarkable, I must admit."

Sam said, "If you look to your left, you can see the very top. Let me tell you, I would not want to live all the way up there. In the seventies, a number of people lost their houses right off the top of it." He went on, "They say there was some kind of lake effect that washed away the underside of the dune, and the houses slid off their slab foundations and down the side of the dune."

"Just goes to show you," Catherine answered. "Build your house on rock, not on sand. But here we sit, with nothing but sand under us," she said, laughing.

"You don't have to worry. For one thing, the lake has receded considerably since then. And your house is far enough back so that could never happen," Sam assured her. The conversation was nearly over then as their attention turned to the horizon.

They sat on the deck overlooking the lake until it was nearly dark. Conversation was sparse, even for the MacMurtles, because the view was so spectacular that it absorbed all their attention. Sunsets on Lake Michigan, Catherine realized, were so varied and spectacular they could not be surpassed. She was mesmerized by the one they experienced this particular evening. The day had been warm and hazy, and the humidity apparently diffused the sun's rays into a great prism of colors which reflected on the water, entertaining many watchers for more than an hour. Homemade ice cream, decent neighbors to share with, some of nature's abstract painting lighting up the sky, and rhythmic waves lapping at the sand; what more could she want? Catherine was more at peace this evening than she had been for many months.

After the sky had turned completely dark, Sam offered to take Catherine on their boat the following afternoon if the weather permitted. She thought that would be nice. Then they said good night, and Catherine headed across the dune to her cottage.

It had gotten rather late, so she undressed and jumped into bed. She picked up the *Tribune* to work on the puzzle for a bit. She felt she would get a good night's sleep after a relaxing evening.

Chapter 38

Not Again

She began to toss and turn just around three o'clock—the witching hour, as it is sometimes called. She opened her eyes to see Zach leaning over her. Not again, she thought. Will he never leave me?

"Westie," he called, as if from a very deep cavern. "Westie, I need you. Come to me. Come die, Westie, die. You know how. You know how. Die, Westie, die!"

Then everything changed and Zach was gone. On the bed next to her lay another figure. She was afraid to look, but slowly turned to see Tina, at no particular age. Catherine couldn't tell if she was four or twenty-four. Tina was pallid like marble, cold, and crying. "Mom, I need you. Help me, Mom. Die with me. Mom, please, come to me." As Tina's ice-cold arm began to encircle her neck, Catherine awoke with a start. The wind was whipping through the open window, and the sheet wrapped around her neck was cold. She tore it off but did not close the window. She needed the reality of the water's roar.

Catherine lay staring into the darkness for hours. She was afraid of sleep, afraid to move. She lay sweating, hardly daring to breathe. Fear enveloped her. Now she was afraid of herself; she feared her response to these summonses. What would she do in the morning? Or tomorrow evening?

When light began to show through her open window, she knew she must try to get up. She felt tears come with the approaching day. "Oh, God. What am I going to do?" she cried aloud.

She shuffled her way to the phone, not even stopping to put on a robe, and punched in her sister's number. When Gwen's groggy voice answered, Catherine gushed her miserable night into her sister's ear.

"My goodness, Kate, I can't be there but you shouldn't be alone. Call Phillis. At least you have a past connection with her, and she's such a nice person."

"Oh, man, I can't. Oh, I don't know. She'll preach to me for sure. Shit! I hate this. I hate my life." She emitted a deep sigh, paused for a few moments, and then added, "Okay, I'll call her. What the hell. Why not? What do I say?"

"What did you talk about the last time she called you?"

"I don't remember. I think I hung up on her."

"Oh, Kate, you didn't!"

"Well, I didn't really, but I felt like it. I was very short with her. That's all I remember right now."

"Give her a call, Kate. Do lunch with her or something. Relax a bit if you can. I know letting go of the two most important people in your life must be extremely difficult. Give yourself a break."

"Yeah, well, you don't know the half of it. But okay, I'll give Squeaky a call."

"Kate! You're not going to call her Squeaky, are you?"

"Don't worry, sis. Later. Thanks." Catherine hung up. She quickly searched for the number Phillis had given her and punched it in before she lost her resolve.

Catherine, even in her present mood, could not help but smile and tried to suppress a giggle when she heard Phillis' voice. "Hello,"

Phillis squeaked.

"Hello, Phillis, this is Catherine. I want to apologize for calling so early and for my curt response to your phone call a couple of weeks ago," Catherine began.

"Hey, don't give it another thought. I'm glad you called. As a matter of fact, I was just thinking about you." This was an unexpected response. Why would this woman she knew forty years ago be thinking about her? *Ask later*, she thought.

"I have an entirely free day, Phillis, and I thought maybe we could meet for lunch or something."

"Kate, that would be great. Do you have any place in mind?"

"I haven't been here long enough. I thought you might have a favorite."

"Well, it's a beautiful day, so how about eating outside? I know a nice little restaurant on the river that has a deck, and good sandwiches, salads, and other fare. Does that sound good?"

Do they have Guinness on tap? she wondered.

It sounded fine, but how was she going to manage eating? If they had soup, maybe she'd be able to get that down. And Catherine had one other concern. "Phillis," she began, "I know you don't approve, but I wonder if they serve beer there."

"Funny that you should mention it. I do approve, and yes, they do." Phillis laughed at the somewhat expected comment.

"Things have changed a little, I take it? Your approval of drinking, I mean."

"We have a lot to talk about, Kate. I think you may find my past interesting. Anyway, I'll pick you up. Twelve-thirty okay?"

"Fine." Catherine gave Phillis her address. "I'm the last house at the end of the street. I'll be watching for you."

The women had not seen each other since they'd been in their teens, and Catherine was not sure what to expect. Squeaky had been a bit heavy, as she remembered, but not so much that she couldn't be a cheerleader. In their purple and gold uniforms, Phillis had had to put up with another nickname that some of the boys had given her—"Moby Grape." How she took it all, Catherine never could figure out. She'd been perky; she'd worn her hair long, almost to her waist, and often in a ponytail. Most of the girls had expressed envy at the beautiful long hair Phillis swung behind her perky smile and freckled nose. It was blonde, like the hair of so many of the kids of Dutch ancestry.

She and Kate had been friends, but two girls could not have been more different. Kate had always been the sarcastic one, the cynic/ agnostic; Phillis had been dogmatic, a devout believer trying to convert everyone in her path to Christ, and none more than Catherine. This had been the one great bone of contention between them. "Only stupid people are Christians," Kate had often said. And now this stupid person approved of beer.

The line at Cozy Cove was not long, and they were seated within ten minutes.

Kate took a close look at her friend. The freckles were still there, but the very blonde hair was short—it could not have been more than an inch and a half long all over. Large gold hoops topped by diamond studs hung from pierced ears. The diamond on her finger could have been Liz Taylor's. Phillis was svelte and walked with a confidence Kate had never seen in her before. Not that Phillis had not been self-assured, but this was a new kind of confidence—more mature, more worldly. Catherine realized this was a very sophisticated and beautiful woman sitting across from her.

"The years have been very kind to you," she said.

Phillis smiled. "Only some," she said. "You're looking pretty good yourself, in spite of the grief you've just experienced. Gwen filled me in a bit. Kate, let me just say I'm so sorry."

"Thanks, Phillis."

The young girl waiting on them arrived with her pad, ready to take their order. "Can I get you anything to drink?"

"Do you have Guinness on tap?" Catherine queried.

"We do, but only in the downstairs dining room. Up here we have it in bottles."

"Really? You can't run downstairs and get a pint?"

"I'm afraid that's not our policy," the girl said apologetically.

"Tell your boss for me, that he's got an incredibly stupid policy."

The waitress attempted a smile and asked if Catherine would like a bottle of Guinness.

"Certainly not. I'll have a draft Guinness. Ask your manager."

"I'll check." She turned to Phillis, who had been taking all this in with a grin.

Catherine really hadn't changed all that much after all, she thought. "I'll have the same, if possible."

Catherine turned to Phillis and said, "So, you've become a drinker?"

"I've learned to enjoy all of God's gifts," she replied. "What shall we eat?"

They perused the menu. Phillis settled for the lunch special of fish and a salad; Catherine ordered the minestrone. When their dark beer arrived, they toasted one another and the success of their renewed friendship.

Catherine couldn't leave the last statement by Phillis alone. "So, Phill, if you feel we should enjoy all of God's gifts, one of them is marijuana. What do you think about that?"

"I think you're baiting me," she retorted, laughing. "I think it should be legalized so that people who need it can get it without having to skirt the law or get others into trouble for getting it for them."

"It's been a long time since we were friends. Apparently we've both been through a lot of changes," was Catherine's only response.

She was awed by this Phillis who could never again be referred to as Squeaky, although the voice was the same.

Their lunches arrived, and Phillis bowed her head. Catherine waited in silence; this she knew about. Even Tina had been known to pray before her meals and sometimes William had done the same but, out of deference to her, had omitted the gesture in public.

"I'm kind of surprised your name is 'Ver Hage,' Phillis. I surely thought you would have married your high school sweetheart, Todd Strom."

"I did marry him," was her response. "Don't look so surprised. I divorced him five years later."

Catherine raised both eyebrows. "You did what? You, who preached virginity, fidelity, one husband forever to everyone?"

"Yes. Embarrassing isn't it? Well, it's not a pretty story in some ways; one of those that make us eat our words, you know. God moves in mysterious ways, you might say. But I cannot say God intended for me to be as stupid as I've been. I made a wrong choice by marrying Todd, and I knew it on our wedding day."

Catherine's interest was more than piqued. She was suddenly so glad she'd listened to Gwen's advice and called Phillis. The lunch was beginning to taste pretty good. If this woman could sin with impunity— well, hell, what was she feeling so guilty about? The women each took a long sip of beer and looked one another in the eye.

Catherine broke the silence. "I have a rather sordid past, as you might well guess from the kind of kid I was. I don't know how much Gwen told you; I'm working on getting over a lot of difficult things. But you bowl me over."

"I don't tell just anyone my story, Kate. But in your case, I don't mind, if you want to hear it. May be it will help you."

Catherine put up her hand. "Oh no, you don't. I don't want to hear it if this is just another conversion attempt."

"Listen, Kate, I do not convert people. I have learned, and should always have known, that's it's God's job, not mine. I think you might feel better if you know that I've also had some struggles that gave me a lot of stress and guilt."

"Yeah. Well, I know about guilt," she replied, then leaned in to listen.

"I married Todd right after we graduated from college. We'd gone to different schools and only seen each other a few times a year. When we graduated, we hurried into marriage even though I had qualms about it—"

Kate interrupted. "What? If you weren't sure, why—"

"Another big error on my part. I thought that if you'd slept with a boy, you should marry him. As if sex made you married already."

"You mean that goody Squeaky had sex before marriage?" Kate blurted, almost too loudly.

"Shh. Listen, Kate. Either listen completely, or I won't be able to do this," Phillis said quietly, giving Kate a look. Then she continued, "We got married and moved to a small town in Minnesota where Todd got a job as a social worker. We lived in an apartment for a year and found a nice Presbyterian Church to attend. After a few months, we realized we weren't getting as much out of the church as we knew we needed, but we weren't sure what to do about it then. We were doing fine with each other, and were quite happy for that first year.

"One Sunday, a couple from church approached us and asked if we'd like to join their Bible study group once a week. We were enthusiastic, and agreed right away—even met with them and a few others that evening. All seemed well for a while. Then I learned that Todd was spending his lunch hours with this Karl Snoop. That was the name of the guy who'd first approached us.

"At any rate, Todd was coming home with stories about the spiritual victories Karl had won over the years. He'd healed all kinds of people, had cast out demons, had preached to fellow workers and single-handedly converted them—stuff like that. Karl gave Todd all kinds of CDs by preachers who taught the stuff Karl was doing, and Todd spent hours locked in his study listening to them. I didn't know what they were about, but soon Todd brought them out and wanted me to listen. I didn't think too much of any of this; if anything, I figured all this Bible study and fellowship would do Todd a lot of good.

"I listened to some of the tapes. The emphasis on healing and using the power of the spirit for personal reasons triggered a red light for me. The stress on submission, especially by wives to husbands, made me really uncomfortable. I don't have a problem with the headship concept, but what these guys were preaching was closer to slavery.

"After a couple of months, I learned that Todd was using his lunch hours to spend time with Karl at his office. Todd would come home all excited with stories about Karl's wonderful healings that week. He explained the process in detail, especially the parts about casting out demons. I was incredulous. Todd became furious when I challenged him on this. He informed me that Karl and his wife Mary were the finest Christians in the world, and I had no right to question their authority. When Todd stopped going to church, he explained that the church did not understand the workings of the spirit, so it was best to stay away. I learned from others that Karl had been kicked out of various churches for attempting to cast evil spirits out of fellow Christians.

"Then one day Todd came home and informed me that he'd submitted himself to the higher authority of Karl. 'What?' I asked. 'What does that mean?' Todd smiled and said that from now on he would bow to the authority that Karl had over him, and would do whatever Karl advised. I had no idea what this would mean until it was time for us to buy a new refrigerator. I told Todd we needed one, and he said he would consult with Karl to see if that was all right."

Catherine had been listening without interruption up to this time, but now she exclaimed "What?" loudly enough for all the patrons to hear. Phillis quickly put up her hand.

"Shh. Please, Kate. This is hard enough for me to tell. Just let me finish. You may want to hear this."

"Okay, sorry. Go ahead. It's getting very bizarre."

"I know; that's the point. Anyway, Todd came home that evening and told me it was not a good time for us to spend that kind of money. Karl had said we should not get a new refrigerator. As far as Todd was concerned, that was that. The next day I went out and bought one, and had it delivered and loaded by the time Todd got home. Well, let me tell you, the roof nearly blew off the house when he saw what I'd done. I told him that if he wanted to submit to Karl, that was his business, but I certainly did not, and I needed a new fridge so I got one. Todd started yelling and screaming at me. If he was in submission to Karl, then I was too, by default, because I was his wife and supposed to live in submission to him. He used various texts from the Bible, especially from Ephesians, to prove he was right. He nearly threw a tea kettle at me, but restrained himself, and I could see the effort on his face. I told him I had never placed myself in that position, and especially not to this weird guy. He called me a rebellious woman and stalked out of the house. He didn't return that night.

"After that, things got really strange. Todd would come home at all hours of the day and night. He never called, but always said he was late because he had the Lord's work to do. We would get phone calls at odd hours, and I would hear Todd giving advice to others. When I asked about that, he told me some young guy, whom I'd met, had put himself under his authority and he had to advise him whenever the kid called, and this kid was a drug addict. I asked him what I was supposed to do since I had to get up at six to go to work. No answer. I finally resorted to unplugging the phone when he wasn't looking.

"He never stopped trying to get me involved with Karl—who, by this time, had surrounded himself with about six young men like Todd and gotten them to stop going to their respective churches in favor of attending Karl's Bible study sessions. Todd asked me to attend a picnic one Sunday, promising that it was just a nice get-together over some good food. He promised there would be no preaching or anything I would not like. He begged me to come, so I did. No sooner did we get to this couple's house than Karl seated himself in the center, pulled out his Bible, and began to preach. He then called for wine and bread, and proceeded to officiate at his own communion service. I left; enough was enough. Todd had lied to me. We had quite a row when we got home.

"All these men were speaking in tongues and healing everyone they could find. Todd even ran after ambulances and told people in the emergency rooms they didn't have to go through this, that God would heal them. Mary Snoop once told me that God gave special learning and reading powers to men once they were converted, because they were supposed lead their wives. So even if the wife had learned the Bible from her youth on, the man would still—within weeks—know more than her.

"At some point I began to question myself. I wondered if Jesus wanted me to be like them. I prayed and cried, but nothing happened to change me into what these people had become. I never spoke in tongues, although I was told it would happen if I just opened my mouth and made any old sound. That really turned me off; it didn't sound like spiritual intervention to me. I did try it, though. Nothing. Of course, I didn't have enough faith.

"Finally, one day, I got a call from Todd saying that he'd been fired from his job. As it turned out, he took a client to Karl on his lunch hour instead of transporting her to the county home as he'd been instructed. He'd taken her first to Karl to cast out her evil spirits. This was a seriously schizophrenic young woman, and she reported the event—it scared the life out of her. Many other such incidents were suspected.

"To make a very long story short, Todd became totally dominated by Karl and his cronies. He was seldom home and, if he was, he'd be lying belly-down on the floor with arms outstretched half the night, praying, or kneeling in front of one of the windows which he claimed faced east and had become his private altar. He always did these things in the middle of the night. Everything had become so weird that I thought I was going to lose my mind. No more money, except mine, came into the house.

"We couldn't pay our mortgage, but Todd was not concerned. He spent his days with Karl, or reading books by the same kind of people, or listening to their CDs. I was offered money for our mortgage by my own pastor, to whom I'd gone for help. He finally advised me to leave Todd to preserve my own spiritual peace and sanity. I found the strength to do that only because of his advice. I never believed divorce was the answer, but now I saw no other way."

"I guess not," Kate finally added. "I guess not."

"Yes. Well, I've felt guilty about having married Todd when I felt, on our wedding day, that I shouldn't. I felt guilty about getting a divorce. I sometimes wonder, even now, if he was the better Christian, or if I was totally wrong. I know I wasn't, but those doubts surface occasionally."

"I can't answer that, but it sounds to me like Todd was caught up in a cult. This Karl Snoop person sounds like really bad news."

"So many weird things went on during those five years, I can't even begin to tell you. One time we went to Todd's cousin's wedding. These were people from a good church background. Some of the relatives had also been involved in this neo-Pentecostal movement, on the fringe of which Todd and Karl operated. Anyway, this aunt comes up to me and says, 'What a wonderful husband you have!' I still can't believe my own rude response. 'Really? You haven't lived with him, have you?'"

Catherine giggled. "Sounds like a perfect reply to me."

"No; too rude for me. But I learned a lot, too. I do not proselytize anymore; I know what it feels like to be cajoled into believing something you can't, and to have people constantly trying to shove it down your throat anyway. It's absolutely nauseating."

"You've got that right. What about this Ver Hage man you are now married to? What's he like?"

"Gary is wonderful. He's kind and considerate. He asks my advice; I ask his. We have a great mutual respect. We go to a Presbyterian church together, and have learned that God is in charge of saving people. We just have to live a Christian life and be prepared to answer questions. You have any questions, Kate?"

"Maybe later. What a lot of crap you've been put through," Catherine's responded. "Still, my guilt is more serious. Sorry, Phill, but my only child is dead, and I'm convinced it's all my fault."

"How can you think that? Surely you loved her."

"I did, but I spent too much misplaced love on somebody else, and now I have nothing. It's all my fault."

"Well, I know guilt. Just believe me, that's all I can say. It plagues me far too often. I pray to our Savior every time it threatens to overtake me."

"Yeah, well, I do not wish to grovel before something I neither know nor understand."

"I'm so sorry for your loss. Do you want to talk more about it? Can I help?"

"Nope and nope."

"What do you do to keep busy, Kate? I mean, on a day to day basis?"

"I've been buying furniture. I walk the beach. I swim. I read. Sometimes I even turn on the TV. I also got an invitation to a class reunion. Did you?"

"I did. Are you thinking of going?"

"Surely not. I could tell them all something that would blow their pants right off their behinds. I think I'll forego the pleasure."

"I wonder if it might help you to get involved in some kind of volunteer work."

"Gwen has mentioned that. I don't think so; I'm not much good for something like that right now. I need some time, I think."

"When you're ready, let me know. I know some agencies that could really use your talent and experience."

"I'm not a Christian, Phillis. Don't even try to set me up with some church agency."

"That was not at all what I had in mind. I know you."

"Well, we'll see. I'll call if I need you. Thanks for having lunch. It was really—well, it was really enlightening. Thanks for trusting me with your story." Kate moved to pick up the tab but Phillis got to it first.

"I insist, Kate. I'm so glad we could reconnect. I hope we can do this again sometime—and on a lighter note next time."

"Sounds good. Until next time, then." Kate left Phillis to pay the bill and walked to her car. On the way home, Catherine wondered if Phillis would understand guilt a bit better if she'd murdered Todd.

Chapter 39

Warren

"You're sister really ought to get a grip, you know. She's been out here for two months already, and she's still crying on the phone to you every other day." Warren Konynbelt took another sip of coffee as he waited for a response from his wife. Gwen turned from her dishes to glare at him and said nothing. "Oh, come on Gwen. Can't we get over the past and get back to where we were? Can't we just have a civil conversation? I told you I was sorry. I really am sorry. What can I do?"

Gwen went back to her dishes. She stared out her kitchen window to at the gloriously blooming back yard. The wildflowers offered a rich array of colors that did her heart good. Warren had done a superb job of making her garden thrive. She loved that the butterflies had come back again this year. But her heart had been hardened against her husband, and she found it very difficult to be civil towards him. Months had passed, and she still felt frozen. The wasted years, when she might have had the brood of children she'd always wanted, grieved her more than she could bear. She found forgiveness impossible, even though she desperately wanted it. The stone in heart would not move.

"I guess there's nothing you can do," she answered quietly. When the phone rang, she wiped her hands on the towel hanging from the stove handle. As she walked to the phone, she noticed the sneer on Warren's face. If it was Kate, she would have to take it in the other room. She didn't want to see or deal with Warren's impatience with her sister's problems. Helping Kate was somehow helping herself. She picked up the receiver. "Hello."

"Hello. Is this Gwen Konynbelt? This is William, Catherine's friend from Brigantine. Do you remember me?"

"William! Of course I remember you. How are you?" She was surprised to hear this most welcome voice.

"I'm fine. I don't live in Brigantine anymore. You might know that, since I put my house up for sale before Catherine did. I live in Pennsylvania, in my old home town, where I have some friends and acquaintances."

"It's always good to be near some familiar faces, especially after a major change in your life."

"Yes, and that's why I called. About the major change, I mean. I think I'd like to see Catherine again. I'm not sure yet, but I'd like to know how to reach her if I do decide to get in touch. Would you be able to give me her information?"

"I need to warn you, William; Catherine is not doing very well. You may be just what she needs right now, but you do need to know that she's having some serious issues with the loss of both Tina and Zachary."

"I'm not surprised. I would hope she'd have some issues, especially about Zachary."

"Why would you say that?" Gwen thought Kate's serious grief would rather be over her daughter. What William said surprised her.

"Oh. Never mind. I just thought that after forty years...well, you know." He wasn't sure why he'd said what he did; now he didn't know how to get out of it. His suspicions about Catherine's last night with

Zach had never left him. He'd become convinced that he needed to know the truth about Catherine if he were ever to trust her or befriend her again. "I called because I miss her company more than I thought I would. That's all. And I believe she must need a friend. Not that you haven't been a wonderful support for her."

"You're babbling, William. Is there something you aren't telling me?"

"Not really. I just think I'd like to see Catherine sometime, that's all. Do you think that would be all right?"

"Yes, of course, William. As I recall, you were the one who broke off the relationship, but never mind. Listen, she lives in Good Heavens on a wonderful piece of property overlooking Lake Michigan. I'll give you her number and address. When you see her, be kind. She's easily agitated."

"I imagine she is," William answered. "By the way, Gwen, would you please not tell Catherine I called? I'm not sure when I'll be able to come out there, and I want to talk to her without her anticipating my arrival. What do you think?" He didn't want any expectations; he wasn't even sure he was going to contact her. He certainly wasn't going to tell anybody about his dreams.

"It's up to you, William. I won't say anything if you don't want me to." Gwen gave him Catherine's information and hung up.

Warren looked at her quizzically. "Who was that? That old guy Kate used to hang out with on the island? Wow, she really knows how to hook them, doesn't she?"

Gwen answered with a phrase she never used. "Shut up, Warren" Their relationship, which had always seemed close to perfect to Catherine—and had seemed so to Gwen, too—had deteriorated to this. When trust is lost, most of a marriage is lost. Gwen was hanging by a string, a very thin one. Warren tiptoed around her as much as he was able, knowing how deeply his betrayal had damaged their relationship.

Neither was sure what the future would bring for them. Neither wanted to talk about it in detail lest too much be said, precipitating the final break. But they both knew the time would come when something would have to be done and said. Gwen poured herself a cup of coffee, set it on the counter next to her, and continued her dishwashing.

Warren could not stand the silence. For lack of anything better to say, he asked, "Why not just use the dishwasher, Gwen?"

"Washing helps keep my fingernails in shape." No further discussion followed. Gwen let a few tears roll down her cheeks, wiped them away with a fury, and tried desperately to continue her chore so she could avoid thinking about both her husband and her sister, whom she was dying to call. But she had promised William.

William looked at Catherine's address and phone number. He shook his head and folded the paper neatly into fourths, went to his study, and placed it in the right top drawer under a stack of canceled checks. He was a packrat, he knew. And unduly fastidious.

He was afraid he might dream again that night, so he took an extra sleeping pill to ensure a dreamless sleep.

Chapter 40

Plans

Catherine drove up her steep driveway, parked the car, and looked at the clock on her dash. She realized she'd spent most of the best part of the day listening to Phillis. She knew Phillis had experienced pain, but she couldn't imagine feeling guilt over leaving a jerk like Todd, especially after what he'd put her through. "Those Christians," she muttered to herself. "They feel guilty even if they're the only ones doing the right thing. Go figure." If Phillis only knew what she, Catherine, had done. *Wow, what a number that would do on her*, Catherine thought. "Better not let that cat out of the bag just yet," she said to no one.

"Hey, you got a cat?" she heard someone call. *Oh shit*, she thought, *not them again*. She turned to see Sam lumbering up her drive with a bag that was dripping water. "Hi! I'm glad I caught you home. Been out on the boat and caught a really nice salmon. I filleted it and thought you might like a piece. The fresher the better. And Betty wants to know if you have plans for Thanksgiving. It's just a month or so away, you know."

She did her best again to stay sweet, a word she'd never applied to herself before. "Well, Sam, with this unusually warm autumn we've had, I can't say Thanksgiving crossed my mind yet. It is quite early, isn't it? I guess I'll have to see what my sister has in mind."

Sam handed her the dripping bag, which she took and held away from her body. "Thanks, Sam. I think I'll freeze it for another day, though."

"You're very welcome. Don't think for a minute you have to spend a holiday alone. We would love to have you over. Just say the word." Sam grinned. "Ta-ta for now, then." He moved on across the dune to his own drive, and disappeared behind the shrubs.

Catherine sighed and went around to the deck. She climbed the five steps from the dune and dumped the bag in the garbage container before she opened her slider. Then she thought a cold dip would do wonders for her head. She wanted to clear it of the afternoon. She was sort of glad Phillis was around and had had a bit of grief in her life, but she was still uncomfortable with her constant references to her faith. In some ways, Phillis hadn't changed at all.

As she got out of her clothes and pulled on her black tank suit, she wondered about Warren and Gwen. Had Doug had been told about his "brother"? He was living on the West Coast, so probably not; let sleeping dogs lie and all that.

Catherine stepped out onto the deck and descended to the beach, shivering in the cool October air. It was unseasonably warm for that time of year, but not warm enough to be nearly naked on the beach, and surely not warm enough to swim. But Catherine held her breath and ran into the icy water. The lake did not become deep enough for a good swim for several yards, so she dipped her body under the water to get the full effect and moved as rapidly as possible to the deeper area. She swam vigorously for twenty minutes, and then hurried out. Goose bumps stood out all over her untanned skin and she shuddered with the cold, yet felt exhilarated at the same time. Her head was clearer. She rushed back up the stairs. On her way into the house, she thought better of her earlier decision and reached into the garbage can to retrieve the fish.

At the sink, Catherine turned on the cold water, unwrapped the filet, and dumped it in. She thought she'd poach the salmon; she could save the leftovers for a salad sometime later in the week. She put on a pan of water for the fish, and then took out a small saucepan and placed some butter, olive oil, freshly squeezed lemon, chopped onions, garlic, and dill in it for a sauce, and turned the burner to low. Then she placed the fish into the water. She had some potato salad and lettuce left over to balance out her meal. While she waited, she took the morning paper out to the deck. She knew she should not sit too long; neither the fish nor the sauce required a lot of cooking.

When she thought all was ready, she filled a plate with a little of each and took it, as well as cutlery and a napkin, out on the deck. She went back in and poured herself a big glass of cold Pinot Grigio. She thought she was finally truly hungry and began to attack the fresh salmon, but three bites of fish and four swallows of wine later she began to gag. She was so angry with herself that she forced another large forkful of salad and fish down her throat, quickly following it with a gulp of wine.

Some of the fish landed in the garbage after all. She knew she'd had enough. The rest of the plate would have to be put away for another time. She covered all the leftovers and put them in the fridge. But she kept the wine, and carried the half-empty glass to her sunroom. There she thought about what her friends had told her about themselves. So far, no one had suffered or did suffer as she did, she was sure.

Just before she thought herself ready for bed, the phone rang. She took her time answering it. She could see from the caller ID that it was an out of state call. She picked it up, but all she heard was a click as the phone went dead. She thought to check what number it was, but she really didn't care. She poured more wine and retreated back to the deck, dropped into the lounge, watched the reflections on the water, and sipped. She wanted oblivion, but knew the danger of working at it. Maybe that's what Tina had wanted, too, but had not known the danger. Maybe.

She thought she'd fallen asleep when her thoughts turned to William. It was almost as if she could see him. She called his name. He was not there, of course, but his face was in her head. Then everything changed, and she was out on a boat with Sam and Betty. They were fishing. Catherine didn't care for fishing but somehow she felt exhilarated, as if something were about to happen. She felt a tug on her line. She pulled but there was no movement. She called out, "Hey, Sam, I got snagged."

Sam took her pole and pulled. "This is no snag. You have something big. Work it." He showed her how, and soon she saw a large fish. Then she recoiled in horror. The fish's head was William's, smiling, with a hook in his mouth. She shook with the terror of it and almost fell out of her lounge chair. The night was dark, and there was not a light on in her house. She stumbled through the slider and flicked on the kitchen light. "William!" she breathed into the air. Then she picked up the phone. She thought that, perhaps if she called his old number, there would be a message giving his new number. She began to dial, but her reticence to talk to him overpowered her, so she hung up and poured herself another glass of the cold white wine. She knew she should get some sleep, but fear of another nightmare kept her up.

She turned on the TV. She had despised television her whole life, but now it had become her pacifier. Tony Soprano was struggling with his therapist again. *Why doesn't this woman just get rid of him?* Catherine thought. The episode turned on his guilt. He was experiencing panic attacks and was not sleeping well over the murder of a young thug. She knew the feeling. And she knew she had to get back to Dr. Landman. It was almost as if *The Sopranos* had a message just for her tonight. Not likely, but it certainly seemed that way to Catherine in her agitated mood.

Tony called himself a soldier. He believed he had a right to murder people who deserved it. He knew the law would not take care of those who offended him, so he and his mob had to take care of things themselves. Catherine empathized, but still felt just as guilty as Tony. What could she do?

She took a dose of nighttime aspirin and tried to get some undisturbed sleep. But Zachary appeared on the beach, coaxing her to come down. "You need to be dead too," he kept saying. "Come and join us. Come to the water and be clean. You'll feel much better." Her great fear upon waking was her strong inclination to follow Zach's advice, her unnatural desire to walk into the lake and never turn around.

In the morning she called Dr. Landman.

Chapter 41

Sam's Story

While she was in the shower trying to wash the night out of her hair, out of her eyes, out of her skin, the doorbell rang. She hoped it was Gwen promising to go to therapy with her. She wrapped her robe around her and went to the door only to find Betty. "I'm so sorry to disturb you, but we're going for a boat ride in about an hour. We'd love you to come." Catherine felt panic creep up her neck and numb her face. What if William was in the water out there? She knew this was absurd, and decided meeting her fear straight on might be good. With some evidence of struggle in her voice, she said she would go. "Great," Betty answered. "And by the way, would you like to do some fishing while we're out?"

"No!" Catherine almost yelled. "I do not do fishing!" She was immediately sorry and said, "I'm so sorry, Betty. I had a really bad night. I'd love the ride, but no fishing, okay?"

Sam and Betty had discussed their new neighbor's often strange behavior—walking on the beach at night, sleeping in her lounge chair and waking them with her screams. They thought a nice boat outing would be good for her. They wanted to offer what peace they could to what they perceived to be a very troubled woman. They hoped to find the reason for Catherine's anguished cries at a later date, so they decided to stay close.

At the marina Sam, helped the women into his twenty-eight foot boat. It was lovely, Catherine thought—white and blue, with "Dune Runner" painted on the back and side. The MacMurtles couldn't tell her enough about their wonderful find. Used but well cared for, the boat had cost a pittance. It slept four, and even had a flush toilet. "I wouldn't have had it without the flush toilet!" Betty laughed. Sam explained that he would love to take her to Chicago, but Betty would go nowhere she could not see shore. She also wore two bracelets to protect against possible seasickness. *She's not a good candidate for boat ownership*, thought Catherine.

"How are you today?" Betty asked out of the blue. They'd just backed out of the slip, and Sam was heading into the river.

"I'm fine, Betty. Why do you ask?"

"I just thought you looked a little peaked this morning. I hope you're well," she answered.

"I'm fine. I don't always sleep well, that's all." Catherine did not appreciate Betty's questions; she felt these people were nice enough, but a bit too nosey.

"I've noticed you've lost quite a bit of weight since you arrived. I'd love to know what diet you're on. I could stand to lose a few pounds myself," Betty giggled.

Catherine was not amused. "I eat simply," was all she said, and turned to view the shore.

Eating seemed to be a preoccupation with Sam and Betty. The very word brought up a myriad list of wonderful places to get the best hamburgers ever and, oh yeah, the greatest ice cream and malts to die for, mouthwatering pasta, and so much more. They regaled Catherine with food stories for the next hour.

The lake was placid this morning. Tiny whitecaps appeared from time to time, but they were mostly a result of others' wakes. There was the slightest hint of a gentle breeze; just enough to sweep through one's hair and cool the neck from the unusually warm late-autumn sun. Although jackets were a must out on the water, no one wore much more than summer clothes on this balmy day. Catherine did not wear shorts, but had on capris. Sam wore his white captains' shorts, and Betty her usual tight black capris and a sweatshirt. Everyone was very comfortable.

Catherine thought she would change the subject, and so asked Sam where he had grown up. This, unexpectedly, brought out a loud guffaw from Betty. "Ha! Wait until you hear Sam's story," she exclaimed.

"Now, Betty. Maybe Catherine doesn't want to hear it," Sam admonished.

But Catherine did want to hear it, and told them she would love to. It would give her more to talk to Dr. Landman about, for one thing. And, oddly enough, she was beginning to enjoy other people's tales.

Sam began, "I come from West Virginia. My father was a coal miner. We were poor. You know the reputation. As a dentist said to friend of mine when he was ready to put a cap on her front peg of a tooth, 'I can leave it like this and you can live in West Virginia.' Ha ha, right? Anyway, I'm the youngest of eleven children. Two died in childhood, so there were nine of us." Catherine felt a response was not appropriate, so she stifled the urge.

"I never knew my parents," Sam confessed, eliciting a surprised "What?" from Catherine.

He ignored it. "My father died while my mother was still pregnant with me. He was killed in a mining accident—nothing unusual back then, you know. Anyway, right after I was born, the mining company came to my mother and offered her a check as compensation. The shock of it all, the grief, I guess, and postpartum stress seemed to pile up on her, and she had a stroke. Died right at the feet of the messengers from the mine."

"Oh my goodness!" Catherine interjected.

Sam looked at her and continued. "Yes, well, that left nine orphans. The oldest was eighteen; I was two weeks. The neighbors came to our house to offer condolences. Everyone was very kind but, as it turned out, they were a little too kind. About nine neighbors came over one evening and made an offer. They had decided that one couple would take two of us kids, another would take one, another three, and so on. My brothers and sisters were aghast, and my oldest brother said he would get back to them and asked them all to leave. Then he sat the family down to discuss their situation.

"The mining company had given us enough money to keep the family going for quite a long time. My brother said that if the rest agreed, he would stay and take care of them all until he was twenty. Then my next oldest sister would be eighteen, and she could take over. Each older child would take his or her turn until we were all grown. He asked how many were in favor of that over what the neighbors had proposed, and it was unanimous that we stay together. The neighbors were informed of our decision, and that's how I grew up. My brothers and sisters were my parents. I will always be grateful to them."

"Wow," was all Catherine could say. "Wow," she said again. Then, after a minute's reflection, she asked, "What about the state? Child protective services?"

"In the mountains of West Virginia, sixty-five years ago? No such thing, and I can never be thankful enough. Can you imagine what they would have done to us? Separated, and one foster home after another? No thanks. God took care of us just right, and equipped each one of us with the gifts needed to do the job. We all grew up pretty well." Sam smiled as he steered the boat into a channel leading to a smaller lake.

The rest of the trip featured Sam and Betty pointing out the enormous homes along the shoreline, specifying who owned what, who they were, and how much they were worth. Catherine fully understood Sam's interest in wealth; he'd known enough of the opposite, she was sure.

Chapter 42

Meeting

William parked on the street below the dune. He watched Catherine get into her car and floor it on her way down her drive and onward. He took the opportunity to drive up to her house, just to see where she lived now and what kind of place she had. He was very impressed with the blue-and-white house—much more than a cottage—which sat perched on the dune overlooking this enormous lake. At least she wasn't on top of one of these super-high ones, he mused. He turned his car around just as someone appeared on the front steps of the house next door. He was in no mood to introduce or explain himself, so he too floored his car on the way down and out. He was not ready to let Catherine know he was here yet.

Catherine felt fully equipped to see Dr. Landman even though Gwen had not been able to join her. Her head was filled with stories of other's hardships and guilt, each filed away under her own creative headings. She was ready to tell Dr. Landman about "The Liar," "The Cultist," and "The Orphan." She also believed not one of these people had as much to feel sorry or guilty about as she had, but this was not something Dr. Landman would ever know the full facts about. A crime with impunity is what she had, and impunity is what she intended to keep.

"So, Ms. Cedar, it's been a while. How have you done with your assignment?" *He looks smug*, she thought. *How conceited he is about this!*

"I'm very proud of what I found out about other people," she answered.

"Proud?"

"I discovered that my sister, whom I always thought perfect—a perfect marriage and all—is married to a totally dishonest man who has been so with her since before they married. She only found out a few months ago, as I understand it, and she is devastated."

"And you're proud about this? How does that make you feel? The fact that your perfect sister is devastated and you're proud?"

"Well, I'm just proud to have gotten it out of her; I'm not happy— for her sake, of course. But I'm relieved to know that she knows suffering, that I'm not the only one. Although I must add that hers is bad, but mine is infinitely worse."

"How can you be sure of that?"

"I just know. No one can be suffering like I am. No sleep. No appetite. No escape from accusing dreams."

"What do your dreams accuse you of?"

"Hmm. Well, for example, the other night, I dreamed I'd gone fishing with my neighbors and had caught a really big fish. When I reeled it in, it turned out to be a fish with William's head and a hook through his mouth. I screamed myself awake."

"And William is…"

"He's the man who was my only real friend on Brigantine."

"What do you make of this dream?"

"You tell me. That's why I'm here. I'm sure I can't figure it out."

"Perhaps you miss him. Perhaps you'd like to reel him in as your own companion."

"You mean I want to marry William?"

"Maybe; I'm only offering one suggestion. I don't know what kind of relationship you had with him, so that's my best guess."

"Well, I also found out that my high school friend, the Christian who had always tried to convert me, married her high school sweetheart and divorced him. It turned out he got involved with a kind of cult group. She couldn't live with the demands on her and she left him. Then she married another man and joined a different church."

"Does she suffer guilt over all this?"

"She says she does, but how can you feel guilty over leaving an abusive situation? I'd think she'd feel relief."

"Does she believe divorce is an option, according to her faith?"

"Well, no. I guess that's it, then."

"Why do you think you have a premium on pain and guilt?"

"These people are not losing weight or sleep, for one thing."

"Are there any others with whom you've interacted since the last time we talked?"

"Yes. I went for a boat ride right after the fish nightmare. I thought it might be good to face my fears head on, although I did decline to do any fishing, Anyway, my neighbor told me about the death of his parents, which left him and eight siblings to fend for themselves. He doesn't suffer from guilt; as a matter of fact, the man is so jovial that I don't think he knows how to suffer. But he does feel a tremendous debt to his siblings. He was the youngest, you see."

"Did his parents die in an accident?"

"His father was a miner and died in an occupational accident; his mother was overwhelmed and died of a stroke when he was only two weeks old. His siblings became his parents. Each took over when he or she turned eighteen, and were set free of the obligation when they turned twenty. That's how they kept the family together."

"That's quite a story. What a task for those kids. How did hearing this make you feel?"

"Wow. That's all I could think to say. Just wow."

"Do you think talking to these people has helped you in your own struggles?"

"Not really. I admire some for what they accomplished in the face of difficulties, but I still carry this guilt over my daughter. I can't get beyond it."

"Get a dog."

"What? A dog?"

"A dog will take up some of your time, and you'll have something to think about besides yourself. It will also help keep you company at night. Maybe some of your nightmares will abate."

"A dog, you say? Hmm, a dog. I never thought of that. At least I won't be alone, right?"

"Right."

"Well, I'll think about it."

Catherine left Dr. Landman's office feeling better than she had in a while. Talking about other people, maybe getting a pet—all ways to get away from herself—helped. She decided to stop for a hamburger. She couldn't let the moment pass, since she felt hungry and could think about purchasing a dog. She walked into the Morning Glory café, bought a local newspaper, and sat in a booth. She turned to the classifieds before she ordered. She didn't need to look at a menu; she was going to eat. A hamburger, fries, a salad, coffee, and water with lemon. Then the classifieds.

The food arrived just as she found the pet section. She took a huge bite of her burger, and it tasted good. The dogs for sale were all very young puppies. She took another bite. The dogs up for adoption were too old. She thought a one-year-old dog would be about perfect; old enough to have learned some manners, yet young enough to become attached to her. She found an ad for the local humane society and decided to stop there on her way home. Then she noticed another adoption ad from an agency that helped girls who had serious problems and absent parents. Apparently they were in need of volunteers to help some of the girls get their GEDs. She munched on her salad as she thought about her own needs. She was more than qualified to help. Maybe she would stop there first, before the dog place. She took down the address.

When she looked down at her plate, she realized with great satisfaction that she had eaten a full meal. She gave the waitress a generous tip, as if the girl had had anything to do with her eating.

Chapter 43

They Meet

William knew it was called stalking these days, so he decided to back off and find a nice beach to enjoy for an hour or so. He found Catherine just as gorgeous as when he'd left Brigantine. She appeared to be thinner, but even that enhanced her beauty. He missed her sarcasm and laughter; he missed his dinners out with her. William just plain missed Catherine, and he thought some solitary enjoyment of the beach would help him find the courage to talk to her, or find the resolve to go home and forget about her.

He watched his GPS to find water; he knew it had to be west. He drove down Main Street, took a left, and cruised along the river. Very few people were out. A few elderly couples huddled together, wearing the first winter clothing, on benches along the riverfront. The air was very cool. William parked his car near the public beach where the river emptied into the lake, walked through the gate, which now had no attendant, and onto the long public beach. He tried to imagine this place filled with children and parents. He looked to the right and saw the empty camp ground which, a few months earlier, had been teeming with every kind of RV imaginable and even a few small tents. William knew this was one area of town Catherine would not frequent during the bustling summer months.

He decided that he needed a nice stroll along the beach instead of sitting. He peered back at the lighthouse and the long pier. There were a few people walking, and some men casting fishing lines. It was getting colder as the day began to draw to a close. William wrapped his arms around himself and shivered. He saw a tall woman with a large beige dog walking down the boardwalk toward the beach. The dog kept jumping on the huge stones lining the walk. It sniffed all the crevices, and occasionally came up with something in its mouth. The woman kept pulling it back. She insisted each time that it drop whatever it had garnered from the rocks.

William couldn't tear his eyes away. Then he caught his breath. He'd recognized Catherine, and it was too late to run or hide. She stopped short a few yards from him, her mouth agape. Then she pulled the dog to her and made it sit without taking her eyes off William. It was as though she were in a trance. William wasn't sure what to do.

Catherine, on the other hand, was sure she was having some kind of waking dream. She was afraid to move or make a sound. *What if the nightmares had become hallucinations?* she thought. William moved toward her with slow, deliberate steps. When he was within earshot, he said, "Catherine?"

She recognized his voice. She held very tightly to the dog, who pulled on her leash to run to William. She knew the dog could not be hallucinating with her. "William," she dared to breathe, "is it really you?"

"Catherine," he repeated.

The large goldendoodle jumped, out of control, at William—into his face and scratching his arm before Catherine was able to pull her away. She was a little embarrassed about her new dog, but much more flustered at seeing William.

"I'm so sorry," she apologized. "This is Dune. I just got her yesterday. They told me she was well-behaved, but as you can see...." She pulled on Dune's training collar until she sat, panting to get at William one more time. Her long tongue hung, drooling, from her friendly face.

"It's all right, Catherine. I'm all right, really. Well, I didn't mean to run into you so soon. Okay, that didn't come out right at all. What I mean is—"

"Stop, William. How did you ever find me?" she interrupted, and then paused. "Oh, wait, don't tell me. Gwen, right?"

William nodded.

"You sure have a way of using my family."

"I know. This time I'm at fault, but I was so sure I needed to see you."

"Really? Why would that be?" Catherine gave an extra pull on the leash and took a deep breath just to get herself under control. William found his tongue paralyzed as he stared at the woman who had so disturbed his sleep. She quietly added, "As I recall, you refused to speak to me by the end of the summer. You returned none of my phone messages, and left Brigantine without a goodbye or forwarding address. Why would you want to see me now?" Her matter-of-fact tone warned William to be very careful.

"This will sound very strange, and I'm not sure if you'll find this entirely credible, Catherine. But I had a dream about you." William blushed when he said this. He knew it must sound juvenile or ridiculous. He was embarrassed, and Catherine could see it.

"William, do you believe in dreams?"

"I don't know. I guess that's why I'm here."

"Hmm, I wonder... Do you suppose there might be dream messengers, like maybe dream angels or something?"

"Or dream demons?" William added with a nervous chuckle.

"Was your dream that bad?" Catherine wanted to know. She shuddered at the reminder of her own worst nightmares. A demon could certainly account for them, but she knew better. She also knew not to continue this conversation.

"It was more disturbing than bad. There was more than one."

Catherine pulled a pack of cigarettes from her shirt pocket. She took one out, lit it, and drew a long drag into her lungs. When she let it out, she saw William's surprise. "What? That I smoke? Always intended to once I got old enough. No big deal."

William sighed. This woman never ceased to amaze him. Sometimes he wished he had the courage to be this outrageous.

The smoke brought Catherine back to her old self. "So William, it's getting late, nearly dark. Want to have an early supper? Where are you staying, by the way?"

"I'm at the new Hilton on the river—introductory prices and all. Yes, an early supper would be nice. Do you have a favorite place yet?"

"No, but we can go to the Cozy Corner overlooking the river. We can walk from here. It'll give us a nice view of the river and a private booth."

Catherine stopped by her car to deposit Dune and opened the windows a bit. They walked in silence. Neither was quite sure what to say. Small talk was out of the question, and more than that would need to wait. And each was acutely aware of the other.

When they'd descended to the lower level of the restaurant and been seated in a booth with a wonderful water view, they hid behind their menus until Catherine began to laugh out loud. William peered over the top of his menu at someone he thought he knew. He'd forgotten how unpredictable she could be. One minute quiet or gloomy, the next laughing or dancing. Her menu began to bob up and down as her laughter increased and became more uproarious—enough to call attention to them. William was amused or embarrassed; he wasn't sure which. He lowered his menu and smiled. "What's so funny?" he asked.

"You and me, of course. Here we are, a couple of old farts, so to speak. We've known each other for a year or more by now. We've been friends, we've experienced a ton of life together, and now we're hiding behind our menus because we don't know what to say to each other. Teenagers do that, not us!"

"I guess you're right, Catherine. I'm just aware of imposing on your space. I hadn't intended to meet you on the beach. I guess I'm embarrassed at myself. But you're right; let's order, talk, and enjoy this time, if we can."

Catherine tried to control herself. Her nervous reaction to William's unexpected presence made her unable to control her laughter. Even as she ordered, a giggle erupted. The young waitress smiled with what seemed like contempt, but her voice was very friendly. Catherine ordered the seafood salad, even though she knew the shrimp had to have been frozen at some point. William ordered the grand salad and a side of fries. Each had a glass of the white house wine. As William bent his head in a silent blessing over his food, Catherine smiled at his consistency. Fries and a prayer. It was William, all right.

William broke the silence. "I drove by your house, Catherine. It's a wonderful spot you found. It lacks the smell of the ocean, but my goodness, what a lake. And what a view you have."

"Really? What did you do? Case the place while I was out?" She popped a rich green leaf of spinach into her mouth.

"Not exactly. I sound like a stalker, don't I?"

"You not only sound like one, but you are."

"Well, no. I was doing a drive-by a second time and stopped for a better look. A man came down the next drive waving his arms at me. I wasn't sure what to do, so I rolled down my window."

"Yes, that would be Sam. Always on the lookout."

"Oh? So, anyway, he asked if I was looking for you. I said I just wanted to see where you lived, that I'd been your friend in New Jersey. He absolutely insisted I come up to his deck and see the view you both had."

"I believe you. He would never have let you leave without first having accommodated his curiosity. Friendliness is his and Betty's way of finding out everything about everybody. He must have asked you about your relationship to me."

"He hinted about it. I just told him we were friends once, but had lost touch. That's all."

The waitress hovered over them, and then asked, "How's it tastin'?"

Catherine burst out laughing again at this question. A shrimp shot from her mouth like a projectile and landed on the floor at the stunned girl's feet. "Everything is fine. I'm so sorry; I seem to have the giggles. Please forgive me." And with that she waved the girl away.

"Why'd you come, William?" Catherine composed herself and continued the conversation, saying, "You mentioned dreams, I think."

"Yes. So very strange. The first one was you and me in Brigantine on the beach. You were flirting with me, and I was a bit embarrassed. In the second, Bernice came to me. I have no idea where I was, but it felt familiar. She told me to go see you. Can you believe that? Weird. Anyway, I didn't know what to make of it, but I couldn't get you out of my mind. So here I am. I'm not sure why."

"I've had a few dreams myself, William. Only one was about you, though. I'll tell you about it later. Anyway, I think Zach is trying to kill me. He's in my dreams, always threatening me or telling me to die. It's awful. Then Tina is there, both as a little girl and later. She wants me to come to her. I hear her crying 'Mommy' over and over. It makes me crazy—so much pain. I don't know how long I can go on."

"You're carrying a tremendous burden, aren't you, Catherine?"

"Grief over losing one's only child is a burden. You'd better believe it."

"And your burden due to Zach's sudden death?"

"What do you mean, William?"

"Well, he's in your dreams, trying to make you die, you said. Why would he?"

"That's what I can't figure out."

"Aren't you feeling a bit of grief over his death? Even though you finally found him to be the scoundrel everyone told you he was?"

"What is this, a psych session? No. As a matter of fact, I'm profoundly thankful that he's no longer on this earth."

"Catherine, you've lost the two people who were most important in your life for the past twenty-five years and more. Surely your dreams have to do with those severe losses, or perhaps because of the nature of those losses. I mean, one suicide, the other as a result of a dinner you prepared. The trauma you suffered must be profound, don't you think?" He popped a fry into his mouth.

"Of course. Was it your fear of my reaction to the trauma that sent you running, William?"

"Maybe."

"Well, let's finish our food and decide what's next over coffee. I mean about you, here, now."

They ordered coffee and pie for dessert. William had always adored key lime pie, and it happened to be the special. Catherine joined him. They ate their dessert in silence, each enjoying the sweet tartness. Catherine found she was not overwhelmed with negative feelings this evening, and had a pretty good appetite. What she would experience when she got home alone she didn't want to consider. At least she had Dune, who was now sleeping comfortably in the back of her car.

When they finished, William took the check before Catherine had a chance to pick it up. He insisted; she acquiesced. When they got outside, they had to decide what to do next. It was dark as they walked back to the beach parking.

Catherine broke the silence first. "Why don't you follow me in your car and come see my place? We can talk for a bit."

"Catherine, I didn't mean to impose on you—not on your time or your privacy. Perhaps I'd better go to the hotel."

"Nonsense, William. You're here let's talk, so let's get it over with."

They walked to Catherine's car, where Dune had awakened and sat happily nibbling on the arm rest.

"Oh, no. Dune. Bad dog," Catherine scolded as she held up a piece of torn leather. "Now I have to get this repaired. Bad Dune. Bad, bad dog," she scolded again. Dune jumped forward, landed on her shoulder, and began licking her face with a long, wet fury. Her wagging tail made her entire body wiggle.

"She loves you," William observed. "I think she's apologizing."

Catherine managed a smile, patted then gently pushed the big curly creature back into the seat, and got into the car. "Let's go," she said to William before closing the door.

William followed Catherine to her cottage. He could see just enough in the darkness to note its size and appeal. He knew this must have cost her at least half of what she'd earned from her sale of the oceanfront house. When she ushered him through the front door, which she hardly ever used, he was delighted by the tasteful decor and immediately impressed with the difference in style from her Brigantine house. He commented, "Wow, Catherine. You certainly changed your style."

"Don't you like it?" she asked.

"I like it very much, but it's such a change for you. So modern, so geometric; I love the bright red sofa and white chairs. The hardwood floors are outstanding, and the fixtures—well, it's very contemporary, but not cold. You know what I mean?"

"Of course I know what you mean. I changed everything to keep from anything reflecting my life in Brigantine. I did it on purpose."

"How much of Brigantine do you mean to erase, Catherine?"

"Only the pain, William, only the pain. Let's see the rest of the house and then sit and chat."

William was impressed with the deck, the spectacular view, the change in Catherine's style, and the size of the lake, which he had not quite expected. After the tour, they sat in the living room with cups of coffee. Dune lay contentedly at Catherine's feet, panting loudly, drooling on the floor, and looked up to Catherine every few seconds to see what would be happening next. Catherine patted her head and continued her conversation with William.

"You have a wonderful house, Catherine. I'm sure you'll be very happy here."

"Don't be so sure. I have terrible nightmares. Tina is constantly on my mind."

"I can understand that. But what about Zachary? I mean…well, I'm not sure what I mean. Do you have really awful dreams about him too?"

"Why in the world do you want to know that?"

"I told you—many years of waiting and yearning, and then the horrendous discovery about your daughter. I thought maybe some of that would cause your nightmares."

"What did you come here to find out, William? What exactly are you thinking?"

"I wish to know why I've dreamed about you and why I miss you."

"Then why all these questions about Zach?"

"Well, Catherine, I just want to know if he's out of your system, I guess."

"I hate him. I hate the memory of him. I hate your asking about him. And, yes, as I said, he's been in the nightmares. He is the nightmare. He wants me dead. Anything else you need to know?"

"I guess not. I think I'll go. Thank you for showing me your house, Catherine." William gulped the last bit of coffee, placed his cup on the glass side table, and stood to leave. Catherine also got up, as did Dune. They walked William to the front door.

"What's next, William? How long do you plan to stay?"

"I could go back anytime, but I guess I'd like to know what you think."

She hesitated, and then admitted, "I think it would be nice to have you around for a while."

"All right. I'll be at my hotel for at least a few more days. I'll call tomorrow and we can decide what to do."

They said goodbye. William got into his car and backed down the drive very slowly. As soon as he was out of sight, Catherine called Gwen.

"So, Gwen, who do you suppose showed up on the beach this afternoon?"

"Not a clue, Kate. Who?"

"Not a clue, huh? You were the one who gave him my whereabouts."

"Really? William is there?"

"Yes."

"You're not mad, are you?"

"I guess not, but I wish you would have told me. I'm having a hard enough time without this kind of surprise. We went out for dinner, and now he's back at his hotel on the riverfront."

"How long is he staying?"

"I don't know. We may talk tomorrow. I don't know anything right now."

They said their goodbyes and retired to their respective beds for the night—one to her dreams, the other to a husband who seemed a stranger.

Chapter 44

Baby Steps

Gwen turned her back to Warren as she settled into bed. She thrust her left fist under her pillow, flung her right arm over her head, pulled her right knee almost up to her chin, and stretched her left leg out as far as it would go. Warren placed himself on the far end of the huge king-sized bed and also slept on his side. Neither said good night. This had been their routine ever since Gwen found out about Warren's deception. She often shed quiet tears over the waste of the past forty years, but she also shed tears over her inability to forgive. She desperately wanted something of Warren back in her life, but she didn't know what or how to get it. Months had passed, and their communication was still so terribly limited.

She had not found out who the mother of Warren's son was; she wanted to know, but she was afraid to. She had not asked, and he volunteered no information. *Just think, he could have been my son instead of hers*, she often mused. She'd found it intolerably difficult to deal with Tina's death and Catherine's subsequent grief because her own grief still weighed so heavily on her. Catherine could not have carried any of Gwen's misery with her; there was so much misery in her own life.

And, to add to the dilemma, Zachary's death was a complete mystery, especially since Catherine seemed totally immune to it. How did that make sense after all those years of waiting and yearning? After all those months together, doing the most absurd things? Old folks like them should not have behaved like a couple of unrestrained lovers, casino hoppers, and who knew what else. Gwen's life had turned around completely in the past year, and she felt she'd lost herself in the process. She tossed and turned in her bed, and finally got up.

When she got to her kitchen, she opened the fridge to take out the milk, but spied the bottle of white wine and decided to go for that instead. The row of dark maple cupboards across from the appliances shone with the reflection of the hall light. She took a large wine goblet out of a cabinet, filled it halfway, and took it into the living room where she dropped into the comfortable old recliner. She reached for her Cosmopolitan magazine, which she indulged in once or twice a year, and flipped it open. "How to Please Your Aging Man" was the first article. She thought she would barf. "How about my aging man pleasing me," she mumbled more loudly than intended.

Warren tripped down the last two steps coming from the bedroom when he heard his wife's comment. "What, Gwen?"

"Where did you come from?"

"What do you mean? Same place as you. Our bed. What are you doing down here talking to yourself?"

"I couldn't sleep. I thought I'd have a glass of wine and read my magazine for a while."

"Well, Gwen, since we're both awake, could we talk for a while?"

"Warren, I'm so tired of it all."

"So am I, Gwen. What can I do to make us whole again? I don't know what to do." Warren bent his head, held his face in his hands, and squeezed it as if to change it, as if a different look might help. "I was so afraid of losing you. I was so scared; I couldn't tell you. I was going to tell you after we were married, but I was still so afraid. I was afraid I'd lose you." Tears began to flow. "And now it looks like I have anyway," he sobbed.

"I'm not sure how this is all going to play out, but I don't think I want to start over without you at this late date. We're going to have to find a way through this mess of mistrust. I have to find a way to forgive you; you have to find a way to earn my trust."

"How? I don't know how," Warren whispered.

"Maybe we should consider counseling," Gwen offered, knowing it would take a long time and a lot of hard work to get back even a little of what they'd had.

"Yes, I guess we could try that." Warren would never have agreed to such a thing in the past, but the situation he had created left him no choice.

"All right then. Go back to bed, Warren. I'm going to finish my wine."

Warren lumbered back up the stairs and Gwen took a long swallow. It made her feel giddy almost immediately. She was not a drinker, but she enjoyed the feeling and took another. By the time she'd emptied the glass, she was feeling quite mellow and leaned back in the chair. Soon she was asleep. When Warren tiptoed down to check on her, he saw her sleeping peacefully and decided to leave well enough alone.

Chapter 45

Work

"Well, Dune." Catherine patted her companion's head as the dog slobbered puppy slime over her foot. "What should we do with William?" Dune jumped up and tried to climb into her lap. Catherine laughed and pushed the dog away. "You're too big, Dune. You can't sit on my lap, even though you're still a pup. Lie down." The big dog panted in her face and slowly backed down. Catherine went into her bedroom and patted the large dog bed she'd bought to let Dune know where she should lie down. She dropped a doggie bone on the bed to help Dune get comfortable. Then she changed, brushed her teeth vigorously, washed her face, and got into her own bed. She hoped to have an undisturbed night.

Her mind began to race as soon as she turned off the light. Thoughts careened around her brain. *What if William thinks I'm a murderer? What if Zachary succeeds in getting me killed? Why is William asking questions about Zach? How can Tina ask me to come to her? Why? Is there an afterlife? If so, does Zach have access to Tina there?*

After more than an hour of this, Catherine sat up in her bed. "I have to get a grip. I have to find some way to get my mind off myself," she said to no one, but Dune believed her new mistress was talking to her and bounded off her bed, took one great leap, and landed on Catherine, who let out a great yelp of surprise. "My, my, Dune, you're a huge comfort—and a huge pain. My legs feel like they're going to break. Move, you big lummox." With that, Catherine pushed her pet off her legs and to the side. "All right, then. Sleep there, next to me. I'm sure that'll keep both of us in better spirits." Dune snuggled in, and Catherine did likewise.

For the first time since she'd left Brigantine, she had an undisturbed night. When she woke up in the morning the bedcover was wet with drool, and Dune had slept with her head on Catherine's legs. Now she had to get the circulation back in them. But cramps and pins-and-needles felt better than fear and angst in the morning, so she patted Dune's head and thanked her for the comfort.

After coffee, Catherine went to the phone and searched for Phill's number. She pushed the buttons and waited for the rings to cease and the high pitched voice to answer.

"Hello."

"Phillis, it's Catherine. How are you?"

"Oh, hi, Kate. I'm fine. Yourself?"

"Great. I've been thinking about this volunteering business. I wonder if you could connect me with someone or somewhere that might be able to use my skills—tutoring or something."

"Yes. I'm so glad you've decided to do this, Kate. I think I have just the place for you. Let me look up the number."

Catherine could hear Phillis rummaging around and leafing through paper. Finally she came back. "Here it is. This is a rescue mission—a mentoring kind of service. They also work with young girls in trouble or without homes of their own; the parents are in jail or unfit. Most of the kids are in foster care. Most need help with basic skills, which is where you come in."

"Okay. What do I do?"

"I'll give you the number and the name of the best person to talk to. Just tell her I gave you her number, and use me as a reference. You'll have to go through some background checks and such, but as a teacher, you know about those things. Do you think you might want to work one-on-one with a troubled girl?"

"Yes, Phill, I think that would be just the thing right now. God knows I've done enough of that sort of thing in the past—all those years in public ed."

"Right, Kate. That's why I thought you might like this. I mentioned your name already, so they won't be surprised to hear from you. Don't worry though; I made no promises, only said you might want to volunteer someday."

"Yeah, people do like to mess in my life. Not that I don't appreciate this, Phill, but Gwen gave out my address, and an old friend has shown up and is kind of stalking me, and you tell total strangers I'd like to volunteer someday. You're all right, I know, and you all mean well. But I feel like...I don't know, like everyone thinks I'm helpless. I'm not, you know."

"Kate, if anyone is not helpless, it's you. I think everybody knows that. But you've been through some major trauma and a big move. We care about you and are trying to be your friends."

"Okay. Thanks for the help. Where do I go?" Phillis gave the information, and Catherine hung up with the appropriate thank yous. She decided to call the number before she could rethink the whole thing and back out.

Chapter 46

Angry Pair

"My name is Kashata. You don't look like somebody I'm going to like," the girl almost snarled at Catherine.

"You know, I don't think I'm going to like you either. So we're even. But you need help with reading, and I'm an expert reader, so I'm going to teach you."

"Maybe I don't want any help."

"Tough. You're going to get it."

When Catherine had first laid eyes on the African-American girl with the beautiful skin tone—almost amber—she sensed the hostility as though it oozed out of her pores. Catherine had received some information to help her understand her pupil.

Kashata was twelve, almost thirteen. She'd been terribly abused and neglected in early childhood, and in foster care since she was four. She knew little or nothing about her parents except that one was in jail; the other's whereabouts were unknown. Drugs and alcohol were major factors. She might have experienced sexual abuse in at least one of her foster homes; she'd been removed from two for suspicion. Catherine read her background and listened to the social worker before accepting this assignment, and she had no qualms. Hostile teens were not new to Catherine West-Cedar. She'd earned her stripes after forty years in the classroom.

When Catherine told Kashata she was going to help her no matter what, the girl had looked her in the eye and asked, "Why?"

"Because you need it, and I can give it. That's why."

So the tug-of-war began. Every Wednesday at four o'clock, Catherine was to meet with the reluctant Kashata. Her biggest challenge was to find the right material to get the girl's interest. After that it would be a piece of cake.

Kashata had been in eight different foster homes. Before that, who knew what she'd experienced. Catherine knew it would take a mountain of patience to crack the protective shell Kashata had built around herself.

When Catherine heard about Kashata, she decided to prepare. She had begun at her local book store, The Bookman, and picked up every teen-related magazine she could find. She also asked the clerk for any books the store carried that might interest teens or be part of teen reading lists. She bought bags full of materials. When she got home, she hauled her stuff inside. She laid out the magazines in alphabetical order beginning with *Blue Jean*, then *Cosmo Girl*, *Girl's Life*, *Odyssey*, *React*, *Seventeen*, *Teen Ink*, *Teen Magazine*, and *Teen People*. She'd also bought news magazines, including *Time*. She'd also purchased some Dr. Seuss and *Where the Wild Things Are*, just to get a feel for Kashata's reading level.

When it came to books, she scratched her head. Her English-teacher conscience drove her to her own cache. She added *Jane Eyre*, *David Copperfield*, *Oliver Twist*, the abridged *Les Misérables*, *Anna Karenina*, *Pride and Prejudice*, *Their Eyes Were Watching God*, and *To Kill a Mockingbird*, as well as the short stories of George Mac Donald, some fairy tales, and C.S. Lewis to her pile of books from the store. She wasn't sure about all of them, but she thought if she had enough variety,

Kashata would be able to browse and choose. So she'd also bought the Harry Potter series, the Lemony Snicket books, *A Little Princess, Black Beauty, Anne of Green Gables, A Wrinkle in Time, A Tree Grows in Brooklyn, Dicey's Song, Where the Red Fern Grows, Old Yeller*, and a few of S.E. Hinton's and Roald Dahl's books.

As she perused the great pile, for some reason she remembered the quote from Ecclesiastes that read, "of making many books there is no end." *Wow, that is certainly true*, she thought, and knew there were so many more Kashata could use. Then she went to her computer and ordered the Sunday edition of *The New York Times*. Now she felt ready. "Let the little shit come," she said aloud.

That same evening, she treated herself to a shrimp cocktail and a large bowl of potato salad. These were her favorites, and she knew if anything would go down, these two would. The fact that she had a new goal and friends also helped her mood.

While she got ready for bed, she turned on the television. The news, as usual, was filled with tragedy. Three teens had been in a serious crash which had killed two of them; all had been drinking. A jeweler and a customer had been shot in his store in broad daylight, right in Good Heavens, and no one had heard the weapon fire. The broadcaster mentioned how upset the town was that a murder could take place in such a fine community.

"Give me a break," Catherine muttered. She seldom read the front page of the newspaper or watched the news these days—too much violence and pain. But this evening she'd wanted a little diversion, and now she was sorry she'd turned the thing on.

Her nightmare was much more focused this time. It came directly from the news she'd watched, but still caused her enormous pain. Kashata and Tina were in the car, and been the two teens killed in the crash. Catherine was called to identify the bodies. The coroner lifted the sheet, and she screamed as she recognized the mangled bodies of the two beautiful young women.

She woke on the floor with a crash which sent Dune yelping into the kitchen. She sat up in a daze, sweat pouring from her armpits and under her breasts. Even her back was wet. The worst was flipping off the bed. She knew she could really have been hurt, and thanked whomever there might be that she was not.

She shook her head vigorously to get rid of the memory of the dream, slowly got herself to her feet, and limped into the kitchen. One leg had been bruised in the fall. Dune sat under the table, whimpering.

Chapter 47

Vulnerability

The following morning, tired and afraid, Catherine reacquainted herself with her doctor. She needed to talk; she needed a listener, and knew no one with whom she could discuss her dreams except her doctor. But she also buoyed herself up to be less vulnerable than she felt. She called as soon as she knew his office would be answering, and thankfully there had been an opening. Cancellations are wonderful for procrastinators who wait until the last minute, and this had been Catherine's habit. Even her stylists got used to her last minute demands.

"Well, Dr. Landman," she began, "I think you'll be proud of me." Catherine sat down in the big easy chair, folded her long legs under her, and smirked into his face.

"Why do you say that, Catherine?" he asked.

"I say that, doctor, because I've done a lot of good stuff."

"Do you care to talk about this?"

"You bet I do. I got a dog. Her name is Dune."

Doctor Landman nodded.

"Yes, and I reacquainted with an old friend from Brigantine. He's staying in town for me," she said, grinning.

"Okay."

"And I've begun working with a young girl who needs help learning to read."

Doctor Landman could see the pride on Catherine's face, commended her on her progress, and then inquired, "What about your dreams? Any more of those?"

"Well—" Catherine hesitated. She didn't want to admit to any more dreams; she wanted to be done with this doctor and with her dreams. She decided not to talk about the particularly violent one she'd had last night, but instead went back to a night earlier that week. "I did have a dream recently."

First she related the news story she'd seen on TV, and then described her dream. Doctor Landman took notes, nodded, and asked if there had been any more. Catherine wavered, and then asked, "What do you make of this last one?"

"The news made a deep impression on you. You're still grieving for your daughter. A new child has entered your life, and you must deal with her. It all comes together in your subconscious. Makes sense, don't you think?"

"Yeah, I guess it does."

"Is there more? Any other dreams or fears you haven't talked about yet?" he persisted.

"One." Catherine took a very deep breath and stared at Dr. Landman. She coughed, cleared her throat, said nothing, and stared.

She'd dreamed she was a little girl of five or six. She'd been asleep, and was suddenly awakened by a noise in her room. When she dared to open her eyes, a very tall figure was coming toward her from the darkest corner of the room. She remembered she'd always feared looking into that corner at night. She pulled her knees up under her chin, grabbed the blankets, and pulled them over her head. But she felt them snatched out of her hands and pulled off the bed. She was cold, and she shivered; she tried to scream, but could not make a sound. The figure was soon upon her, and she could smell Zachary's breath. He was so tremendously big and she so small, but when it happened, the awful thing little girls know nothing about, she felt the most searing, burning pain. Her legs were so wide apart the muscles hurt, and then she knew how much Tina had hurt. In the middle of the dream, in the middle of the assault, she knew she was dreaming, and she knew she felt what Tina had felt. Then, just as suddenly, the pain left and she felt a great rush of pleasure. Then she'd awakened to a vile and hateful disgust for herself. Catherine went to the bathroom to vomit, but nothing would leave her. How could she have dreamed such a thing? It was as though she'd betrayed her daughter all over again.

Now she was faced with the dilemma of how much to tell her doctor. She would not use names or let on that she'd known her attacker. She left Tina out except to say she believed that Tina might have had a similar experience a few months before her death. And that was the story she offered him.

He raised an eyebrow. "You never mentioned your daughter had been raped. Why not?"

"I've been in denial. I can't think about it."

"And you knew the rapist?" he asked.

"I never said that! Why in the world would you think that?" she hurled at him, utterly upset, hoping she had not given too much away.

"Your face, your hesitation, your voice, your hatred; they all suggest it, I'm afraid."

"Well, you can be as afraid as you like, but you're wrong. And I'm in much better shape now than I was a month ago. I have friends, I have a dog, and I have a purpose. So I don't think I'll be seeing you anymore." She delivered this little speech with mock confidence, hoping he would not see through this too.

"All right, Ms. Cedar, as you wish. But your dreams persist, so you might want to rethink this decision. Apparently there's something very important you're not telling me. Think about it."

"No. But I am a bit better. May I have that drawing you did of me now, please?"

"No, Ms. Cedar. I'm going to hang on to that a while longer."

"Please! It's by far the ugliest image of myself I've ever seen. Please let me have it," she pleaded.

"No, and I'm sorry you find it so disturbing. You may wish to think about that for a while. Be sure to call when you need me again. I'll be here." He stood up, put out his hand, and waited.

Catherine knew when she was bested. She got up, went to the door, and left without a word or acknowledging the offer of his hand.

Chapter 48

Plans

"Gwen?"

"Yes, Kate. What's up?" came the tired voice on the other end.

"You sound tired. No problems, I hope."

"Warren and I had a difficult night. We both found it hard to sleep, so we got up and started talking. I'll tell you about it sometime soon, but right now I'm too exhausted to think."

"Okay, Gwen. I just want you to know that I'm done with Doctor Landman and I've started working with a needy girl—teaching her to read." Catherine had to let Gwen know she was doing well; no need to say anything about the dreams. She hoped her new employment and William's friendship would help eradicate them from her nights, and so she'd called Gwen after her session with Dr. Landman to let her know there was no reason to worry about Kate anymore. "And, by the way," she continued, "everyone is invited to my place for Thanksgiving dinner."

Gwen didn't have the energy to pursue any of this, so said thanks and hung up.

Hmm. Kate wondered. *What was that about?* She was curious, but too caught up in her own fearful night to be as nosy as she normally would be. She hated being alone after such a dream; it kept coming back to her when she was not involved with someone else.

She called Dune to her, put on her leash, and took the dog outside, turning to close the sliders but not bothering to lock up. No one did, really; there was no need. Then she began her descent to the beach looking left and right to see if anyone was out. Then she released Dune to make her way to the beach, a flurry of red fur caught in the wind as the dog raced down the dune, back paws almost ahead of the front ones. Catherine was sure the dog would somersault the rest of the way, but Dune was sure-footed enough to keep her balance. Soon she was swimming in the cold, early-November waters of Lake Michigan.

The wind blew Catherine's hair into her eyes, and she squinted against the sun and wind. She wrapped her coat snugly around her and held it in place with both arms. *This is almost as good as the ocean*, she mused. How she loved rough weather, the big waves pounding the shore and wind whipping her hair, almost lifting her off her feet. Now she felt close to Brigantine, even though the whitecaps were not as high, nor the pounding as strong. She knew it was still a fearsome stretch of water in front of her, and this gave her great comfort. The joy and delight in her dog's romping in the wild waves and on the wet sand inspired her to feel some joy herself. What had she done without a dog all those years? The infectious fun Dune was having lived in Catherine's body too, and she ran down the beach against the wind, feeling the pleasure of the cold pressure. *This was a battle worth waging; me and the wind*, she thought. In this she felt one with her pet, who bounded out of the water to jump on Catherine and lick her face, leaving heavy globs of wet sand on her jacket. She was almost able to forget her dream of the night before. Almost.

It was about three in the afternoon when she and Dune finally got back to the house, and both were tired from the exhilarating romp.

Dune flopped on the rug in front of the sink, almost becoming one with the mat; Catherine sat in one of the leather Eames chairs and sucked in a great breath in an attempt to ward off the memory of the night. After ten minutes she got up, went to the sink, and filled her kettle with water for tea. When it whistled, she dropped a chamomile tea bag into a two-cup pot, filled it with the hot water, and got out her favorite mug. She had bought it at the Tate art museum in London years ago. She loved it because of the memories as well as its shape. She wrapped her hands around the warm cup after having poured her tea and carried it to her chair where she sat with her legs under her, looking out at the lake.

Kashata was due to arrive at four-thirty, so Catherine felt she could relax for a half-hour. Then she would prepare her lesson and set up the display of reading materials. Dune settled down, her drooling mouth on Catherine's feet. The one thing Catherine hated about her new friend was the slime, but she was trying to learn to tolerate it.

Chapter 49

A New Dilemma

When Kashata and her social worker knocked on the door, Catherine woke up with a start. "Oh, no, I fell asleep," she yelled. She shot out of her chair, upsetting Dune and tripping over the dog's hind legs. Luckily, she caught herself on the dining table so she didn't fall. When she arrived at the front door, she tried to straighten out her face and hair before opening it. But when she looked into the face of the girl standing before her, she wondered why she'd bothered.

Kashata's scowl was pronounced, and she oozed defiance. She was clad in dirty jeans with holes in both knees, which hung from her protruding hip bones. Her top had once been a t-shirt, but was now a raveled, very shortened version of its former self. The tiny pearl sticking out of the girl's navel was still covered with some of the blood produced by a recent piercing.

"Come in," she said with little conviction or warmth; both her startled awakening and the look of her student put her off. She offered a chair to Kashata and her escort, Mrs. Graham, a tall, heavy, but muscular woman with skin only a shade darker than Kashata's. She was dressed in a beautiful grey suit which hung so right and was so properly tailored that it might very well have come from a posh New York store—maybe even Prada. The contrast between the two made Kashata look younger and shabbier than she really was. Mrs. Graham—Catherine never knew her first name—crossed her long, shapely legs, folded her hands in her lap, and gave Catherine a good once-over.

"You look pretty capable," she said.

"Well," Catherine replied, "you look more than capable yourself."

Mrs. Graham smiled at this and told Kashata to pay attention to Mrs. Cedar.

"It's Ms. Cedar," Catherine corrected.

"Yes, well, Kashata would do well to pay attention nonetheless."

Catherine invited the girl to come into the dining room and take a seat at the table. She went to the pile of books and magazines placed on the floor, grabbed her very old version of an early elementary McGuffey's Reader, and sat next to Kashata as she opened the book to the first lesson. Kashata shot a look at the page and then at Catherine. "What kind of stupid pictures are these?" she inquired, pointing at one of the children dressed in clothing from the 1920s.

"Never mind the pictures; let's concentrate on the letters, on the words they make, and on the story they produce together."

Catherine began with sounds, and then progressed to combinations of sounds, and on to words and meanings. She wasn't sure how much Kashata already knew, so took it from the beginning. Kashata was initially appalled. "I know this kind of stuff," she yelled. But when it came to multisyllabic words and compound sentences, she was a little less sure of herself. Mrs. Graham sat quietly and listened.

This routine continued for a few sessions.

Catherine's efforts were met with displeasure and disdain at first, and then with reluctant interest. When, after three such meetings, Catherine placed some of the magazines out for Kashata's perusal, she saw real interest on the girl's face. Mrs. Graham was always in the background, making sounds of approval or disapproval, but Kashata paid no attention to her at all.

At the fourth tutorial, in the middle of the lesson, Kashata had stopped her work, looked defiantly at Catherine, and said, "I hate you."

Catherine, undaunted and without skipping a beat, answered, "Good. I hate you too. Now let's get on with what we're here for." When the lesson was over, Catherine looked the girl squarely in the face and offered a proposition. "Listen, Kashata, let's form a club. We'll call it 'The Mutual Hate Society.' It's just you and me. We agree to hate each other and never mention it again—we just know that about each other. What do you say?" She held out her hand to shake; Kashata spat into her hand and placed it firmly into Catherine's.

"Sounds like a plan to me, Cathy," she replied, her eyes gleaming with superiority.

Catherine removed her hand slowly. She wanted to wipe her right hand on Kashata's pants, but instead she put both her hands on Kashata's face, pushing her cheeks together to make her look fishy. "Never call me that again," she said very slowly. "Understand?"

Right behind them, Mrs. Graham said in an equally chilly voice, "And, Ms. Cedar, never do that again. Understand?"

Catherine laughed and said okay, but Kashata beamed. It seemed to Catherine that their relationship improved after that session. Kashata loved to spend the first ten minutes playing with Dune, who made an immediate friend of the girl, and ten minutes of each lesson paging through a magazine. She settled down to serious reading and discussion after that, and after six sessions in three weeks, asked to take one of the books home with her. She managed to read *Old Yeller* in a weekend. When Catherine quizzed her on the book, Kashata answered correctly and sensitively each time. Next, Catherine gave her *Black Beauty*. This time Catherine asked her to write a one-paragraph response to the novel. Kashata handed in the paper in a few seconds. It read, "Black beauty is about me. I am black beauty, 'cept I ain't dead yet."

Catherine had to fight back tears when she read these lines. There was a depth of understanding about the horse's plight that the girl had grasped in comparing it to herself. Catherine looked down at the paper and nodded her approval, murmuring, "Yes. Yes." Then she handed the paper back.

"Can I read *Jane Eyre* now?" Kashata inquired.

"I'm not sure you'll like it. It's about a poor orphan girl, and—"

"I know what it's about," Kashata interrupted. "I checked it on the Internet at school. I'm ready for it, don't you think, Teach?" This was the address of choice she used since the "Cathy" incident.

Kashata was advancing in leaps and bounds, and Catherine knew she was ready for that level of reading. She wondered if it might be a catharsis; after the girl's response to *Black Beauty*, she thought it might, so she offered it to her. Catherine was quite thrilled at the progress she had seen in her pupil. What a bright young woman she was. *Why hadn't she excelled before this?* Catherine wondered.

Chapter 50

William's Choice

"Yes, William. Everyone is coming here for Thanksgiving. Gwen, Warren, Doug, Kashata, Sam, Betty—and hopefully you."

"I really wasn't planning on staying quite so long, but since I only have to pay by the month, I guess I could extend my stay until December at least," William said, more to himself than to Catherine. He'd agreed to stay through October and had taken a winter rental near the lake—an old, refurbished cabin that could have done with a lot more updating, but it was available on very liberal terms, so William had taken it. He didn't care for the odor of mildew he noticed every time he entered the cabin, but somehow he didn't notice it after about ten minutes.

"Well, you've only been here for a few weeks, and we've only seen each other a few times. Do stay. Let's go out for dinner tonight. What do you say?"

"I say okay. Where shall we go?" William delighted in rekindling his friendship with Catherine.

"Let's find a dark bar and grill with a cozy booth and drink a lot of wine." Catherine felt better this day than she had in a long time. Kashata had been very good for her the last few weeks, and the dreams, although still gory, ghostly, or tempting her to suicide continued, she was better able to negotiate her way through her days than she had previously. She'd managed to regain a few lost pounds and wasn't gagging on her food as often. Good food was easier to swallow with good red wine, so she kept plenty of that on hand. And even Sam and Betty had become tolerable.

They'd found a lovely bar and grill that seemed to be just the place for them. The sign on the window read, "The Best Kept Secret in Good Heavens." They were in the mood for cozy and private, so they asked for a booth. The place had the most inviting, dark booths Catherine had yet seen in the small town. They parked themselves in one and smirked at their adolescent behavior. Then Catherine beamed. Finally, she felt something like her old self again.

They both ordered steaks, home fries, and salad. Catherine doused her steak with A-1 Steak Sauce in the hope it would go down easier. The bottle of Shiraz was perfect, and they ordered a second before the meal was finished. She knew she wouldn't be able to handle dessert, but she encouraged William to go ahead while she ordered coffee; he thrived on desserts.

After dinner, they decided to sit on Catherine's deck overlooking the beach and the lake and enjoy the autumn air. Neither cared about the time; neither had anything special to get early up for in the morning, and neither had had a solid night's sleep in a long time. They often put off going to bed. Sitting together on the deck, one might have taken them for comfortable old lovers, but they sat feet apart on the divan. Most people had put their summer things away by this time; in fact, most people had left the lake area and retreated back to their city homes for the winter. Catherine and the MacMurtles were the only ones left on their road, so she and William were quite alone, enjoying the coolness which had finally descended on the area. October had been unseasonably warm, but it seemed that November had restored the briskness Catherine had been looking forward to.

The sun had set long ago. The moon glimmered on the water, illuminating the horizon line; all else was black. The sound of the lake was not dissimilar to the sound of the surf at the shore, but it was weak in comparison. Still, it brought a kind of comfort to the desperate souls.

"Why don't you just stay here tonight? It's late and we don't have to think about you driving home alone in the dark," Catherine suggested.

William looked over at her. "If you give me another a glass of wine, I might be able to say yes," he responded.

"Sure. Coming right up." She jumped off the divan and slipped into her kitchen to retrieve a bottle of Yellow Tail Cabernet-Merlot, a corkscrew, and two large crystal stemware glasses. She handed the bottle to William, stood in front of him until the cork popped, and held the two glasses while he filled them. She handed one to him and reassumed her seat, cradling her glass in her hands. Nothing needed to be said. They enjoyed their wine and each other's company while listening to the roar of the lake. After about a half-hour, William broke the silence.

"I can't help but wonder, Catherine," he began. He turned to look at her, even though the darkness made it impossible for him to see her expression.

"What have you been wondering, William?" Catherine whispered.

"Well, don't get mad—but about Zachary. Did he have one of those injectors to use in case of an emergency? You know, an EpiPen."

"Why do you ask, William?" she inquired as objectively as she could.

"Well, most very allergic people carry them, and I wondered why Zachary had not alerted you if he had one. I don't know why, but sometimes I just wonder."

"Hmm," she murmured, and then laughed. "Yes, he did have one. Yes, he did tell me. No, I couldn't save him, because he told me too late and I couldn't find it."

"Ah. Of course."

"What do you mean, 'of course'?" She was getting irritated now.

"I mean, I can see that you might not have been able to locate it if he'd stored it in his room or something."

"Yeah, well, he did have it hidden. Remember, he didn't want anyone to know his weakness. Now can we just drop the subject?"

"I'm sorry I brought it up. Yes, let's drop it. Tell me about your pupil."

"Huh. It's funny, but we have what is a variation of the Mutual Admiration Society. Remember that song from the fifties?"

"I do."

"Well, we have a Mutual Hate Society. She told me she hated me, so I told her I hated her in return and we formed this pact so our feelings wouldn't get in the way of her studies. It seems to be working. She's very bright and seems eager to read."

"Sounds a little unusual, but coming from you, I'm not surprised. I admire your spontaneity and daring. Very creative, too. I'm sure the girl is very fond of you."

"I doubt it, but she is progressing nicely. Let's go to bed, William. Suddenly I feel exhausted."

"Me too."

They got up simultaneously and went into the house. Catherine locked the doors behind her, offered William some clean towels, and began turning off the lights.

"Excuse me, Catherine," William said in the semidarkness, "but where is my room?"

"Oh, that's right; you haven't been here that often. It's right down this little hallway."

As William turned to go to his room, he announced, "By the way, Catherine, I'll leave very early so I can shower and change at my place. Don't make breakfast or bother about anything for me."

"Right, William. Good night, then," she called after him. To herself she murmured, "You old prude."

"What did you say?" William called from the entrance to the guest bedroom.

"Nothing, William. Just good night." She hoped he really had not heard.

About three in the morning—the witching hour—Catherine heard the all too familiar voice.

"Come, Catherine. Come to me. You know you can't resist." When she heard these words, she looked into a dark corner of the room, which held an eerie light. From its depths, Zachary appeared with a noose in his hand. "Don't resist, Catherine. It's time. It's your turn." She tried to get out of bed, but a small, strong hand held her. She turned to look into Tina's tear-stained face. "Mommy, Mommy, Mommy," she cried, then swelled into a hideous likeness of Tina as a fifty-year-old or older whore with lipstick the color of long-dried blood smeared all over her mouth, and eyes covered with bright blue shadow and outlined with thick black lines. Her clothing was black but she was nearly naked. Her grip had become stronger, and now she dragged Catherine from the bed. "Okay, Zach. She's ready. I've got her." Zach grinned and came toward her with the noose. Catherine screamed, wrenched herself loose, and ran from the room, knocking into the door on her way to her living room. She collapsed on the sofa, somehow aware that they could not follow her out of her bedroom, although she didn't know why.

Then she felt another's hot breath and heard someone calling from far away. "Catherine, Catherine," the male voice said, but she couldn't open her eyes. Then the voice seemed nearer. "Catherine, wake up! Catherine!" She heard the last more clearly, and struggled again to open her eyes. She saw William, and a wave of relief came over her. She opened both her eyes and clutched at him.

"They were going to kill me. They were going to strangle me," she sobbed to him.

"Catherine, take a breath. Who was going to kill you?" The sound of his voice soothed her, and even in her turmoil, she wondered why.

"Zach and Tina. They're together now, and Tina is much older and they want me to join them so they can kill me," she rattled without taking a breath. Then she fell back on the sofa, exhausted. "Oh, William, what am I going to do?" she asked softly. "What am I going to do?"

"There's really only one thing you can do, Catherine."

"What? What is it?" She grabbed his shirt and twisted the front of it, as if she would never let him go. "Tell me!" she yelled in his face. "Tell me!"

"Confess," he said flatly.

"What?"

"Confess what you've done, then pray for forgiveness. You'll be freed from these dreams."

"Why? What have I done? I loved and lost. What is there to confess?"

"Catherine," William began, "really. You can't keep hanging on to your guilt like this. How did Zachary really die? Allergy, yes. But why did you use peanut butter? Confess, Catherine, or this will kill you."

"Oh, how do I do this? Okay, I planned the murder. I knew. I wanted him to pay. No one else was going to hold him responsible. Someone had to do it, so I did. For Tina. You understand, don't you, William?"

"No Catherine, I don't. It is not our place to wreak vengeance. I'm sure you know that, or you wouldn't be plagued by these nightmares. They're your salvation, you know. The nightmares are what will save you, what brought you to this point."

"Am I done now, you think? Do you forgive me?"

"I'm not the one. You have to go to the God whom you've offended."

"I don't know any god."

"Perhaps you should just bow to the ground as Raskolnikov had to do in *Crime and Punishment*. You've offended creation. The Creator will see you, whether you believe in him or not. Begin there."

"Will you go outside with me?"

"When you're ready."

"Now. While I have the nerve."

They walked down to the beach through the night, arm in arm. Dune, surprised, flashed past them with exuberant energy. At the bottom of the stairs, Catherine let go of William and kneeled, and then bent and lowered her head to the sand. "Forgive," she said. "Please forgive me."

She got up, wiped the sand from her face, and began to cry. "Do you think your God knows me, William?" she asked through her tears. "Will your God be able to forgive a murderer?"

"Catherine, my guess is He already has." He took her arm and steered her back up to the house. The phone was ringing when they got inside, and William answered it.

"This is Betty from next door. I saw lights and heard some commotion. Is everything all right with Catherine? She's not sick, is she?"

"No, Betty. She's better than she's been in a long time. Thanks for your concern, but Catherine is fine. Goodbye."

William poured each of them a glass of wine, and they sat quietly together in Catherine's living room, awaiting the morning light.

Chapter 51

Kashata's News

"I'm feeling really good today, Kashata, so tell me about your book."

It had been a week since the event with William. Catherine was doing a bit better each day, but knew she would not be able to forget her past just because she confessed. She would still have moments of doubt and guilt because she was human. William had warned her about this, but so far, so good.

"I can't tell you about the book because I didn't read it," Kashata announced.

"Oh? Would you like to talk about that?"

"You sound like a shrink, Ms. Cedar." Kashata had begun addressing Catherine with respect about two weeks earlier, and it felt like a milestone. Also, Mrs. Graham now left them alone together, and only appeared to drop Kashata off and pick her up again. But today, the social worker had come in with her, and Catherine knew something was up.

"Go ahead and tell her, Kashata," Mrs. Graham urged.

"I'm probably not going to be able to come here anymore," was all Kashata offered. She didn't look at Catherine, but kept her eyes glued to the floor, where one tear fell. Catherine raised an eyebrow, and then looked up at Mrs. Graham questioningly.

"Kashata is being removed from her present foster home; she'll be placed somewhere else. But very few foster homes are available right now, so placement out of the area is the only possibility."

"Oh, that's lousy. Why?"

"Because they hate me, that's why!" Kashata yelled into the floor.

"Ms. Cedar, Kashata's foster mother isn't sure she can deal with a teenager and the particular problems they have in the family right now. She's also lost her job, and has so far been unable to find another. Her husband walked out on her for good; her son is in college and doesn't come home much anymore, and she has a teenaged daughter of her own. She asked to have Kashata removed so she can concentrate on her problems and probably move from the area within the year. It's very sad, but that's the way it is."

"The system stinks," Kashata and Catherine said almost simultaneously. Kashata shot a surprised glance at Catherine, who began to laugh, and they laughed together at their mutual disdain. But they both knew the system was not the only problem; the difficulty was with people who could not or would not commit to long-term parenting. There were many who did, Mrs. Graham emphasized, but Kashata had not yet had many.

Catherine shook her head, and then shook it again. She couldn't believe the thought that had just dropped into her mind.

"You know, Thanksgiving is next week, Mrs. Graham. Kashata is planning to be here. How are we going to work that out? Do you think the system would be able to approve me as a viable foster parent in a very short period of time?"

"I was hoping you'd suggest that. In fact, I've already looked into the possibility, and I can pull some strings. In fact, I've already set the ball rolling. Thank you, Ms. Cedar. We'll be back as soon as we get everything in proper legal order. Someone from my department will come by to inspect your house and perhaps ask some questions. Will you be home tomorrow?"

"Wait a minute, Mrs. Graham," Catherine cautioned, putting up her hand.

Kashata saw this and, without blinking, yelled, "See! I told you she wouldn't go for it. She's backing out already!"

"Wait a minute. I was going to ask Kashata if she wants to stay with me," Catherine said very firmly.

"Oh." Kashata was visibly embarrassed. "Oh," she repeated. "Yeah, I guess so."

"All right, then. Let's get things in motion." Catherine beamed at the girl.

Mrs. Graham took Catherine's hand, shook it so hard that Catherine winced, and thanked her profusely. Then she put her arm around Kashata's shoulder and escorted her out the door. "I'll start reading a new book right away, Ms. Cedar," Kashata called over her shoulder.

When Kashata was in the car with her headphones on, already moving to the beat of the music, Catherine called Mrs. Graham back to the steps. "Yes, what is it?" she asked.

"I just was wondering," Catherine began, and then hesitated. "I was wondering if...well...I was wondering if Kashata could be adopted. If she's legally free from her parents, I mean."

"Are you serious? You want to adopt Kashata? Why?"

"I thought, for a brief moment, that if she's going to live with me anyway, I might as well be her legal guardian. I might as well give her a total commitment—something she's never had, as I understand it. I might as well be her mother; someone she can call mother for the rest of her life, if she wants to. The first part of her life hasn't been so hot, and I think the rest should offer her the opportunity to make it. She'll have a home she can come to." Catherine hesitated. "I can love her, you know" she whispered to Mrs. Graham.

"Yes, I'd hoped that was what I was observing. She is free; her father gave up his rights years ago and is still in prison." Catherine flinched slightly. *He's not the only one*, she thought. "Her mother sold her for a fix when Kashie was four, and that's when the state stepped in. Luckily for her, a neighbor called us in after having witnessed her being sold. But I must warn you, there will be problems. Kashata may never allow you to get close to her; she'll have serious attachment issues, as all such children do. They've learned not to trust anyone."

"What a rotten life. Poor kid. I'd like to give her a bit of what she should have had all her life. I will not renege nor turn her out. Ever."

"I believe you, Ms. Cedar. We need more people like you. Think it over for a couple of days. If you're still sure, it can and will be done, and soon. Trust me." She shook Catherine's hand again, and then they were gone.

Catherine went into the house, raking her hands through her hair. She dropped into her recliner and said aloud, "What have I done? What have I done?" Then she grinned from ear to ear. "Look what I'm going to do!" she yelled into her living room.

She sat for a while, contemplating her decision. She knew it was impulsive, but she also knew it was necessary. This girl had been thrown away too often. She knew there would be tremendous issues and problems to deal with, and that maybe Kashata had been damaged beyond repair in some ways. Yet Catherine knew she could be strong enough to support the girl.

Her only worry was herself. What if she had one of those horrible nightmares while Kashata was in the house? How would she be able to explain? And, even more seriously, she thought that perhaps a murderer had no right to raising a child, even one already in her teens. What kind of role model would she be? But if Zach were still around, she would always worry about him raping another young woman, and no one would believe her if she told what she knew about him—not without proof, not without Tina. So she must have done the right thing. Surely she was fit to help Kashata; she'd asked for forgiveness, after all.

These troubling thoughts coursed through her mind for the remainder of the afternoon. She sat for hours thinking about all the ramifications, all the possibilities. She got up twice to fill her wine glass. She watched the sunset, and looked off into the darkness that followed. Finally, at nine o'clock, she went to the phone.

Gwen had just said goodbye to her son when the phone rang again. "Hello, Kate. I'm glad you called."

"Damn that caller ID, Gwen. I'm never ready to be that quickly identified when I call."

"I'm sorry, Kate, but it does offer a tremendous benefit if I don't want to talk to someone."

"How many times have you done that to me, I wonder?"

"Never. I'm glad you called because I just got off the phone with Doug, and he's coming for Thanksgiving. So we'll all be there." Gwen sounded positively happy.

"Good. That's not why I called, however. I have some news. But first, how are you and Warren doing? I keep thinking about you, hoping it'll somehow work out."

"Thanks, Kate. We had a really long talk, and we're seeing a counselor. I've forgiven him for his lies—at least in my head. My heart can't seem to do it yet. I look at him sometimes and I see the old Warren. Sometimes I write down the good memories as they come—all the really wonderful times, and how I miss them. I want that back.

"But other times I look at him, and all I can see is the deception, the huge betrayal, and I hate his face. But the good memories are beginning to win, I think. So we're on our way back in some fashion.

"I'm sorry; I'm just talking and talking. Thank you for asking about us. What's your news?"

"I'm going to adopt Kashata" Catherine blurted into the phone, unable to contain her excitement.

"What? Are you out of your mind? You said she hated you." Gwen was incredulous. What was her crazy sister thinking?

"Well, that's just a way she has of protecting herself from being hurt by another adult. We agree that she'd like to live with me, so that's the first step. She's being kicked out of her present foster home again! She needs to know there can be permanency, and I'm going to try to give her that. Am I nuts?" She hoped Gwen would affirm her decision; she knew she would need her support.

"Yes, you are, but you're right. Are you sure you're up to it? This is for life, you know. I know you know that, but I worry about you and your nightmares."

"I know. Of course, I've thought of all that. William has been a great help, and I haven't had a dream for about a week. Anyway, I wanted you to know." Catherine stood with her fingers crossed, waiting for the response she hoped for from her sister. It came.

"I'm sure you'll be a wonderful mother to her, Kate. Let me know when and if I can help. Congratulations. I hope it happens soon."

Catherine was thrilled. "Thanks, Gwen. Thank you so much."

Chapter 52

What If?

"No, Zach, I am not coming," she said in her sleep that night. "I'm never coming. Leave me." When her dream apparition had gone, she slept soundly. She awoke feeling more refreshed than she had in months, and she was hungry.

She called Sam and Betty to invite herself to their daily restaurant breakfast. She showered and dressed, and then went to her living room and opened the drawer in the Chinese black lacquered cabinet to remove a fifty. She felt it only fair to treat her neighbors this morning. Feeling good felt really good.

They ate at a little place near the riverfront called The Pavilion. There were three booths along one side of the room, four or five tables on the other side, and two bar tables with stools in the center. Betty directed them to one of the tall tables, announcing that this was their usual spot. Catherine would have much preferred a booth.

The place only had one window in the front, so it was relatively dark, even on this bright, sunny November morning. The unusual weather delighted everyone. Michigan has never been known as predominantly sunny; it's considered the grey-sky state. But the sun reflected Catherine's mood. She ordered eggs, bacon, potatoes, and toast, as well as juice and coffee. When she poured what seemed like half a bottle of ketchup over her potatoes, Sam and Betty watched openmouthed. They only had ever seen Catherine pick at her food, make excuses for her lack of appetite, and eat extremely small portions of whatever was on her plate. Now she dug in like a truck driver at a greasy spoon after hauling a load for twelve hours straight.

When she finished, she wiped her mouth, asked for more coffee, and then opened the conversation with, "You're probably wondering why I invited myself this morning." She looked at her friends, who seemed to be all ears. "Well, the real reason I'm here..." She paused to see their reaction. So many people had experienced the scam which seemed like a social evening, but which turned into a sales pitch for a pyramid-scheme home-products company, that Catherine thought she would try it out on Sam and Betty. They didn't bite; they just smiled and waited. Catherine chuckled. "One reason," she continued, "is because we need to talk about Thanksgiving Day plans at my house. I hope you'll be able to come."

"Oh, yes, let's. What shall I bring? I love to bake. How about a few pies?" Betty offered enthusiastically.

"Yes, her pies are the greatest. I like to make garlic mashed potatoes. Shall I make a batch of those?" Sam volunteered.

"Both sound absolutely delicious and will be very welcome," Catherine said graciously. "But the real reason I want to talk to you is because I've also invited a young girl. She's thirteen years old and will be the only person of that age there. It could be very difficult for her, but I thought if everyone is prepared and makes a special effort to include her on her own level it would be very helpful."

"Is this the girl you've been teaching reading to?" Betty queried. "She looks to be a very nice young lady. And drop dead gorgeous, I might add!"

"I'll say. Sure, we'll be happy to meet her and share a great meal with her. How many are coming?" Sam wanted to know. He wanted to be sure he made too many potatoes so he could take some home. Sam loved that dish.

"About seven or eight, no more than that," Catherine said after counting silently on her fingers. "And I guess I might as well tell you that Kashata is going to be living with me. Her present foster parents can't keep her, so she'll also be your neighbor."

Sam and Betty smiled through mouthfuls of eggs and bacon and nodded their approval. When breakfast was over, Sam offered Catherine congratulations on her decision, and Betty promised to be nearby to help if Catherine needed her. They'd turned out to be real neighbors.

Things moved along extremely rapidly. Catherine's house was inspected, as well as her person—looked over, questioned, considered as to age, health, and mental stability. Dr. Landman had not been consulted; no one had mentioned Catherine's visits with him. Mrs. Graham assured Catherine that all was going well, but was progressing rapidly because Kashata needed a new and permanent home as soon as possible. Also, the agency was desperate to get her off the books. The home study was done as soon as Catherine had mentioned her willingness not only to foster, but to adopt. Catherine suspected the latter was probably more the case than the former. She couldn't blame them; they were so overloaded with serious cases.

The one thing that stumped Catherine was the requirement to secure an alternate legal guardian for Kashata if anything happened to her. She was not sure she would be able to do this. She considered William, but dismissed him in favor of a woman. She thought of Phillis, but dismissed her, too, in favor of someone a little less zealous. She knew she wasn't being fair to Phillis, who had proven her value to Catherine in the past few months, but she couldn't feel otherwise. So she called Gwen.

Chapter 53

The Announcement

Thanksgiving Day arrived along with a ton of snow. Catherine's guests had a time trying to get up her steep drive. Snow-clearing equipment was not out yet, and neither were salt trucks. The summery weather had persisted until early November, so the sudden and radical change caught everyone off guard. "This feels more like Christmas than Thanksgiving!" Kashata exclaimed when she looked out over the lake in the early morning. Catherine cradled her coffee mug and groaned. Not that she didn't love snow; she did but, like everyone else, she wasn't prepared. She hoped William's Prius would be up to the task.

Catherine stood next to Kashata, looking out over the pristine whiteness of the beach, and smiled. How could one not smile at the beauty of the freshness, the purity of the falling snow dropping into the water like little stars. It was as though a thick cloud of glory had come to cleanse the earth of its summer humidity. Narnia must have been as glorious to the eyes of the children when they'd first entered. Kashata's eyes glittered at the spectacle she was observing. The first days of snow are always magic.

Catherine put her arm around Kashata's shoulder and whispered,

"Today we tell them about your adoption. We'll make an announcement right before dessert. What do you say?"

"Gwen already knows, doesn't she?" Kashata asked.

"She does, but not the others. We'll make it a celebration, yes?" Catherine looked down and saw a question in her eyes.

"What?" she asked. "What's wrong? Why do you look like that?"

"Nothing. I'm just excited about everything, that's all," Kashata answered.

After a few minutes, she cleared her throat to get Catherine's attention. "Do we still have The Mutual Hate Society?"

"I don't know. What do you think?"

"Well, do you still hate me?" Kashata wanted to know.

Catherine shrugged, and then let out a short laugh. "I never hated you. Those were just words to even things out with you."

"Oh. I probably don't hate you anymore, either."

"Good," Catherine answered. "Let's get the cooking started." She pulled out pans and ingredients; utensils for stirring, pouring, cutting, and basting; and then the bird, which had been sitting in the refrigerator since Tuesday. There were squash to cut and boil, sweet potatoes to bake, and a rutabaga to peel, cube, and boil. And there was stuffing to make. Kashata got out onions, celery, walnuts, apples, bread crumbs, rice, and chicken broth. She began to chop while Catherine lathered olive oil and butter onto and into the bird. Pots were filled with boiling water, casseroles were filled with vegetables, and salt, pepper, sugar, brown sugar, cinnamon, and all kinds of wonderful fresh herbs were put out to be added to the proper dishes at just the right times. Cranberries and orange zest had been cooked the night before, along with sugar and chopped nuts. One JELL-O mold with pineapple stood in the refrigerator so Midwestern taste buds would not be disappointed. The guests were expected at two, and Catherine planned to prepare and put the hors d'oeuvres out at the last minute. The shrimp cocktails waited proudly in white and red succulence beside the very tightly covered JELL-O, although Catherine really couldn't have cared less if the stuff tasted fishy. Still, these people were her guests.

Then, out of the blue, Kashata announced, "Oh, by the way, I'm pregnant."

A rutabaga dropped into the sink with a thud, and a spray of blood followed, making the thing look like a small severed head. Catherine screamed. Kashata, thinking the scream was a response to her announcement, sat on the floor, yelled, "I knew you would hate me for this!" and bawled her eyes out. Catherine tied a washcloth around her cut finger and bent down to comfort Kashata. "I screamed because I cut myself," she said quietly. "I do not hate you, and I want to know more about what you just said. Let's sit and talk." With this Catherine gently led the girl to a chair.

"Tell me again. What did you say?" Catherine asked.

Kashata wiped the tears from her eyes and cheeks, and blew her nose in the tissue Catherine had given her. She looked so terribly vulnerable that Catherine almost embraced her as she would have a small child. She knew Kashata might well refuse that kind of embrace, so she held herself in check. The girl began, "I think I'm pregnant."

"I don't mean to be simple here, but why do you think that?" Catherine did her best to keep her voice calm and very gentle. She knew she was walking on thin ice when it came to Kashata, and especially now, if this were true.

"I missed my period last week. I never miss," she almost wailed.

"Yes? Anything else?"

"You won't kick me out if I tell?"

"Kashata," Catherine said, "I've made up my mind. I've made a promise. You will never get kicked out again. Never out of my home, no matter what. Do you understand? Never."

"Not even with a baby?"

"Not even. Now tell me how you know you're pregnant."

"I haven't had my period. I never miss. Not since I started. Never," Kashata said in a kind of moan.

"Will you tell me who the father is, or what circumstances put you in this situation?" Catherine almost whispered, her face close to Kashata's. She knew how sensitive this conversation was.

"No, no. It was just a boy I thought I liked. He came home from college with my foster brother one weekend. It was nothing, and I never thought it would end up like this. Other times it never did. It was only one time with him."

Other times? Catherine felt weak. This was a wrinkle—no, a deep crease—she had not anticipated. Her Thanksgiving happiness was over; now she had a teenager and an infant to consider. How could she deal with this? She knew she was dealing with a severely traumatized child; she'd been told about Kashata's earlier abuse. But she had not even thought this possible when she promised a permanent home. She needed to think, but there was no time. She couldn't go back on her promise; Kashata would never have a chance at life if she sent her off now. And the baby? No, that was not possible.

"Kashata," she began, "we need to do some serious talking about this and the options that are available to us, but right now we need to fix dinner. People are coming and we won't let them know anything is amiss. Can we do that?"

Kashata nodded, wiped the tears from her eyes again, blew her nose one more time, and straightened up. "I'll cut the vegetables," she said, and got up to begin her chores. She washed her hands and face. Her sniffling continued, but Catherine knew she should not embrace this girl. For now, her support would be mostly verbal and physical presence.

The two scraped and cut, peeled, mixed, stuffed, boiled, baked, chopped, sliced and poured until it looked like they would have a wonderful dinner in spite of the earlier upset. The kitchen smelled festive.

The phone rang; Catherine wiped her hands and ran to answer it.

"Hi, Kate. I just wanted to call and wish you a very happy Thanksgiving." Phillis sounded happy. Catherine was glad to hear her old friend's voice.

"Why, thank you, Phill. You've been on my mind for the last couple of days. What are you two doing today?" Catherine had intended to call Phillis for days, but had totally forgotten in the excitement of preparing to become a mother again.

"We're going to a fancy-schmancy restaurant. I made the reservation over a month ago because it's so very chic, and only the very chic go there," Phillis responded.

"Oh yeah? Going into town? Well, why don't you call the place and tell them you've had a better offer. I'd love to have you come here. I've got a wonderful meal cooking and, if you're lucky, there might be leftovers to take home. I'll don my best outfit and be more chic than your very chic."

Phillis laughed. "Catherine, I didn't call to wangle an invitation. Really."

Catherine harumphed into the phone and said sarcastically, "I know that, Phill. Just come."

"I'll ask Roger if he'd like to do that. Hold on."

Catherine held the phone while she heard muted conversation in the background. Then Phillis was back. "We'd love to come. What time is best?"

"We eat at three o'clock sharp. Hors d'oeuvres and libations at two."

"We'll be there, thank you. Catherine, what can I bring?"

"Your sweet self and your man," was the reply, and Catherine hung up. "Well, that makes two more for dinner," she said to Kashata, "but it looks like we'll have enough to feed ten more." Kashata managed a slight grin and continued her chores. Dune had ensconced herself right under Kashata's feet, anticipating dropped food. *The Crumbs on the Table* were a reality for the big dog.

Chapter 54

Feast

At a little before two o'clock, they began to come. Gwen and Warren showed up first; they lived the greatest distance away and so left early in case traffic or snow should slow them down. This had not been the case, so they were about a half-hour early. Gwen went right into the kitchen to help. Catherine had her arrange the hors d'oeuvres, and Warren began uncorking wine bottles. When she finished, Gwen went to Kashata and began helping her empty bags of chips, jars of salsa, and containers of dip into the little bowls set out for them by Catherine. Soda bottles, a water pitcher, ice, and glasses came next. All the while, Gwen chatted amiably with Kashata about nothing in particular but everything in general—from the weather to school subjects to clothes.

Catherine prepared the shrimp cocktails and shot a glance across the kitchen at Gwen and Kashata from time to time. She knew who her choice for guardian would be. Her former jealousy of Gwen's relationship with Tina surfaced for a moment, but diminished with the realization that Kashata needed as much love and human commitment as she could get. She was not going to deny her this burgeoning relationship with her new aunt. She swallowed her pride as she threw another shrimp into the bowl.

Just as Kashata was pulling the sweet potatoes from the oven, the doorbell rang. Sam and Betty rushed into the kitchen, followed by Catherine. "Wow, what a smell!" Betty observed. "Heavenly," Sam added, setting his bottle of white Zinfandel on the table next to the shrimp, after which he proudly lifted his garlic mashed potatoes above his head and placed them on the counter. There was no room left for the two pies Betty was carrying, so Catherine placed them in a cupboard for later.

Catherine urged them to help themselves to drinks and hors d'oeuvres. They filled plates and proceeded to the living room, where Gwen had gone to entertain them. She introduced herself and began a lively conversation with the MacMurtles about lake living, and Catherine realized that she had more than one reason to be a bit envious of her sister. Small talk with strangers had always been extremely difficult for her. Gwen simply introduced herself, asked a few questions, and before long she had the newcomers engaged in good conversation. Warren also admired Gwen's gift for this.

Soon the others came. Catherine encouraged each new arrival to partake of the sumptuous appetizer buffet and invited them to find a seat in the living room, where extra chairs had been placed the evening before. Catherine, as hostess, made the introductions. "This is Gwen, my sister, her husband Warren, and their son, Doug; William, a friend from Brigantine; Phillis Ver Hage, my friend from high school, and her husband Roger. These are my next door neighbors, Sam and Betty MacMurtle. And last but best, this is Kashata, soon to be my legal daughter." Kashata blushed and withdrew to the shadows. She'd thought she'd be introduced at dessert and was caught off guard. Everyone turned to look at the girl with undisguised surprise. Gwen smiled and clapped, infecting the rest, who soon joined in.

Catherine looked at Kashata, who was looking down at the floor. She rescued her by asking Kashata to help her begin bringing the entrees to the table. Gwen quickly got up to help with the serving, and the rest took their cue and moved to the dining room.

Place cards had been set out, so the guests found their seats easily. All the vegetables, condiments, stuffing, and serving pieces were brought to the table, followed by Catherine carrying an enormous platter with an equally enormous browned bird, which she set in the middle of the rest of the food. She'd seen to it that the table would be large enough to hold everything by purchasing a huge piece of plywood to fit over the regular tabletop a week ago.

There they'd all gathered—the couple who delighted in knowing everything about everyone and imposing on another's space when least expected; the woman who was trying to come to grips with a deceiving husband; the elderly man who had erotic dreams about his hostess, to his embarrassment; the damaged child carrying a child; the pious Christian bitten by someone who had seemed to have gotten it all wrong, with her new husband beside her; and the nephew who knew nothing yet of his half brother. They held hands in Thanksgiving communion. The hostess, the murderer, asked William to say a prayer.

"Our Father in Heaven," he began, "thank You for this wonderful day, and for each of the people You have gathered together at this table. Look into our hearts and lives to help us as You see need. We praise you for the bounty you have bestowed on us today. We ask Your blessing on this food and on the hands that have prepared it. Grant us grace in all the days You have allotted us. Bless Your holy Name. For Jesus' sake, in whose name we pray. Amen." A subdued "Amen" echoed from some of the others.

Catherine pulled the turkey platter to her, picked up the great knife and fork, plunged them into the bird, and began to carve. The lake roared and swirled in the rising wind of the late November day, and Catherine's guests swelled into happy conversation, laughed at one another's stories, and filled themselves with food and wine.

Dune placed herself behind William after Catherine had commanded her to lie down, and soon inched herself forward to reach a piece of food William had dropped. She used her forelegs to move slowly in any direction where the smallest crumb might fall to the floor. She too hoped to fill herself under the lavishly laid table. Of course, there were those who had taken note of the dog and dropped morsels to the floor on purpose, just to experience the Dune's thankful delight.

When the pies— apple, pumpkin, and coconut custard—came out, no one had room. William got up to take a walk on the deck, and was followed by Warren. The men stood looking out over the now-turbulent water, enjoying the chill after a sumptuous meal which had made them very warm. Others retreated to bathrooms, and still others relaxed by tipping back chairs and engaging in superficial, idle conversation. Doug turned on the TV to watch a game, knowing his father would soon join him. Kashata ran to the small half-bath and vomited, hoping no one had heard her.

A few hours later, back at the table, the guests treated themselves to coffee, tea, more wine, and a slice or two of pie. Some indulged in three slices—it was Thanksgiving, after all, and the pies were so gorgeous. During dessert Catherine explained the decision she and Kashata had made about legal adoption but didn't elaborate. She wanted to spare her soon-to-be daughter from having to deal with painful details.

Soon the guests began to leave, all with small leftover packages Catherine had made for them. Gwen and Warren said their goodbyes, complimented Catherine on a wonderful meal and great company, and departed. The Ver Hages left next, with a sincere thank-you for having invited them. "So much warmer than a restaurant," Phillis commented, and Roger heartily agreed. "So nice to have met you and all your friends, Catherine—or shall I say Kate." Catherine thought Roger a pretty decent guy. Good for Phillis. Todd Strom had not suited her at all.

Catherine looked into the dining room and saw William and the

MacMurtles in deep conversation. She hoped it would end soon so Sam and Betty would go home. When the conversation finally came to a close, Betty ran into the kitchen with stacked plates. "I'd love to stay and help with the cleanup," she announced as she began to rinse the plates she'd deposited on the counter, but Catherine said she'd have none of it. Betty began to protest when William entered the kitchen behind her, put on a recently discarded apron he found lying on the kitchen floor, and announced that this was the one thing he and Catherine had always done together. Betty smiled, put down the plates, and told Sam that they should be going.

Kashata asked Catherine if it would be all right to take Dune out to the beach for a walk. She put on some boots and a heavy old coat with a hood. The girl and dog ran down the steps and onto the snow-laden beach with great energy, leaving William and Catherine to do the dishes, clear away the leftovers, and talk.

Chapter 55

William Has Plans, Too

"You know, Catherine," William began as he placed the turkey platter on the counter, "I like it here on the lake. It's a lot like the ocean in many ways. I'd like to stay and renew our friendship—if you can see your way clear to doing that."

"What exactly do you have in mind, William?" she asked. She didn't look his way because she felt the old wariness creep into her stomach and chest.

"The old cabin I've rented has an option to buy. It's old and small, but very adequate for my needs. I thought I might buy it. I'll keep my place in Pennsylvania so I'd be able to spend time there as well."

"What do you want from me, William?" Catherine felt easier after what he'd just said; he probably had no commitment in mind.

"Just your opinion and your friendship," William replied, sensing Catherine's tension.

"I haven't seen your place, William, but I'd love to. And you know I'll be your friend, just like in Brigantine—if that's what you're asking."

"No more than that," he replied. When they'd finished the dishes, William retrieved his coat and said, "Perhaps you could stop by tomorrow morning. I'll have coffee and we can look the place over. What do you think?"

"I have to check with Kashata first. I'll give you a call." With that, William thanked her for the delightful meal and left.

Catherine went out to the deck to see what her dog and soon-to-be daughter were doing, calling their names. The wind blew the words back into her face; neither responded. She put her thumb and index finger in her mouth and whistled so loudly that it could have been heard in Chicago. At that, the dog and child immediately turned their heads, looking up to see Catherine motioning for them to come back. Dune took off in a flash, her red coat flying in the wind as she rushed to obey her mistress. Catherine reveled in the sight of this beautiful creature's joy as she tore up the dune, tail straight out in her hasty pursuit of obedience. Kashata lumbered more than walked up the dune, at least forty steps behind the dog. Dune thumped her tail against the wooden rail as both she and Catherine anticipated Kashata's arrival.

Chapter 56

A Baby Wrinkle

It was early evening, and the sun was setting. The brilliant orange-and-pink sky behind the amber and black beauty of the girl presented a scene that brought tears to Catherine's eyes. Her tears came easily these days, but they were joyful and in response to a beauty had eluded Catherine for a long time. Now she silently thanked whatever god there might be for this surprise happiness.

Her involvement with Kashata's needs minimized her nightmares and anxieties. Her grief had given way, in part, to concern for another person. The nightmares in which Tina beckoned to her, crying as a small child, standing by her bed, were almost a thing of the past, but she still dominated too much of Catherine's sleep. Zach seemed to be gone for good, but the empty wound Tina had left was still pretty raw. But even Kashata could not put Tina to rest, and Catherine believed no one and nothing ever would do that.

Now she turned to the girl, smiled, and ushered both Dune and Kashata into the house, hurrying to shut out a cold blast of wind. It was warm and redolent with the smell of the recent feast, guests, and the heat from the fireplace. Coziness oozed through Catherine's body, as well as a feeling of satisfaction. Kashata shed her wrap, letting it fall onto the kitchen floor. Dune took the opportunity to fetch it and carry it off to the bedroom, where she proceeded to roll around on it until chewing it made more sense.

"Do you really want Dune to eat that jacket?" Catherine asked without reprimand.

"I don't care," Kashata shrugged.

"All right then. We'll just call it a special canine Thanksgiving indulgence." Catherine laughed at the sheer insanity of it, yet they allowed the dog the pleasure of tearing the jacket to shreds. They sat down at the kitchen table, and Kashata shot a glance into the bedroom where her jacket was being pulverized.

"I hate that jacket," Kashata confided. "My last fosters bought it for me at the Salvation Army store. Cost them all of two bucks."

"You know what, Kashata? Tomorrow is a big sale day. I think we'll go to the mall and buy you a proper jacket. I'd love to see you in leather. What do you think?"

"Are you serious? Yeah, I think so!" she replied, laughing.

"Okay. Tomorrow morning we go to William's place, and then we have lunch out and shop. How does that sound?"

"We have to go to that old man's place?" Kashata questioned.

Catherine suddenly paled as Tina came crashing into her memory. "Old man" was Tina's exact phrase for William before she'd become his friend. *What did this portend?* Catherine wondered. She worked to get hold of her emotions and continued.

"Before we call it a day, we have something we need to discuss, right?"

Kashata nodded and fidgeted in her chair. "I guess," she murmured.

Catherine knew this would not be easy, but she forged on in the hope Kashata would be wise enough to take good advice. "Kashata," she began, "about this pregnancy. We need to make some decisions.

First, we have to find out if there is a pregnancy, and then we have to decide what to do about it."

"What do you mean?" Kashata asked, wary of the intimation in Catherine's words.

"Well, first we have to decide if you're going to have this baby or not."

"Of course I'm going to have the baby. I'm pregnant. If you're pregnant, you have a baby, don't you?" Kashata shot back.

Catherine felt the tension, but forged ahead anyway. "You know, Kashata, there are ways to keep from having a baby, especially for someone as young as you. Maybe you'd like to speak to a counselor about the options. I could take you to Planned Parenthood."

"Do you mean...? No, I will not murder my baby! That's what you mean, isn't it?" Kashata suddenly went out of control. Her face was red, and her fury launched her from her chair and sent her into her room with a powerful, crashing slamming of her door. Dune jumped three feet in the air, and then hid under the dining room table, whining.

Catherine grabbed the edge of the table to steady herself. She cringed at the thought of Kashata having an abortion, and self-doubt immediately descended on her. *What if I really am a murderer at heart?* she wondered, and then shook her head vigorously to expunge the thought. Kashata's reaction was a surprise; Catherine had not known nor anticipated this side of her daughter-to-be. She waited, struggling for self-control. When she felt strong again, she went to Kashata's door and knocked.

"May I come in, Kashata?" she asked quietly through the closed door which her ear was pinned to in an attempt to hear what the girl might be doing. Catherine heard nothing. She waited, and then called one more time. "Kashata, please let me in so we can talk about this."

"You want to talk about murder?" was the response.

"No, I want to talk about you and your future." With this, Catherine opened the door. She saw the child lying prone on the bed, her face buried in the pillow. The small room didn't yet have any personal touches which revealed its occupant; its walls still wore the somber beige that was there when Catherine had bought the house. Very neutral, but not especially happy. The bed cover was white down, and it too begged for some color. Even the small wicker dresser and nightstand were white. Very nice, very clean—very nondescript. The only color in the room came from the window dressing, which was a simple green sheer hanging from ceiling to floor.

Catherine approached the bed, sat down, and placed a hesitant hand on Kashata's head in the attempt to quiet the volatile spirit within. She lifted her head to look at Catherine, who said, "I'm sorry, Kashie. I had no idea how you felt. I didn't mean to be so insensitive."

"I let my temper fly, didn't I?" Kashata admitted with an impish grin on her face. Catherine realized that she really didn't understand this girl—one minute rage, the next almost joking.

"Dune almost jumped to the ceiling," Catherine said without a smile.

"Sorry. But I am going to have and keep this baby. She's a gift from God," Kashata apprised Catherine.

"Really? From God? You believe in God?" Catherine was amused. "What has God ever done for you?" The memory of a scene from *Crime and Punishment* invaded her thoughts. If Kashata answered "everything," Catherine was sure her mind would explode. She tensed at the idea.

But Kashata surprised her.

"I'm here," she nearly sang at Catherine, her smile dissipating Catherine's automatic aversion to anything smacking of god. "And I've got you." Kashata jumped from the bed and twirled and danced around the room. "And now I'll have a child of my own. How good does it get?"

"Well," Catherine answered, "that depends on how you look at it."

"I look at it as a gift from God," Kashata responded. "I love my baby. I do!"

"Kashata, sit down here on the bed, beside me. We really need to talk about this."

Kashata sat as requested, folded her hands in her lap, and asked, "Are you thinking of throwing me and my baby out?"

"No, but you're thirteen years old. You're still a child, and you're carrying a child. This is a problem."

"I don't think so. I'll be fourteen before she's born, anyway. If I were Jewish, I'd be an adult by now."

"Kashata." Catherine tried to appeal to the girl's sense of logic. "Listen. You are not Jewish and you are not an adult yet. For the sake of your child, wouldn't it be better if she or he had a stable home with a mother and father who would love the child and be able to care for him or her properly?"

"What do you mean? I love her. Her father doesn't know, so he doesn't matter anyway. I don't know what you mean."

Catherine knew she had to tread lightly now. She focused for a minute on the room, but was really staring at nothing. Her gaze took in the light green curtains, the beige walls, and the bed, but her eyes didn't register the details; they were turned inward. She saw a future filled with two children—one in diapers the other in jeans and a backpack heading off to school. She saw and feared a loss of her personal freedom. She saw the possibility of a new beginning. She wondered about her own strength and competence to take on this much in her sixties. But she saw and felt love, amazed and aghast by what she saw and knew.

"Kashata," she began again, "what I meant was that you could love your child so much that you would give it up for adoption to a wonderful family, one who needs a child just like yours to love and raise. That's what I meant."

"No! She's mine! She's a part of me! She'll look like me. Nobody else I know looks like me. Nobody else is like me. No! Please don't make me." Kashata was pleading and yelling at the same time as huge tears rolled down her cheeks, and there was a kind of threat in her voice that Catherine didn't like. So Catherine finally said what she'd known she'd say all along.

"My child, I will be your mother, and I will be your baby's grandmother. I'll take care of both of you for as long as you need me. Don't cry anymore," she finished, putting her hand on Kashata's shoulder. The girl's cries turned to a whimper and then she smiled.

"You will?" she whispered as she turned a tear-stained baby-face to Catherine.

"As long as I possibly can, I will. I promise. However, if we are to be a family, we need to be able to trust each other. You won't tell who the father is, so how do I know this won't happen again?"

Kashata shot Catherine a look of pain. She lowered her head and quietly said, "Because I'll be living with you. Then it can't happen again."

"Oh my god," Catherine whispered. "Oh my god, you poor child."

"Yeah, well, at least I'll have my own daughter. At least that."

"Yes. At least," Catherine sighed. Then she enfolded the child in her arms, and they sat like that for a few minutes. "Now let's get some sleep so we can see William and shop tomorrow. I need to think this all out too, Kashata. And you must not tell anyone about this yet. First we get a confirmation from the doctor, then I adopt you, and then maybe we'll tell others. Okay?"

What a Thanksgiving this has been, Catherine thought as she settled into her chair. Then, once she was sure Kashata was asleep, she picked up the phone and took it into the living room, as far from Kashata's room as the small house would allow. She dialed a number, hoping she was not disturbing anyone so late.

Chapter 57

Commitment

Gwen was tired after the huge dinner and two-hour drive home. She wanted nothing more than to brew a nice cup of tea, watch a half-hour of *House Hunters*, and go to bed. Warren expressed the same sentiment, so he put the water on while Gwen got out of her clothes and into her nightgown and robe. Her warm, fur-lined slippers helped her find the right level of relaxation, and she sighed with satisfaction as she lowered herself onto the overstuffed yellow-and-green-striped sofa. Warren changed too, and came to sit beside her. He took her hand in his and brought up the right channel. It was just ten o'clock; the show would begin any minute. Then the kettle whistled, and Warren got up to make the tea as Gwen filled a tray. They again settled down together. It had been a good Thanksgiving Day.

The house to be hunted this evening was in the Detroit suburbs. The housing market had grown a bit soft, so the young couple on TV was anticipating getting a lot for their money. Gwen loved watching the house hunters walk through the homes and make comments, and since the show was taking place in Detroit, she was doubly interested. But just then, the phone rang. "Shall we let it go?" Warren asked. "Let the machine get it?" When it did, Gwen heard her sister's voice.

"Hey, Gwen. I know you're there. Please pick up." The demanding voice grated on Warren, who told Gwen to ignore it. She didn't; she knew Catherine too well to ignore that tone of voice. Catherine would call in the middle of the night if she felt like it. Gwen gave Warren a look and reached for the phone.

"All right, Kate. What is it?"

"I'm working to get this adoption done posthaste, but I need something from you."

Gwen's heart thumped. She'd anticipated this, but worried about Warren's response. "Okay, Kate, let's have it," she responded.

"I know this isn't the way to do this, but I don't have a lot of time. I need someone to take care of Kashata if anything should happen to me. I need you, if you agree, to sign a document stating that."

"You're asking a lot, Kate. I need to discuss it with Warren, of course. We aren't young anymore either, you know. Will the agency accept us?"

"Of course! I was accepted, wasn't I?"

Gwen had known this was coming, but now felt uneasy about the possibility. But she knew that she would not be able to refuse taking care of this new niece, should that possibility arise. How to get it past Warren was her greatest concern.

"Kate, I need to talk to Warren. Can I let you know tomorrow?"

"Yes, Gwen, but I want the thing completed by Christmas. The social worker said it could be done, but we need to expedite all the requirements. Hey, I bet Warren thinks he owes you big time and will agree in a minute." Catherine neglected mentioning the possibility of a second child. One thing at a time, she thought.

"Well, don't be too sure. And I don't think that would be a good way to go; it sounds too much like blackmail. But we'll see. I'll call you tomorrow."

Gwen didn't want to confront Warren with this information and this request after a long day and right before bed. She hung up and returned to the living room, where she sat down to watch what was left of the show. Warren sat in his big lounge chair, enjoying a last beer, and asked, "Who was that?"

"Oh, just Kate. Wanted to know if we arrived home safely."

"Really? What else?"

"Not much. Just some stuff about Kashata."

"Like what?"

Gwen didn't want to tell him, but felt pushed. "Not much. Just about the adoption requirements and stuff."

"Uh-huh. I like that girl. Do you think Kate would want us to be legal guardians? I'd love to do that, you know."

Gwen's jaw dropped. "Really?" she replied, her face disclosing her surprise by one eyebrow raised almost an inch higher than the other.

"Yes. Why that look? We can act as godparents and be available if the need ever arises. You think I'm not capable of that?" He considered his wife's disbelief and knew it was not ill founded. He wanted desperately to be happy with her again, and he also felt Kashata's need. He would also like to be a kind of father figure to her. He wasn't sure why he felt that way, but he did. "Look, Gwen, let's pray about it and talk it over."

"Of course. Yes, of course."

They spent another hour discussing the ramifications of this possible major change in their lives. Warren explained his feelings and convictions about Kashata, and Gwen nodded in agreement. She too had felt a strong pull to the girl. She was glad Kate had made the decision to adopt, and was thrilled that Warren had taken the stand he had. They prayed quietly for guidance and strength and then went to bed, anticipating telling Kate their decision in the morning.

Chapter 58

Aches

Catherine got up early the day after the big feast. She wanted to get everything put away and in order before waking Kashata and getting ready to visit William. After she bent to put the serving platter away, she felt a dull pain in her back as she began to stand. She'd felt it a few times before during the last couple of weeks, but chalked it up to age. After all, she was no youngster, and some aches and pains were to be expected. She felt pretty lucky; she had always been exceptionally healthy. She rubbed the area of discomfort as she straightened up the rest of the way, made a pot of coffee, and started for Kashata's room. Before she could get there, Dune bounded out and almost knocked Catherine over. The big dog had made her permanent sleeping quarters next to Kashata's bed; the two had become nearly inseparable. Kashata followed Dune, but with a lot less exuberance. Catherine smiled and said good morning; Kashata only smiled. She took one look at the kitchen and commented on the work Catherine had already done.

"I had some help from William," Catherine answered.

"Oh, yeah. The old man did stay a while."

"Must you always refer to him as 'the old man'?"

"I don't must, but I do rather. Did you ever take a close look at him? That man is old!" Kashata pronounced, laughing. Then she said, "Just joking. Just joking. Can I have some coffee?"

"Coming up. Go sit."

The older woman and the girl sat quietly in the sunroom overlooking the now-frozen beach, each cradling a mug of hot coffee. Dune wagged her tail and settled herself with an audible thump under Kashata's chair. The sun peeked out, promising a lovely late fall day, but was soon overpowered by great, grey clouds. "So much for sunshine." Catherine mused.

Kashata shot her a glance and jumped from her chair, almost overturning her coffee cup, and ran to the bathroom. Dune followed, seeming to sense the urgency. Kashata retched and vomited until the coffee and more were gone, and then flushed it away, turned to the sink to clean her mouth, and grimaced at the discomfort. *It must be worth it,* she told herself.

Catherine set out some crackers, soft-boiled eggs, and a fresh pot of coffee. She also made a small pot of herbal tea to help Kashata's morning sickness. Then she rubbed her aching back and sat awaiting the emergence of the child and dog from the bathroom.

"If I even look at food, I'm going to be sick again," Kashata wailed as she considered the table. Dune anticipated a nice snack from Kashata's generous hand, and so settled under the table and waited. Catherine insisted Kashata eat some crackers, which would settle her stomach. The tea would help, too. Kashata frowned but acquiesced, eating a few saltines and swallowing a cup of the tea. Then she picked up one of the soft-boiled eggs and began to peel.

Catherine looked on with amusement, wondering what had changed the girl's mind about eating. When Kashata deftly slipped the egg under the table into Dune's open, waiting mouth, Catherine sighed, "Must you feed that dog all the time? She's going to be as big as a house if you keep this up." Kashata shrugged and popped another cracker into her mouth. She stared at Catherine as she popped the other egg under the table. *This is just a very small taste of what's to come*, Catherine thought. This child and her child were going to take Catherine's energy and patience beyond her accustomed limits, she was sure. She took a deep breath, as if to buck up for this future storm. Tina had been so easy to raise, but this girl was no Tina.

They took Lake Shore Drive to get to William's house. Catherine kept her eyes open for the pink mailbox William had told her to find. While driving the scenic route, Kashata said, "I want to go to church on Sunday."

"Oh?" Catherine replied. "Where did that come from?"

"I've been thinking about it for a long time," Kashata said, "and it's time. I need to go to church."

"What for?" Catherine asked.

"I want to pray. I want to sing," was the quiet response.

"Why? Can't you do that without going to church?"

"No. I want to do it with God's people. To worship Him."

She said it in such a way that Catherine knew the pronoun was a capital *H*.

"I see. You trust this god of yours, then?"

"He's almost the only one I trust, besides my other mother."

"Which other mother do you trust?"

"Used to trust. She's the one who taught me about God and about Jesus. And she loved me, too."

Catherine felt a pinch of disappointment at this. She'd held a faint hope...but she knew better. It was too soon anyway, she told herself. "Why didn't this person keep you, then?" Catherine asked, almost afraid but feeling the need to know.

"She would have, but she died. And her husband wasn't a Christian, so…"

"I'm so sorry, Kashata. Maybe I can make up for your loss in some small way. Maybe just a little."

"Yeah, whatever."

"Listen, William likes to go to church. Maybe he'll take you sometime. We can ask."

"If you're going to be a real mom, why won't you go with me?" Kashata shot a look at Catherine that pierced her heart. What should she say now?

"You know what, Kashata? Maybe I will—sometime. I'm not ready yet. I have to have some time to think about this religion stuff. Maybe soon; we'll see. But William—"

Kashata interrupted. "The usual."

"What do you mean by that?"

"You know, the brush-off. No church with you."

"That's not fair, Kashata. I'm working on it; I'm just not ready yet. You don't want me to be a hypocrite, do you?"

Kashata shrugged. She said no more, and soon they were heading up the long, steep drive to William's little cabin. *What a view*, Catherine thought, *but what a drive in winter!* William anticipated their arrival and was already at the door. It had turned very cold, and he shivered as he opened the door. He noticed for the first time how much older Catherine was than the child-woman, as he perceived Kashata to be.

"Nice little dive," Catherine said as she quickly took in the interior. "Lots of potential, I'd say. And your view! To die for, as they say." The lake lay before them, swirling its wintery waves onto the beach which was already covered with a light dusting of snow. The sun had just come out, and it sent long shadows from the dune growth across the white beach. Catherine was mesmerized by the spectacular sight. *This is not the ocean*, she thought, *but it certainly holds its own charm.* She turned when she heard Kashata address William.

"Miss Catherine said you would take me to church," the girl stated.

"Will you?"

William turned to Catherine with a bewildered expression. Catherine was not looking at him, but at Kashata. "Miss Catherine?" she said. "Where and when did 'miss' enter the scene?"

"I have to call you something if we're going to be adopted. I can't call you mom, and I can't call you Catherine, out of respect, so I thought 'miss' sounded pretty good. I've been thinking about it for a while."

"Have you?" Catherine responded, probably sounding a little more sarcastic than she intended.

William quickly interjected, "It sounds like a good compromise to me," at which Catherine turned on him, her expression stating that it was none of his business. She squelched the urge to voice her thought, swallowed hard, and said, "Yes, well, it'll do for now. And perhaps William would like to answer the question about going to church."

"Catherine," he began. He paused to look at Kashata, and then continued. "It might be more comfortable for Kashata to go with Phillis. What do you think?"

"Ah! I never thought of her. Kashata, what do you think? Want to try Phillis?"

"Whatever." After a long pause she added, "I guess that would be okay for now."

Having tentatively settled that question, William and Catherine sat down to coffee and discussed the possibilities of his new place. Kashata declined coffee, opting instead to get Dune to run on the beach with her. Dune had become a regular companion, even riding along wherever they went.

After a half-hour on the beach, Kashata opened the back door to let herself and the wet dog in. Dune shook herself vigorously, knocking over a small table and spraying sand, snow, and water over everything else. Catherine was ready to shout, but William quickly interposed, saying, "Well, you two seem to have had a great time. What fun to experience the joy of this place, plus the exuberance of youth through the activity of these two young creatures!" Kashata laughed more at Dune than at William's comment, although it did a lot to dispel Catherine's obvious disfavor.

"Let's shop, Miss Catherine," Kashata said, and shot out the door with Dune in tow.

Catherine looked at William. "What have I gotten myself into?"

"I'd say you've gotten yourself into a wonderful new adventure, Catherine. I just hope I can be a little tiny part of it." He laughed; she raised an eyebrow and then smiled.

"I'll keep that in mind. I promised Kashata a new leather jacket, so I'd better get moving. Nice place, William. You'll love it here, I'm sure." With that she put on her coat and walked out the front door.

"Yes," William said to himself. "I wonder what my role will be this time."

Chapter 59

Back to Square One

"I thought Zach was gone for good, and then last night he was back. I almost let him take me with him."

"What do you mean, Ms. Cedar?" Dr. Landman chewed the end of his pencil as he studied the anguish on Catherine's face.

"Well, since I've had Kashata at my house and William back in my life, I haven't had so many nightmares. Tina visits from time to time, but not in a disturbing way. She hasn't asked me to join her, for example, in a long time. Then last night, after I'd had a particularly good day, he came again. I was really tired and fell right to sleep. Then I heard him call me. 'Westie' he said, three or four times, until I answered. I asked him what he wanted. He stared into my eyes and sort of hypnotized me, I think. He told me he wanted me to go with him, to go down to the lake. I remember getting up and putting a long sweater on. I filled the pockets with stones and a large ceramic vase I broke into little pieces. It seemed to weigh enough—"

"You get this idea from Virginia Wolf?" Dr. Landman interrupted.

Catherine shot him a look of despair. "I don't know; it was just part of the dream. I felt a desperate need to be done with all the guilt and horror, so I went down the stairs to the beach. Zachary was on the beach and kept beckoning me, laughing and urging me on. 'We'll be together forever,' he kept saying, laughing. He led me down to the water, which was cold and swirling and very black. I kept walking; I was mesmerized. He didn't go into the water—he hovered above it, but kept leading me. I went in. I felt nothing, not even wet. I kept walking until I heard my name called from some very far away place, but I instantly knew it was a safer voice than Zach's. The voice kept calling, and then I woke up and found myself waist deep in the coldest water I've ever known. I began to cry uncontrollably. I remember turning and seeing a figure on my deck, yelling at me to come up. So I called out,   Don't worry, honey, I'm on my way,' and then yelled, 'Tina, is that you? Have you been sent to save your mom?' But the girl was not Tina, of course. It was Kashata.

"Dr. Landman, I never wanted her to know about my nightmares, but now she does. What am I going to do? What if it happens again? What if Zach wins the next time?" Catherine was beside herself with the fear of her own death. She was exhausted from telling her story and having had another horrible night, and she was terribly nervous about Kashata's involvement. She called Dr. Landman's office before six in the morning, demanding to see him. Now she lay back in the large chair wailing to him to help her.

"Ms. Cedar," he began, "I can give you some pills to help you sleep, and I can give you others to calm your thoughts and nerves, but I cannot help you with Zachary. I don't know what your problem concerning him is, but I know you haven't told me all I need to know. What are you hiding?"

Catherine fought her angst. Her doctor obviously sensed her turmoil, her desperate attempt to hide the truth, but she could never tell him—she knew that much. He'd probably surmised it. So she said, "He was an idol of mine. For forty years I obsessed about him, at Tina's expense. I had to find a way to let him go, that's all. And now, in death, he won't leave me alone."

"Ms. Cedar, as you say, this man is dead. He can't do anything to you. You are the problem. 'The fault, dear Brutus, is not in our stars, but in ourselves.' It can't be more clearly stated than that."

"I see. Well, I guess I'll go." She got up, took her coat and marched out, slamming the door behind her. Then she realized she might need some of the pills he'd mentioned, and abruptly reentered the office. "Sorry about that," she said. "I'm really not myself today. Do you think I could still get some of the pills you mentioned?"

"Ms. Cedar, you are enough to make any doctor swear. I've already written out your prescriptions. Take them." He handed her a couple of slips of paper. She took them, embarrassed, and thanked him. Then she turned again to the door. Before she left, he said, "if you'd like, I could meet Kashata and have a talk with her. That's up to you, of course." She nodded and left.

Chapter 60

Church

Phillis was surprised by Catherine's request. "Of course we'll take the child to church," she said.

"Good. What time shall I drop her off?" Catherine was very brusque, but Phillis assumed Kashata might already have become a bit of a burden, so she asked no questions.

"The service begins at eleven; bring her by about ten-thirty or so. I'll try to introduce her to some people her own age."

"Thanks, Phillis. I'll pick her up around twelve-thirty?"

"Fine, Catherine. Are you all right?" Phillis heard an edge in Catherine's voice and hoped it was not something to do with Kashata.

"Yes, why?"

"Nothing, really. I thought I heard a little edge in your voice."

"Yeah, well, Phillis, I didn't sleep well last night, so I guess I'm a little tired. I'll take a nap later, and then I'm sure I'll be fine. Thanks for agreeing to take Kashata on Sunday. It means a lot to her to go to church, it seems."

"I'm glad to do it. I'm glad she's a believer. It'll help a lot."

"Yes, so you say. Later, then." Catherine hung up.

Phillis mused, *Maybe it will help you a lot, too,* and went back to her morning baking.

Catherine was satisfied with the progress she'd made that morning. She was again beginning to feel a little like her old self. Now all she had to do was convince Kashata there was nothing wrong. Sleepwalking was natural for some people and, for Catherine, this was only the second time in her life it had happened. With the pills and the help of her doctor, Catherine could assure Kashata she would be all right.

Catherine went over to Sam and Betty's to retrieve her daughter and her dog. Both were seated in the kitchen, one by the table the other under it. "Thanks so much for giving Kashata and Dune some breakfast. I had to see the doctor.

"Kashie, are you all right?" she queried. Kashata shot her an indulgent look and responded with, "You all right?"

"I'm fine. We'll talk about it when we get home. Are you ready?"

"Why don't you stay for a cup of coffee, Catherine? Don't need to hurry away, do you?" Betty asked. "Your family is quite comfortable. Look at Dune enjoying that rawhide under the table. What a precious animal. Our dog, Cubby, died a year ago. We still miss him. Won't you sit for a few minutes?"

Catherine acquiesced and sat down next to Kashata. She thought it best not to argue and not to run off too soon. She wanted Kashata to feel everything was all right after the previous night's debacle.

Betty poured Catherine a cup of fresh coffee. Sam walked in from wherever he'd been and took a mug for himself before he sat down at the table. He looked at the faces of the three women. "Would you girls prefer to be alone?" he inquired. No one answered, so he shrugged and settled back in his chair.

"I hope everything went well at the doctor," Betty said. "I hope it wasn't anything serious." Catherine knew Betty wanted to know every detail. She wasn't about to let her know what kind of doctor Geoff

Landman was.

"Yes, Betty, thank you for asking. I got a prescription, and all is well." Catherine took another sip of her coffee, peering over the rim at Kashata. The child was handing half a cookie under the table to Dune, who would soon be as big as a brick outhouse, Catherine was sure.

Betty regaled them all with stories of her important acquaintances in town; Sam smiled and nodded in agreement from time to time. Finally, Catherine interrupted.

"Thanks for everything, both of you, really, but we must be on our way. C'mon, Kashie. Get your dog and go home."

Kashata's time with Catherine had been short. So far, there had been school and adult companionship. She enjoyed her new home, the beach, the dog, and her own private room. But she wanted friends, too. At least she would not have to start in a new school; she was especially thankful for that. Her life had been one move after another, one set of family members after another. There had been only one person who'd truly loved her, and others who had tolerated her, used her for money, or abused her. She knew what men were after, and trusted not a single one.

Her physical beauty was her curse. She'd discovered early on that many of her so-called mothers took her in for the money, so she'd lost trust in them as well. Today she was happy with her new black leather jacket, but she had a lump in her stomach regarding Catherine. What in the world had all that been about last night? And what doctor had she run to so early this morning? It all seemed terribly fishy to Kashata that Saturday morning in late November.

Chapter 61

The Shrink

When they got home, Catherine asked Kashata to sit down, and they did so together, looking out over the water. It seemed a lot less threatening in the bright daylight but, even so, Catherine shivered for a moment at the sight of it. "I have some explaining to do," she began. "I guess I really frightened you. I really frightened myself, Kashie," she said with a little laugh. She wondered what Kashata was thinking; there was no response from the girl. Catherine forged on. "You may as well know the truth. The doctor I went to see this morning is a psychiatrist."

Kashata looked at Catherine and squinted. "You see a shrink?" she asked.

"I do, ever since my daughter died. I needed help with the nightmares I've been having. The thing is, since you came into my life, I haven't had any at all. I dream about my daughter, of course, but no nightmares and no sleepwalking—until last night."

"Why last night, all of a sudden?"

"I don't know, Kash. I don't know."

"Was it your daughter? Does she want you to die?"

"No, no, it wasn't my daughter. It was someone else, someone

I used to know. Someone else was out there calling me to die. Someone very evil."

"How come you knew somebody that evil?"

"I didn't know how evil he was until a short time before he died. And I thought the nightmares were gone. But last night was one of the worst, because I could not force myself to wake up."

"You woke up because I called you?"

"I think so. I heard you in the distance."

"If I hadn't been there, would you have drowned, do you think?"

"I don't know. I don't want to think that way."

"Hah!" Kashata almost shouted. "You know what that's called? It's providence. That's what it was, providence!"

"What? What the hell is providence?"

"Hey."

"I'm sorry. Kashie, I'm working really hard on changing and being what you need me to be. Now tell me what you mean by providence."

"It means God took care of it for us. It means He's in charge, always."

"Uh-huh. Well, I went to my doctor, and we talked about it. He gave me some medicine to help me sleep and keep the nightmares away, so we should be fine now. Oh, by the way, I've made arrangements for you to go to church tomorrow with Phillis Ver Hage and her husband. She said she would introduce you to some young people there. How does that sound?"

"Lily-white, I guess."

Catherine laughed. "I don't think so. She doesn't go to church in town; she goes to a big church a few miles north. A very diverse crowd attends there."

Kashata agreed to try it. She was sure it had been God's doing to awaken her and lead her out to the deck in the middle of the night. And she knew she needed and wanted to be with other people who believed what she did. She doubted she'd make any real friends, but she would give it a try.

Then Catherine brought up what Kashata didn't want to hear. "Listen, dear. We need to work on getting the adoption done very soon so we can take you to a doctor and see you safely through this pregnancy."

"I wish I could do this alone," she murmured. "I hate doctors. I don't trust them."

"Why? They're there to help," Catherine tried to assure her.

"I won't go if it's a man." As far as she was concerned, no man would ever touch her again.

"Ah. We'll find a woman then. Will that make you more comfortable?"

"I guess. I just hope God will turn out to look more like a woman than a man when I finally see Him." Catherine had no response to this.

That Saturday ended on a much better note than it had begun. Kashata asked another girl she knew from school to walk on the beach with her. Catherine had a long talk with William, who was always ready to come for a cup of whatever she had. Dune wore off his extra Thanksgiving calories running and playing with the girls, and a promise had been made by Mrs. Graham to do everything in her power to get the adoption expedited—maybe even before Christmas. Gwen's call accepting her and Warren's role as legal guardians had been a great comfort to Catherine, and would certainly help in court.

In the early evening, Kashata and her friend Jolene had lain side by side on Kashata's bed and gone through the magazines Catherine always ordered. They giggled and laughed, oohed and aahed at the fashions and the models, but especially the young rock stars. The favored group right now, they both agreed, would have to be the Jonas Brothers. Jolene thought Kevin was really hot, even though he was the oldest. She loved his sexy mop of dark, curly hair. Kashata realized she enjoyed looking, but still felt very squeamish at the thought of physical contact.

Catherine had not intended to listen, but the house afforded little privacy, so she could easily hear most of the girls' chatter. It delighted her. Her cottage had begun to take on the sound of a home.

Before she went to bed, after driving Jolene home, she took her sleeping pill and prayed for undisturbed sleep. She was never sure to whom she prayed, but some kind of mental activity asking for whatever she needed was becoming a habit.

Chapter 62

Church and Guilt

While Kashata was at church with the Ver Hages, Catherine took the opportunity to take a long walk on the beach with Dune. The chill air caressed her face, the only part of her body left uncovered. Her vigorous pace was easily matched by the big dog, who found it most welcoming and strange to be out on the beach with Catherine instead of Kashata. Dune kept in step with her, continually looking up into her face to detect any change or new command. The two were in perfect harmony. Catherine walked to think, while Dune walked to enjoy her life.

Catherine had made her commitment; she had given her word. She knew how it felt for someone to go back on a promise. She thought about that pain, and what it would do to this girl she had embraced. Suddenly all her years of waiting for Zach to come back flooded her brain. She shook her head vigorously to empty it of him, but without success. Betrayal, brutality, death, remorse, grief and guilt. Great guilt.

Guilt and grief stopped her in her tracks and forced her eyes out to the water. Her tears flowed as full and heavy as the waves slapping the beach. Dune sat quietly at her feet, waiting for the storm to pass. Catherine thought about her troubles and rued the years wasted on empty hope, on a broken idol. She felt hatred, but it was not directed at Zach. She loathed herself, she loathed her years, she loathed her lack of understanding Tina. She wanted nothing more than to walk into the lake until the water joined her tears and covered her head. Dune licked her leg, reminding her of another.

As she came back to reality, she was reminded of her talks with people who had come through excruciating times. She finally understood why Dr. Landman had asked her to listen to them. If they could go on, if they found goodness after pain, maybe she could, too. Kashata was the answer. And yes, even with all her issues, she was worth it. And then the baby. How would she cope? One thing was certain; she would not have time to feel sorry for herself.

The sky suddenly opened, and rain poured down, drenching Catherine and the dog in seconds. The wind had also picked up. The sound of the fury whistled around Catherine's head and whispered in her ears, sounding like "Murder! Murder! Murder! You murderer!" The wind howled the message through her hair, into her skull, and deep into her brain until she ran to elude it. Dune raced ahead of her, up the stairs to the safety of the deck, and sat wagging her tail in anticipation of Catherine's arrival. She ran blindly to the steps and recognized them only by chance. Her terror of herself and her fear of her own guilt drove her up the stairs and out of the rain. The wind followed her into the house until she closed the slider. She fell into a chair and wept with fear and exhaustion. Dune continued her consolation, licking the limp hand that hung over the arm of the chair.

Catherine was asleep when Kashata came home.

"Hey, Miss Catherine, wake up!" She poked Catherine's arm to awaken her, and she sat up with a start. She looked at Kashata as if she had never seen her before, and then shook the agitation out of her head and tried to smile. Kashata was so excited that she didn't even notice the empty look, the still-wet hair, or the crooked smile.

"Guess what!" she exclaimed. "The church is great. It's really big, and they have drums and guitars and a sound system that's awesome. Two black girls sang gospel, and a whole group of kids sang praise songs. Then I went to a youth group that met in a kind of a coffee shop. They had chili dogs and pop and all kinds of things. It was so sweet. I can't wait to go again. Phillis even said she would take me to the Wednesday evening get-together anytime I want. Can I go?"

Catherine had time to pull herself together while Kashata went on about her church experience. As she came out of her stupor, she realized that were it not for this girl, she would not be sitting where she was. She roused herself with gratitude and took the child's hand. "I'm so glad, Kashata. Of course you can go. You should go any time you want."

That night, Catherine took an extra pill to make sure she would sleep soundly. The false was so much better than the real right now that the extra help given by this medication was the balm she needed. She wished she could find the peace that the child had. *Both children*, she thought. Even Tina had had something Catherine didn't understand. She had had a kind of strength Catherine didn't know. What was it? What is it about Kashata? Surely not this God thing. William too, for that matter.

She lay down, knowing she would be in oblivion within a few minutes. She said her little prayer, hoping something out there had heard, and dropped off into a place where there were no dreams.

Chapter 63

Adoption

Monday morning brought news neither Catherine nor Kashata could believe; there was to be a final hearing and finalization of the adoption the second week of December. "Before Christmas!" they said at the same time, and laughed. Catherine grabbed the girl's hands and danced through the kitchen, around the table, into the living room, and back again. Dune danced before, behind, and in-between, almost tripping Kashata and then Catherine.

Catherine felt as if this child would be her salvation; Kashata laughed as she twirled around the furniture, knowing she would never be thrown out of a house again. Permanence. She could hardly believe it. And then they sat down and cried together—neither knew how long nor why. What an unlikely pair, this thirteen-year-old girl and sixty-year-old woman. Catherine figured she would be seventy when Kashata was in her twenties. Well, that would be just fine, as long as she kept her health.

Thanksgiving vacation was over. Kashata sang as she dressed for school, and Catherine listened with envy. Her guilt still hung on her like the albatross on the mariner, even though things were a lot better in her life. She felt that, but she knew it was not over. She called William.

After dropping Kashata off at school, she drove to his little cottage. William met her at the door, coffee in hand. She hurried inside and took the cup he offered her. "Good to see you, Catherine," William said.

"Yes. Me too," she replied.

"Sit down, Catherine. I know you have something on your mind."

"I heard from our social worker early this morning that the hearing for the adoption is going to be in two weeks."

"Wow. Who would have thought this would go that fast? Are you both ready for this?"

William the realist. Catherine answered, "We both laughed, danced, and cried when we heard. But now, as you suggest, I'm not so sure. I still feel so awful about it all. I almost walked into the lake yesterday while Kashata was at church. Ironic, isn't it? She's at church singing her lungs out, and me, the one who's supposed to be her parent, is thinking about death."

"Catherine, you've got to resolve this."

"I know, William, but I don't know how. If I confess, nobody will believe me, and if they do, I'll go to jail. What good would that do anybody? If I don't, I go on being a danger to myself and others, I think. That shrink was no help. Now what?"

"I have only one answer. Your problem is with your maker. Not jail, not confessing to the authorities, not anything or anyone else will make you free. Go to Jesus. Tell him what you told me."

"I don't like him, William. I can't do that."

"What does that mean, 'I don't like him'?"

"Too much crap I've heard, maybe."

"What kind of crap?"

"You know, stuff that contradicts. Stuff that's too judgmental, stuff that doesn't jive with tolerance. Like, for instance, my English master's professor who always wrote as a Christian and called herself one.

Anyway, one day she came to class and said that her partner of sixteen years had walked out on her and she was devastated. We understood that, of course. Then she proceeded to tell us she was a lesbian and not about to live the rest of her life without sex. That was a picture I didn't need in my head. The last few weeks of class we got to hear all about her association with Wicca, about her mother abusing her when she was a child, about her family disowning her when she announced her preference, and so on. She invited us all to join her church, which was Episcopalian but embraced Wicca and alternate lifestyles. In the meantime, I hear about Christians constantly judging gays and judging each other. Now why should I get on my knees to the founder of this kind of contradictory behavior?"

"We are not perfect; we just know our need for grace."

"Well, this Episcopalian-wiccan lesbian and her judgmental Christian family showed me enough of grace to know I don't need it."

"Catherine, Tina had grace. You brought her to church. What does that mean?"

"Tina was soft; weak, in a way. I thought that kind of support would be good for her, and it was."

"Tina was not weak. She was strong, but confused. She had faith, but didn't trust you anymore. When Zach…well, that was more than she could bear. But she always knew who really loved her." William sighed. "I have the feeling though that He loves you too. That professor was as confused as anyone can be. She misrepresented Christianity. You must believe that. Anyway, I'll be here as long as you need me. That's the most I can do."

"Nobody's asking you for anything else, so shut up already." Catherine sat quietly for a while and tried to empty her brain of the conversation. How she hated hearing about Tina, Zach, and Jesus. Finally, she turned to William.

"Let's go to bed, William. I always feel good about that. What do you say? After all this time, it would do us both good, don't you think?"

"No, Catherine! Sex is not the answer!"

"Well, shit. You're still such a prude."

"Not so much as you think. I'd love to, believe me, but no. Not now, not like this. You've got to get yourself straightened out." William felt like he'd been handed a grenade and he wanted nothing more than to pull the pin, but he knew it would only blow up in his face and hers, so he resisted. "Catherine, go back to your shrink, go to Phillis, go to your sister. Get on your knees, do what it takes, but do not fall into your old patterns. There's only death there. You know that."

Catherine wept, then dried her tears, drank her cold coffee, and left. No word of departure; she just slammed the mug down, breaking it, wiped her eyes, and exited.

Great elation followed by great despair made her so tired she could hardly turn the key in the ignition. Even so, she wasn't sure what to do. She decided to go home and collect Dune, who had not even been fed yet. Then she thought she'd go out and buy herself something really extravagant, and something for Kashata, too. She knew she'd feel better after that.

William watched her go. He shook his head and went back into his house to clean up the mug fragments.

Catherine fed Dune, and then bundled him into the car and took off for her favorite store. She collected a number of outfits to try on. As she stripped to her underwear, she felt the old, now-familiar pain in her back and belly. It had become a frequent companion. "Need to eat more," she murmured while pulling a blue cashmere sweater over her head. She tried on at least ten tops, five pairs of pants, a skirt, and a dress, and then bought most of them. She also shopped for Kashata. Three full outfits later, Catherine went to her car, dropped the packages in, and drove off to the pet store. Dune became the happy recipient of three pig's ears and a rawhide bone the size of her own tail.

It was time for lunch, so Catherine went to the local Red Robin and ordered a large salad with shrimp, a glass of white wine, and coffee. Her stomach approved of the meal, and the twinge of pain was gone. Her thoughts, too, were more cheerful. She took out her cell and pushed the familiar button.

Chapter 64

Apologies

When she walked into Dr. Landman's office, she wore the contented smile he'd had her working toward. He offered his hand and asked her to sit down.

"How are you feeling, Catherine? You look a lot happier than the first time I met you." He was already scribbling on his pad. "What about—Kashata, is it? Yes, what about her? How has the process gone so far?"

Catherine was pleased she could offer some good news. "We have our hearing in two weeks. She and I should be a legal family before Christmas."

"I'd say that's a pretty good present for both of you. I understand your smile today. Congratulations." He paused. "What about the nightmares and sleepless nights? Have the medications been of any help?" he asked.

"Yes, they've been a tremendous help. I have no trouble any more," she lied.

"Really?" he said with a raised eyebrow. "None at all?"

"Well, maybe a little from time to time, but nothing to be worried about," she answered.

"You're doing well, then?"

"Yes, very."

"So why are you here today?"

"Oh, that. Well, I stormed out the last time, so I came to say I'm sorry about that, and also that I won't be needing you any more, except maybe for refills on my prescriptions. You're free of me, in other words." She smiled sweetly at him.

"Uh-huh. I hope you're right. You do look a bit better. Maybe Kashata is just what you need."

"She's made a tremendous difference." She didn't have to lie about this.

He sensed her honesty and scribbled on his pad. Then he tore the page off and held it up for Catherine to see. "How do you like this one?" he asked.

"Wow," was all she could answer. There she was, sketched in black and white, looking almost radiant. "Wow," she said again. "Can I have this one?"

"You can have both of them." he replied, and went to his file cabinet to retrieve the first drawing he had done of her. "I don't think we're finished. There's still something lurking that you can't talk about. I think you may need to return. But for now, here they are—you can see the change yourself. Hang on to them. I'll be here whenever you or Kashata need me."

They shook hands. The session had only lasted a half-hour. Catherine was thrilled to have the drawings in her possession. She knew that only a few sessions were far too little to do much good, but she would not tell the truth about her problem to this guy or anyone else.

The fact that William knew was a confirmation that she could not only trust him, but that he was tuned in to her. He knew her and seemed to understand her. The "fat little wimp," as Zach had referred to him.

Who would have guessed?

She thought about William all the way home. He was the only person who'd guessed the truth. He was not judgmental, and he gave advice sparingly. Who was this man who was not even susceptible to seduction? What did he have that gave his apparent wimpiness such strength? Should she listen to him? She shook her head vigorously at the appalling thought of kneeling and praying to someone she thought was too stupid to defend himself against the most inhumane death she could imagine. Who in the world would do such a thing? She shook her head again and, instead of turning to go home, she continued down Lake Shore Drive, and then turned to pick up Kashata from school and show her the many purchases she'd made. This thought made her smile with pride. It was good to have stuff to fall back on.

Chapter 65

A Family

The big day had finally come. Gwen and Warren were to be there, as well as Mrs. Graham. Kashata put on her best outfit; she loved the denim miniskirt and jean jacket Catherine had bought for her, and adored the striped tights and long shirt. While she pulled on her new leather boots, she thought about how quickly her life had changed in the past few months. She could hardly believe what was happening to her. From telling Catherine she hated her to becoming her daughter was almost too much to take in. Not only that, but Catherine was even willing to care for her baby. Wow. And today it was all going to be made legal. Who would have thought it?

Phillis, too, had been invited to the hearing, but couldn't make it; she had a prior engagement. Kashata knew how busy Phillis was with her volunteer activities. She'd gotten so much good stuff from her new church, and appreciated Phillis's help in getting her involved. William, of course, wouldn't miss it. Kashata even had taken a liking to the old man. Everything was working. God did do everything! She'd always known it.

Catherine pulled a green jumper on over a pink cashmere sweater.

She knew she had better look her best today. When she pulled her short boots on, she nearly fell to the floor with the twinge which had become more than a twinge. She knew she'd have to go to the doctor about it soon. She braced herself for the hearing, praying she would not have a pain while in the courtroom. She was very proud of the way she'd made everything work.

When they were both ready, Kashata put on her leather jacket and Catherine put on her new faux fur, which looked as much like real mink as possible, and then held Kashata's hand all the way to the car. Betty and Sam were on the deck, waving and yelling "Good luck!" The day was so cold that even Dune had refused to go out for more than to do her duty. They left her in the house while they went to get themselves properly familied—"unconditionally connected," as Mrs. Graham had put it.

Catherine had already made doctor's appointments prior to the hearing. She had scheduled Kashata with a woman gynecologist the following week, and herself with an internist a week later. All would be done before Christmas; all would be well before Christmas. Peace on earth for Catherine and Kashata.

The hearing went exceptionally well. Mrs. Graham gave a wonderful report and recommendation. Gwen and Warren showed their joy at having been chosen as guardians, Kashata said all the right things about school, her commitment, her excitement at having a home of her own, and a mother; she even told the judge about Dune and her friends at church. Catherine, of course, was in rare form, and humbly stood before the judge professing her devotion to Kashata and her commitment to giving the girl a real home after all the years of shuffling from one to another. She even shed tears when the judge told her how impressed she was with all these people, especially Kashata and Catherine and their apparently genuine love for one another.

All the papers were signed and notarized, pictures were taken, and congratulations were offered. Kashata and Catherine were family for the rest of their lives; it was a done deal. Catherine, "Hallelujah!" Then she took everyone, including Sam and Betty, to the Red Lobster and ordered lobster dinners for everyone to celebrate. Kashata was overjoyed to see that Phillis was there, and had brought Jolene as well. The girls hugged each other and laughed.

When Kashata pinched a claw with the nutcracker, a spray of water hit Sam right in the eye. He didn't know what hit him, and barked his confusion into his napkin. Everyone laughed, and Sam soon recognized the accident and laughed as well.

The dinner celebration was the success of the season. Faces were red with the flowing wine, and stomachs ached with the pleasure of the meal. Jaws tired from talking and laughing. Kashata's baby must have smiled her first smile at the joy of the day. It was her day too, after all.

When they got home, Catherine broke out a bottle of champagne. She gave a small glass to Kashata because it was a special day, and even filled a small bowl for Dune, who lapped it up gratefully and proceeded to gag, bark, and fall on the floor, legs splayed, belly attached to the tile. Catherine put on some fifties music and swung Kashata around in some sort of jive dancing until all three collapsed on the sofa together, Dune having gathered enough strength to climb aboard. The laughter didn't cease until two in the morning.

Chapter 66

Doctors

Kashata's trip to the doctor nearly did her in. She was so nervous that Catherine was tempted to give her a tranquilizer. She didn't, but she did make Kashata a cup of chamomile tea accompanied by lots of reassuring talk before they went. Kashata holed herself up in her room for almost an hour before they were to go, and Catherine didn't know what she was doing. Kashata did a lot of being alone, said it was prayer, and really seemed to believe in it. *Silly child,* Catherine thought. *She'll get over all that in due time—although Phillis never had.* Confusion made Catherine push those thoughts aside and pour the boiling water over the tea bags. A nice cup of tea, as all the BBC programs said, is always good to bring one back to reality and calm.

Kashata drank her tea, put her jacket on, and fidgeted with the zipper as Catherine went out to warm up the car. Dune slept under the table, not at all concerned about the women. The winter sun shone in the eastern window, just catching the dog's back. The warmth relaxed her enough to put her to sleep, and she sighed her comfort.

Kashata shivered with dread. She abhorred the idea of seeing this doctor, of having someone dig into her again. Perhaps she could take a pill to numb her into sleep; she didn't want to know what was going on. She decided she was going to ask if she could be put to sleep for the exam.

Catherine honked the horn. Kashata finally came out of the house, closed the door, climbed into the car, dropped her head against the backrest, and let out a long, drawn-out sigh. "It's going to be all right," Catherine reassured her.

"That's what you think," Kashata whispered back. "Do you think I could be tranquilized for this?" she asked.

"Probably not. Let's go. You'll be fine. I'll stay with you. You'll be fine," Catherine said again.

Kashata was not fine. After she'd disrobed and put on the gown, she looked at the stirrups and she panicked. Catherine had to hold her down to keep her from running away as she screamed her defiance and fear. "Kashata, honey, you need to do this for your baby. She needs to have the doctor evaluate her progress. You need to be safe. Please quiet down. Please." Kashata tried, but shook with fear when the doctor came in.

The woman looked kind enough, and she spoke kindly. But when she told Kashata to scoot down to the edge of the table, she knew she had a troubled patient on her hands. Kashata's resistance would not help the exam, so she took time to talk with Kashata, to soothe her fears as best she could, and assure the girl the procedure would be over very soon. Catherine nodded her agreement.

After Kashata had settled down, all went fairly well. The baby was doing fine, and Kashata seemed to be healthy, although extremely young. The doctor recommended abortion, but Catherine would not hear of it. "This baby is a gift from God," she heard herself say. The doctor smiled her assent. Kashata was dressed and ready to go in a matter of minutes.

"That wasn't so bad," she said when they got to the car.

"Well, you seem to be fine, the baby is fine, and you go back in a short while. Get yourself ready. In the meantime, there's Christmas to celebrate."

"And your doctor's appointment, Ms. Catherine. Don't forget your doctor's appointment," Kashata reminded Catherine.

"Yes, Kashie, I'm well aware of it. It's on the calendar and, if I forget, I'm sure you'll remind me." She smiled at the girl who had tried to be brave. *What terrible things had been done to her?* Catherine wondered. Now was not the time, but Kashata was going to have to talk—if not to Catherine, then to a therapist. Even though she was reluctant to be honest with Dr. Landman, she believed her daughter was more in need of counseling than she had been. That was one more thing the near future held.

Catherine kept her doctor's appointment as she had promised, no happier about the prospect than Kashata had been about hers. Her back ached too often for her to be comfortable, and the twinge was pretty much a constant now.

After the initial examination, she was told she needed to have an MRI. Then the waiting began. She was nervous and jittery, wondering what the tests would reveal. Kashata was not aware of a change in Catherine; Christmastime was busy and wonderful for her. Catherine threw herself into the preparations partially for Kashata's sake, and partially to keep her mind off her health concerns.

Kashata had a family; she had adults being nice to her and giving her gifts. William spent a lot of time with them, and Kashata found him to be kind and understanding, even though she still perceived him as an old man. Catherine sent the girl to spend a weekend at Gwen's while she had the little room next to Kashata's made into a nursery. She knew it was very chancy, but she had pink lacy curtains hung, pink lamps resting on white little tables, and little pink booties on the bassinet. The rest of the room was painted light yellow with powder-blue trim, just to be on the safe side.

When Kashata came home, Catherine ushered her into the little room, where the expectant mother jumped and yelled with delight. She could hardly contain herself as she fingered the furniture, stroked the curtains, and put the booties on her fingers. "Wow," she said. "Wow. Do you think the baby's feet will be this small? Wow!"

Catherine had thought Kashata would be happy, but she was overwhelmed with her response. This had been all so simple to accomplish, yet had so profound an effect.

Chapter 67

The News

New Year's Eve had been simple—just Jolene, William, and the Konynbelts. They'd played games and danced around the tree as the ball fell in New York City. They hugged and kissed, and then went to their respective beds.

The doctor's office had called on January 5, asking her to come in that afternoon to talk. William had offered to come along. They were so close now that she was afraid she might say yes one of these days, but she needed to do this alone.

After taking Kashata to school, she lingered in a hot tub until she was sure she was as wrinkled as an old dried apple, and probably as red. But the hot water gave her comfort, so she was in no hurry to get out. Then she dressed, put on her goose-down jacket, Thinsulate gloves, and heavy boots to take Dune out on the frozen beach. It was snow-covered, but enough was negotiable for a nice walk. Her breath came in puffs of white mist, and Dune's tongue hung above the frozen sand in the apparent hope of acquiring a frozen taste of something dog-yummy. The seascape was otherworldly; great blocks of ice had formed with the last storm. Evil crevices, deep, dark, and foreboding, loomed between the ice sculptures. Frozen sand offered a beige topping on some of the icy pillars, and the beach was hard as slate. Catherine found the beauty almost spiritual. She sighed, let the thought go, and ran up the stairs, slipping a bit only once.

She made herself some hot soup for lunch and gave half to Dune, who slobbered it all over the floor in her enthusiasm over such a gift. Catherine took the time to clean up before she dressed. Her fur coat covered her body for the trip. She was finally ready and on her way. Dune found her place under the table and happily slept while awaiting the women's return home.

Catherine ran up the stairs to the doctor's office just to prove how fit she really was. *How could anyone as healthy as me be sick?* she thought. She pushed her fears aside. She was sure it was nothing, and smiled as she walked into the office. The doctor offered his hand and asked her to sit down.

"I'm sorry, Ms. Cedar—Catherine. We see some suspicious areas in your abdomen and will need to do a biopsy. I hope it's not a malignancy, but I want you to be prepared. It doesn't look good."

"Crap," she said.

When she got to her car, she stared straight ahead at nothing. "So," she whispered, "this is my punishment. Okay, you unknown god of William and Kashata, be that way." Her voice grew louder with each successive word. "But don't get any fancy ideas about me just because I'm here. I am not praying. I'm just talking to you." Then she broke down in a waterfall of tears she never knew she had.

Chapter 68

Wedding

William grinned from ear to ear when he heard her say "I do." Catherine had been elusive and unwilling for too many years, but would finally be his wife. What joy and what pain. Kashata stood up for her, and Doug, Gwen's son, stood up for William. Catherine had bought full-length faux minks for each member of her party. Even William wore his made-for-a-man fur with a winter-white gardenia in his lapel. Catherine and Kashata also wore small fur caps and small gardenia corsages on their wrists.

They stood on the cold, late-winter beach below Catherine's house, willing the time to be short. The wind had picked up, although the morning had almost promised spring. Dune ran along the water's edge and shook herself dry onto those glorious hunks of fur hanging from her people. Grinning was attempted, but the cold seemed to have frozen expressions in place.

The wedding was very short and the party very small—Gwen without Warren, Doug, and Kashata. No one else witnessed the ceremony, but Reverend Wisekirk from Brigantine had agreed to fly to Michigan to marry these two diverse individuals. He knew them and he wanted to see them attain some semblance of normalcy. He smiled at William's obvious joy.

Catherine, however, didn't smile. She felt no confidence in this rash agreement she'd made, but she thought, *What the hell, I'll be gone soon enough anyway, why not give everybody what they want?* And so she said "I do" and ran to the stairs to get out of the cold. The wedding party followed with much cheering and laughing. Why they'd gone to the Rainy Day Café for burgers, salad, and soup was also a mystery, but it seemed like just the right place for this little party. Catherine had arranged it.

The next morning, she awoke with the sharp winter sun streaming through the window. She rubbed the sleep from her eyes and looked over at her new husband. He'd been awake for quite some time, relishing his luck in this new adventure. It had been a year since he'd appeared on the beach in Good Heavens.

Catherine began to laugh. "What a couple of old farts we are!" she exclaimed. "Who would have thought you were capable of all that?"

"Don't be silly, Catherine; we're married. We can do anything we want. I never had so much fun in my whole life."

"But we're old. We're supposed to be done. And me with cancer, yet."

"That's enough! We've been given a gift. We're not as old as our numbers suggest, and I pray your illness might still go into remission. Let's enjoy what we've got—and no more nonsense talk." He smiled, looking at this new wife he couldn't imagine he'd ever get even six months ago.

Over a breakfast of soft-boiled eggs, lean, crisp bacon, and whole-grain toast, the newly-weds sat quietly, indulged in their newfound delights, and sipped strong coffee. Without warning, Catherine broke the comfortable silence. "So, what do you think of being married to a murderer, William?" He nearly choked on his toast.

"Where in the world did that come from?" he asked.

"You know. Zach, peanut butter, revenge for my daughter's abuse. Just thought I'd see what you thought of it now that you're tied to me."

"My dear Catherine, we've been over this, and I thought we were done with it. You confessed, you repented, and you should leave it. We decided no one need know—and no one need talk about it anymore."

"Do you suppose your God has forgiven me for murdering Zach?"

"I know that God forgives those who confess and repent. You and God are the only ones who know what's really in your heart about all this."

"Okay, just checking. Because I sometimes think that this illness is a punishment for what I've done. I can't help but think that maybe this is my final punishment since the law was never involved."

"Catherine, you're sick because people on this fallen earth get sick. We all suffer from these evils. Please don't think God is punishing you—although I believe He may be using this to get your attention. That would be a gift in disguise. Try to think of it that way, if you can."

"Well, William, I can't, and you know I can't. But I think the power of the universe is after me. I can't help it. Let's leave it, okay?"

"For now, yes. I'll keep praying for remission just the same, if you don't mind."

"Do whatever you want privately; I don't want to hear about it. But let's get back to basics. We're really going to enjoy this marriage thing, aren't we?"

"You can count on it, my dear."

Chapter 69

An Odd Family

William, after the wedding, formally adopted Kashata, and a tentative, pasted-together family was established. They all shared Catherine's comfortable cottage.

The baby had arrived—another gift. Not anticipated at first, but fully welcomed. A gorgeous bundle of squealing flesh named after both Tina and Catherine herself. Tina-Kate would be as beautiful as her mother. How could this thirteen-year-old have done so well and known to be so sensitive?

Good Heavens was not cosmopolitan; summers brought tourists of various ethnicities, but winters saw the native "Whitelandia" in full bloom. Kashata's deep bronze complexion, as well as that of little Tina-Kate, and their large, dark, golden eyes stopped people on the street. There is beauty in all people, but whatever had contributed to Kashata and her daughter made people catch their breath when they saw them. This had been Kashata's curse as well as her blessing, for it had brought her a child she adored and a family she craved.

Kashata was the legal child of two rather weird old folks, but she thought she'd died and gone to heaven. Then reality had raised its ugly head with Catherine's cancer diagnosis. William should have been appalled by it; his first wife had died of cancer, and it had devastated him. Now he was willing to take on a second wife already in the grip of the disease. No one could figure him out—except Catherine.

She came to know that he craved adventure, family, and her impulsiveness. She had known that about him when they reconnected, and she had somehow suspected his need long before that. What she had not understood was her need for him. She found in sedate, slightly pudgy little William the stability and safety she'd always craved. Their wedding night was a complete surprise. Had she guessed, she would have done it long ago.

What she'd imagined to be boring she found to be more warm and exciting than anything Zachary Bekker had ever been able to give her. In her sixties and facing a fatal illness, she was finally given the life she'd needed in her twenties. She exulted in the gift, however brief it portended to be.

William marveled at the women in his life, and prayed every night that it all might last a lot longer than the doctors' prognosis.

Chapter 70

Faith Issues

Now Kashata's tiny daughter had grandparents. How had she deserved all this wealth? After the pain was gone and the wonder of a new life had been accepted, Kashata thanked her God. The wisdom of this girl who'd endured abuse, rejection, loss, and cold fear was a miraculous phenomenon.

Catherine was confused by it, but William quietly smiled. Kashata always gave credit where credit was due, and William knew exactly where and why. This was the one thing about both that infuriated Catherine. She hated their primitive, stupid views because she could not understand them, nor could she dismiss them. Their shared faith made her nervous. She'd made William promise he would not try to talk to her about any of it after they were married, and he smiled his dumb, knowing smile when he'd agreed. Kashata, in her naïve consistency, bragged how her Divine Savior had blessed her, regardless of Catherine's atheistic views.

Kashata bundled little Tina-Kate up a few days after the baby's birth, begged William to give her a ride to town, and marched into the Rainy Day Café. William made her promise to call. "Got your cell phone, Kashata?" he asked.

"Of course!" she replied as she undid the baby seat and took her child out into the cold. William felt a little apprehensive about this excursion, but believed Kashata needed the outing. She barely knew Rita Rocket, but instinctively knew she needed to show her her special prize—her very own daughter.

Chapter 71

An Odd Café

The day Kashata walked into the café, located just off Main Street in Good Heavens, Rita Rocket guessed the child needed a friend, perhaps a confidante. That was Rita's strength; she believed she could read most people within the first ten minutes of meeting.

Run by Rita Rocket, the café was a novelty. It was tiny and uninviting with its grey clapboard exterior and small dirty windows. And Rita herself was a novelty. Her name alone was enough to draw bewildered attention, but her sun-drenched flaming hair and penetrating, deep-green eyes set her apart from anyone else in that blond, Northern European community.

Rita smiled when Kashata came in with her little bundle and put out her arms to receive the baby. The first time Rita had ever seen Kashata, the girl was draped in fur—covered from head to toe in a fine, silvery-white coat. When she removed the coat, Rita was shocked to see how very pregnant the child was. She said nothing nor stared as she took the orders and served the little wedding party. Now this kid was in her café with her kid, grinning from ear to ear and willing to hand her baby over to Rita. The little baby carryall sat on the table as Kashata slid into the booth and Rita rocked Tina-Kate in her arms beside the young mother.

"She's gorgeous, isn't she?" Rita cooed as she took in the small, perfect features.

"I know. She's mine!" Kashata shot back. "And she's totally related to me."

Rita recognized a cry for recognition and family when she heard it. "Of course she is; she looks exactly like you. You're a lucky mother." The elderly couple in the next booth stared. Their expressions betrayed their incredulity at the youth of this girl whom Rita had just called "mother." Kashata saw the look and the stares, but she didn't care. She was too enamored of her tiny daughter to let any negative reaction bother her.

"And guess what? I never have to go to school again!" she said loud enough for all to hear. She looked over at the eavesdroppers, raised an eyebrow, and then offered them a huge, white-toothed grin. They turned to their burgers and sniffed. "Who cares," she said to Rita, and then informed her quietly that Catherine was going to home school her in English and social studies, with William offering his expertise in math and science.

"My guess is that you're in very good hands," Rita remarked, handing the squirming infant back to her mother. "I imagine school would be a bit difficult under the present circumstances. But what will you do for friends?"

"Yeah. I still have a friend." She paused. "Except," Kashata's voice now dropped to a whisper, "except that Mama Kate has cancer."

Rita stopped clearing dishes, threw down her towel, and stared at the girl. So that was the fly in the ointment. She had thought something was not quite okay, but this was worse than anything she could have imagined.

"Oh dear. I'm so sorry. I am truly so sorry. What can I do for you?"

"Pray," was the quick and certain response.

This was the one thing that Rita could not nor would not do. "Kashata," she said, "I'll do anything, but not that."

"Okay. That's okay. Catherine won't either, so William and I take care of it."

"Let me at least explain a little," Rita offered.

"If you want to, okay, but it's all fine with me. Everybody in their own time and way."

When Rita talked about herself, Kashata realized they had much in common.

Chapter 72

Rita's Story

Rita grew up in Chicago. Her small home on Seventy-Eighth Street was both a haven and a hell. Mrs. Rocket was a saint, and Mr. Rocket was a devil—especially where his daughters were concerned. Rita voiced her memories of her father, referring to him as a brute with an iron fist, a leather belt, and a harsh voice. Her mother tried to assure her girls that he only meant to protect them, but both girls grew up with an inordinate fear of men and a hatred of their father and the God he spouted about from his pious Roman Catholic perch. The abuse had emotionally crippled the girls as well as their mother.

Rita told Kashata she'd married exactly the same kind of man. "Go figure," she said. She added that her sister, Rachel, had never married and eventually died of brain cancer. "Why?" she asked Kashata, expecting no answer.

"I'm sorry you had a rotten childhood. I know about that. I gotta go now. See you later." With that she bundled up her baby, made a quick call to William, and left the café.

It was not easy for Rita to forget, having resurrected the memory of her father. As soon as she was eighteen, she'd left home for New York.

She waited tables at two places, diners really, but the tips were enough to keep her. Eventually she'd been able to move up to a better restaurant and earn enough to rent a small, clean apartment in the Village. She kept in touch with her mother, of course, and learned that soon after she left her father had lost his job, become very depressed, and walked out one day. He never came back.

When her sister got sick, Rita spent many days traveling back and forth from New York to Chicago—sometimes by plane, often by car. They were long, arduous trips. But eventually hospice had to take over, and that had been a short stay. From diagnosis to death was only eight months. Rita's mother was heartbroken, so Rita took her to live with her in New York for a while. As is often the case, her mother missed her old friends, her neighborhood, and her church, and so moved back to Chicago after only three months. But those few months together had done both women a world of good. Rita railed against God and man for a long time, and finally lost her faith. Her mother hung on to her long-established Catholicism by a thread. "At least I have that," she said. What else is there?"

Her father had professed his love for his family immediately after he'd been to confession; he'd beaten and emotionally abused them after he had been to the bars. His love was spoken, his hatred was felt. He never remembered the extent of the harm he'd done, and found it difficult to believe when they, through tears, dared to tell him. His touch was feared and loathed when he was drunk, and ironically craved when he was sober. He could not show his love; he could only speak it.

Rita sat at the counter, holding back tears as she thought again about her childhood. When she remembered her few years in New York City, her expression changed. They had been good years, but there was one morning she knew she would never forget, and that memory made her cry. *Who would have guessed*, she thought, as she remembered the happy little dog.

On clear summer mornings, Rita sat on her stoop having coffee. She let her thoughts wander, sometimes hardly noticing her surroundings, but other times keenly aware of the people going by, the smoke rising through the grates in the street, and the little black-and-white mongrel leading its docile gentleman, dressed in his impeccably tailored Brooks Brothers, suit to the tree just in front of her house to take its long, luxurious morning pee. She often saw, but paid no attention, to the man, the dog, women with little dirty kids, crying babies in strollers, men with lunch pails and hard hats. She loved to sit and think of nearly nothing. She smiled, enjoying the bitter brew warming her throat. The people were always there in the summer, but once winter blew its way across the city, she wasn't there any more either. Then she would take her coffee to the window and watch snow-covered streets collect skidding cars to its curbs as desperate drivers attempted to miss both the curbs and each other. But summer in the city was magic. Rita enjoyed early mornings the most, before the heat of the day sent too many for cover.

She was not sure how many summers she'd indulged herself in this morning activity, but one summer day she'd been especially alert. She'd seen him before, but had taken no particular notice, and couldn't say what made her aware this particular day. Perhaps the rumble of his cart over the broken pavement, which revealed cobblestone of more than a hundred years prior, struck her ear. The length of his heavy black wool coat in the sweltering heat also burned another, older time into her consciousness. She dropped her cup with a clatter and a crack on the sidewalk below. At the sound, he seemed to awaken from his thoughts. He looked at the shattered cup and spilled coffee near his feet with a look that suggested that the cup and the accident had been his doing. He slowly bent to pick up a shard, turned it over in his bony hand, looked at her for the first time, and slowly dropped the shard into his basket, ignoring her entirely. He didn't see her as she saw him; he seemed to see through her. She said nothing. She blinked into the sun, trying to process what had happened. He leaned into the handlebar of his garbage-laden cart and pushed it down the street, out of her sight. She felt hot tears behind her eyes which she kept back with effort.

The following morning, she tensed when she heard the clatter again. She realized it was a familiar sound to which she had never before paid the least attention, but she couldn't ignore it again. When he had passed her, she put her new coffee cup on the top step and stood up to follow him. Down one street and up another they wandered together, she out of his sight, although she could have walked beside him for all he knew or cared. They passed Magnolia, the cupcake bakery, which had lines out the door and around the block; he took his time to go around the people, and then to the back to fill a paper bag in his cart with what he could glean from the large garbage container. Then he reappeared, put the bag in his cart, and resumed his slow trek. *Where?* Rita wondered. She continued to keep pace, but at a safe distance.

At a filthy little greasy spoon, he repeated his garbage collecting from the depths of a huge, smelly dumpster and moved on again. After about an hour of slow walking and scavenging, he stopped at a dark little alley between buildings so close together that only a thin ray of light penetrated its depths. He turned into it and pushed his laden cart, which scraped the walls of both buildings—but only slightly—to the filthy, paper-strewn end. He kneeled down, opened a small flap of a large cardboard box which had, at one time, contained some great appliance, and retrieved a wriggling, scraggly dog with a rope for a collar and leash. The little thing wiggled its entire body with obvious delight at seeing the old man. He petted and kissed the dog, held it to his breast, and caressed it incessantly, offering it small tidbits from his bags. His eyes poured his love over the entire creature. He nestled it inside his long black coat and grinned at the warm little body so close to his.

She knew that old man. The coat was his favorite purchase from the Salvation Army store when she was only ten; it hung around him like a rag now. The little bump of a dog hidden inside was held close to the old man's heart. She realized she hated him.

Rita turned, stepped away from the alley, and wept. Her tears were the tears of a child. If only he had loved her when she was little as he loved the little dog.

Chapter 73

Gwen's Sorrow

William and Catherine settled into married life more easily than either had anticipated. It was a natural complement of opposites. He never tired of her impulsive ways and rather earthy talk; she felt a warmth and security in his love she'd hoped for and had believed would never be hers. She considered herself too wild and independent to be able to sustain that such a relationship. But here it was—and in her sixties, no less. Six months into their marriage, six months into parenthood and then grandparenthood, almost six months into her cancer treatment, the two sat in the little room overlooking Lake Michigan having breakfast together. Catherine was thin but had kept her hair. She was hungry this morning, and ate with a relish that gave William great joy.

When the phone rang, neither of them felt the urge to answer it. "Let it go to the machine," both said at once, and laughed.

"Hi, Kate. I need to talk to you. Can you give me a call soon?" It was Gwen. Catherine looked at William and he nodded. She knew, by the sound of Gwen's voice, she would have to call right away. She took a last swallow of her coffee and walked into her kitchen. Gwen was the epitome of the satisfied woman, but had ups and downs, having suffered from mood swings her entire adult life. Catherine was in no mood herself to indulge one of Gwen's emotional downs, but the sound of her voice this morning suggested something a more serious. She punched in the familiar numbers and waited, tapping her foot on the tile. When she heard the phone pick up she didn't wait for a hello.

"So, what's up, Gwen?" She heard Gwen begin to sob and almost lost her temper. "What the hell? What is it, sis? It can't be that bad."

"Warren's gone," Gwen sobbed into the phone.

"Gone? What do you mean, gone?" Catherine demanded.

"Catherine, he left me. He walked out last night."

"What? He'll be back, Gwen. Just give him time."

"No, Kate. He wants a divorce. He says he can't stand the guilt. I tried to explain that I forgave him, but he says he still feels guilty for having lied to me all those years. Now that I know the truth about the vasectomy before we were even married—well, he says he feels it every time he looks at me. He says he can't stand it."

"So let the bum go, then. He's been dishonest from day one. Lying about his illegitimate son, lying about his vasectomy, letting you go through all that infertility stuff. He's not worth one tear."

"Maybe, Kate, but thirty-five years is a long time. I thought we were fine."

"You weren't fine after all that. I'm sorry, Gwen, really. But I thought he might be having a problem when he didn't show up for the wedding. Why don't you drive down and spend a few days with us?"

"Oh, Kate. You're so crowded with Kashata and Tina-Kate. I don't know," Gwen whined. Catherine hated whining. However, Gwen had been there for Catherine when she needed her most, and she wanted to be a help to her sister.

"Okay. Listen, Gwen. Get down here and I'll make sure there's room. Just do it."

"Thanks, Kate. Maybe I will. Thank you, dear."

"All right. See you when? This afternoon?"

When they hung up, Catherine walked back into the sun room where William had already anticipated the problem. "Good god, William—" she began.

"Catherine."

"Oh, yes. Sorry. Good gracious, William. Gwen and Warren have broken up."

"My goodness. I thought as much when I heard your conversation. How awful after all these years."

"And to think that I was always a little jealous of them. One never knows. No one ever knew he was living that lie about having a son and a vasectomy before they were married. What a louse he turned out to be."

William sighed. "Is she coming here?"

"Yes. I thought I'd call Sam and Betty to see if she could stay there for a time while they're in Florida. What do you think?"

"Sounds like a good plan to me."

Gwen arrived at three that afternoon. It was Saturday, so traffic had been almost non-existent. When she entered the house, Catherine was ready with a big hug, a hot cup of tea, and ears ready to listen.

Warren had gotten up that morning, packed a bag, come downstairs, and announced he was leaving. He explained his reason and left. Gwen was in shock; she couldn't even respond. She just gaped at his retrieving back. Soon she came to herself, realized what had happened, and called Catherine.

"So," Catherine said, "what you need to do is rest quietly, try to make sense of it, and find a haven of peace in which to accomplish this. I called Sam and Betty. They're in Florida for the next month or so, and they've graciously opened their house to you. They said you can stay as long as you need to."

"Oh, Kate, should I? I mean, do Sam and Betty really mean for me to live there? How very kind of them." Gwen's voice still had a whiny note, but Kate turned a deaf ear to it.

"Just sit for a while, have your tea, and I'll take care of everything. You'll be all right, Gwen. I promise."

Chapter 74

Cancer

That year's winter crept by with mounds of snow blocking the view of the frozen lake, as well as the house where Gwen was trying to make sense of her life. By March, Catherine had been receiving chemo for four months and felt like a wrung-out dishrag. Gwen anticipated spring with the hope it would afford both her and her sister a semblance of renewal. She survived on the thought that her husband would soon return to her. Catherine could not understand this; she thought Gwen should just say good riddance to the bum.

From the treatments, Catherine had had little pain, some discomfort, minimal nausea, and no hair loss, and for all this she was thankful. William praised his Lord each new day he had with Catherine, but she didn't want to hear about it. She was sure no God was behind any of her blessings, as William called them, but that science and medicine were her saviors. She didn't even believe He was behind this curse of cancer. No one was to blame; it just was. She thanked her doctors, medical technology, and the love of her family for her sustenance. She even thanked Gwen, who'd kept her from thinking too much about herself and more about trying to keep her sister from falling apart. If anyone knew about the pain of deception inflicted by someone beloved and trusted, it was Catherine. At least Gwen didn't have to do anything about it, as Catherine had. Gwen didn't have to deal with guilt, either. *Lucky Gwen*, Catherine thought. *Even her catastrophes are milder than mine.*

And now this miserable disease was rocking her life. For the first time in all her years she felt utterly out of control. She'd been able to control her students, her colleagues, her daughter—to some extent, anyway—most of her lovers, and even Zach, at the end. But now, even William was able to slip lovingly from under her controlling hand. He took her for her treatments, he took her out to lunch, he told her when to go to bed, and ushered her there if she refused. She was helpless under his resolute care. She could not understand this; he'd always seemed to be such a wimp, but there was a quiet, irresistible strength in him that confounded Catherine but completed her as well. She knew she should resent his control and her willingness to accept it, but she felt such peace and comfort with him that she willingly rested in his care. It seemed to Catherine that William did everything for her sake while holding the reins tightly.

Cancer was a curse to be sure, but a blessing that brought out the best in their marriage at the same time. Life was a paradox for Catherine this winter of her sixty-second year.

Kashata was also a mystery. She doted on Tina-Kate, studied diligently, obeyed William in everything, and took complete control of Catherine's kitchen. Why and how had this abandoned and abused child become so reliable and pliable? Kashata's friendship with Rita Rocket, the woman who ran the Rainy Day Café, was certainly an influence, especially when it came to the cooking. But that was not the answer to the thirteen-year-old's ability to function so well. William, of course, attributed it to Kashata's faith, and Catherine laughed at that. How could a child possibly have faith in some unknown male being when everything in her experience had been worse than awful at the hands of men she was supposed to have trusted? The whole business was absurd, and Catherine often said as much. William smiled at her denial and resistance, but didn't argue. *He should*, she thought, *but he didn't. So*, Catherine reflected, *maybe he agrees, but quietly presses on in case I'm wrong*. It was bewildering, all of it. She had never in her life had this much time to think, and it was most unsettling.

Chapter 75

Renewal

One morning in late April, Gwen arrived for her afternoon tea with Catherine. She sat with a sly grin her usually rather dour face. Catherine knew something was up, but waited for her sister to explain. Gwen took a sip of tea and then put her cup into the saucer without so much as a clink. "Guess what, Kate," she began. Catherine said nothing, raised an eyebrow, and waited. Gwen swallowed hard, fidgeted in her chair, and finally burst out with her news.

"I'm officially divorcing Warren!" she exclaimed.

"Is there another way?" queried Catherine.

Gwen dismissed the expected sarcasm with a wave of her hand, swallowed one more time, and continued. "I have to get the divorce because I met someone."

"Oh?"

"Yes."

"Is that it? Are you going to tell me the rest?"

"Okay, but I want you to be happy for me."

"How do I do that without the details? I make no promises, but I'll support you in any decision you make if you really believe this person is worth it."

Gwen swallowed again. "I met him at Rita's place. Remember when I drove Kashie and Tina-Kate there last month?" Catherine shook her head. "No, of course not. Anyway, this man was there in a booth by himself. He noticed Kashie and the baby, of course, and smiled and commented on the lovely little girl. We smiled, and he invited us to sit with him. He looked harmless enough and rather lonely, so we did. Kashata sat in the corner, hugging the wall, but did offer him a tentative smile. I saw something in his kind face and warm brown eyes that attracted me. As it turned out, he's a pastor, widowed for ten years."

"A pastor. It figures."

"What's that supposed to mean?"

"Never mind. Go on, please."

"Well, we talked a bit, and I learned that he was senior pastor at the Methodist church in town. His wife died of heart failure ten years ago, and he never thought of marrying again."

"Until now? Because of you?"

"Kind of, yes."

"And your hope of Warren returning is…"

Gwen smiled a wry smile. "I guess that's over."

Catherine smirked. "Uh-huh. So what if he does come back. Then what?"

"Then nothing. I'm done with that deception, Kate. I'm moving on, that's all."

"Okay. In that case, I wish you the best."

"Thanks, Kate. I was hoping you'd say that."

"Does this pastor have a name?"

"Yes. His name is Oscar Plug. Reverend Oscar Plug."

"You could become Gwen Plug?"

The sisters looked at each other and both began to laugh.

When Gwen left, Catherine got up and got out her new coping

device. Kashata was out with a friend from church, Tina-Kate was well into her mid-afternoon nap, and William was doing volunteer work at Love Inc., his new Christian service project. Catherine loved this time alone to indulge herself. Neither William nor Kashata knew anything about it, and they didn't need to know. Catherine found the time comforting, especially in the face of her chemotherapy treatments.

"Catherine, what are you doing?" She sat up with a start at William's voice. She had not heard him come in so had not had time to extinguish her smoke.

"What the hell? What are you doing, sneaking up on me like that?"

"I'm not sneaking; I came home early and I find you out here like this."

"Like what?"

"Catherine, what are you doing?" he repeated.

"I'm smoking, William."

"I can see that, but what you're smoking is a problem."

"Problem? This is a problem for you? I'm smoking marijuana. So what?"

"So what? It's illegal, that's what."

"Medicinal is not illegal. And I find a great deal of comfort in it."

"What you have is not prescription. It is illegal."

"Oh, who cares. I like it and I'm going to do it. It makes me feel good."

"And to hell with me, whether I like it or not?"

"No, William, I do not want you in hell, but it's none of your concern. So just leave me alone, okay?"

"It's my concern if you have illegal stuff in our house. It's also my concern if Kashata finds out. What about that?"

"She's not going to find out, but if she does, I'll explain that it's part of my therapy. Let me deal with my illness as best as I can. Just leave me alone about this."

William shrugged; he had no answer. Catherine continued to surprise him, but this time he felt injured and a bit betrayed as well.

"Look, William, I'm sorry you had to find out like this. I used to smoke all the time long ago, and I always loved the way it made me feel. So I decided that I want to feel that kind of good again, especially because I'm sick, so please indulge me in this."

"You have to do what you have to do, Catherine. I'll leave you to it, but I don't like it."

"You don't need to. Just don't bother me about it."

"Fine." William resigned himself to accepting another aspect of new wife, despite his serious reservations.

"Are you going to tell your doctor?" he asked.

"No. It's none of his business. When I see him tomorrow we'll just go through the routine exam results and go from there. I feel really good right now, so I'm not saying anything about anything."

William let it go. What else could he do?

Catherine's visit to her doctor turned out not to be routine at all.

Chapter 76

Happy Prognosis

"Catherine, William. Good to see you both this morning. How are you feeling today, Catherine?" The doctor had his laptop open, ready to pound in whatever she said.

"Good," she replied. "Really good."

"Okay! I like to hear that," he said without looking up. He entered a bit into his computer, and then continued, "Your last test results came back. It seems we have a strange and uncommon situation." The familiar fist of fear immediately squeezed Catherine's stomach, and William grabbed her hand. The doctor noticed their reactions and quickly continued. "The last X-rays showed no tumors. No sign of cancer whatsoever. We can't figure it out, but that's how it is. You seem to be in complete remission." The couple was incredulous. They looked at one another for a full ten seconds, and then simultaneously burst into laughter. Catherine's doctor smiled, but warned them that further tests would be needed to verify the new findings. "In the meantime, let's be thankful for what we see, and continue the treatments for the time being. I'd like to schedule Catherine for another evaluation tomorrow."

The final tests also showed no further cancer, and Catherine was

declared "cured." She couldn't believe it. What luck!
William could believe it. What a blessing!

Chapter 77

Years

Kashata walked into the café kitchen, grabbed her apron, and readied herself for the regulars, who would be showing up shortly. She expected the school bus to drop Tina-Kate off within the next hour. Rita said goodbye and left for the day, so Kashata was in charge of the café with the help of a new girl named Jane.

Not many customers ever occupied the café, but those who did were loyal. From time to time, new people would show up out of curiosity at the unique name, and inevitably come back for more. Kashata had become an innovative cook; Rita had always been very good at simple, comforting food, and Jane was encouraged to bring her skills to the kitchen. The three women worked well together. Even seven-year-old Tina-Kate was allowed to suggest menu items that children would favor.

Today, Kashata would cook while Jane waited tables. Both young women were students at Fair Valley University. The part-time work suited them and provided extra income.

Kashata had turned twenty a short time ago. Tina-Kate was almost seven and in first grade. Catherine had been a cancer survivor for nearly seven years, and Gwen had been Mrs. Oscar Plug for five. All seemed well. William had never adapted to Catherine's penchant for smoking, but he didn't interfere and was thankful for the years he'd been given with her as his wife.

When the first mid-afternoon customer appeared, Kashata squealed and gave her a big hug. Phillis Ver Hage had been a big help in Kashata's life, a top-notch lady, and a good Christian friend for both Catherine and Kashata. She'd introduced the girl to many young people at church. Catherine, as usual, opted to stay as far away from this aspect of her friend as possible. Kashata still attended the church group for college kids, and had friends there from the time she was thirteen.

Kashata ushered her to a booth and sat down. Phillis said, "So, Kashie, tell me how things are in your life. I haven't spoken with you for quite some time."

"I know. I'm okay. Catherine has been having a little discomfort, and William and I are pretty worried, but she says it's nothing. Tina-Kate is doing great in school and loves it, so that's good. I like most of my classes. I only have one more year and then...I don't know."

"It's hard to know what will be available for you, but I'm sure you'll be fine. Teachers are needed." Kashata smiled and then asked Jane to make them a cup of tea. No other customers were expected for another half-hour, so Kashata decided to relish the time with her friend. "I'm not sure I want to teach. I'm not sure what I want to do, really."

Jane brought the tea just as the door to the café opened and a very tall African-American man walked in. He looked around and frowned before sidling up to the counter, finding a stool, and sitting down slowly, still looking around. Finally he asked Jane, in a booming voice, "You the only lady working here?" Both Phillis and Kashata turned to look at this loud stranger. She didn't know why, but Kashata felt a familiar knot form in her stomach. Jane told him only that business was light and no one else was needed. The man cast a furtive look around and ordered black coffee with a piece of pie, he didn't care what kind.

Kashata and Phillis continued their conversation. "It's so wonderful that Catherine had such a miraculous remission from her cancer. I pray all will remain that way for a long time to come," Phillis said.

"William, of course, was overjoyed as I was, but now we're not so sure. If it has come back we can't complain, since God has given us these wonderful cancer-free years, you know. It's also given Tina-Kate a chance to get to know Catherine, and me a chance to get my life together while Kate and William watched their granddaughter. All blessings." Kashata smiled rather ruefully into her tea cup.

"Amen!" Phillis responded, but Kashata still seem worried knowing Kate was not feeling as well as she had.

"Ben has been around again too. Remember him? My former foster brother? He's continually bugging me about who Tina-Kate's father is. It's none of his business. I think he believes his friend is. It's none of his business!"

"Are you ever going to let anyone know? I mean, what about Tina-Kate herself?" Phillis asked tentatively.

"Yeah, I've thought about it. She asks, but I just can't. Not yet. I can't."

The man at the counter slurped from his coffee and listened intently to the conversation of the two women. He smiled, wiped his mouth and got up to leave, taking another quick look around before walked out the door, letting it slam shut behind him.

Phillis raised an eyebrow. "Wonder what that was all about," she said. Kashata shook her head and remained silent. She wondered too, but didn't know what to think. When the door opened again, in came the little girl with the great big smile just like her mother's. She leapt onto Kashata's lap, grabbed the teacup with both hands, and finished the contents in one swallow. Phillis smiled at her childish exuberance. Kashata hugged her daughter and asked her how her day had gone.

"Mommy, I'm the best speller in the whole class!" she squealed.

Catherine had commented many times on the brilliance of her granddaughter, so Kashata was not surprised every time Tina-Kate came home with accolades and great grades. Kashata too had become a top-notch student, acquiring wonderful scholarships and top-of-her-class grades. In spite of her desperately poor beginnings, she'd overcome at least some of her negative experiences. Her academics were fantastic, her mothering a surprise, but her personal and emotional life was often in turmoil.

She spent many hours in prayer, desperate to feel "normal," as she put it. She still kept most of her issues to herself, not willing or able to share them. Counseling had helped a bit in getting a handle on her past and why she felt so betrayed, but her greatest comfort was her faith. Only William understood that, and he'd become her greatest advocate. Catherine had her own contributions, of course, but didn't or wouldn't accept the "stupid" faith, as she put it, of her family members. Kashata had found some good friends at church and the university, but no one to whom she would confide her innermost thoughts or issues from her past. No one knew who Tina-Kate's father was, and no one dared to ask. Kashata let people know that this was not a path to tread with her.

When she'd met Rita Rocket some six years before, she'd found a kindred spirit. Rita knew what it was to survive abuse. She knew betrayal at the hands of those who ought to have protected her, and this gave the two women, almost a generation apart in age, a bond no one else quite understood.

Chapter 78

A New Customer

Little more than a week after his first visit, the tall, good looking man returned. Again, he chose to sit at the counter. This time he came for lunch and ordered Rita's best, a large burger with the works, homemade potato chips, thick and greasy with homemade ranch-style dipping sauce, and a large bowl of mac and cheese. For dessert he ordered coffee with sugar and cream and two slices of blueberry pie. He ate slowly, looking around the tiny café as he ate.

Rita watched him from the corner of her eye as she served her other customers. The gentleman did swivel on the stool to take a closer look, and seemed very interested in everyone who came in. His ears were tuned in, and his eyes were all over the café.

When he finished, he lingered over his coffee. Rita went behind the counter and asked him if he'd like a refill, which he did. As she topped off his cup, she got up the nerve to ask if there was anyone special he was looking or waiting for. He smiled. "No, not really. Just new in town and interested, that's all."

"Interested in the people in this café?" Rita wanted to know.

"Interested in everything. I'm liking this place. Good food, a friendly lady—you—and inexpensive. It all works," he remarked, smiling.

"You seem to be looking for someone," Rita ventured.

"No, not really. I'll just finish my coffee, thank you." With that, she knew she'd been dismissed. He lingered over the last refill longer than necessary. Rita felt a bit of discomfort at the man's constant looking around. He stayed far beyond the amount of time her customers usually stayed, and soon all the others were gone. She was left alone in the small place with this stranger.

"Would you like anything else?" she asked.

"No," was his terse reply as he picked up his cup and took another slow sip. Rita went to the back and began cleaning the grill as she kept a wary eye on the customer. Soon Kashata would be coming in, and Jane was expected as well. At least there would be two of them, although she knew she really had no reason to feel as she did. He appeared and behaved like a gentleman, exhibiting no threatening behavior at all. Yet...

When Kashata bounded through the door with Tina-Kate in tow, the man took a sharp turn and stared at them. He registered a look of pain and dismay, Rita thought, but he quickly got up and left.

"Hey, Rita. Wasn't that the same guy that was here about a week ago?" Kashata asked as she watched his back go through the door.

"Yeah," she answered with a sigh.

"You look like you don't like him. Anything happen?"

"No. He had lunch and took a long time about it, that's all. Look, Kash, I'm going home soon, but I'll stay until Jane shows up. You can close early if you want. I don't think we'll have too many more customers today. It's been pretty slow."

"You worried this guy is going to come back?"

"Don't know. He looks okay, but he seems a bit too interested in something here. I'd rather be careful."

When Jane arrived, Rita left. The rest of the afternoon went by with few customers. The tall, dark gentleman didn't return, but even if he had, Kashata was prepared to close shop when he did. She knew about being careful where men were concerned.

Chapter 79

It's Back

Catherine bent double with the pain. William had not yet gotten up, so she made as little noise as she could. The stab of pain in her belly was like a sword being thrust in and through. She had not experienced so much pain before, although she'd already surmised what was happening. "It isn't fair!" she sighed. "Why now?"

William shuffled out of the bedroom, rubbing his eyes. "What's not fair?" he asked.

"Will, I'm sorry I woke you up. I was just talking to myself. Nothing, really." Catherine was not aware she'd spoken out loud. The pain subsided almost as quickly as it had struck, so she could stand straight up and look William in the face with a smile. "I'll get the coffee on," she said as she moved toward the sink.

"No, you sit. I've got it." William turned on the tap and filled the glass pot, placed the works inside, measured out five spoons of coffee, replaced the lid, and put it on the stove to perk. It had taken Catherine months to find the glass percolator, but she had insisted on getting a non-electric machine since she loved the flavor, the sound of it perking, and the fact that if there were a power outage she could still make coffee on her gas range.

She watched her husband of seven years masterfully take over the kitchen with an insistence she'd never yet been able to overcome and smiled. She didn't want this to end.

When he brought her the first cup of the morning, she took it gratefully, poured in a bit of cream, and lifted it, hot and steaming, to her mouth. The first tiny sip was heaven. She smiled as William cradled his own cup across the table from her. Then she felt the beginnings of another stab. She quickly ran to the bathroom so William would not see her double over. The pain was a bit less searing, this time but it made Catherine fearful. She knew she'd have to address it—get tested and tell her family. But the dread of it vanquished her as she stood in the small half-bath, staring in the mirror. William knocked on the door.

"Kate, are you all right?" he called.

"How long have I been in here?" she asked as she opened the door.

William put his arms around her and whispered, "Don't worry, Catherine. We'll work through this together."

He knew, she thought. *He always knows.* "Okay," she replied, and let him hold her for a moment longer before she extricated herself from his arms and poured them a second cup. Coffee wasn't going to heal her, nor were her daily smokes and glass of wine, but they sure helped her get through her days. She called them her little blessings, and would let no one criticize her minor indulgences.

Her enormous blessings, she knew, were her family. Late in life, the loves of her life.

Kashata, despite of her turbulent youth, was flourishing, and little Tina-Kate was loved, pampered, and spoiled, and knew nothing of abuse, thank God. Catherine thought these things as she struggled with her own fears. She subconsciously thanked a god on a near-daily basis, but would have been horrified to have admitted this to anyone, including herself. What god? She understood none of this strange phenomenon that seemed to surface unsummoned.

"Why are you guys hugging and whispering?" Kashata asked as she shuffled into the kitchen. Her pale blue robe, bootie-slippers, and disheveled hair indicated she'd just barely awakened. As she poured herself a cup of coffee, she looked inquiringly at her parents. "Well?" she asked.

"Nothing, Kash," Catherine lied. "Nothing but a good morning, and thankful for it. How are you?"

"Fine."

"Tina-Kate still sleeping?" William wanted to know.

"She's playing with Dune in her room; I just checked on her. We'd better get ourselves together. I have an early class, so I need to get Tina-Kate ready soon." Kashata took her coffee with her to her daughter's room. William and Catherine looked at one another, neither sure what to tell Kashata, if anything.

"Let's get you to the doctor as soon as possible," William suggested. Catherine nodded but could not hide a tear. It was her body, and she surmised the worst.

Chapter 80

Him Again

Following her last class of the day, Kashata left the campus of Fair Valley University to get to the Rainy Day Café to relieve Rita. When she opened the door of the tiny café, she stopped. There he was again. It seemed that when he was there the room was too full, making it difficult for Kashata to breathe. She didn't know why. It had been a few weeks since she'd seen him; she thought he'd gone back to wherever he'd come from.

And here he was again, sitting at the counter. Rita stood across the counter from him, smiling. They were talking and laughing when Kashata walked in, but stopped abruptly when they saw her. Rita didn't appear to be in any hurry to be going home; she didn't excuse herself, take off her apron, or even particularly acknowledge Kashata's presence. She simply nodded and continued smiling at the big, darkly handsome man.

Kashata's defenses shot up. *What is going on here?* she wondered. *Rita must be crazy!* The man turned to look at Kashata, who was still standing in the doorway. "Ain't you coming in, honey?" he asked.

"Don't call me honey," she shot back. "I'll come in when I'm ready."

"Oops. Sorry. Don't let me keep you from your job. I'm leaving anyway." With that he picked up his coat, which had been flung on the stool next to him, stood, and leaned over to whisper a loud goodbye in Rita's ear. Kashata moved aside to let him pass. She could not believe what she had just seen and heard.

"Rita!" she said in a stentorian voice. "What is going on here? You and this guy?"

"Hey, I can be nice to anyone I want. I'm sorry, Kashata, but I don't need your approval." Rita's voice was not kind.

Kashata didn't quite know how to respond. Had she been betrayed, or was she just overly sensitive? If she was, she wasn't even sure why. "I'm sorry, Rita," she said. "I just thought we were a little scared of him, that's all. What made you change your mind?"

"He's been in here a number of times, when you were at school or home or wherever. Anyway, we got to talking, and he really is quite a nice gentleman. I like him, that's all. Nothing to be afraid of." Rita's tone sounded almost apologetic, yet she knew she'd better leave it alone for now. But she added one bit of information she hoped would not upset the girl. Rita did what she wanted regardless of other's thoughts, but she didn't want Kashata suspicious or fearful of this man. She wanted to be as up front with her as possible to keep the friendship from breaking. So she added a detail she knew Kashata would figure out soon anyway.

"By the way," Rita continued, "not that it's any of your business, but since we're friends, I've had a couple of evenings out with him."

"You're dating him?" Kashata didn't know why, but this news devastated her. Her friend dating this guy that gave her the creeps. Why? Why did he make her so uncomfortable?

"Yeah, I am." Rita began undoing the knot at the front of her apron. "He's gorgeous, for one thing," she said, working on the knot and not looking at Kashata. "And he's different than any other man I've known. I feel I can trust him," she added, now looking Kashata in the eye.

"Just the same, I hope he doesn't come here when I'm here alone."

"Kashata, you don't have anything to be afraid of. He's just fine."

"Yeah, well, you don't know that, do you?"

"I think I do."

"You can't be serious. How long have you known him?"

"Kashata, what is your problem? You've never reacted like this to any other customer. Is it because he's African-American? What?"

This was the first time in their relationship that the two women were at odds with one another, and neither liked it. Kashata finally answered, "Yes, maybe that's it. A reminder of my past, maybe. I'll get my apron and start work. You go ahead; I'll be fine."

Rita got her coat and left after taking one last hard look at her young friend. *"Hmm."* she mused to herself. *"I wonder."*

She was planning to see the man again that evening. Perhaps she would ask him a few questions then.

Rita didn't go right home; instead, she drove north to the mall. She wanted to look her best. She had to admit that was really quite taken with Adam Jackson, who had offered only very sketchy information about himself. She knew he'd been married, and that his wife had been in prison, and had died of an overdose soon after her release. She also knew he'd been a party to his wife's use of drugs at one time, but he swore he was clean and had been for twenty years. All pertinent information, but something important was missing. She could feel it in all her discussions with him. Why was he in Good Heavens? Why had he stumbled on the Rainy Day Café when few out-of-towners knew about it? These were all questions she would need to have answered this evening.

As she walked through the mall, she knew she had to really outdo herself this evening. The best way to get a guy to talk was to make him totally engrossed in one's delicious appearance. Rita knew what to do and how to do it.

Chapter 81

Revelations

Adam drove his 2003 tan Mini Cooper to Rita's modest home on Ottawa Place. The small white-and-grey ranch needed repair, especially the front lawn. It looked like it might need a new roof as well. Adam sighed. He knew the little café could not possibly bring in enough money to sustain a decent living. But Rita seemed to love the place, and he figured she needed it to feel the control she wanted over her life. He walked to her bright-red front door—her one concession to beautifying her home—and rang the bell.

He waited. He rang again. He waited. Should he ring again or wait? He waited.

Finally the door opened, revealing a vision in green and red appeared. The lime green dress and pearls were the perfect complement to Rita's auburn hair. Nothing was overdone, but the woman looked good enough to consume.

"Wow," he said. "You look amazing!"

"Thanks," she said, smiling. "So do you." He'd bought a new navy sports jacket and wore it with an off-white turtleneck and tan pants. He knew he looked as good as she did. "Ready?" she asked.

He offered his arm, opened her door and slid into the driver's seat. He couldn't believe his luck, being out with this incredible lady. They drove along Lakeshore Avenue to the next town. He had made a reservation at Pereddies, the great Italian place next to the art gallery. Good food, good ambience, good service, great company. What a joy. When he'd begun his search, he had not expected this extra perk. But here he was, and he'd found even more than he had hoped for.

They ordered the Gorgonzola salad to share, then had the baked brie—the ultimate appetizer. They ate slowly, savoring every bite. Rita drank a glass of Pinot Grigio, but Adam preferred water with lemon. Rita didn't want to disturb the warm feeling, and so decided to save her questions for dessert. They ate shrimp risotto as they conversed about the café, the lakefront, the political issues of the day and, the weather.

For dessert, they had Italian wedding cake and coffee. Rita felt a bit tense because she had some serious questions to ask this man. As she stirred her coffee she smiled and continued looking down at her cup as she plunged in. "Adam," she began, "why did you come to Good Heavens?" He had told her he'd wanted to see the lake, but she knew there was more to it. He could have gone to Chicago, seen the lake, and enjoyed the lovely city.

"I told you," he said. "I wanted to experience the lakefront."

"There's more to it than that; you know there is. What is it?" She took a bite of her cake, looked him in the eye, and raised her fork to indicate he'd better come clean. "You came to my café, which a tourist would never find on his own. You stare at Kashata when you think no one's looking. Why?"

He took a deep breath, put down his fork, and swallowed hard. "I'm not sure I should tell you; I'm not sure what I should do. I really think you'd be upset," he answered.

"Try me."

"Rita, I really like you. I never thought I'd meet anyone I like this much again. But that's not the reason I'm here." He hesitated, looked around the room, looked at his plate, took a sip of coffee, and then looked at Rita. "I'm Kashata's father," he said almost in a whisper.

"Hmm. You think that surprises me?"

"What? You suspected?"

"Yes. You look at her; you look like her. I put two and two together. She's terrified of you. Why would that be?"

"I don't know if I can talk about it. It's a horrible story, and I've tried to find her to ask forgiveness."

"I probably wouldn't be shocked but, of course, you don't owe me an explanation."

Adam took a deep breath, sipped his coffee, cleared his throat, and began.

"Her mother was the most beautiful woman I had ever seen. We were young, in our teens. We got married after having known each other barely four months. We ran around with a crazy bunch of people, wild people. Drug addicts, pushers, pimps, you name it. We became addicts too, of course. She was in much worse shape than I was, but we were both bad off. Her parents had completely disowned her because she was married to a Black man.

"Anyway, she got pregnant, and Kashata was born. We were thrilled at the time, but as she began to grow up, our lives were spiraling downward. I left the apartment when Kashata was barely four. Sandy, her mother, was totally out of control—hooked on heroin and in desperate need of money to support her habit. She used our baby to get it."

"Oh my god!" Rita breathed. "Poor baby. Poor Kashie. And you knew?"

"I was told by some friends. I wanted to do something, but I couldn't," he whined.

"Bullshit!" Rita yelled into his face. Other diners, shocked at the sudden outburst, looked over at them. One man stood and asked for an apology. "Sorry," Rita murmured, then went on to Adam, "How could you possibly not do something? How?"

"I was as stoned as Sandy; I didn't have the ability to think or care. I ended up in jail. A friend called child protective services and they picked up Kashata. She was in foster care until this lady adopted her. Sandy went to jail and died there. That's it, the whole ugly lot of it. I'm clean. I have been for twenty years. I had to see if Kashata was all right. It took me a long time to find her."

"She doesn't know who you are, are but something in her brain triggered an inordinate fear of you the minute she saw you. Why would that be?" Rita could not wrap her mind around what she'd just learned. She'd been abused herself, but nothing like this.

"She might have memories of me. She's apparently very bright and, somewhere in her subconscious, she might remember."

"Did you ever—"

"No! No! Absolutely not. Crap, this is so hard. I wanted to find her because I want her to forgive me. I can't live with this awful guilt anymore." Adam had tears in his eyes now. Their conversation was barely audible but, even so, other diners were beginning to take notice. Tears, recriminations, and one loud outburst were enough to alert sensitive ears to something unsavory.

"We've got to get outta here, Adam." Rita stood and put on her coat and walked out without waiting for Adam to pay the bill. She waited for him outside the gallery and smoked a cigarette. She couldn't believe what had happened to Kashata. She inhaled deeply, let go a stream of smoke, and began to cry softly for her friend. She'd wanted this to be a special evening with this great new guy, but it had all gone up in smoke.

Chapter 82

New Pain

While sitting in the waiting room, her heart pounded so loudly she was sure others could hear it. William held her hand, thinking about his own fears. How could he lose a second wife to this dreaded illness? Wasn't God ever going to let him off this painful merry-go-round? He closed his eyes and silently prayed. Catherine sat, took very deep breaths to help her stay calm, and quietly said "please" into the air for any god out there to catch and answer.

When her name was called, she attempted to get up. William stood, offered his hand, and tried to help, but Catherine was paralyzed by fear. She tried once more to bounce forward, pulling on William's hand. When she finally stood, he led her into the doctor's office.

There was a painting on the wall behind the white-clad physician—a whirl of circles and ovals in incandescent blues and greens, with intermittent patches of white and yellow. It depicted nothing but movement, pattern, and nausea to Catherine. She could not look at the doctor. She was mesmerized by the painting—floating into its colors, sickened by the movement of the spheres in her attempt to deny the truth.

"I'm so sorry," he was saying, and proceeded to lay out the

possibilities, treatments, and prognosis as Catherine whirled around and around inside the painting. She thought she'd heard, but decided she had not heard a thing. William looked at her and realized he had more to deal with than physical illness. "Kate," he said. "Kate. Please listen so we can decide what to do. Kate," he said again.

"Decide what to do?" she asked as though she were inches away from reality. "Decide what to do? William," she said as she came to herself, "there is nothing to do." She got up, shook the doctor's hand, and left the room. William smiled an awkward grin at the doctor in a sort of apology, and hurried after her.

She was already sitting in the car when he caught up. Her expression was almost serene. "Well," she said when William slid behind the wheel, "I guess this is it. I guess this the end. I guess we'll have to make the most of it and really live it up every day because, this time, each day is the last, isn't it?" She looked William in the eye. He felt tears; she smiled. "We've had a wonderful go of it, old friend. Let's not ruin the last days with tears. Home, James!" she ordered jauntily and sat back in her seat.

Catherine didn't know where her jubilation came from. She couldn't tell if it was the result of abysmal fear and denial, or a true sense of ultimate peace given by the God she'd so often invoked and equally often denied. She didn't care. Home, her girls, her husband were to be enjoyed in a measure not known before, and even Dune was going to become the focus of her days, however many were left. There would be no treatment, no radiation, and no chemicals to degrade her quality of life from now on. It would be just Catherine, her family, and whatever hardships and pain accompanied that pleasure. She felt so thankful to be alive she couldn't wait to get home and embrace those living beside her.

William sensed her mountain of jubilation and feared the deep valley to come. He drove in quiet peace, prayer, and knowledge of fulfilling days to come, as well great depths of pain and despair.

Chapter 83

"I Hate You"

Kashata knew nothing of the new development in her family; she was caught up in school, work, and her daughter. She had learned, through no fault of her own, to take Catherine and William somewhat for granted. She attended church on Sundays as usual, had coffee or lunch with Phillis when time allowed, went out with friends from school on an occasional weekend, and led a generally uncomplicated life. This was still relatively new territory for her, and she loved the routine of it.

Her life took a turn about a week after Catherine had had her doctor appointment. What she had never expected happened; her mother was going to die. She had inadvertently witnessed one of Catherine's awful episodes of pain, and assumed it had just been a bad stomachache from something Kate had eaten. But it was worse than that. William tried his best to let her know in his quiet, compassionate way, but Kashata reeled with the news. She had fully believed that the miracle would last. Why hadn't it? Then the worst blow had come from Rita.

She had to ask William to pick Tina-Kate up after school one more time. "Rita says it's urgent, William. I'm sorry." She flung on her coat and ran for the door. "I'll be back in no time. Promise," she called over her shoulder as the door slammed behind her. She drove down the dune and onto Lake Shore, making the turn toward the east side of town on Fourteenth Street. When she arrived at the Rainy Day Café, she saw Rita's car parked out front. She didn't recognize the other one parked a half block away. A new customer, probably. Rita motioned Kash to sit in the booth as she poured coffee for each of them, and then slid into the booth opposite her. There was no one else in the café.

"So, what's all this about?" Kashata asked.

Rita took a sip of her coffee. "Hot," she remarked. "Good and hot." A slight pause followed, and then Rita plunged in. "Do you remember that man who was here a while ago—the tall, dark guy you didn't like?"

"Yeah. What about him?"

"Well, I've been seeing him. I've been seeing a lot of him."

"What? I thought he was gone."

"No, he's around. I've been with him. I like him, Kash, and I think you might like him too when you know him."

"And why should I bother? To know him, I mean."

Rita hesitated. "Kash, his name is Adam. He's your father."

A bomb exploded in Kashata's head. Tears sprang to her eyes and fear gripped her as her stomach turned, threatening eruption. But then clarity surfaced. She knew and had known. "What?" she whispered. More audibly, she hissed, "What is he doing here?"

"He wants to see you," Rita explained, "and I said I would help him."

As Rita spoke, he entered quietly from the kitchen door. "He just wants to ask your forgiveness. He's so sorry," Rita said, but Kashata's eyes were riveted to the apparition behind the counter.

"I hate you!" she shouted. "I hate both of you!" She stood and turned to Rita. "How could you betray me like this? How could you be with this demon? How?"

"Kashata, please. He's not the man you knew. Give him a chance."

"You like him? You're with him? Are you nuts? How could you do this to me? I thought we were friends!"

"Kashie, I'm not doing anything to you; I'm doing it for me. I need a life, and I've found it. This is a good man. I don't owe you my life, I don't owe you my future, but I hope you might be able to forgive."

Then the deep voice began to plead. "Kashata, I never knew how bad it was. I didn't know what your mother was doing until it was too late. I couldn't stop her. I was too fried myself. Please. Could you possibly...forgive me?"

Kashata shook with fear, anger, hatred, and a deep feeling of betrayal. "Never. You were never my father, you were my devil! Fathers protect their children. I hate you. I hate everyone who associates with you! You have no right to mess in my life again. Don't ever—" She grabbed her coat, ran out the door, and tore the car away from the curb at breakneck speed. She didn't know where she was going. Tears flowed from her eyes, searing pain circled her abdomen, and nausea threatened. She drove and drove. When her cell rang she stopped, blew her nose, rubbed her eyes, and answered. "I'm sorry, William," she stammered. "I just got some really bad news. What should I do?"

The voice on the other end asked what the trouble was. "I can't tell you, but I need to talk to somebody, I think."

"Can you go to Phillis?"

"I don't know. Maybe. I'll try. Can Tina—"

"She's fine. She's a great diversion for Catherine, and I'm on my way to fix dinner. Do what you need to do, but please be very careful, Kashata, especially driving when you're upset. We'll all be waiting for you."

Maybe there is such a thing as a father, Kashata thought after she hung up with William. *Maybe there is, but it certainly does not have to be someone you're related to, that's for sure.* She sat back in the seat and waited for peace. She needed time. She tried to pray, but "my Father" stuck in her throat. She prayed but not to the Father, but only to the Son this time, and even that was short, self-centered, and full of fear.

Chapter 84

The Last Straw

When Kashata heard from Catherine that Rita was going to marry Adam, she spat into her cup. "This is the last straw," she exclaimed.

Catherine said only, "Well, I guess you won't be working there anymore." It was early morning, a month after the initial confrontation. Summer was almost upon them, and tourists would be soon. Rita would be swamped. The man might be a help to her; Kashata certainly wasn't going to be.

"I haven't gone since I saw him there; you know that. I know how to hate, and now I have the object of my hatred in front of me all the time. If I just go for coffee, there he is!" she spat at Catherine.

"Neither your sarcasm nor your venom become you, my dear. You'll have to work on these intense feelings. Please don't wait too long. What about your God? Doesn't He have something to say about this? I mean hating and forgiving and all?

"I can't. Leave me alone." Kashata took her cup to the sink.

"By the way, who said you were in charge of Rita's life?"

She nearly threw the cup onto the counter as she called for Tina-Kate to hurry. She left in a huff as though Catherine were to blame for it all. William shuffled in from the bedroom looking like a large plaid-robed maid who'd left her mop on her head. His puzzled expression told of his having heard most of the ranting. "What was that all about?" he queried. "Still Kashata's father?"

"Yes. You know, William, it pains me to see this. It reminds me of my failure with Tina. When Robert showed up, she also went crazy and said I'd betrayed her. It's all coming back to me in Kashata."

"No, Catherine, no, no, no. Not the same at all. A few parallels, but not the same. Tina had no childhood abuse, and she had a very good mother. An horrific event culminated in her death. Not the same. Kashata had no protector, no childhood, and no mother, but she has all that now. Don't go back there and accuse yourself. Be thankful for what we have now and, I assure you, Kashata is eventually going to do what she must to be healed. You'll see."

"Will I live that long, William?" she asked.

"We'll see" was all he could answer. William kept his feelings well under wraps. He didn't want to add to Catherine's pain, but he felt a real disappointment at the new diagnosis. Perhaps he knew better somewhere deep in his soul, but right now he wondered, *How could God do this to me?* He felt a deep bitterness in his gut almost every morning. He'd finally found the passion he'd craved, and it was to be taken from him far too soon. The fact that he was in his seventies made no difference to him. He had the appetite of a forty-year-old, if not younger, man. Catherine had awakened this in him. Why would God want him to be without it, as well as the warm family love he'd found? And what about Kashata? Just another abandonment? The last straw was her friend's betrayal in marrying her father. What would this do to her faith?

William often found himself wandering the beach alone these days while his wife took drug-induced naps. He could not pray. He wept often, but alone. His strength was saved for the three women. William felt his weakness weigh on him like a cross of steel.

Chapter 85

Phillis

"I am not your counselor, Kashata. I'm not equipped to help you in the way you need." Phillis loved Kashata like a daughter, but felt the burden of what Kashie asked of her today was too heavy.

Kashata had done a lot of thinking. She'd not been able to go to her parents for the advice she needed; they were already too burdened. She found her peace in her car, driving long distances, sometimes with Dune in the seat beside her. Sometimes Tina-Kate was in the back, but she had been instructed not to chatter because her mother needed to think. Sometimes Kashata got up early in the morning went off driving in checkered pajamas and bare feet. She would return an hour or so later, sit at the breakfast table with a cup of coffee, and offer no explanation. No one asked for one, either. A spirit of silent turmoil had entered the little house on top of the dune.

Then, one morning, Kashata knew where to go.

"I'm only asking for advice, Phillis, not any counseling. Just tell me what you think I should do about this father who has showed up and wants me to forgive him. How do I do that? Why should I? What right does he have to ask?"

"Kashata, you know as well as I do that guilt and fear are healed through forgiveness. Without forgiveness, there is no healing. The burden just stays, grows, and often kills. Forgiveness, like love, is more doing than feeling. Just do it. Find your strength in your faith. You are forgiven; forgive in return. Nothing is so bad that it cannot be forgiven. Just do it. That's all I can give you. But you already knew that, right?"

"I guess. I've been running away from it. All I've felt for the past few weeks is hatred and betrayal. Maybe I can, someday." She thanked Phillis for listening and her advice. She knew she had more than a father and friend to forgive; she also had to deal with Tina-Kate's father. It was all too much for today, but maybe tomorrow she would begin.

She found, on her way home, that she could say a little prayer. "Help," she said in the quietness. "Give me strength."

Chapter 86

A Father's Confession

When Kashata received the letter, she began to tear it up, but then she remembered her prayer. She fingered the envelope and looked at the printed words—"To my daughter, Kashata." She felt her stomach squeeze into a ball. William had become her father, and she wanted no one else on earth to claim her. When she finally tore the thing open, she closed her eyes and took out the letter.

> My dear child, I cannot tell you how much I regret my life and what I made of yours. I have no claim to you or your daughter, I know that. But I need your forgiveness. Nothing else. Just a hint of forgiveness so I can go on living my life with Christ. Yes, I am a believer. I know also that without forgiving those who have done you the most harm, you won't find the peace you need, either. So I beg you to meet me one last time. Maybe we can make it work—the peace of forgiveness, I mean.
>
> Adam

She didn't know why, but suddenly tears erupted into a flood and she shook from head to toe. She could not stop until it seemed all the moisture in her body had been drained. Then she went to the bathroom, washed her face, sat on the closed toilet seat, and prayed. "Okay, then. I guess with Your help I may be able to do this," she said aloud, and called Rita.

Chapter 87

Return to Brigantine

Sam and Betty knocked on the door. William answered to find his neighbors grinning and holding a large, dripping bag which they offered to him. "This is for you and your family. I just caught it, had it filleted, and thought you might enjoy it for dinner."

"Thank you. Come in." William took the offering, holding it far out in front of him while Dune followed, lapping up the trail. It was salmon—Catherine's favorite. Sam and Betty knew this, and they also guessed something was not quite right in their neighbors' lives. There had been little communication for quite some time. The offering was given in hope of finding out what the trouble might be. They liked to know stuff.

Catherine was sitting sunning herself, looking out over the water. She was wrapped in a wool throw even though the temperature had climbed well into the seventies. She was smoking, and the rich sweet aroma told all. Sam looked at his wife, raising an eyebrow. She shrugged in response. "Well," he said, "maybe we should go."

"Have a cup with us first," William suggested. "Catherine will join us soon, and we can visit. It has been a long time, hasn't it?"

"Well, William, we haven't really spoken since we got back from Florida. I hope all is okay here," Betty answered.

"You're right; we haven't. It is high time we did. Can I offer you coffee? Tea? What?"

Catherine shuffled into the kitchen, her wrap wound tightly around her. She smiled her hello and sat down, all with effort. "We owe you an explanation," she said. "You've been such good neighbors, so let me fill you in. My cancer is back, and this time it's terminal."

"Oh my god," they said in unison, truly astonished. "What can we do to help?" Betty asked.

"Nothing. Just be here. And thanks for the dinner. You've already done enough," William consoled his sincerely devastated guests.

"Tell you what," Sam began. "Let me have that Coho back and I'll grill it and bring dinner to you this evening. How about that?"

Catherine and William smiled. Who were they to deny their neighbors the opportunity to serve? William went to the pantry to retrieve a plastic bag, into which he dropped the dripping fish, and handed it to Sam. "Thanks, Sam. What a great help this will be," he added.

They chatted over coffee as best they could before Sam and Betty went off to their own house.

"That was good of you, Catherine. Letting people who care about you know is really a good thing. Thanks."

Kashata and Tina-Kate arrived back from school just in time to run into their neighbors carrying a large platter covered in aluminum foil, exuding aromas of fish and spices as well as small puffs of steam.

Kashata was more animated than she'd been in weeks, and her parents were happy to see it. Tina-Kate jabbered about school, her friends, and her joy at learning to swim in the lake. With summer upon them, Kashata had taken the time to get Tina-Kate involved in a swim group at the Y, which would be invaluable training for lake safety later in the year.

Sam and Betty stayed for dinner. Wine was served, laughter accompanied the eating, and for the first time in quite a few days there was warmth and happiness floating from the beams to the floor. Dune's tail tapped out a joyful rhythm on the floor as everyone dropped small morsels of fish from time to time. The change appeared to be due to Sam and Betty, but the reality lay in Kashata's resolution to add forgiveness in response to her own salvation. She knew it would take time, but she was going for it. She also knew what else she needed to do. Ben's friend had to be told.

The conversation turned to Catherine. Her illness was upon her, but she had had some really good days; both she and William were glad to have them. What a difference even one good day meant to them.

Catherine had been in touch with Gwen, who was having a fulfilling second marriage with Pastor Plug. Gwen hated to hear what Catherine had to say. She too wanted to be helpful, but there was nothing to be done except wait and offer comfort as needed. Nobody approved of Catherine's decision to smoke pot, but no one dared oppose her, either. She was the one who was sick, and anyone who knew Catherine at all knew that opposing her would only result in a tongue-lashing which would end in nothing but humiliation for the opposer. Leaving Kate to her own choices was safest, Gwen knew. She'd done what she could to get her sister back to some normalcy in Michigan, but that was it. Now she prayed for another recovery; the little family would suffer from the loss of her sister.

After dinner and clean-up, Catherine excused herself to sit once more in the sun room to rest. Sam and Betty took their leave. Kashata sat at the kitchen table with her daughter, doing homework together. William joined Catherine.

"That was a really good time, Kate. We got to laugh and enjoy ourselves again."

"You calling me 'Kate' is great, William. I love it." She turned to him. "Do you know what else I'd love? Something I want?"

"Anything you want. Just say it. If it's in my power to give, it's yours."

"I'd like to see the ocean one more time. Sit on Brigantine beach, watch the ocean swells, hear the gulls, and watch the pipers scramble after beach food."

"Catherine, what an idea. How lovely. Let's do it!" William had not thought of it, but now he delighted in the possibility. That Catherine wanted to go gave him anticipation of renewed health, at least for a time.

"Yes, William, lets," she answered.

The preparations for the trip east didn't take long; they knew they had to make the best of the good time that Catherine was having. She was not free from pain, but she was able to negotiate her way through her days with relative ease. They would fly from Grand Rapids to Philadelphia, and drive to Brigantine from there. They would stay in one of the luxury suites in the Borgata, as close to Brigantine as the casinos got. William surprised Catherine by ordering first-class seats on the plane.

Both Kashata and Tina-Kate helped with the packing. It didn't take long, since carry-on was all they needed. Everyone was in a good mood prior to the trip. This was to be a great last hurrah for both Catherine and William, and everyone knew it.

Gwen and Oscar stopped by to say bon voyage. It was as though they were travelling to China instead of to New Jersey, there was so much hullabaloo. Phillis promised to help out with Tina-Kate whenever Kashata had classes. Sam and Betty would look after the house when and if needed. All was set and, on the appointed day, William and Catherine drove to the airport with Kashata and their granddaughter. They kissed each other goodbye at the security area.

When they arrived in Philadelphia, Catherine was exhausted. Instead of driving directly to Brigantine, William booked a room at the airport Hilton. They rested there for the remainder of the day and that night. They were both tired but happy at the adventure they had planned. After a meal of decent clams over pasta with wine, delivered by room service, Catherine slept a drugged sleep. William put up his feet and watched TV until he too fell asleep.

The following day was Sunday. William let Catherine sleep in, left a note, and went off to the early morning service at Tenth Presbyterian, the center city church he knew from his past in Philadelphia. When he returned, Catherine was up and dressed. She looked radiant, considering her plight. They ordered a light breakfast, ate it leisurely, ordered their car, and got on their way.

There was little traffic on the Atlantic City Expressway; William drove the speed limit the entire way. Cars passed them left and right. Sometimes an inappropriate gesture from a passing driver or passenger was directed at William, but he couldn't have cared less. He was with his Catherine, and they were heading to the place where they'd met. They were, in a way, heading home.

"I love the blown-glass fixtures and sculptures here, William. I'm so glad we decided to stay here instead of a little motel. Look at the view of the ocean." Catherine was in her element; William could only smile and enjoy the moments.

They took special advantage of the spacious facility they'd rented for the week. Room service helped whenever Catherine was too tired to go to one of the island's restaurants. They ate sumptuously, even though Catherine's appetite was often miniscule. William helped finish anything she could not. She was losing weight on this trip; he knew why, but refused to acknowledge it. He was gaining, and refused to acknowledge this as well. They were honeymooning again. Who cared about anything else?

They decided to spend the entire final day of the vacation on the beach. They rented chairs and a blow-up mattress-sized float for

Catherine to nap on. They went to the Fourteenth Street beach, parked, and slowly made their way over the walkway between the dune grasses to the very edge of the water. There they set up camp for the day. The hotel had packed lunches for them, and they'd brought wine in a large thermos to hide the contents, since no alcohol was allowed on the beach.

"We're back in Brigantine. Who would have thought it!" Catherine exclaimed. "Smell that sea air. No lake, no matter how big, can compare with this. I am absolutely in love!"

"You are right, my dear. There's nothing quite like it. Nothing at all."

"You know, William, I haven't mentioned it before, but I might—just might—have prayed to your God last week."

"What do you mean, 'prayed'?"

"I don't know. But I asked for a sign, something that showed me everything would be all right, something that would help me accept and feel happy and now, well, here we are. And man alive, am I happy!"

He took her hand in his. "I'm happy too, Kate. Happier than I've been in a quite some time. Thank you for your prayer. God is good."

"I guess," she answered. "I need to take a nap now. Do you mind?"

She lay down on the float, placed the rolled-up towel under her head, and closed her eyes. The wine, the food, and the sleeping pill had done their best; Catherine was asleep in no more than ten seconds. William smiled as he looked at his wife, overjoyed that she was with him again on this magical island they loved.

The sun was warm and bathed William in relaxation. He let his book fall to the sand as he too was lulled into sleep. The pleasant sound of the lapping waves, the rhythm of the ocean's movement, the silence of a quiet beach with few other bathers, and the gentle sound of Catherine's breath offered William a peace that allowed a profound and dreamless rest.

All was very still; no other people were on the beach. There was only a sound of rushing waters. The sky was not as bright as it had been. Water covered William's underside, even though his chair was many inches above the sand. He awoke with a start and turned to Catherine. She was not there. The mattress was not there. High tide had must have come in, and suddenly William panicked. He stood and looked out to sea. There it was. He could see it; he could see her. He yelled, "Catherine!" And again, "Catherine! Oh God, let her hear me."

When she lifted her head as if to turn, her entire body turned instead and she was dumped from the float into the ocean. She bobbed up in the waves for a brief second or two, and then was gone. Not a ripple was left behind.

William screamed an inaudible scream and dropped on knees. He collapsed and shriveled into what looked like skin without bone and lay in a lump on the beach. His salty tears mingled with the salt water of the tide that had taken his love away. She would feel no more pain, he knew.

But his was palpable.

Chapter 88

Epilogue

The little cottage on the dune was emptier than it had been for years. An old man and an equally old dog walked the beach together each morning. Every Tuesday, a lovely dark woman and her equally lovely daughter came to spend the day with the man and his dog. A tall blond man—Ben's friend, Tina-Kate's father, and now Kashata's husband—often accompanied them. They smiled at the old man and embraced him with affection each time. The dog attempted to jump up on them, but his hindquarters only allowed him to reach their knees, and fell away wagging his still fully-furred tail furiously. Happiness radiated from the now-blind but faithful animal. The man smiled as he ushered his family into the house. He was very old. He knew, as they all knew, that he would soon leave this earth. He would finally see the face of the greatest Lover the world has ever known.